# Billy Liar

### KEITH WATERHOUSE

# The Loneliness of
# The Long-distance Runner

### ALAN SILLITOE

*with Introduction and Notes by*

### DAVID ELLOWAY B.A.

## LONGMAN

# LONGMAN GROUP LIMITED
## London

*Associated companies, branches and representatives*
*throughout the world*

*Billy Liar* © Keith Waterhouse 1959
*The Loneliness of the Long-distance Runner* © Alan Sillitoe 1959
*Introduction and Notes* © Longman Group Ltd (formerly Longmans, Green & Co Ltd) 1966

First published in the Heritage of Literature Series 1966 by arrangement with Michael Joseph Ltd. and W. H. Allen & Co.

New impression 1975

Twelfth impression 1979


ISBN 0 582 34885 4

*Printed in Singapore by*
*Singapore Offset Printing (Pte) Ltd.*

## CONTENTS

*Billy Liar*

## ONE

Lying in bed, I abandoned the facts again and was back in Ambrosia.

By rights, the march-past started in the Avenue of the Presidents, but it was an easy thing to shift the whole thing into Town Square. My friends had vantage seats on the town hall steps where no flag flew more proudly than the tattered blue star of the Ambrosian Federation, the standard we had carried into battle. One by one the regiments marched past, and when they had gone—the Guards, the Parachute Regiment, the King's Own Yorkshire Light Infantry—a hush fell over the crowds and they removed their hats for the proud remnants of the Ambrosian Grand Yeomanry. It was true that we had entered the war late, and some criticised us for that; but out of two thousand who went into battle only seven remained to hear the rebuke. We limped along as we had arrived from the battlefield, the mud still on our shredded uniforms, but with a proud swing to our kilts. The band played 'March of the Movies.' The war memorial was decked with blue poppies, the strange bloom found only in Ambrosia.

I put an end to all this, consciously and deliberately, by going '*Da da da da da da da*' aloud to drive the thinking out of my head. It was a day for big decisions. I recalled how I could always cure myself when I got on one of those counting sprees where it was possible to reach three thousand easily without stopping: I would throw in a confetti of confusing numbers or, if they didn't help, half-remembered quotations and snatches of verse. '*Seventy-three. Nine hundred and six. The Lord is my shepherd, I shall not want, he maketh me to lie down. Four hundred and thirty-five.*'

It was a day for big decisions. I had already determined,

3

A*

more for practical reasons than out of any new policy, to clip the thumb-nail which I have been cultivating until it was a quarter of an inch long. Now, lying under the pale gold eiderdown, staring up at the crinoline ladies craftily fashioned out of silver paper and framed in passe-partout (*they* would be coming down, for a start) I began to abandon the idea of saving the clipping in an ointment box; I would throw it right away, without a backward glance, and from now on, short nails, and a brisk bath each morning. An end, too, to this habit of lying in bed crinkling my toes fifty times for each foot; in future I would be up at seven and an hour's work done before breakfast. There would be no more breath-holding, eye-blinking, nostril-twitching or sucking of the teeth, and this plan would start tomorrow, if not today.

I lay in bed, the toe-crinkling over; now I was stretching the fingers of both hands to their fullest extent, like two starfish. Sometimes I got an overpowering feeling that my fingers were webbed, like a duck's, and I had to spread them out to block the sensation and prevent it spreading to my feet.

My mother shouted up the stairs: 'Billy? *Billy! Are* you getting up?' the third call in a fairly well-established series of street cries that graduated from: 'Are you awake, Billy?' to 'It's a quarter past nine, and you can stay in bed all day for all I care,' meaning twenty to nine and time to get up. I waited until she called: 'If I come up there you'll *know* about it' (a variant of number five, usually 'If I come up there I shall *tip* you out') and then I got up.

I put on the old raincoat I used for a dressing-gown, making the resolution that now I must buy a real dressing-gown, possibly a silk one with some kind of dragon motif, and I felt in my pocket for the Player's Weights. I was trying to bring myself up to smoke before breakfast but this time even the idea of it brought on the familiar nausea. I shoved the cigarettes back in my pocket and felt the letter still there, but this time I did not read it. '*He scribbled a few notes on the back of a used envelope.*' The phrase had always appealed to me. I had a pleasing image of a stack of used envelopes, secured by a rubber band, crammed with notes in a thin, spidery hand-

4

writing. I took the used envelope out of my pocket with the letter still in it and thought up some jottings. '*Calendars. See S. re job. Write Boon. Thousand??? See Witch re Captain.*' Most of these notes were unnecessary, especially the bit about seeing Witch re Captain; that, along with the calendars, always a part-time worry, and the other bit about seeing S. re job, had kept me awake half the night. As for Thousand??? this was a ghost of idle thinking, the last traces of a plan to write a thousand words each day of a public school story to be entitled *The Two Schools at Gripminster*. Having conceived the plan in early August, I was already thirty-four thousand words behind on the schedule. There were long periods of time when my own ambition was to suck a Polo mint right through without it breaking in my mouth; others when I would retreat into Ambrosia and sketch out the new artists' settlement on route eleven, and they would be doing profiles of me on television, 'Genius—or Madman?'

I put the ballpoint away and shoved the envelope back in my pocket, and on the cue of cry number seven, by far my favourite ('Your boiled egg's stone cold and *I'm* not cooking another'), I went downstairs.

Hillcrest, as the house was called (although not by me) was the kind of dwelling where all the windows are leaded in a fussy criss-cross, except one, which is a porthole. Our porthole was at the turn of the stairs and here I paused to rub the heel of my slipper against the stair-rod, another habit I would be getting out of henceforth. Shuffling there, I could see out across the gravel to the pitch-painted garage with its wordy, gold-painted sign: 'Geo. Fisher & Son, Haulage Contractors, Distance No Object. "The Moving Firm" Tel: 2573. Stamp, Signs.' The sign was inaccurate. I was the son referred to, but in fact the old man had gone to great trouble to keep me out of the family business, distance no object. What really got on my nerves, however, was the legend 'Stamp, Signs' which was almost as big as the advertisement itself. Eric Stamp had been the white-haired boy of the art class when we were at Strad-houghton Technical together, and was now my colleague at Shadrack and Duxbury's. It was his ambition to set up in the sign-writing business full-time, and I for one was not stopping him.

Anyway, the fact that the garage doors were not open yet meant that the old man was still at home and there were going to be words exchanged about last night's outing. I slopped down into the hall, took the *Stradhoughton Echo* out of the letter-box, where it would have remained all day if the rest of the family had anything to do with it, and went into the lounge. It was a day for big decisions.

The breakfast ceremony at Hillcrest had never been my idea of fun. I had made one disastrous attempt to break the monotony of it, entering the room one day with my eyes shut and my arms outstretched like a sleep-walker, announcing in a shaky, echo-chamber voice: 'Ay York-shire breakfast scene. Ay polished table, one leaf out, covahed diagonally by ay white tablecloth, damask, with grrreen strip bordah. Sauce-stain to the right, blackberry stain to the centre. Kellogg's corn flakes, Pyrex dishes, plate of fried bread. Around the table, the following personnel: fathah, mothah, grandmothah, one vacant place.' None of this had gone down well. I entered discreetly now, almost shiftily, taking in with a dull eye the old man's pint mug disfigured by a crack that was no longer mistaken for a hair, and the radio warming up for Yesterday in Parliament. It was a choice example of the hygienic family circle, but to me it had taken on the glazed familiarity of some old print such as When Did You Last See Your Father? I was greeted by the usual breathing noises.

'You decided to get up, then,' my mother said, slipping easily into the second series of conversations of the day. My stock replies were 'Yes,' 'No, I'm still in bed' and a snarled 'What does it look like?' according to mood. Today I chose 'Yes' and sat down to my boiled egg, stone cold as threatened. This made it a quarter to nine.

The old man looked up from some invoices and said: 'And you can start getting bloody well dressed before you come down in a morning.' So far the dialogue was taking a fairly conventional route and I was tempted to throw in one of the old stand-bys, 'Why do you always begin your sentences with

6

an "And"?' Gran, another dress fanatic who always seemed to be fully and even elaborately attired even at two in the morning when she slunk downstairs after the soda-water, chipped in: 'He wants to burn that raincoat, then he'll have to get dressed of a morning.' One of Gran's peculiarities, and she had many, was that she would never address anyone directly but always went through an intermediary, if necessary some static object such as a cupboard. Doing the usual decoding I gathered that she was addressing my mother and that he who should burn the raincoat was the old man, and he who would have to get dressed of a morning was me. 'I gather,' I began, 'that he who should burn the raincoat——' but the old man interrupted:

'And what bloody time did you get in *last* night? If you can call it last night. This bloody morning, more like.'

I sliced the top off my boiled egg, which in a centre favouring tapping the top with a spoon and peeling the bits off was always calculated to annoy, and said lightly: '*I* don't know. 'Bout half-past eleven, quarter to twelve.'

The old man said: 'More like one o'clock, with your half-past bloody eleven! Well you can bloody well and start coming in of a night-time. I'm not having *you* gallivanting round at all hours, not at your bloody age.'

'Who *are* you having gallivanting round, then?' I asked, the wit rising for the day like a pale and watery sun.

My mother took over, assuming the clipped, metallic voice of the morning interrogation. '*What were you doing down Foley Bottoms at nine o'clock last night?*'

I said belligerently: 'Who says I was down at Foley Bottoms?'

'Never mind who says, or who doesn't say. You *were* there, and it wasn't that Barbara you were with, neither.'

'He wants to make up his mind who he *is* going with,' Gran said.

There was a rich field of speculation for me here. Since my mother had never even met the Witch—the one to whom she referred by her given name of Barbara—or Rita either—the one involved in the Foley Bottoms episode, that is—I won-

7

dered how she managed to get her hands on so many facts without actually hiring detectives.

I said: 'Well you want to tell whoever saw me to mind their own fizzing business.'

'It *is* our business,' my mother said. 'And don't you be so cheeky!' I pondered over the absent friend who had supplied the Foley Bottoms bulletin. Mrs Olmonroyd? Ma Walker? Stamp? *The Witch herself?* I had a sudden, hideous notion that the Witch was in league with my mother and that they were to spring some dreadful coup upon me the following day when, with a baptism of lettuce and pineapple chunks, the Witch was due to be introduced to the family at Sunday tea.

Gran said: 'If she's coming for her tea tomorrow she wants to tell her. If she doesn't, I will.' My mother interpreted this fairly intelligently and said: 'I'm *going* to tell her, don't you fret yourself.' She slid off down a chuntering landslide of recrimination until the old man, reverting to the main theme, came back with the heavy artillery.

'He's not bloody well old enough to stay out half the night, I've told him before. He can start coming in of a night, or else go and live somewhere else.'

This brought me beautifully to what I intended to be the text for the day, but now that the moment had come I felt curiously shy and even a little sick at the idea of my big decisions. I allowed my mother to pour me a grudging cup of tea. I picked up the sugar with the tongs so as to fall in with house rules. I fingered the used envelope in my raincoat pocket, see S. re job. I cleared my throat and felt again the urge to yawn that had been with me like a disease for as long as I could remember, and that for all I knew *was* a disease and a deadly one at that. The need to yawn took over from all the other considerations and I began to make the familiar Channel-swimmer mouthings, fishing for the ball of air at the back of my throat. The family returned to rummage among their breakfast plates and, aware that the moment had gone by, I said:

'I've been *off*ered that job in London.'

8

The replies were predictable, so predictable that I had already written them down, although not on a used envelope, and had meant to present the family with this wryly-humourous summing-up of their little ways as some kind of tolerant benediction on them after they spoke, which according to my notes was as folows:

Old man: 'What bloody job?'

Mother: 'How do you mean, you've been offered it?'

Gran: 'What's he talking about, I thought he was going to be a cartooner, last I heard.'

Another of Gran's whimsicalities was that she could no* or more likely would not, remember the noun for the person who draws cartoons. She threw me a baleful glare and I decided not to bring out the predictions but to carry on as I had planned the night before or, as the old man would have it, the early hours of the morning, tossing and turning under the pale gold eiderdown.

'That job with Danny Boon. When I wrote to him,' I said.

I had often likened the conversation at Hillcrest to the route of the old No. 14 tram. Even when completely new subjects were being discussed, the talk rattled on along the familiar track, stopping to load on festering arguments from the past, and culminating at the terminus of the old man's wrath.

'What job with Danny Boon?' This line—together with a rhubarb-rhubarb chorus of 'What's he talking about, Danny Boon'—was optional for the whole family, but was in fact spoken by my mother.

'The job I was *tell*ing you about.'

'What job, you've never told *me* about no job.'

It was obviously going to be one of the uphill treks. The whole family knew well enough about my ambition, or one of my ambitions, to write scripts for comedy. They knew how Danny Boon, who was not so famous then as he is now, had played a week at the Stradhoughton Empire. They knew, because I had told them four times, that I had taken him some material—including my 'thick as lead' catchline which Boon now uses all the time—and how he had liked it. ('Well how do you know he'll pay you anything?' my mother had said.) They

9

knew I had asked him for a *job*. Thank God, I thought, as I pushed my boiled egg aside with the yolk gone and the white untouched, that they don't ask me who Danny Boon is when he's at home.

'Why does he always leave the white of his egg?' asked Gran. 'It's all goodness, just thrown down the sink.'

The remark was so completely irrelevant that even my mother, always a willing explorer down the back-doubles on the conversational map, ignored it. Shouts of 'What about your job at Shadrack and *Dux*bury's?' and 'Who do you think's going to *keep* you?' began to trickle through but I maintained my hysterical calm, wearing my sensitivity like armour. Above everything I could hear the querulous tones of Gran, going over and over again: 'What's he on about? What's he on about? What's he on about? What's he on about?'

I took a deep breath and made it obvious that I was taking a deep breath, and said: 'Look, there is a comedian. The comedian's name is Danny Boon. B- double O-N. He does not write his own scripts. He gets other people to do it for him. He likes my material. He thinks he can give me regular work.'

My mother said: 'How do you mean, he likes your material?'

I brought out the heavy sigh and the clenched teeth. 'Look. This pepper-pot is Danny Boon. This salt-cellar is my material. Danny Boon is looking for material——' I turned the blue plastic pepper-pot on them like a ray-gun. 'He sees my flaming material. So he flaming well asks for it.'

' 'Ere, rear, rear, watch your bloody language! With your flaming this and flaming that! At meal-times! You're not in bloody London yet, you know!'

'He's gone too far,' said Gran, complacently.

I went: 'Sssssssss!' through my teeth. 'For crying out loud!' I slipped back a couple of notches into the family dialect and said: 'Look, do you wanna know or don't you? Cos if you do ah'll tell you, and if you don't ah won't.'

They sat with pursed lips, my mother heaving at the bosom and the old man scowling over his bills and the Woodbine ash filling up his eggshell. The radio took over the silence and filled it for a moment with some droning voice.

'Try *again*,' I said. I took another deep breath, which developed into a yawning fit.

'You just eat your breakfast, and don't have so much off,' my mother said. 'Else get your mucky self washed. And stop always yawning at meal-times. You don't get enough sleep, that's all that's wrong with you.'

'And get to bloody work,' the old man said.

I pushed back the polished chair, about whose machine-turned legs I had once had so much to say, and went into the kitchen. It was five minutes past nine. I leaned against the sink in an angry torpor, bombing and blasting each one of them to hell. I lit a stealthy Player's Weight, and thought of the steel-bright autumn day in front of me, and began to feel better. I breathed heavily again, this time slowly and luxuriously, and began to grope through the coils of fuse-wire in the kitchen drawer for the old man's electric razor. I switched on, waited for a tense second for the bellowed order from the lounge to put the thing away and buy one of my own, and then began my thinking.

I was spending a good part of my time, more of it as each day passed, on this thinking business. Sometimes I could squander the whole morning on it, and very often the whole evening and a fair slice of the night hours too. I had two kinds of thinking (three, if ordinary thoughts were counted) and I had names for them, applied first jocularly and then mechanically. I called them No. 1 thinking and No. 2 thinking. No. 1 thinking was voluntary, but No. 2 thinking was not; it concerned itself with obsessional speculations about the scope and nature of disease (such as a persistent yawn that was probably symptomatic of sarcoma of the jaw), the probable consequences of actual misdemeanours, and the solutions to desperate problems, such as what would one do, what would one actually *do*, in the case of having a firework jammed in one's ear by mischievous boys. The way out of all this was to lull myself into a No. 1 thinking bout, taking the fast excursion to Ambrosia, including in hypothetical conversations with Bertrand Russell, fusing and magnifying the ordinary thoughts of the day so that I was a famous comedian at the Ambrosia State Opera, the only stage personality ever to reach the rank of president.

Propped up against the gas-stove, buzzing away with the old man's razor, I began to do some No. 1 thinking on the subject of the family. This usually took a reasonably noble form: riding home to Hillcrest loaded with money, putting the old man on his feet, forgiving and being forgiven. My mother would be put into furs, would feel uneasy in them at first, but would be touched and never lose her homely ways. Grandma married Councillor Duxbury and the pair of them, apple-cheeked, lived in a thatched cottage high up in the dales, out of sight. That was the usual thing. But this morning, in harder mood, I began to plan entirely new parents for myself. They were of the modern, London, kind. They had allowed, in fact *encouraged*, me to smoke from the age of thirteen (Marcovitch) and when I came home drunk my No. 1 mother would look up from her solitaire and groan: 'Oh God, how dreary! Billy's drunk again!' I announced at breakfast that I was going to start out on my own. My No. 1 father—the old man disguised as a company director—clapped me on the back and said: '*And* about time, you old loafer. Simone and I were thinking of kicking you out of the old nest any day now. Better come into the library and talk about the money end.' As for Gran, she didn't exist.

The thinking and the shaving finished concurrently. I switched off and began brooding over the matter of the black bristles under my chin which, shave as I might, would never come smooth. I dropped back into my torpor, a kind of vacuum annexe to the No. 2 thinking, and began scraping the back of my hand against the bristles, listening to the noise of it and wondering whether there was something wrong with me. The old man came through into the kitchen, putting on his jacket on his way to the garage.

'And you can buy your own bloody razor and stop using mine,' he said without stopping. I called: '*Eighty-four!*' supposedly the number of times he had used the word 'bloody' that morning, a standing joke (at least with me), but he had gone out. The business of going to London was shelved, forgotten or, as I suspected, completely uncomprehended.

I went through the lounge and upstairs. My mother, as I passed her, chanted automatically: 'You'll-set-off-one-of-these-days-and-meet-yourself-coming-back,' one of a series of remarks tailored, I liked to fancy, to fit the exact time taken by me from kitchen door to hall door. There had been a time when I had tried to get the family to call these stock sayings of hers 'Motherisms.' Nobody ever knew what I was talking about.

Swilling myself in the bathroom I found the business of the bristles on my chin leading, as I had known it would, into a definite spasm of No. 2 thinking. I wondered first if I were developing ingrowing hair, like those people whose throats tickle every six weeks and who have to go into hospital to get it removed, and then I ran through the usual repertoire, polio, cancer, T.B. and a new disease, unique in medical history, called Fisher's Yawn. Nowadays these attacks, occurring more or less whenever I had a spare minute, usually culminated at the point where I began to wonder what would happen if I were taken to hospital, died even, and they found out about the calendars.

My mother shouted up the stairs: 'You'll never get into *town* at this rate, never mind London! It's after half-past nine!' but by now the calendar theme had me in its grip, and I staggered into my bedroom, gasping and clawing for breath, doing some deep-level No. 2 thinking on the subject.

It was now September. The calendars had been given to me to post about two weeks before Christmas of the previous year. This meant that this particular problem had been on the agenda for over nine months or, as I sometimes worked it out, six thousand five hundred and twenty-eight hours. The calendars were stiff cardboard efforts measuring ten inches by eight, each bearing a picture of a cat looking at a dog, the legend 'Rivals' and, overprinted in smudgy olive type, 'Shadrack and Duxbury, Funeral Furnishers. Taste'—then a little star—'Tact'—and another little star—'Economy.' They were prestige jobs for Shadrack's contacts, people like the directors of the crematorium and parsons who might ring up with a few tip-offs, and for good customers like the Alderman Burrows Old People's Home, with whom Shadrack and Duxbury's had a standing account. I had omitted to post them in order to get at the postage money, which I had kept for myself. I had hidden the calendars in the stockroom in the office basement for a while and then, tired of the hideous reel of No. 2 thinking where Shadrack lifted the coffin lid and found them, had gradually transferred them home. A few I had already destroyed, taking them out of the house one by one at night and tearing them to shreds, dropping them in a paper-chase over Stradhoughton Moor and sweating over an image of the police picking them up and piecing them together. I had got rid of fourteen in this way. The rest were in a tin trunk under my bed. There were two hundred and eleven of them.

I dressed, making another mental note to look up *Every Man's Own Lawyer* and find out the penalties for this particular crime. 'Pay attention to me, Fisher. I have thought very carefully about sending you to prison. Only your youth and the fact that your employers have spoken so highly of your abilities...' Tying my tie, I began to imagine myself in Armley Jail, impressing the governor with my intelligence, making friends with the padre; and for a short while I was back on the No. 1 thinking, a luxury I could ill afford at half-past nine on a working morning.

'Billy! If you're not out of this house in five minutes I shall push you out!'

I put on my jacket and pulled the old japanned trunk from under the bed. The piece of stamp edging was still in position across the lid. A long while ago, when it had contained no more than the scribbled postcards from Liz and a few saccharine notes from the Witch, I had started to call this trunk my Guilt Chest. Any grain of facetiousness there had been in this description had long since disappeared.

I lifted the lid gingerly, jolted and disturbed as usual by the vast number of calendars there seemed to be, stacked dozens deep in their thick brown envelopes, addressed in my own broad handwriting to Dr H. Rich, P. W. Horniman, Esq., J.P., the Rev. D. L. P. Tack, the Warden, Stradhoughton Workpeople's Hostel. Beside the calendars, nestling in their own dark hollow of the Guilt Chest, were the love letters, the bills the old man had given me to post, the aphrodisiac tablets that Stamp had got for me, the cellophaned, leggy copy of Ritzy Stories, and the letter my mother had once written to Housewives' Choice. I could picture her sitting down with the Stephens' ink bottle and the Basildon Bond, and I could never explain to myself why I had not posted the letter or why I had opened it under cover of the Guilt Chest lid. *'Dear Sir, Just a few lines to let you know how much I enjoy Housewife's "Choice" every day, I always listen no matter what I am doing, could you play (Just a Song at Twilight) for me though I don't suppose you get time to play everyone that writes to you, but this is my "favourite song." You see my husband often used to sing it when we a bit younger than we are now, I will quite understand if you cannot play. Yours respectfully (Mrs) N. Fisher. PS. My son also write songs, but I suppose there is not much chance for him as he has not had the training. We are just ordinary folk.'* The debates I had had with my mother on the ordinary folk motif, in long and eloquent streams of No. 1 thinking, would have filled Housewives' Choice ten times over.

Snapped together by a rubber band, like the used envelopes I had fancied for myself, was the thin pack of postcards that Liz had written to me on her last expedition but one. They were matter-of-fact little notes, full of tediously interesting details about the things she had seen in Leicester, Welwyn Garden City and the other places where whatever urge possessing her had taken her; but at least they were literate. I felt mildly peculiar to be treasuring love letters for their grammar, but there was nothing else I could treasure them for. Sometimes I could think about Liz, think properly on the ordinary plane, for a full minute, before we were both whisked off into Ambrosia, myself facing trial for sedition and she a kind of white-faced Eva Peron in the crowd.

I took one of the calendars out of the Guilt Chest and stuffed it under my pullover. If I was going to London in a week it meant that I had one hundred and sixty-eight hours to dispose of two hundred and eleven calendars. Say, for safety, two calendars an hour between now and next Saturday. I took out another three and crammed them half under my pullover and half under the top of my trousers. Rummaging in the Guilt Chest, I spotted the flat white packet of supposed aphrodisiacs, the 'passion pills' as Stamp, shoving them grubbily into my hand in a fit of remorse, fear and generosity, had called them. I put Liz out of my mind and began thinking about Rita and then, making a definite decision, about the Witch. I put the passion pills in my side pocket and bent to close the Guilt Chest, the calendars stiff under my ribs and the sharp corners showing through the cable-weave of my pullover. I replaced the stamp edging, four inches from the handle on the right-hand side, pushed the trunk carefully under the bed and went downstairs, feeling like a walking Guilt Chest myself. In the hall I put on my outdoor raincoat and buttoned it to the waist before going into the lounge.

'He'll be *buried* in a raincoat,' said Gran, almost, in fact completely, automatically. She was rubbing viciously at the sideboard with a check duster, a daily gruelling which she imagined paid for her keep. It was to the sideboard that she addressed herself, because my mother was in the kitchen.

It was long past any time at all for a working morning. The last late typists, their bucket bags stuffed with deodorants and paper handkerchiefs, had clacked past on their way to the bus shelter. A morning hush had settled over the house. There were specks of dust in the sunlight and the stiff smell of Mansion Polish. The radio emphasised the lateness with an unfamiliar voice, talking about some place where they had strange customs; it was like going long past one's station on the last train.

I called: 'I'm off, mother!'

'Well don't hurry yourself, will you?' she called back, following her voice into the lounge. I paused with my hand running up and down the brown bakelite finger-plate on the door.

'Might as well give my notice in today, if I'm going to London,' I said. My mother pressed her lips together in a thin purple line and began bundling up the tablecloth, taking it by the corners to keep the crumbs in.

'You want to make up your mind what you *do* want to do!' she said primly.

'I *know* what I'm going to do. I'm going to work for Danny Boon.'

'Well how do you know, you've never done that sort of thing before. You can't switch and change and swop about just when you feel like it. You've got your living to earn now, you know!'

She was trying to talk kindly, making a real effort at it but drawing the effort back, like someone whispering across a bridge. I was touched, fleetingly. I said, trying hard myself: 'Any road, we'll talk about it later,' a gruff and oblique statement of affection that, I could see, was received and understood.

I left the house, ignoring the old man who was messing about with the lorry in the road outside. If I can walk all the way down Cherry Row without blinking my eyelids, I told myself, it will be all all right. I kept my eyes wide and burning long past Greenman's sweet-shop, past the clay cavities where the semis were not built yet; then Mrs Olmonroyd came past, spying. I clapped my eyes shut and wished her a civil good morning. I felt the calendars under my jacket and wondered why I had brought them out and what I was going to do with them, and what I was going to do about everything.

T W O

'The very name of Stradhoughton,' Man o' the Dales had written in the *Stradhoughton Echo* one morning when there was nothing much doing, 'conjures up sturdy buildings of

honest native stone, gleaming cobbled streets, and that brackish air which gives this corner of Yorkshire its own especial
*piquancy.*' Man o' the Dales put piquancy in italics, not me.

My No. 1 thinking often featured long sessions with Man o'
the Dales in whatever pub the boys on the *Echo* used, and there
I would put him right on his facts. The cobbled streets, gleaming or otherwise, had long ago been ripped up with the tramlines and re-lined with concrete slabs or tamacadam—gleaming tarmacadam I would *grant* him, stabbing him in the chest
with the stocky briar which in this particular role I affected.
The brackish air I was no authority on, except to say that
when the wind was in a certain direction it smelled of burning
paint. As for the honest native stone, our main street, Moorgate, was—despite the lying reminiscences of old men like
Councillor Duxbury who remembered sheep-troughs where
the X-L Disc Bar now stands—exactly like any other High
Street in Great Britain. Woolworth's looked like Woolworth's,
the Odeon looked like the Odeon, and the *Stradhoughton
Echo's* own office, which Man o' the Dales must have seen,
looked like a public lavatory in honest native white tile. I had
a fairly passionate set piece all worked out on the subject of
rugged Yorkshire towns, with their rugged neon signs and their
rugged plate-glass and plastic shop-fronts, but so far nobody
had given me the opportunity to start up on the theme.

'Dark satanic mills I can put up with,' I would say, pushing
my tobacco pouch along the bar counter. 'They're part of the
picture. But'—puff, puff—'when it comes to dark satanic power
stations, dark satanic housing estates, and dark satanic tea-
shops——'

'That's the trouble with you youngsters,' said Man o' the
Dales, propping his leather-patched elbows on the seasoned
bar. 'You want progress, but you want all the Yorkshire tradition as well. You can't have both.'

'I want progress,' I retorted, making with the briar. 'But I
want a Yorkshire tradition of progress.'

'That's good. Can I use that?' said Man o' the Dales.

Anyway, satanic or not, it was the usual Saturday morning
down in town, the fat women rolling along on their bad feet

like toy clowns in pudding basins, the grey-faced men reviewing the sporting pinks. Along Market Street, where the new glass-fronted shops spilled out their sagging lengths of plywood and linoleum, there were still the old-fashioned stalls, lining the gutter with small rotten apples and purple tissue paper. The men shouted: 'Do I ask fifteen bob, do I ask twelve and a tanner? I do *not*. I do not ask you for ten bob. I do not ask you for three half crowns. Gimme five bob, five bob, five bob, five bob, five bob.' Frowning women, their black, scratched handbags crammed with half-digested grievances, pushed through the vegetable stalls to the steps of the rates office.

Off Market Street there was a little alley called St Botolph's Passage, the centre of most of Stradhoughton's ready-money betting. Besides the bookies' shops, the stinking urinal, the sly chemist's with red rubber gloves and big sex books in the window, and the obscure one-man businesses mooning behind the dark doorways, there was a pub, a dyer's and cleaner's, and Shadrack and Duxbury's, tasteful funerals. Many were the jokes about St Botolph and his passage, but even more were those about the dyers and the undertakers.

The exterior of Shadrack's, where I now paused to take my traditional deep breath before entering, showed a conflict of personalities between young Shadrack and old Duxbury, the two partners. Young Shadrack, taking advantage of Duxbury's only trip abroad, a reciprocal visit by the town council to Lyons (described by Man o' the Dales as the Stradhoughton of France), had pulled out the Dickensian windows, bottle-glass and all, and substituted modern plate-glass and a shop sign of raised stainless steel lettering. Thus another piece of old Stradhoughton bit the dust and the new effect was of a chip shop on a suburban housing estate. Councillor Duxbury had returned only just in time to salve the old window-dressing from the wreckage, and this remained: a smudgy sign by Stamp reading 'Tasteful Funeral's, "Night or Day Service"' (which, as my other colleague Arthur had said, needed only an exclamation mark in brackets to complete it) and a piece of purple cloth on which there was deposited a white vase, the shape of a lead weight, inscribed to the memory of a certain Josiah Olroyd. The reason Josiah Olroyd's vase was in Shadrack's window and not in the corporation cemetery was that his name had been misspelled, and the family had not unreasonably refused to accept goods ordered. The Olroyd vase always served to remind me of a ghastly error with some coffin nameplates in which I had been involved, a business that was far from finished yet, and it was with this thought uppermost in a fairly crowded mind that, ninety minutes late, I entered Shadrack and Duxbury's.

The shop bell rang and, behaving exactly like a Pavlov dog, Stamp got up and began, elaborately, to put on his coat.

'Must be going-home time, Fisher's come,' he said.

I ignored him and addressed Arthur.

'Is he in?' I jerked my head towards Shadrack's door.

'Just come in this minute,' said Arthur. 'You can say you were in the bog.'

I hissed with relief and flopped down at my desk, between Stamp and Arthur. Every day, sitting tensed at the front of the bus, pushing it with my hands to make it faster, I had this race to the office with Shadrack. Duxbury didn't matter; he never came rolling in until eleven and in any case he was so old that he could never remember who worked for him. It was Shadrack, with his little notebooks, and the propelling pencil rattling against his teeth, who gave all the trouble. 'It's been noticed that you were half an hour late again this morning.' He always said 'It's been noticed.' 'It's been noticed that you haven't sent those accounts off yet.'

'I'm off to tell him what time you came in,' sniggered Stamp, and I was obliged to murmur 'You do,' the passing acknowledgement of his feeble jest. Stamp called himself a 'clurk' and did not go very much beyond jokes of the Mary-Rose-sat-on-a-pin-Mary-Rose variety. He now started on his morning performance.

'Hey, that tart on telly last night! Where she bent forward over that piano! *Coarrrr*!'

It was the first duty of Arthur and myself to nip this quietly in the bud.

'What make?' said Arthur innocently.

'What make what?'

'What make was the piano?'

Stamp sneered: 'Oh, har har. Some say good old Arthur.'

We got down to our work, what there was of it. Shadrack and Duxbury's was dull and comfortable as offices go. It was done throughout in sleepy chocolate woodwork, which Shadrack, dreaming of pinewood desks and Finnish wallpapers, had not yet got his hands on. Our task was to do the letters, make up the funeral accounts, run the errands and greet prospective customers with a suitably gloomy expression before shuffling them off on to Shadrack. September was a quiet month and Saturday was a quiet morning; we all had our own pursuits to work on. Stamp, head on one side, tongue cocked out of the corner of his mouth, spent most of his time making inky posters for the youth club *'Have you paid your "subs"? If not, "why not"!!!'* Arthur and I would sit around trying to write songs together, or sometimes I would tinker with *The two Schools at Gripminster.*

'You couldn't see what make it was, she was bending too far over it,' Stamp said at last. I did not look at him, but I knew that he was describing a bosom with his hands.

'Penny's dropped,' Arthur said.

'Penny-farthing more like,' I said. 'It's been earning interest while he thought that one up.'

'Write that one down,' Arthur said.

'Joke over,' said Stamp.

There was nothing in the in-tray. I got *The Two Schools at Gripminster* out of my desk drawer and stared vacantly at what I had written of my thirty-four thousand words. ' *"I say, weed! Aren't you a new bug?" Sammy Brown turned to greet the tall, freckle-faced boy who walked across the quad towards him. Sammy's second name was appropriate—for the face of this sturdy young fellow was as brown as a berry. W. Fisher. William Fisher. The Two Schools at Gripminster, by William Fisher. William L. Fisher. W. L. Fisher. Two-School Sammy, by W. L. P. Fisher. Two Schools at Gripminster: A Sammy Brown Story by W. L. P. Fisher. The Sammy Brown Omnibus.*

*W. Lashwood Fisher. W. de L. Fisher.'* I looked at it for some time, thought *'William Fisher: His Life and Times'* but did not write it down, then put the paper back in the drawer. The four chunky calendars under my pullover hurt my chest when I leaned forward over the desk. I began thinking of Danny Boon and the letter I had better write to him, and about Shadrack and the letter I had better write to *him*.

'I've got something unpleasant to say to our Mr Shadrack this morning,' I said to Arthur.

'You've got something unpleasant to say to our Mr Shadrack this morning?' repeated Arthur, dropping into the Mr Bones and Mr Jones routine in which we conducted most of our exchanges. I decided not to tell Arthur just yet about the London business but to while half an hour away in the usual manner. 'Anything I say to Mr Shadrack would be unpleasant,' I said.

'Kindly leave the undertaker's' Arthur said.

'Tell me, Mr Crabtree, what are the Poles doing in Russia?'

'I don't know, Mr Fisher, what are the Poles doing in Russia?'

'Holding up the telegraph wires, same as everywhere else.'

'That's not what these ladies and gentlemen have come to hear.'

I jumped to my feet, clutching the ruler from my desk. 'Have a care, Mr Crabtree! If I fire this rod it'll be curtains for you!'

'Why so, Mr Fisher?'

'It's a curtain rod.'

'I don't wish to know that.'

Stamp plodded in: 'Same here, it's got whiskers on it, that one.' We had explained to him fifty times over that that was the whole bloody *point*, but the idea would not sink in. It always led Stamp to his own jokes.

'If a barber shaves a barber, who talks?'

Arthur and I, deadpan, said : 'Who?'

'Joke over,' Stamp said, weakly. He went back to the poster he was doing for a pea-and-pie supper out Treadmill way.

Arthur started typing out the new song we had written. I got going on the letter.

*Dear Mr Boon,*
    *Many thanks for your letter of September 2——*
*Dear Mr Boon,*
    *Yes! I should be delighted to come to London——*
*Dear Mr Boon,*
    *I will be in London next Saturday——*

The idea of being in London next Saturday, put down on paper and staring me in the face, filled my bowels with quick-flushing terror. For as long as I could remember, I had been enjoying rich slabs of No. 1 thinking about London, coughing my way through the fog to the Odd Man Out Club, Chelsea, with its chess tables and friendly, intelligent girls. I was joint editor, with the smiling 'Jock' Osonolu, a Nigerian student, of the club's sensational wall-sheet, modelled somewhat on the lines of the Ambrosia *Times-Advocate*. I would live in a studio high over the Embankment, sometimes with a girl called Ann, a Londoner herself and as vivacious as they come, but more often with Liz, not Liz as she actually existed but touched up with a No. 1 ponytail to become my collaborator on a play for theatre in the round. Sometimes I could see myself starving on the Embankment, the tramp-poet; and now, sitting at my desk, the idea of *actually* starving on the Embankment suddenly presented itself to me. I switched over into the No. 2 thinking with a grinding of the points inside my stomach and there I was, feeling for the actual pangs of hunger and counting the hot pennies in my pocket. Five shillings left, one egg and chips leaves three and nine, doss down at Rowton House, two and nine. Evening paper twopence-halfpenny, breakfast a tanner, call it two bob, two bob, two bob. I do not ask for ten bob, ladies, I do not ask you for three half crowns. Gimme two bob, two bob, two bob, and back I was on the No. 1, the poet stallholder of Petticoat Lane.

The door-bell tinkled and we put on our funeral faces but it was nobody, only Councillor Duxbury. He crossed the floor to his own office with an old man's shuffle, putting all his thought into the grip of his stick and the pattern of the faded, broken lino. A thick, good coat sat heavily on his bowed back, and there were enamelled medallions on his watch-chain. At the door of his room he half-turned, moving his whole body like an old robot, and muttered: 'Morning, lads.'

We chanted, half-dutifully, half-ironically: 'Good morning, Councillor Duxbury,' and directly the door was closed, began our imitation of him. 'It's Councillor Duxbury, lad, Councillor Duxbury. Tha wun't call Lord Harewood mister, would tha? Councillor, that's mah title. Now think on.'

'Ah'm just about thraiped,' said Arthur in broad dialect. The word was one we had made up to use in the Yorkshire dialect routine, where we took the Michael out of Councillor Duxbury and people like him. Duxbury prided himself on his dialect which was practically unintelligible even to seasoned Yorkshiremen.

'Tha's getten more bracken ivvery day, lad,' I said.

'Aye, an' fair scritten anall,' said Arthur.

'Tha mun laik wi' t' gangling-iron.'

'Aye.'

We swung into the other half of the routine, which was Councillor Duxbury remembering, as he did every birthday in an interview with the *Stradhoughton Echo*. Arthur screwed up his face into the lined old man's wrinkles and said:

'Course, all this were fields when I were a lad.'

'—and course, ah'd nobbut one clog to mah feet when ah come to Stradhoughton,' I said in the wheezing voice.

'Tha could get a meat pie and change out o' fourpence——'

'Aye, an' a box at t' Empire and a cab home at t' end on it.'

'Ah had to tak' a cab home because ah only had one clog,' said Arthur.

'Oh, I'll *use* that,' I said, resuming my normal voice. '*Bastard.*'

'Bar-steward,' said Stamp, automatically.

Every Saturday night I did a club turn down at one of the pubs in Clogiron Lane, near where we lived. It was a comedy act, but not the kind of thing Danny Boon would be interested

24

in : a slow-burning, Yorkshire monologue that was drummed up mainly by Arthur and me at these sessions in the office. Arthur was more interested in the singing side. He did a turn with the band at the Roxy twice a week, Wednesdays and Saturdays, trying vainly to get them to play the songs we had written between us. When my own turn was finished I would hurry over to the Roxy to listen to him, pretending that I was whisking from one theatre to another to catch a promising act that I was thinking of booking.

As for Stamp, he did nothing at all except loll about in the Roxy, waving his arms about and mouthing 'Woodchopper's Ball' when the band played it.

'Saw that bint you used to knock about with 's morning,' he said, when the Duxbury routine was over.

'You what?'

'That bint. Her that always used to be ringing you up.'

I ran flippantly back through the sequence of disasters, Audrey, Peggy, Lil, that bint from Morecambe. A depression grew inside me as I traced them back almost to my schooldays. When I recognised the depression, I knew whom he was talking about.

I said lightly, knowing what was coming: '*What* bint, for Christ sake?'

'That scruffy-looking one. Her that always wore that suède coat.'

I poured unconcern into my voice. 'Who—Liz What's-her-name?'

'Yer, Woodbine Lizzy. Randy as a rattlesnake, isn't she? She hasn't got a new coat yet.'

So Liz was back in town. I liked the phrase 'back in town', as though she had just ridden in on a horse, and I toyed with it for a second, so as not to think about her. Drive you out of town. City limits. Get out of town, Logan, I'm warning you for the last time.

It was a month ago since she had left last, with only a chance good-bye, and this time there had been no postcards. It was part of the nature of Liz to disappear from time to time and I was proud of her bohemianism, crediting her with a soul-deep need to get away and straighten out her personality, or to find herself, or something; but in less romantic moments I would fall to wondering whether she was tarting round the streets with some American airman. I had no real feeling for her, but there was always some kind of pain when she went away, and when the pain yielded nothing, I converted it, like an alchemist busy with the seaweed, into something approaching love.

'Where did you see her?' I asked.

'*I* don't know. Walking up Infirmary Street,' said Stamp. 'Why, frightened she's got another boy friend?' he said in his nauseating, elbow-prodding way.

I said carefully: 'Thought she'd gone to Canada or somewhere,' naming the first country that came into my head.

'What's she come back for, then?' said Stamp.

I was trying to find a cautious way of going on with it when Arthur came to the rescue. He had been handling the switchboard.

'Never use a preposition to end a sentence with,' he said.

I often told myself that I had no friends, only allies, banded together in some kind of conspiracy against the others. Arthur was one of them. We spoke together mainly in catchphrases, hidden words that the others could not understand.

'I might ask you to not split infinitives,' I said gratefully, in the light relieved voice.

'Hear about the bloke who shot the owl?' said Arthur. 'It kept saying to who instead of to whom.'

'Shouldn't it be Who's Whom instead of Who's Who?' I said, not for the first time that week. Even our ordinary conversations were like the soft-shoe shuffle routine with which we enlivened the ordinary day. I was perfectly aware that I was stalling, and I turned back to Stamp.

'Did you speak to her?'

'Speak to who?'

'To whom. Woodbine Lizzy,' I said, burning with shame for using the nickname Stamp had given her.

'No, just said hullo. She was with somebody,' he said, as though it did not matter. But it was my first bit of emotional

26

meat this morning, and I was determined to make it matter, and to get the pain back inside where it belonged.

'Who was she with?'

'*I* don't know, I don't ask people for their autographs. What's up, are you jealous, eh? Eh?' He pronounced the word 'jealous' as though it were something he had dug up out of the garden, still hot and writhing.

The door-bell tinkled again. 'Shop,' called Arthur softly, getting up. A small woman, all the best clothes she had collected together on her body, peered round the door. 'Is this where you come to arrange for t' funerals?'

Arthur walked respectfully over to the counter.

'Ah've been in t' wrong shop. Ah thought it were next door.' She leaned heavily on the counter, her arms folded against it, and began to spell out her name.

I got up, stiffly, feeling the calendars under my pullover, and the waft of cold air when I separated them from my shirt. 'Off to the bog,' I muttered to Stamp and went downstairs among the cardboard boxes of shrouds and coffin handles. I pottered aimlessly among the wreath-cards and the bales of satin lining, looking for something worth having, and then went into the lavatory.

The lavatory at Shadrack and Duxbury's had a little shaving mirror on the door, where Shadrack could inspect his boils. More as a matter of routine than anything else, I put my tongue out and looked at it. There were some lumps at the back of my throat that I had never noticed before. Putting the subject of Liz on one side, I began putting my tongue between my fingers, seeing if the lumps got worse further down and wondering if this were the beginning of gingivitis which Stamp, with some justice, had suffered the year before. The sharp pain in my chest I located as the edge of the calendars shoving against my ribs. I checked the bolt on the door again, and took the calendars out from under my pullover. They were dog-eared now, with well-established creases across the envelopes. The top one was addressed to an old mother superior at the nunnery down by the canal. I took out the calendar and folded the envelope in four, a surprising bulkiness. I rammed the envelope into my side pocket, where the passion pills were, and held the calendar in my hands, the other three firmly gripped under my arm.

There was a brown-printed page for each month. The months tore off, and at the bottom of each month was a quotation. I knew some of them by heart. *'The only riches you will take to heaven are those you give away'*—January. *'Think all you speak, but speak not all you think'*—February. *'It takes sixty muscles to frown, but only thirteen to smile. Why waste energy'*—April. I tore the leaves off one by one and dropped them into the lavatory. When I had reached October, *'It is a gude heart that says nae ill, but a better heart that thinks none,'* I decided that that was enough for the time being and pulled the length of rough string that served for a chain. As the screwed-up pieces of paper swam around in the water I tried hurriedly to count them, January to October inclusive, ten pages, in case I had dropped one on the floor for Shadrack to find and investigate. The water resumed its own level. To my horror, about half a dozen calendar leaves, soggy and still swimming, remained. I began gnawing at my lower lip and checking the signs of panic, heart, sweaty palms, tingling ankles, like a mechanic servicing a car. I flushed the lavatory again but there was only a heavy zinking noise and a trickle of water as the ballcock protested. I perched myself on the side of the scrubbed seat and waited, staring at the mother superior's calendar. *'Those who bring sunshine to the lives of others cannot keep it from themselves'*—November.

I could hear Councillor Duxbury clumping about upstairs, aimlessly opening drawers and counting his money. Without much effort, I drifted into Ambrosia, where the Grand Yeomanry were still limping past the war memorial, their left arms raised in salute. *'It is often wondered how the left-hand salute, peculiar to Ambrosia, originated. Accounts differ but the most widely-accepted explanation is that of the seven men who survived the Battle of Wakefield all, by an amazing coincidence, had lost their right arms. It was necessary for them to salute their President——'*

The stairs creaked and there were footsteps on the stone

28

floor outside. Somebody rattled the loose knob of the lavatory door. I waited for them to go away, but I could hear the heavy breathing. I began to start up a tuneless whistling so that they would know the booth was engaged, and to back-track through my recent thoughts to check that I had not been talking to myself. The door-rattling continued.

'Someone in here,' I called.

I heard the voice of Stamp: 'What you doing, man, writing your will out?'

It was the kind of remark Gran would shout up the stairs at home. 'Naff off,' I shouted, as I would dearly have loved to shout at Gran in the same situation. Stamp began pawing at the door. If there had been a keyhole he would have been peeping through it by now.

'No writing mucky words on the walls!' he called. I did not reply. The last few words were breathless and accompanied by a scraping noise on the floor, and it was obvious that he was jumping up and down, trying to peer over the top of the door. 'Naff off, Stamp, for Christ sake!' I called. I stood up. The soggy little balls of paper were still in the lavatory but I dared not pull the chain again while Stamp was still there. I picked up the other calendars from the floor where I had put them and stuck them back inside my pullover, trying not to let the stiff paper crackle. Outside, Stamp began grunting in what he imagined to be an imitation of a man in the throes of constipation.

'Bet you're reading a mucky book,' he said in a hoarse whisper through the door. I let him ramble on. 'Bet y'are, bet you're reading a mucky book. *"His hand caressed her silken knee——"* ' and, excited by his own fevered images, he began to mouth obscenities through the cracks in the deep green door.

There was another sound on the stairs, this time the furry padding of light suède shoes, and I could imagine the yellow socks and the chocolate-brown gaberdines that went with them. I heard the nasal, nosey voice of Shadrack: 'Haven't you anything to do upstairs, Stamp?' and Stamp, crashing his voice into second gear to simulate something approaching respect, saying: 'Just waiting to go into the toilet, Mr Shadrack.'

'Yes, it's thought that some of you spend too much time down here. Far too much time,' said Shadrack. He picked at words as other people picked at spots.

Shadrack was not the stock cartoon undertaker, although he would have made a good model for other stock cartoons, notably the one concerning the psychiatrist's couch. He was, for a start, only about twenty-five years old, though grown old with quick experience, like forced rhubarb. His general approach and demeanour was that of the second-hand car salesman, and he had in fact at one time been one in the south. He was in the undertaking business because his old man was in it before him and old Shadrack had been, so to speak, young Shadrack's first account. After that he rarely attended funerals and would indeed have found it difficult in view of the R.A.F. blazer and the canary-coloured pullover which, sported being the word, he sported. But he was useful to the firm in that, besides having inherited half of it, he could get round old ladies. He was a member of most churches in Stradhoughton and to my certain knowledge was a card-carrying Unitarian, a Baptist, a Methodist, and both High and Low Church.

'You'd better get up into the office,' I heard him say to Stamp. 'I've got to go out.'

Stamp shuffled off, murmuring inarticulate servilities. I called: 'Is that you, Mr Shadrack?'

He either did not hear or did not choose to hear, but started fidgeting among the coffin handles, just outside the lavatory door.

'Is that Mr Shadrack?'

'Yes, there's someone waiting to come in there,' he said testily.

'Shan't be a minute,' I called in the high monotone of a man hailing down from the attic. 'I was wondering if I could see you before you go out?'

'What?'

The voice I had chosen was beginning to send ridiculous. 'Was wondering if I could *see* you, 'fore you go out.'

Shadrack called back: 'Yes, I've been thinking it's about time we had a little talk.' Perched in my cold cell, I wondered miserably what he meant by that and skimmed quickly through a condensed inventory of the things he might know about.

'Well I can't see you now, Fisher, I've got to arrange a funeral. You'll have to come back after lunch.'

Every Saturday afternoon, after the firm had closed for the day, Shadrack started messing about with a drawing-board he kept in his office. He was trying to design a contemporary coffin. So far he had not had the nerve to try and interest Councillor Duxbury in the project, the Councillor being an oak and brass fittings man, but he spent a lot of time drawing streamlined caskets, as he called them, on yellow scratchpads. One thing he had succeeded in doing was fitting out the funeral fleet, including the hearse, with a radio system. When there was a funeral Shadrack would sit in his office saying 'Able-Peter, Able-Peter, over' into a microphone. So far as I could remember, nobody ever answered him, and I could not think what he would have said if they had, except: 'Divert funeral to Manston Lane Chapel, over.' He kept a copy of *The Loved One* in his desk, but only to get ideas.

I called: 'Righto, Mr Shadrack.' I did not know whether he had gone back upstairs or whether he was still prowling about outside. Not to take chances, I flushed the lavatory again. When the water had flowed away there were two little balls of paper still floating about. I took the thick, folded envelope out of my pocket and, my face disfigured by nausea, scooped the two soggy leaves of calendar out of the lavatory. I stuffed them inside the envelope and crammed it into my pocket. Then I unbolted the door. Shadrack was standing immediately behind it, and he glanced me up and down like a customs officer as I passed.

Upstairs, Arthur had his raincoat on, waiting to go out for coffee. Before I could speak, Stamp called: 'Here he is! Reading mucky books in the bog!' I reached for my own raincoat. Stamp shouted, hoarsely so that Shadrack could not hear downstairs, 'Let's have a read! What you got, *Lady Chatter-*

*ley's Lover?*' He dived forward and began scragging me around the stomach. He felt the stiff calendars under my pull-over and bellowed in triumph: 'He has! He has! He's got a mucky book under his jersey! *Coarrr!* Dirty old man!'

I seized his wrists and snapped: '*Take* your stinking mucky hands off my pullover, stupid-looking crow!'

'Give us your mucky book,' pleaded Stamp, wheezing in his joke-over way.

Arthur was twiddling the door-handle impatiently. 'Are you coming out for coffee?' I pulled my coat on.

'Don't be all day, you two, I want some,' said Stamp.

'Go to hell,' I said.

'Don't take any wooden bodies,' Arthur called from the door.

'Go to hell,' said Stamp.

### THREE

Stradhoughton was littered with objects for our derision. We would make fascist speeches from the steps of the rates office, and we had been in trouble more than once for doing our Tommy Atkins routine under the war memorial in Town Square. Sometimes we would walk down Market Street shouting 'Apples a pound pears' to confuse the costermongers with their leather jackets and their Max Miller patter.

The memorial vase to Josiah Olroyd in Shadrack's window always triggered off the trouble at t' mill routine, a kind of serial with Arthur taking the part of Olroyd and I the way-ward son.

As we began to walk down St Botolph's Passage, Arthur struck up: 'Ther's allus been an Olroyd at Olroyd's mill, and ther allus will be. Now you come 'ere with your college ways and you want none of it!'

'But father! We must all live our lives according to our

lights——' I began in the high-pitched university voice.

'Don't gi' me any o' yon fancy talk!' said Arthur, reflecting with suspicious accuracy the tone of the old man at breakfast. 'You broke your mother's heart, lad. Do you know that?'

'Father! The men! They're coming up the drive!'

We turned into Market Street swinging our arms from side to side like men on a lynching spree. Arthur held up an imaginary lantern.

'Oh, so it's thee, Ned Leather! Ye'd turn against me, would ye?'

In the university voice: 'Now, Leather, what's afoot?'—and before Arthur could seize the part for himself, I switched accents and got into the character of Ned Leather. 'Oh, so it's the young lord and master up from Oxford and Cambridge, is it? We'll see about thee in a minute, impudent young pup!'

Arthur, piqued as always because I had got the Ned Leather dialogue for myself, dropped the routine. We walked in silence past the pork butchers and the dry-cleaning shops stuffed with yellow peg-board notices, and turned into Moorgate. I was in a fairly schizophrenic state of mind. I was looking into the distance to catch a glimpse of Liz in her green suède jacket, but at the same time tensing myself ready to meet Rita, who worked in the café where we had our morning break. Digging my hands into my pockets I could feel Stamp's little box of passion pills, and this reminded me of the Witch. I was thinking confusedly about all three of them when Arthur began clearing his throat to adjust his voice into ordinary speech. I had noticed before that when he had something unpalatable to say he would preface it with a bit of clowning from either the trouble at t' mill or Duxbury routines.

'My mother's been saying how nice it would be if our families could get together,' he said at length.

'God forbid,' I said.

A star feature of my No. 2 thinking was a morbid dread of Arthur's mother meeting *my* mother. I had once told Arthur's mother, in a loose moment, that I had a sister called Sheila.

'And she wants to send some old toys to the kids as well,' said Arthur.

'All contributions gratefully received,' I said, still flippant.

I wondered to myself why I had ever started it. In the odd bored moments, waiting for Arthur to tie his tie in the quiet ticking house where he lived, I had got Sheila married to a grocer's assistant in the market called Eric. Eric, prospering, now had three shops of his own, two in Leeds and one in Bradford. As conversation lagged between me and Arthur's mother, I had given Eric and Sheila two children; Norma, now aged three, and Michael, aged one and a half. Michael had unfortunately been born with a twisted foot, but medical skill on the part of one Dr Ubu, an Indian attached to Leeds University, had left him with a hardly noticeable limp. Arthur had often asked me to kill my sister off and put the kids in a home, but the long-drawn-out mourning and a Shadrack and Duxbury funeral were beyond me. I felt indignant that his mother should take so much interest in a family of what, after all, were total strangers to her.

'Anyway, don't let your mother come near *our* house,' I said. 'I've told 'em she's in hospital with a broken leg.' This was the truth, not the truth that Arthur's mother was in hospital, but the truth that I, to tide me over some awkward moment, had said she was.

'The trouble with you, cocker, is you're a pathological bloody liar,' said Arthur.

'Well, I've seen the psychiatrist and——'

'Kindly leave the couch.'

We resumed our silence, this one more uncomfortable than the last. I saw that we had a hundred yards to go before the café, and I switched in to the No. 1 thinking for a brief morning bulletin. My No. 1 mother was on: 'Billy, is this another of your *ghastly* practical jokes?' The idea of switching in brought a radio into my mind, a little white portable singing among the rubber-plants on the low-slung shelves as I mixed the drinks before dinner. My No. 1 mother said: 'Do for God's sake turn off that bloody *box*!' but this brought me back to the Vim-scoured face of my actual mother and her letter to Housewives' Choice. Cornered between the Guilt Chest and the spectre of *Arthur's* mother it was with some relief that I saw that we were outside the glassy, glacial doors of the Kit-Kat café and its monstrous, wobbling plaster sundae.

The Kit-Kat was another example of Stradhoughton moving with the times, or rather dragging its wooden leg about five paces behind the times. The plaster sundae was all that was supposed to be left of a former tradition of throbbing urns, slophouse cooking, and the thin tide of biscuit crumbs and tomato pips that was symbolic of Stradhoughton public catering. The Kit-Kat was now a coffee bar, or thought it was. It had a cackling espresso machine, a few empty plant-pots, and about half a dozen glass plates with brown sugar stuck all over them. The stippled walls, although redecorated, remained straight milkbar: a kind of Theatre Royal backcloth showing Dick Whittington and his cat hiking it across some of the more rolling dales. Where the coffee bar element really fell down, however, was in the personality of Rita, on whom I was now training the sights of my anxiety. With her shiny white overall, her mottled blonde hair, and her thick red lips, she could have transmogrified the Great Northern Hotel itself into a steamy milkbar with one wipe of her tea-cloth.

'You know, dark satanic mills I can put up with,' I said as we climbed on the wobbling stools. 'But when it comes to dark satanic power stations, dark satanic housing estates and dark satanic coffee bars——'

'Put on another record, kid, we've heard that one before,' said Arthur in a surprisingly coarse voice.

The Kit-Kat was full of people of the Stamp variety, all making hideous puns and leaning heavily on the I've-stopped-smoking-I-do-it-every-day kind of conversation. Rita was serving chocolate Penguins to a mob of cyclists at the other end of the bar. She waved, tinkling her fingers as though playing the piano, and I waved back.

'Watch your pockets, fellers! See if they measure you up!' This was the standard greeting from the Stamp crowd for any of us from Shadrack and Duxbury's, and the reply was: 'Drop dead.'—'Will you bury me if I do?'—'Free of charge, mate,' and that was the end of the responses.

B*

'No, look, seriously though, you haven't said our old woman's broken her leg, have you?' said Arthur.

'Course I have.'

'She'll go bloody bald, man! What if I'd called at your house and your old woman had asked after her?'

'You would have risen to the occasion,' I said mock-heroically.

'The liefulness is terrific,' said Arthur, entering reluctantly into the mood of banter.

I toyed with the Perspex-covered menu, advertising onion soup that did not exist. 'Think Stamp really *did* see Liz this morning?' I said.

'*I* don't bloody know, man,' Arthur said, adding irrelevantly: 'I've lost track of your sex life.'

'No, I was just wondering,' I said.

Arthur nodded furtively up the bar towards Rita, who was still engaged in primitive verbal by-play with the cyclists. 'Listen,' he whispered hoarsely. 'Which one of 'em are you supposed to be engaged to—her or the Witch?'

'That's an academic question.'

'Well you can't be engaged to them both at once, for Christ sake,' said Arthur.

I turned a wryly-haunted face to him. 'How much have you got *says* I can't?'

'Jesus wept!' said Arthur.

The position with Rita was that I had had my eye on her ever since she moved into the Kit-Kat from a transport café in the Huddersfield Road, her natural habitat. A life of mechanical badinage with lorry drivers had left her somewhat low on the conversational level, but she was a good, or at least a stolid, listener. The previous night, in an eloquent mood, I had proposed marriage and Rita, probably thinking it bad manners to refuse, had accepted. The only complicated thing was that I was already engaged to the Witch, so that Rita's status was roughly that of first reserve in the matrimonial team.

'Well which one of them's got the naffing *engagement* ring?' whispered Arthur.

I said: 'Well, the Witch had it, only I've got it back. I'm

supposed to be getting it adjusted at the jeweller's.' The Witch's engagement ring in its little blue box, I now remembered, was among the items of loot in my jacket pockets. I wondered in a fleeting panic what they would make of it all if I was knocked down by a bus and my possessions were sent home to Hillcrest.

'Who's next on the list—Woodbine Lizzie?' said Arthur.

'No,' I said. 'We can accept no further engagements.'

'Write that down,' said Arthur.

At the other end of the counter, Rita's conversation with the cyclists ended abruptly as one of them stumbled over the tight boundaries of propriety. She pitched her mill-tinged, masculine voice at its most raucous to call back 'Gerron home, yer mother wants yer boots for loaftins!' as she turned away and sauntered down the bar, running the gauntlet of standard raillery as she came to greet us. There was no doubt at all that the Stamp crowd had something to whistle about. Rita was a natural for every beauty contest where personality was not a factor. She had already been Miss Stradhoughton, and she had been voted The Girl We Would Most Like To Crash The Sound Barrier With by some American airmen.

Arthur slumped himself ape-fashion across the bar. 'Gimme two cawfees, ham on rye, slice blueberry pie,' he drawled, a snatch from the two Yanks in a drugstore routine which we were still perfecting.

'Oo, look what's crawled out of the cheese,' said Rita. 'Marlon Brando.'

'If I fire this rod it'll be curtains for you, sister,' said Arthur out of the side of his mouth.

'Yer, cos it's a curtain rod. Tell us summat we don't know.'

'Well come on, love, pour us a coffee,' I said, speaking for the first time.

'Gerroff yer knees,' said Rita without rancour, strolling over to the espresso machine. So far there had been no sign from anybody, her, me, or anybody else, that we were engaged to be married.

Someone out of the Stamp crowd, preparing to leave, called out: 'Coming to the Odeon tonight, Rita, back row, eh?'

Without turning round she called back: 'They wun't let you in, it's an "A" picture.'

Everybody I knew spoke in clichés, but Rita spoke as though she got her words out of a slot machine, whole sentences ready-packed in a disposable tinfoil wrapper. There was little meaning left in anything she actually said; her few rough phrases had been so worn through constant use that she now relied not on words but on the voice itself, and the modulation of the animal sounds it produced, to express the few thick slabs of meaning of which she was capable. In moments of tenderness a certain gruffness, like Woodbine smoke, would curl into her throat, but she had long ago forgotten, and probably never knew, the vocabulary of human kindness.

She slopped the coffee in front of us, Joe's Café style, and rested her elbows on the counter, her bosom—itself a cliché, like a plaster relief given away by the women's magazines—protruding over the bar. She now thought it necessary to make some delicate reference to the fact that we had had a momentous time of it the night before.

'What time did you get in last night?' she said.

''Bout one o-clock,' I said. 'Our old man went crackers this morning. Should've heard him.'

'Me man did as well. I've got to stop in on Monday. Why, did you miss your bus or summat?'

'Yer—'ad to walk,' I said, falling chameleon-like into her own tongue.

'Why didn't you take a taxi, old man, old man?' said Arthur in his Western Brothers voice.

'Oo, hark at Lord Muck,' said Rita. 'You should have gone to Town Square, got an all-night bus.'

This was the sequence and rhythm of daylight love-play as she knew it, a kind of oral footy-footy that was the nearest she could get to intimate conversation.

'No, I like walking,' I said.

Rita said, 'Tramp, tramp, tramp, the boys are marching,' in the derisory tone she used to apologise for putting her tongue to a quotation. 'Anyway, you're lucky, you can always get your shoes mended free.'

I was puzzled by the remark until I remembered, dredging among the fallen platitudes of the night before, an invitation I had made to Rita to come to Sunday tea. The invitation had been make-weight, a kind of free coupon along with the proposal, but in the course of it I had told her that the old man was a cobbler with a shop down Clogiron Lane.

'Oh, yer,' I said. 'Are you still going to the Roxy tonight?'

'Yer.'

'Have I to see you inside, or outside?'

'Are you kidding?'

'Just thought I'd get away without paying,' I said. It was standard, ready-to-use repartee, expected and indeed sought after. 'See you outside, then 'bout nine o'clock. Are you still coming for your tea tomorrow?'

'Yer, if you like. Anyway, we'll fix that up tonight,' she said.

Rita did not know it, but the matter was already fixed. The old man would be called away to inspect a load of Government surplus rubber heels in Harrogate, my mother would take the opportunity of a lift to visit my Auntie Polly in Otley or somewhere, and the tea would be postponed. I had not yet tackled the problem of the Roxy, to which I was also supposed to be going with the Witch. Arthur, by my side, was covering his face with his hands and making quiet cawing noises in a pantomime of amazement. I gave him a quick kick on the foot and felt in my pocket for the little blue box with the Witch's engagement ring in it.

'Try this on for size,' I said, sliding it casually across the counter.

'What, is it for me?' said Rita in her gormless way.

'Who do you think it's for, your mother?'

She opened the box and put the cheap, shiny engagement ring on her finger, as though expecting a practical joke. 'Just fits,' she said grudgingly. 'Why, you haven't *bought* it, have yer?'

'No, he knocked it off out of Woolworth's window,' said Arthur, who had started whistling tunelessly and looking up at the ceiling.

'Oo, it can speak!' jeered Rita. She changed her voice to find the unfamiliar tone of gratitude. 'Anyway, ta. I *won't* wear it now, cos you know what they're like in here.' I could see the picture of marriage forming in her mind, the white wedding, the drawers crammed full of blankets, the terrace house with the linoleum squares, the seagrass stools and the novel horse-shoe companion-set in satin-brass. I felt pleased to have brought her this temporary pleasure, but there was no time to lose, and already I was racing ahead with the No. 1 thinking, breaking the engagement with the big speech about incom-patability.

The glass doors of the Kit-Kat rocked open, and one of the burly lorry drivers with whom Rita had had barren and wintry affairs in the past shambled in. 'Look what the cat's brought in,' said Rita loudly. She slipped the engagement ring into her overall pocket and re-set her face into gum-chewing nonchalance.

I was smiling as we walked back to the office. 'What have *you* got to grin about?' said Arthur.

'Those who bring sunshine into the lives of others cannot keep it for themselves,' I said.

'You what?'

'A quotation from Messieurs Shadrack and Duxbury's calendars,' I said. The calendars were still warm and sharp under my pullover, but they had become a part of my cloth-ing, like an armoured vest.

'You're going to be up for bloody bigamy, mate, that's what you're going to be up for,' said Arthur.

I tried to look as though I knew more than he did about my affairs, and we walked on along Moorgate.

'Have I told you I'm leaving?' I said, putting it as casually as I could.

'Yes, we've heard that one before as well,' said Arthur.

I wondered whether to tell him at all, or whether just to vanish, turning up self-consciously in a camel-hair coat years later like somebody coming home in uniform.

'I'm going to London,' I said.

'What as—road-sweeper?'

'Ay road sweepah on the road—to fame!' I cried in the grandiloquent voice. When it came to the point, I was embarrassed about telling him. I added, in a shuffling kind of way: 'I've got that job with Danny Boon.'

'You haven't!'

'Yup. Scriptwriter, start next week.'

'Jammy bastard! Have you though, honest?'

'Course I have. Don't tell anybody, though, will you?'

'Course I won't. When did you fix *that* up, then?' Arthur was finding it hard to keep the traces of envy out of his voice.

'He sent me a letter.'

Arthur stopped abruptly in the middle of the street and gave me what my mother would have described as an old-fashioned look.

'*Let's* see it,' he said, holding his hand out resignedly.

'What?' I remembered where I had left the letter, in the pocket of the raincoat I used for a dressing-gown, and I wondered if my mother was snooping round reading it.

'Come on—letter,' said Arthur, clicking his fingers.

'I haven't got it with me.'

'No, thought not I'll believe it when I see it.'

'All right, you wait till next week,' I said, trying hard to get into the spirit of jocular injured innocence, but succeeding only in the injured innocence.

'What's he paying you, then?' He was as bad as my mother.

'Wait till next week.'

'No, what's he paying you?'

'Wait till next week. You don't believe me, so wait till next *week*.'

We were back in St Botolph's Passage. I started on an indignant sliver of No. 1 thinking. 'The Danny Boon Show! Script by Billy Fisher, produced by——' Before I could get any further with this, I detected the pale shape of Stamp, hopping about in Shadrack's doorway, making an elaborate show of tutting and looking at his watch.

'Where've you been for your coffee—Bradford?'

'No, Wakefield,' I said, bad-tempered. Stamp buttoned his splitting leather gloves.

'The Witch has been ringing up for you,' he said. 'She rang up twice. I'm off to tell Rita you're two-timing her.'

'Go to hell,' I said.

'Anyway, she said if she doesn't ring back, she wants to meet you at one o'clock, usual place.'

'She'll be lucky.'

'*Is she willing?*' said Stamp, speaking the phrase as though it were a headline. I snarled at him, half-raising my elbow, and went into the office.

### FOUR

At the far end of St Botolph's Passage, past the green wrought-iron urinal, was a broken-down old lychgate leading into the churchyard. St Botolph's, a dark, dank slum of a church, was the home of a Ladies' Guild, a choir, some mob called the Shining Hour and about half a dozen other organisations, but so far as I knew it had no actual congregation except Shadrack, who went there sometimes looking for trade. The churchyard itself had long ago closed for business and most of the people in it had been carried away by the Black Death. It had a wayside pulpit whose message this week was: 'It is Better To Cry Over Spilt Milk Than To Try And Put It Back In The Bottle,' a saw that did not strike me for one as being particularly smart.

I reached the lych-gate at one o'clock, straight after work. The Witch was fond of the churchyard as a rendezvous. We had first met at the St Botolph's youth club and she was a great one for the sentimental associations. She was also very fond of the statues of little angels around the graves, which she thought beautiful. She shared with Shadrack a liking for the sloppy bits of verse over the more modern headstones. I would have liked to have seen her as Stradhoughton's first woman undertaker.

I sat down on the cracked stone bench inside the porch and collected at least some of my thoughts together. The first thing was to get the stack of creased calendars out from under my pullover. My stomach felt cramped and cold where they had been. I pulled the envelope of soggy paper gingerly out of my jacket pocket. Then I bundled the whole lot together and shoved it under the porch seat, where no one would ever look. That seemed to dispose of the calendars. I took out of my pocket the folded carbon copy of a letter I had written to Shadrack on the firm's notepaper when I got back from the Kit-Kat.

*Dear Mr Shadrack,*

*With regret I must ask you to accept my resignation from Shadrack and Duxbury's. You probably know that while enjoying my work with the Firm exceedingly, I have always regarded it as a temporary career. I have now succeeded in obtaining a post with Mr Danny Boon, the London comedian, and I do feel that this is more in line with my future ambitions.*

*I realise that you are entitled to one week's notice, but under the circumstances I wonder if it would be possible to waive this formality. May I say how grateful I am for all the help you have given me during my stay with the Firm.*

*My best personal regards to yourself and Councillor Duxbury.*

I was rather pleased with the letter, especially the bit about being grateful for Shadrack's help, but still apprehensive about the interview it would be necessary to have with him when I had finished with the Witch. I speculated idly on what he was getting at by saying it was about time we had a little talk. I looked out at the church clock and thought: never mind, in one hour it will all be over. I put the letter away again and began thinking about the Witch, the slow and impotent anger brewing up as it always did whenever I dwelt on her for any length of time.

The point about the Witch was that she was completely sexless. She was large, clean, and as I knew to my cost, whole-

43

some. I had learned to dislike everything about her. I did not care, to begin with, for her face: the scrubbed, honest look, as healthy as porridge. I disliked her for her impeccable short-hand, her senseless, sensible shoes and her handbag crammed with oranges. The Witch did nothing else but eat oranges. She had in fact been peeling a tangerine when I proposed to her during a youth club hike to Ilkley Moor, and her way of con-summating the idea had been to pop a tangerine quarter in my mouth. She had not been very much amused when I said 'With this orange I thee wed.'

What I most disliked her for were the sugar-mouse kisses and the wrinkling-nose endearments which she seemed to think symbolised some kind of grand passion. I had already cured her of calling me 'pet lamb' by going 'Jesus H. Christ!' explosively when she said it. The Witch had said sententi-ously: 'Thou shalt not take the name of the Lord thy God in vain.' I disliked her for her sententiousness, too.

Part of the booty in my raincoat pockets was a dirty, crumpled bag of chocolates that had been there for months. I had bought them when Stamp handed over his white box of passion pills. 'You'll need necking fodder to go with them,' he had explained. I took the chocolates out and inspected them. There had originally been a quarter of a pound, but as one opportunity after another slipped by, I had started to eat the odd chocolate and now there were only three left at the bot-tom of the bag, squashed and pale milky brown where they had melted and re-set.

I put the paper bag on my knee. Fumbling about in my side pocket I found Stamp's little box. That too was squashed almost flat by now, and most of the pills had rolled out into my pocket. I took one out, a little black bead that looked inedible. I wondered again where Stamp had got them and why he had given them to me, and also whether I could be prosecuted for what I was doing. 'Fisher, pay attention to me.' I fished around for the most presentable chocolate I could find, and tried to break it in half. It would not break properly. The chocolate covering splintered like an eggshell. It was an orange cream. I stuffed the round little black bead into it and tried to press the chocolate whole again. The result was a filthy, squalid mess. I ate one of the remaining chocolates, and then the second, leaving only the doctored orange cream in its grimy paper bag.

I lit a cigarette and stood up, and stretched. Looking down St Botolph's Passage, I saw the Witch picking her way disdainfully through the swaying little groups of betting men who were beginning to congregate.

I felt the usual claustrophobia coming on as she marched up to the lych-gate, swinging her flared skirt like a Scot swings his kilt; an arrogant and not a sexy swing. I disliked the way she walked.

'Hullo,' the Witch said, coldly. She was always cold whenever we were anywhere that resembled a public place. Later on she would start the ear-nibbling, the nose-rubbing and the baby talk. I said: 'Hullo, dalling.' I could not say darling. I was always trying, but it always came out as dalling.

We sat down together on the hard stone bench, under the spiders' webs. She eyed my Player's Weight viciously.

'How many cigarettes today?'

'Two,' I said.

'That's a good boy,' the Witch said, not quite half jokingly. She had got hold of some idea that I was smoking only five a day.

'Did you have a busy morning, dalling?' I said, giving her the soulful look. The Witch raised her eyeballs and blew upwards into her nostrils, a habit for which I was fast getting ready to clout her.

'Only about thirty letters from Mr *Turn*bull. Then he wanted me to type out an *agree*ment...' She rattled on in this vein for a few minutes.

'Did you talk to any *men* today?' I asked her. This was another idea she had. I was supposed to be jealous if she spoke to anybody else but me.

'Only Mr Turnbull, and Stamp when I rang up. Did you talk to any *gurls*?'

'Only the waitress when we went out for coffee.'

The Witch put on a mean expression. 'Couldn't your friend

have spoken to her?' she pouted. She wouldn't speak Arthur's name, because even *that* was supposed to make me jealous.

'Dalling!' I said. 'Have you missed me?'

'Of course. Have you missed *me*?'

'Of course.'

That seemed to be the end of the inquisition. I grubbed around in my pocket and produced what was left of the chocolates. 'I saved this for you,' I said.

The Witch peered doubtfully into the sticky, brown-stained depths of the paper bag.

'It looks a bit *squashed*,' she said.

I took the chocolate between my fingers. 'Open wide.' She opened her mouth, probably to protest, and I rammed the chocolate in.

'Nasty!' said the Witch, gulping. I craned my neck, pretending to scratch my ear, and glanced out of the porch at the church clock. Stamp's passion pills were supposed to take effect after a quarter of an hour at most. He had once given me a description of a straight-laced, straight-faced Baloo who ran a Wolf Cub pack over in Leeds, and she had started pawing his jacket and whimpering only five minutes after he had slipped her a passion pill in the guise of an energy tablet.

'What were you ringing up about this morning? Anything?'

'Just wanted to talk to you, pet,' said the Witch, wriggling herself into a position of squeamish luxury. 'I've seen the most marvellous material to make curtains for our cottage. Honestly, you'll love it.'

Eating oranges in St Botolph's churchyard on the long crisp nights, or sometimes in the public shelter at the Corporation cemetery, another favourite spot, we had discussed at length the prospect of living in a thatched cottage in the middle of some unspecified field in Devon. At times, in the right mood, I could get quite enthusiastic over this rural image, and it had even figured in my No. 1 thinking before now. We had invented two children, little Barbara and little Billy—the prototypes, actually, of the imaginary family I had told Arthur's mother about—and we would discuss their future, and the village activities and the pokerwork mottoes and all the rest of it.

'It's a sort of turquoise, with lovely little squiggles, like wine-glasses——'

'Will it go with the yellow carpet?'

'No, but it'll go with the grey rugs in the kiddies' room.'

'Dalling!'

The yellow carpet and the grey rugs we had seen in a furniture shop window on one of the interminable expeditions round Stradhoughton that the Witch sometimes dragged me on. They had all long ago been sold, but they had become part of the picture of the cottage, along with the Windsor chairs, the kettle singing on the hob, the bloody cat and also the crinoline ladies from my bedroom wall at home.

We continued on these lines for a few minutes, until, at a reference to the wedding ceremony in some village church that would precede it all, the Witch stiffened.

'Have you got my engagement ring back yet?'

'Not yet, crikey! I only took it in this morning!' The Witch had parted with it suspiciously and reluctantly, not really convinced that it needed making smaller.

'I feel unclothed without it,' she said. She could not bring herself to say 'naked,' yet from her, 'unclothed' sounded even more obscene than she imagined nakedness to be. The reference reminded me that her time was nearly up.

'Let's go in the churchyard, away from all the people,' I said, standing up and taking her cold, chapped hands.

She looked doubtful again, into the dead-looking graveyard. 'It's a bit *damp*, isn't it?'

'We'll sit on my raincoat. Come on, dalling.' I was almost dragging her to her feet. She got up half-heartedly. I put my arm around her awkwardly, and we walked up the broken tarmacadam path that was split down the middle like the crust on a cottage loaf, round to the back of the old church. Behind some ancient family vault was a black tree and a clump of burnt-looked, dirty old grass. Sometimes I could persuade the Witch to sit down there, when she was not inspecting the vault and reading out aloud: 'Samuel Vaughan of this town, 1784;

47

alfo his wife Emma, alfo his fon Saml, 1803.' I threw my raincoat on the shoddy grass and sat down. The Witch remained standing and I pulled her impatiently, almost forcibly, to her knees. By now, even allowing extra time for a difficult case, Stamp's pill should be working.

I stared at her gravely. 'I love you, dalling,' I said in the stilted way that I couldn't help.

'Love *you*,' said the Witch, the stock response which she imagined the statement needed.

'Do you? Really and truly?'

'Of course I do.'

'Are you looking forward to getting married?'

'I think about it every minute of the day,' she said. I disliked the way she talked, tempering her flat northern voice with the mean, rounded vowels she had picked up at the Stradhoughton College of Commerce.

'Dalling,' I said. I began stroking her hair, moving as quickly as possible down the side of her face and on to her shoulder. She started the nose-rubbing act, and I seized her roughly and began kissing her. My lips on hers, I decided that I might as well try to get my tongue into her mouth but she kept her lips hard and closed. She pulled her face away suddenly so that my tongue slithered across her cheek and I was licking her, like a dog. It was not a very promising start.

'Don't ever fall in love with anybody else,' I said in the grave, sad voice. 'Love you pet,' she said, leaning forward and nibbling my ear. I caught hold of her again and started fumbling, as idly as I could manage it, at the square buttons on her neat blue suit. The Witch struggled free again.

'Let's talk about our cottage, pet,' she said.

I counted seven to myself, seeing the red rash in front of my eyes. Obviously the pill was not working yet, or perhaps in the Witch's case I should have given her three or four.

'What about our cottage?' I said in the dreamy voice, containing myself.

'About the garden. Tell me about the garden.'

'We'll have a lovely garden,' I said, conjuring up a garden without much trouble. 'We'll have rose trees and daffodils and

48

a lovely lawn with a swing for little Billy and little Barbara to play on, and we'll have our meals down by the lily pond in summer.'

'Do you think a lily pond is *safe*?' the Witch said anxiously. 'What if the kiddies wandered too near and fell in?'

'We'll build a wall round it. No we won't, we won't have a pond at all. We'll have an old well. An old brick well where we draw the water. We'll make it our wishing well. Do you know what I'll wish?'

The Witch shook her head. She was sitting with her hands folded round her ankles like a child being told a bedtime story.

'Tell me what you'll wish, first,' I said.

'Oh—I'll wish that we'll always be happy and always love each other. What will *you* wish?' the Witch said.

'Better not tell you,' I said.

'Why not, pet?'

'You might be cross.'

'Why would I be cross?'

'Oh, I don't know. You might think me too, well, forward.' I glanced at her face for reaction. There was no reaction, and in fact when I looked at her again she seemed to have lost interest in the wishing well. I tried the lip-biting trick, combined with the heavy breathing.

'Barbara——' I began, making a couple of well-feigned false starts. 'Do you think it's wrong for people to have, you know, feelings?'

The Witch looked at me, too directly for my liking. 'Not if they're genuinely in love with each other,' she said.

'Like we are?'

'Yes,' she said, with less certainty.

'Would you think it wrong of me to have—feelings?'

The Witch, speaking briskly and firmly as though she had been waiting for this one and knew what to do about it, said: 'I think we ought to be married first.'

I looked at her sorrowfully. 'Dalling.' I got hold of the back of her neck and kissed her again. This time, making a bold decision, I put my hand on the thick, salmon-coloured stock-

49

ing, just about at the shin. She stiffened, but did not do anything about it. I moved the hand up, the voice of Stamp floating into my mind, *'His hand caressed her silken knee.'* As soon as I reached her knee the Witch tore herself free.

'Are you feeling all right?' she said abruptly.

'Of course, dalling. Why?' I said, not moving my hand.

She looked pointedly down at her knee. 'Look where your hand is.'

I moved it away, sighing audibly.

'Dalling, don't you *want* me to touch you?'

The Witch shrugged.

'It seems—indecent, somehow.' I leaned forward to kiss her again, but she side-stepped abruptly, reaching for the leather shoulder-bag that she always carried with her.

'Would you like an energy tablet?' I said.

'No, thank you. I'm going to have an orange.'

I saw the red rash again and felt the old, impotent rage. I jumped to my feet. *'Ai'm* going to have an *or-*rainge!' I mimicked in a falsetto voice. *'Ai'm* going to have an *or-*ainge!' On a sudden urge I booted the leather handbag out of her hand and across the grass. It came to rest by an old gravestone, spilling out oranges and shorthand dictionaries.

'Billy!' said the Witch sharply.

'You and your bloody oranges,' I said.

She sat there looking straight in front of her, obviously wondering whether it was going to be worth her while to start crying. I bent down and touched her hair.

'Sorry, dalling,' I said. I put on a shamefaced look and slunk off after her handbag. I started collecting her oranges and things together, looking closely into her open handbag to see if there were any letters from men I might be able to use. There was nothing but her lipstick and a few coins, but on the grass close by I saw something small and gleaming. I recognised it as a miniature silver cross that the Witch used to wear around her neck. Until a few months ago she had never been without it, then she had revealed that it was a present from some cousin called Alec who lived in Wakefield. Under the jealousy pact between us I had made her promise to give it back to him, and according to her story she had done so.

I looked back sharply at the Witch, but she was occupied, dabbing at her eyes with her handkerchief. I slipped the little silver cross quickly into my pocket, picked up her handbag, and strolled back to where she was sitting.

'Sorry, dalling,' I said again. She reached up and squeezed my hand, sniffing deeply to prove that she had finished crying.

'Let's go,' she said.

'All right.'

We walked back along the crumbling church path, through the lych-gate and into St Botolph's Passage. I was beginning to say, 'You know, dalling, I think you have feelings too, deep down,' but the Witch had already resumed the formal attitude she assumed for public appearances. I let the matter drop.

'Are we going looking at the shops this afternoon?' she said as we paused at the corner of Market Street.

My heart sank. On Saturdays, as well as taking her to the Roxy at night, I was expected to meet her two or three times during the day—at lunch-time, during the afternoon, and possibly before I went to the pub for my club turn in the evening. She always said it made her feel wanted, although she had little idea what I wanted her for.

Today I was hoping to get out of the afternoon session.

'I'd love to, only I've got to go and see Shadrack this afternoon, and I don't know what time I'll get through.'

'Please?' She would have said 'Pretty please' if she had had the nerve.

'All right, dalling. About four o'clock. Only wait for me if I'm late.'

'All right, pet.'

Fingering her little silver cross in my raincoat pocket, I watched her down Market Street until her swinging skirt was out of sight.

## FIVE

In the cold sun, on a Saturday afternoon, St Botolph's Passage was just about bearable. It was alive with fat men in dark suits, puffing and blowing over folded racing papers and chucking clean, empty packets of twenty down on the uneven paving stones. Men in raincoats came and went in the vicinity of the shady chemist's, and a swaying, red-faced group continued an argument outside the pub, one of them saying the same sentence over and over again like a blocked gramophone. It seemed to be the same group every Saturday, having the same argument. 'Have you ever realised,' I said to Man o' the Dales—puff, puff—'that your blunt Yorkshire individuals are in fact interchangeable, like spare wheels on a mass-produced car?' At the end of the Passage, by Market Street, there was even a violinist with his hat on the floor, playing 'Pennies from Heaven.' Shadrack and Duxbury's was the only shop with the blinds down, but the door was open and the bell rang quietly when I went in.

The office was cold and dusty now, and looking more like a funeral parlour than usual with the roller blind filtering a green, dead light over the empty desks. I stood hesitating, gaping dozily at the washed-looking photograph of Councillor Duxbury doffing his bowler in front of a horse-driven hearse. It was very quiet. I had a quick, happy notion that they had abandoned the office for ever, or dropped dead in their own coffins or something, but then I saw the thin red glow of the convector heater shining under Shadrack's door. I went over reluctantly and knocked. He was not there. It was probable that he was out in Market Street, selling a Morris Thousand to some fruiterer or other. Shadrack had never quite abandoned his previous trade.

I sauntered over to my desk and sat down heavily, feeling happier because Shadrack was not there. It was, after all, not beyond the range of possibility that he had been run over by a bus. I lit one of my cigarettes and aimlessly opened the drawer of my desk. I stared vacantly into it for a moment, and then made a decision. My desk drawer was a sort of town branch of the Guilt Chest; there were few documents in it that did not cause even a passing spasm of anxiety. I began, briskly, to sort through them, tearing up the unposted funeral accounts first, then the obscene verses about Councillor Duxbury, and the rough notes for a long love letter I had once written to the Witch, daringly mentioning her breasts by name. There were about eight first pages of *The Two Schools at Gripminster*. I stacked them together, tore them through the middle, and dropped them in the wastepaper basket. There seemed to be whole sheafs of quarto with nothing written on them but my name in a variety of handwriting styles. I threw those away too. There was a fragment of dialogue entitled *Burglar Scene*, that I had once thought just right for Danny Boon:

BOON: If I fire this rod it'll be curtains for you.

FEED: W-why?

BOON: It's a curtain rod. Of course, I'm a very respectable man, you know, a very respectable man. My wife and I are in the iron and steel business.

FEED: . . .

BOON: She does the ironing while I do the stealing.

I put this in my pocket together with the beginnings of the letter I had tried to write to Danny Boon. At the back of the drawer there was an old, yellowing piece of foolscap on which I had tried to list all the things that were worrying me at the time. The idea was that I should tick off each item as it ceased to be an anxiety, and when I had finished there would be nothing left to worry me any more.

I looked at the list again, apprehensively. 'Cal. Witch (Capt). Ldn. Hswvs Choice. Namepl. A's ma (sister).' There was nothing on the long list that I could honestly cross off and forget about. I made a decision, and ripped the piece of paper into four, dropping the pieces in the wastepaper basket. There was nothing left in the desk except the long ink stain, the stubs of pencil, and the word 'LIZ' which I had blocked in in careful crayon. I got up and tried to open Stamp's desk, but it was locked. I paced round the office, whistling through my teeth.

One of the habits I was going to get out of was a sort of vocal equivalent of the nervous grimace, an ever-expanding repertoire of odd noises and sound effects that I would run through in time of tension. Alone in my bedroom, seeking refuge in a telephone box, or walking purposefully, purposelessly home along Clogiron Lane late at night, I would begin to talk to myself, the words degenerating first into senseless, apelike sounds and then into barnyard imitations, increasing in absurdity until I was completely incoherent, thereupon I would switch back into human speech with a kind of thought-stream monologue on whatever problem was uppermost in my mind at the time.

I did this now, dropping my cigarette end into Stamp's ink-well.

'London is a big place, Mr Shadrack,' I began, mumbling to myself. 'A man can lose himself in London. You know that? Lose himself. Loo-hoo-hoose himself. Loooooooose himself. Himself. Him, himmmmmnnn, himnnn, himself. Ah-him-ah-self!' Wandering about the office, I started on the odd sounds and the imitations of animals. 'Hyi! Hyi! Yi-yi-yi-yi-yi. Grrruff! Grrruff! Maaa-aaa Maa-aaa! *Maaaaa!* And now——'—taking in a fragment of one of the routines I went through with Arthur from time to time—'and now as Sir Winston *Chur*chill might have said it. Nevah! In the field! Of human conflict! And this is the voiceofemall, Wee Willy Fisher, saying maa-aaa! Maaaa! Maaaaa! Grmp. Grmp. What a beautiful little pig. Hay say, whhat ay *beau*tiful little pig.' I began to repeat this sentence in a variety of tones, stresses and dialects, ranging from a rapid Mickey Mouse squeak to a bass drawl, and going through all the Joycean variations. 'What a batiful lattle pahg. Ah, whet eh behtefell lettle peg.'

I was standing at the open door of Shadrack's office. The room was beginning to echo with my voice. I stopped for a moment and toyed with the idea of going in and having a quick run through Shadrack's desk, but my ankles tingled at the thought. I had a short flash of No. 2 thinking, trapped in Shadrack's swivel chair with the drawer of his desk jammed open. For relief, I turned back to my verbal doodling and began to call his name.

'Mr Shadrack? Mr Shadrack? Ha-*mees*ter Shadrack! Mee-hee-heester Shadrack! Shadrack! Shadrack!' Each time I called, the 'rack' sound bounced back off his streamlined convector stove. '*Shad*rack! Shar-har-har-har-*had*rack! Shaddy-shaddy-shaddy-shaddy-*shad*rack! Hoy! Shadders!'

I was just drawing breath for the second run when Shadrack, who had undoubtedly been listening for the past ten minutes, came into the office through the door that led down to the lavatory. I stuck a finger in my throat and began going 'Ar! Ar! Arrrgh! Sharrgh!' trying to falsify his memory of what he had heard. My first real thought was one of relief that I had not been going through his desk; my second was to turn on him the Ambrosian repeater gun, rather like a machine-gun, which I kept permanently manned for such occasions as this.

'Oh, it's you, is it?' said Shadrack, but without any indication that these words explained, or excused, the din I had been making. Had he heard everything, or had he just come up from downstairs? Even downstairs he could not have failed to hear. Four moves flashed through my mind like a drowning man's life story. One, pretend was singing. Two, pretend not seen him and continue, making it sound like singing. Three, pretend rehearsing play. 'And yet, Lady Alice, even pigs have feelings.' Four, on the No. 1 level, 'I'm glad you heard that, Shadrack. I've been wanting you to hear my views for a long time.'

'Hope my singing didn't put you off,' I said.

'Curious din you were making,' said Shadrack. 'You'd better come into the office.

I followed him into his private sanctum, humming in an embarrassed way.

Shadrack's office was furnished in what he imagined to be American executive style, in so far as he could afford it. He had a metal desk completely free of everything except a black ebony ruler, an unacceptable object to me ever since he had discovered me, or I think discovered me, conducting with it from a record of 'Abide With Me' which he kept on the record-player, another item of luxury. I turned the Ambrosian repeater gun on him again for good measure. On a low, coffee-bar sort of table there were the plans and drawings of the glass-fibre coffin he was working on, and a yellow pad on which he was doodling his ideas for a streamlined hearse. Beyond this, a couple of grey contemporary chairs, the first ever seen in Stradhoughton, and on the wall a boxed print of one of those Chinese horses.

'Come in, siddown, make 'self at home,' said Shadrack. He smiled with his bad teeth, and produced from his blazer pocket a matchbox-sized model, made out of Perspex, of his wedge-shaped coffin. 'Y'know, by the time we're burying you, you'll be going off in one o' these. You know that?'

'Really?' I said, trying to sound interested. I was not fooled by his manner, the well-known friendly word, the boss re-laxing on his Saturday afternoon off. I perched on one of the grey chairs and cleared my throat. 'Arrgh! Sharrgh!'

'Y'see, people don't realise. It's all clean lines nowadays. All these frills and fancies are going out. It's all old.'

'H'm,' I said.

'Same as I tell Councillor Duxbury. You've got to move with the times. It's no use living in one style and dying in another. It's an anarchism.'

'Anachronism,' I said, before I could stop myself.

'Yes, well.' Shadrack turned abruptly to the olive-green filing cabinet and took out a manilla file. He held it up and tapped it. 'Anyway, that's my worry. S'pose you want to talk to me about this letter of yours, do you?' I had an absurd feeling of importance that I should have written a letter and that he should have put it in a file. He put the file, open, on the desk, and I saw that there were several other papers underneath my letter of resignation. I fell to wondering if this was some kind of personal dossier, filled with reports from Stamp and the Witch, and secret spidery mumblings from Councillor Duxbury.

Shadrack perched on his desk, adjusting his tapered slacks

and shooting his cuffs. 'So y're thinking of leaving us, hey, is that it?'

'Yes, well, I *was* thinking, now this opportunity's come up...' I trotted out a wretched, shambling imitation of the speech I had prepared.

Shadrack picked up my letter and examined it. I tried to see what the next paper on the file was. It was one of his yellow memo-sheets with a lot of his writing on it. He frowned over the letter as though he could not read.

'"...now succeeded in obtaining a post with Mr Danny Boon..."' he quoted, and I had an idea that he was going to go through the letter, point by point, getting me to expand. 'Now that's the chap who was on telly the other night, isn't it?'

'That's right,' I said in the encouraging voice.

'Yes, vair vair clever fellow. And you say you're going to work for him?'

'Yes, well, he liked some of the material I sent him and——'

'That's your ambition is it, script-writing?' He was the eager questioner, off-duty, Saturday afternoon.

'Oh, yes, always has been,' I said, beginning to relax and sit back in my chair. 'And of course, there's quite a lot of money in it if you go about it the right way.'

'You get paid by the joke, then, or what? Or do you get a salary coming in each week?'

'Well, it's vair difficult to say,' I said. I had noticed before that I often tended to start imitating the person I was talking to. But Shadrack had lost interest. While I was scrabbling away trying to think of something to tell him, he began murmuring. 'Ye-es, ye-es' absent-mindedly and shuffling the papers in the file. His expression changed to a business one. He got up off the desk and stood behind his chair, putting his full weight on it and swivelling it from side to side.

'Ye-es. Well this letter,' Shadrack began, and it was obvious that we were getting down to the serious business. I looked up intelligently.

'Now you don't need me to tell you that it's vair vair un-satisfactory, a letter like this. Now do you?'

I mumbled, trying to get some action into my voice: 'Oh, I'm sorry to hear that?'

'Vair unsatisfactory. Fact I'd go so far as to say it's unprofessional, Fisher. Vair vair unprofessional.'

Shadrack had a thing about the undertaking business being a profession. I cleared my throat and said: 'Well, I suppose I've got to leave some time——'

'Yes, we realise that. We all realise that. Don't doubt it. Nobody wants to stand in your way, don't think that, and I wish you the vair vair best of luck. But it's felt that you might have gone about it in a more sa'sfactory manner.'

'Oh, in what way?' It sounded like something out of amateur dramatics, the way I said it.

'Well we were hoping, we were *hoping*, that you'd try and get one or two things cleared up before you took a step like this.'

An icy chill, a familiar enough visitor by now, seized me somewhere under the heart. I cleared my throat again and said faintly: 'What——?'

'Y'see, I don't mind telling you that we're vair vair disappointed you've not been to see us be*fore* this. I mean before you wrote this letter. I mean don't think I want to make things *awk*ward for you, far from it, but it has been felt you owe us one or two little explanations.'

It was difficult not to look as though I understood what he was talking about. I said, trying to keep up the equal partners voice of a few moments before, 'Well, I know my work probably hasn't been as good as it might have been. I mean, that's one of the reasons why I think I ought to leave.'

'It's not a question of work,' said Shadrack. 'It's not a question of work at all. It's just a question of what you pr'pose to do about one or two things.'

He looked at me levelly, trying to gauge how much of the message was coming across. Then he said, almost gently: 'Y'see, there's those calendars to be explained, for one thing. I mean, we've never had any sa'sfactory explanation about *that*, now have we?'

I stared back at him, licking my lips. It was no surprise to me that Shadrack actually knew about the calendars. He was bound to suspect, if not to know. I had just been hoping that natural delicacy or some kind of feeling of hopelessness would have prevented him from bringing the subject up. There were many things, in fact, on which I leaned heavily on the reluctant, brooding tact that was Shadrack's speciality. I decided that my best policy was to say nothing, and indeed I had nothing to say.

'I mean, they cost a lot of money to produce, a *lot* of money. We can't understand what you did with them.'

I felt bound to make some sort of effort. 'Well, there was a bit of a misunderstanding——' I began, a story about a fire at the post-office beginning to cobble itself together in my mind.

'It wasn't a misunderstanding, it's just that two or three hundred calendars didn't get posted. To *my* knowledge. I mean, I know you want to leave, I think it's the best thing you could do. I think you're taking a very wise step. We all realise that. But y'see, we've got to get this cleared up and implemented.'

I didn't know, and neither did he, what he meant by 'implemented.' Shadrack had a habit of hoarding words and dropping them into a sentence when they got too heavy for him. It was obvious now that he was going to go on and on about the calendars, probably for half the afternoon, simply because he had never studied the art of hanging the subject. I decided that I was supposed to make some constructive suggestion.

'Well, of course, if it's a question of paying for them——'

'Ah. Aha! Wait a minute. Wait just one little minute. It's not as easy as that. It's not—as—easy—as—that. Y'see, there's the goodwill to consider. What about the goodwill? Those calendars were for goodwill, we can't understand why you didn't send them out. I mean that's what they're there for. I mean, we don't buy calendars so that you can just go out and chuck them on the fire, y'know. That's not what we're in business for.'

He was getting warmed up now. He had stopped fiddling about with his chair and was sitting down, leaning forward over the desk, messing about with the ebony ruler. His eyes glistened.

'No, that won't do at all. I'm afraid you don't seem to apprec'ate it's a vair vair serious business. And then of course there's the other matter.'

'What other matter?' I said dully.

'I think you know vair well what matter. It's no good sitting there saying what matter. There's this matter of the nameplates, isn't there?'

Here I had no advantage at all, and for the first time my mouth sagged. I had suspected, when I considered the thing seriously, that Shadrack knew about the calendars. I felt that he knew something about the irregularities in the postage book, a subject I was surprised had not been ventilated earlier in the conversation. I was fairly sure that he knew about the offensive imitations of Councillor Duxbury but was too inarticulate to mention them. But I would have sworn, willingly, that he knew nothing about the nameplates.

In a way, the nameplates were just as serious as the calendars, if not more so. There were two of them, and I had hidden them in a box of shrouds down in the stockroom. The whole thing had happened during Shadrack's holiday in the summer. I had been supposed to order a coffin nameplate for the funeral of a preacher who had dropped dead in the aisle at Bridle Street Methodist Church. By mistake, thinking about something else, I had put the letters 'R.I.P.' on the engravers' instructions, with the result that they had turned out what was in effect a Catholic nameplate for a Methodist body. I had got the thing hurriedly remade, but too late for the funeral. By a miracle neither Councillor Duxbury nor the relatives had noticed it was missing, and the Methodist minister had been buried in an unidentified coffin. There was nothing to do with the nameplates but hide them, and I had often worried about them, sometimes going into the theological aspects of the affair and wondering if I had committed anything to do with the unforgivable sin. But I would have sworn that Shadrack knew nothing about it.

'Y'see, that's another matter we've got to get cleared up. I don't see how you can leave without getting *that* cleared up.'

He did not make it evident whether or not he knew where the nameplates were. Perhaps he knew only that the body had been buried without a nameplate. I had lived in fear, for some time, of an exhumation order. I decided to sneak downstairs when he let me go and stuff the nameplates under my pullover.

'Well, I can only say I'm sorry if there's been any inconvenience,' I said.

'Inconvenience? Inconvenience? Ha!' He gave a short snort, and entered one of his caves of rhetoric. 'It's not a question of inconvenience, it's a question of what you pr'pose to do about it. S'posing the relatives had found out, what sort of fool d'y'think I'd have looked then? S'posing Councillor Duxbury had found out?' (I felt a slight ray of hope that he was shielding me from Councillor Duxbury.) 'Y'see, I'm vair much afraid that you've been spending too much time acting the fool. You seem to think you're on the music halls, not in a funeral furnishers.'

I was beginning to be possessed by the inward, impotent rage. What did the man want me to *do*? Atone for my sins? Work for another year as penal servitude? Pay for the calendars and the nameplates? Get the goodwill back?

Shadrack looked at the yellow paper in his file where, I was quite ready to believe, he had a list of my misdemeanours scribbled down, like a charge sheet. I expected him to tick them off and start each charge with 'That he did unlawfully...'

'Yes, there's been too much acting the fool in this office. We'll have to get some other system. Y'see, then there's those verses, you never wrote *those* out, now did you?'

Shadrack had once caught Arthur and me writing songs in the firm's time, and had set us to work making up little verses for the In Memoriam column of the *Echo*, a chore he handled for the bereaved on a commission basis. The nearest we had got to the job was an obscene poem about Councillor Duxbury and a couple of lines about Josiah Olroyd in the window: 'Josiah Olroyd has gone to join his Maker. Come inside and join Josiah Olroyd.' Shadrack knew about them both. I was relieved that he was getting on to the minor misdemeanours, but I knew that even those could keep him talking for hours.

'Then there's all that office paper you've been using for your bits and pieces. I mean, that costs money as well.'

'I'll pay for it.'

'It's not a question of paying for it——' In the outer office, the telephone began to ring. Shadrack picked up his extension and found that it was not connected. It was my responsibility to see that it was, last thing on Saturday morning, and he shot me a look of exasperation as he rose to his feet.

'Anyway, under the circumstances I have to tell you, I have to tell *you*, Fisher, that under no circ'stances can we accept your resignation at the moment. Not at the moment. Not until we've got this straightened out. We may even have to take some kind of legal action, I don't know.'

He strode out of his office and went over to the switchboard. 'Shadrack and Duxbury?' I got up and stood in the doorway, running over the bit about legal action and testing it for strength.

Shadrack began talking to some mourning wife in his soupy, funeral voice. I just stood there. He put his hand over the mouthpiece and said: 'Well we'll talk about this another time.' I walked unsteadily to the outer door, twisted the door-handle for a moment, and walked out into St Botolph's Passage. For the first time since breakfast I felt my elusive yawn coming on, and I leaned against Shadrack's window, gasping and gulping. My forehead was sweating, but I was relieved that I had jumped another hurdle. I remembered that I had not gone downstairs after the nameplates, but decided that after all there was little point in it.

I lit a cigarette and started walking down towards Market Street, trying to translate the interview into No. 1 thinking. 'Now look here, Mr Shadrack, there's such a thing as slander——'

It didn't work. I set off home. My No. 1 mother said: 'For God's sake, Billy, why don't you tell the boring little man what he can do with the job?'

I reached Hillcrest at about half-past two to find lunch over and my mother in the kitchen, making notes for a scene about my not being home for meals. It was bacon and egg again, the traditional Saturday feast; the eggshells were in the sink-tidy and there was an air of replete doom about the house. Gran was mumbling to herself in the lounge. The old man was mending something in the garage, or thought he was.

'What time do you call this?' my mother asked as I opened the kitchen door. I knew my part in this little passage and replied: 'Twenty-seven minutes past two, though you may have another phrase for it,' reflecting that my answers were becoming as stereotyped as her questions. 'I've had an exciting morning,' I added, trying to get some uplift into the conversation.

My mother was not having any. 'You seem to think I've nothing else to do but cook, cook, cook,' she said, slipping with disturbing ease into a monologue so familiar to me that I could have chanted it with her, like those two men doing imitations on the radio. 'You come in when you like and expect to find a meal waiting for you, you don't seem to think I'm entitled to five minutes' peace.'

'Peace——' I began, not troubling to think what I was going to say; anything obscure would pass for something clever. My mother cut me short.

'I've not sat down all morning. If I'm not sick!'

From the lounge, Gran shouted: 'If that's our Billy, there's his old raincoat been in the bathroom all morning. It's about time he started hanging his things up.'

I called back: 'What if it isn't our Billy, where has his old raincoat been then?' a grammatical pleasantry whose full subtlety I did not expect to be appreciated. I anticipated, and got, no reply. The old man came into the kitchen from the garage, carrying a shelf.

'And you can start coming home on a dinner-time, instead of gadding round town half the bloody day,' he said, without even looking at me.

'Good afternoon, father,' I said with heavy civility. I was beginning to wonder why I had come home at all.

'And stop being so bloody cheeky. I've just about had enough of it.'

'He wants to give him a good hiding, teach him some manners,' called Gran from the lounge.

I began to feel angry, like a caged animal being taunted with sticks. This feeling, a regular enough occurrence in this house, had several outlets. One course open to me was to revert to what I felt must be my former self or my real self or something, an abusive shadow of the old man. Another, less dangerous move was to introduce the mood of polished detachment.

'What are manners——?' I began, examining my finger-nails. But I had underestimated the strength of the old man's frustration or whatever it was.

'Talk bloody sense, man!' he roared. 'By Christ, if this is what they learned him at technical school, I'm glad I'm bloody ignorant!'

'Ah, a confession!' I murmured, but without any idea that he should hear me. The old man gave me a steady, threatening look. Aloud, I said, 'I'm going upstairs.'

'And keep out of them bedrooms!' Gran called from the lounge.

The bedrooms were nothing to do with her. She was only the permanent guest. I whipped round in a sudden gust of fury.

'*Mind your own bloody*——' I began, then checked myself on the absolute verge of disaster, so abruptly that I physically teetered on my toes.

'You what!' The old man dropped his shelf on the floor and came almost running across the kitchen, face to face with me. 'You what did you say What was that? What did you say?' He grabbed my collar and put his fist close against my face.

'These melodramatics——'

64

'Don't melodram me with your fancy talk!' I was seized, not with fear or anger but with sheer helplessness at the thought that these were beautiful Josiah Olroyd lines and I could not point them out to anybody, or even scoff.

'I merely said——'

'Talk bloody properly! You were talking different a minute ago, weren't you? What did you just say to your grandma? What did you say?'

'Well don't pull him round, that shirt's clean on,' my mother said, anxiously.

'I'll clean shirt him! I'll clean shirt him round his bloody earhole! With his bloody fountain pens and his bloody suède shoes! Well he doesn't go out tonight! *I* know where he gets it from. He stops in tonight, and tomorrow night anall!'

I stood by the sink, looking weary, seeking some facial expression that was not outside the histrionic experience of the family. I searched for something to say that would not sound clever or impertinent. From the lounge I heard Gran muttering, 'Cheeky young devil!' but her voice sounded thick and strange.

'Look——'

'Don't look me! With your look this and look that! And you get all them bloody papers and books and rubbish thrown out, anall! Before I chuck 'em out first, and you with 'em!'

The only way into the conversation was to counterfeit the old man's blunt and blunted way of talking. I set my lips into the same loose, flabby shape and said in the rough voice: 'What's up, they're not hurting you, are they?'

'No, and they're not bloody hurting you, eether,' the old man said, taking over, in his mind anyway, the role of family wit.

He went back across the kitchen and picked up the shelf where he had dropped it. I stood there straightening my tie, not speaking. My mother looked at me, her 'You've done it now' look. The old man turned back.

'Anyway, I've finished with him. He knows where his suitcase is. If he wants to go to London he can bloody well go!'

'Oh, but he's not!' my mother said sharply. She had been

65

dithering for some time, wondering which side she was on, and now she came down on mine, or what she thought was mine.

'I've finished with him! He can go!'

'Oh, but he's not!'

'He's going. He's going out.' The idea was building up attractively in the old man's mind. 'He's going!'

'Oh, but he's not. Oh, but he's not. Oh, but he is not.'

'Look,' I said. 'Can I settle this——'

This time the old man ignored me.

'It's ever since he left school, complaining about this and that and t' other. If it isn't his boiled eggs it's summat else. You have to get special bloody *wheat* flakes for him cos he's seen 'em on television. Well I've had enough. I've had enough. He can go.'

'Oh, but he's not! Now you just listen to me, Geoffrey. He's not old enough to go to London, or anywhere else. You said yourself. He doesn't think. He gets ideas into his head.'

'Well he's going, he can get *that* idea into his head.'

'Oh, but he is not. Not while *I'm* here.'

The old man's anger died down as quickly as it had flared up. 'He wants to get into t' bloody army, that's what he wants to do,' he said.

'Yes, and you want to get into t' bloody army as well,' my mother said.

This exchange of epigrams seemed to mark the end of the conversation. I turned to go.

'Where's he going *now?*' the old man said.

'I'm going to be sick,' I said viciously.

I went into the lounge, expecting Gran to toss her widow's mite into the controversy as I passed. I glanced at her as I walked towards the hall door, and saw at once, with a quick sense of panic, why she was so silent.

I shouted: 'Mother! Quick!' and looked up at the ceiling rather than at my grandmother. She was sitting in her armchair in a curiously rigid position, her yellow face convulsed, her neck ricked back. Specks of foam appeared on her lips and her watering eyes were bulging. She was trying to cry out, but no sounds came. Her skinny hands gripped the arms of her chair and her back was arched as though she had frozen in the act of getting up.

My mother and the old man came rushing into the room. 'Now look what you've done!' my mother cried. The old man dashed over to open the window.

He shouted: 'She's having a bloody fit, can't you see; Get t' smelling salts! Go on, then, frame yourself!'

Glad to get out of it, I galloped upstairs for the smelling salts. Gran's fits, occurring nowadays with increasing regularity, always filled me with dread and, I could not help it, disgust. I had a horror that I would one day be alone with her in the house when she threw one, and I was often haunted by the thought of what I would do in these circumstances. Rummaging around in my mother's dressing-table for the smelling salts, automatically conning the contents of the drawer to see if she had found anything of mine and hidden it, I realised that emerging from my panic was the old thought that perhaps this time Gran would die and there would be no more scenes. I tried to push the thought out by the counting and quoting method: Seventy-four, ninety-six, the Lord is my shepherd I shall not want. Calming a little, I no longer hoped that she was dead but that she was all right, or at least looking all right on the face of it, with the foam wiped off her lips and everything looking normal. I found the green bottle of smelling salts and went downstairs. At the turn of the stairs, scraping my shoe against the loose stair-rod, I told myself that I would count five and that at the end of that time she would have recovered, and I would go in.

I counted slowly, one, two, three, four, five, six. The hall door opened suddenly and the old man was peering round urgently. 'Come on, what you bloody doing?' I jumped the remaining stairs and handed him the bottle. 'Still feel sick,' I muttered. He shut the door in my face.

I walked slowly back upstairs, trying to *make* myself feel sick, but with no success. I went into my room and lay shivering on the bed. I strained my ears to listen for the voices downstairs, and told myself that I could hear the faint voice of

Gran, and that that meant she was all right now. To get the incident out of my head I tried out a piece of No. 1 thinking, concerning my own death and the grief of the family. It tapered out and, feeling more at ease, I began to think aggressively, and then constructively, casting myself slowly into the role of master of the house. There was an insurance man bullying Gran into taking out a funeral policy, but she was too dim to know what it was all about. I came in just as the insurance man was becoming sneering and abusive. 'Would you mind, sir? This lady happens to be my grand-mother.'—'And who are you?'—'Let us say that I have some experience in these matters.'

By now there were definitely voices downstairs, and I heard the old man going out into the garage. He wouldn't be going into the garage if everything were not all right. I breathed in deeply and began to sing quietly to myself. I rolled myself off the bed, stood around indecisively for a moment, then kneeled down and dragged the Guilt Chest out, checking the stamp-edging only perfunctorily and not worrying overmuch whether they had been in it or not. It was time for another decision. I opened the wardrobe and got down the biggest sheet of brown paper I could find. I spread it out over the bed. Then I fell once again into a mild stupor, putting the recent conversation downstairs into some kind of glassy-eyed per-spective. Brooding over Gran's complaint about my old rain-coat in the bathroom, I remembered with a jolt the letter still there in it. I bounded into the bathroom and felt for it in my raincoat-cum-dressing-gown pocket. It was still there. I took it out and tried to remember the way I had folded it. They would surely have mentioned the matter if they had opened it and read it. I smoothed the letter out, and fluff fell out of the creases. I read it again.

*Dear Mr Fisher,*

*Many thanks for script and gags, I can use some of the gags and pay accordingly. As for staff job, well, I regret to tell you, I do not have 'staff' beside my manager, but several of the boys do work for me, you might be interested in this. Why not*

*call in for a chat next time you are in London? Best of luck*
*and keep writing, Danny Boon.*

Read in this light with the old man's threat to kick me out
tentatively expressed if not actually confirmed, it did not seem
after all much to go on. The thought of being in London
began to fill me, once again, with apprehension. I walked back
into the bedroom and took out the pound notes that I had
been hoarding in my wallet. There were nine of them. I
emptied my loose change out on to the sheet of wrapping
paper on the bed: fourteen and sixpence. Nine pounds fourteen and sixpence. But I could not do the complicated sums of
subtracting rail fare, rents, meals and the rest of it. I put the
money away and turned back to the Guilt Chest.

Carefully, I winkled out a stack of about three dozen
calendars and piled them on the sheet of brown paper. There
seemed to be room for more. I got another dozen, and then
wrapped the whole lot up, finding a length of string in the
elephant-shaped vase on the bedroom mantelpiece. They made
a heavy parcel, heavier than I had expected. I closed the Guilt
Chest, putting the stamp-edging in a new position, and went
downstairs, humping my parcel with me. In the hall I picked
up a gramophone record that had been there for days, waiting
to go back to the shop.

I went nervously into the lounge. Gran was sitting in her
chair with a shawl over shoulders, drinking weak tea and
moaning composedly to show that she was still not herself. I
breathed heavily with relief and went through into the
kitchen, where my mother had started making scones.

'Is she all right?' I said gruffly.

'As all right as she'll ever be,' my mother said wearily, in
her martyr's voice. I decided to let it go at that.

She nodded towards the parcel under my arm.

'What's that?'

'Books. Papers. Records,' I said.

'Where are you going with them?'

'Chucking them out, like he told me to,' I said, using my
own martyr's voice.

'Don't be silly,' my mother said easily, and went on baking. I walked out of the house. The old man was still messing about in the garage.

Instead of walking down Cherry Row I walked up it, into Valley Gardens, along Valley Gardens into Moorside Gardens, and along Moorside Gardens past the builders' huts and over the rubbish tip that led steeply down into Stradhoughton' Moor.

Stradhoughton Moor was a kind of pastoral slum on the edge of the town. It was fringed on Moorside by the dyeworks, Stradhoughton Town football ground and some public lavatories. The centre of the Moor was paved with cinders, where generations had tipped their slag and ashes, and where the annual fairs were held. There was a circumference of sparse yellow grass where the old men walked in summer, and I took the path they had worn towards a pocket of stone cottages, mostly condemned, that huddled miserably together in a corner of the Moor. Behind the cottages Stradhoughton Moor rose steeply again, out of an ashpit, to meet the scraggy allotments and, beyond them, the real moors of Houghtondale, such as were illustrated in the Council yearbook. I intended to drop my parcel of calendars down a pothole.

I enjoyed walking here. Given a quiet day I could always talk to myself, and it was easy to picture the cliff-like, craggy boundaries of the Moor as the borders of Ambrosia. The sun was still out, in a watery sort of way, and there was a hard, metal-grey shine on the afternoon. The faint waves of shouting, and all other noises, sounded remote and not very real, as though heard through a sheet of glass.

In Ambrosia, we were settling down to a shaky peace. The reactionary Dr Grover, weakened it was true by his Quisling record but still a power to be reckoned with, had got hold of some letters I had written to Arthur, outlining our plans for taking over the state. Liz, potentially the country's first home secretary, was abolishing the prisons.

I had reached the broken-down cottages by now. 'Mr President,' I said aloud, negotiating the ashpit and wondering whether to drop the parcel of calendars in it to be found, soggy and disintegrating, like a baby's body in a shoe box, 'Democracy is a stranger to Ambrosia. And yet this is a country of democrats. You know what this is?'— I held up the gramophone record I had brought out with me—'It is a ballot paper. Mr President, I will not rest until we have democracy *by vote* in this, er, ancient land of ours.'

I scrambled up the ashpit until I had reached the top of the Moor and was standing on the verge of grass surrounding the allotments. I looked down over the acre of cinders, across the lines of washing and the terrace-end pubs, the grandstand roof of the football ground advertising Bile Beans, and the black stone police station.

'We will rebuild——' I began in the ringing voice. I heard a slight crunching noise behind me, and turned round. A rough path of stone chippings led through the plots of beetroot and big blue cabbages towards the tufty moorland. Staggering along the path like some lost shepherd, doubtless living out his own private dreams as Dr Johnson or George Borrow or somebody, came Councillor Duxbury himself, dabbing his streaming eyes and clutching his gnarled old stick.

My heart missed a beat, and I wondered quickly how many beats it had missed this day, and whether it could only miss so many before you were dead, and if so how far I was off the total. There was nothing to dodge behind, unless I cared to jump back into the ashpit, but in any case he had seen me. I composed my face to look as though I wasn't doing anything, and tightened my grip on the suddenly enormous parcel of calendars under my arm.

Councillor Duxbury came flapping down the stone path, raising his stick in salute.

'Afternoon, lad!' he called in his rich, so-called Yorkshire relish voice.

'Afternoon, Councillor!' I called in the robust voice.

'It's a sunny 'un, this! 'Appen tha's watching t' football?'

'Nay, ahm' just bahn for a walk ower t' moor.' I always talked to Councillor Duxbury in his own dialect, half-mock-ingly, half-compulsively, usually goading myself into internal hysterics when I thought how I would reproduce the conversation to Arthur later.

'What's ta got theer, then? T' crown jewels?' He pointed with his stick at my parcel, his old face set in the serious, deadpan expression that had won him his tiresome reputation as a wag in the council chamber.

'Nay, old gramophone records,' I said, wildly producing the one record I did have, as proof. He did not ask me where I was taking them.

'Aye, ther' were nowt like that,' he said. His memory had been jogged so many times by *Echo* interviewers that he now regarded every statement as a cue for his reminiscences, and no longer bothered to add 'when I were a lad' or 'fot'ty year ago.' 'Ther' were nowt like that. We had to make our own music if we wanted it, else go without.' He rattled on as though he were himself an old gramophone that has just been kicked back into action. I was not sure that he knew who I was. Entirely lost in himself he began to mumble about the Messiah and I let him, full of frothy self-congratulation because I would be one up on Arthur when the next Duxbury routine came up.

'No, ther' were nowt like that.' He stopped at last to wipe his nose, making a ritual of it with a coloured handkerchief about the size of a bed-sheet. He paused between sniffs and shot me what he imagined to be a playful glance, the expression he always wore when he asked people how old they thought he was.

'Does ta think ah could climb down yon ashpit?'

'Nay, tha'd break thi neck, Councillor!' I said, giving him entirely the wrong answer. He gave me a sour look and said: 'Aye, well ah'sll have to manage it, whether or no. Ah'm bahn down to t' police station.'

My heart missed another beat, or rather ceased operating altogether for a second.

'What's ta bahn down theer for, then?' I told myself optimistically that if it were about me he would be going to the town hall, never mind the local police station. Besides, he didn't know who I was.

Councillor Duxbury chuckled. 'We're pulling 't down.'

I gulped with relief, although my heart was still at it. 'Tha's not, is ta?' I said, packing some incredulity into my voice.

'Aye, we are that. All yon cottages anall, they're going. And they won't get *council* houses for three and six a week, neether.'

I shook my head in sympathy, and saw that he was going into another of his reveries. I transferred my parcel from one arm to the other.

'It's all change,' said Councillor Duxbury. 'All change, nowadays. T' old buildings is going. T' old street is going. T' trams, they've gone.'

'Aye,' I said, sighing with him. 'It's not t' same wi' t' buses, is it?' One good shove, I thought, and he would be down at the bottom of the ashpit, where he wanted to be.

'It were all horse-drawn trams, and afore that we had to walk. It's all change. T' old mills is going. T' old dialect, *that's* going,' he said. I suddenly realised that he knew perfectly well that I did not talk in dialect all the time, and also that it was ridiculous to imagine that he did not know I worked for him. To prevent him saying whatever he might have been going to say next, I began to talk, looking desperately down over Strad-houghton Moor.

'Well, progress is all very well,' I said. 'But it's a pity we don't have a Yorkshire tradition o' progress.' I was trying to modify the dialect so that I could drop out of it completely within the minute. I nodded down at the police station. 'I don't mind dark satanic mills, but by gum when it comes to dark satanic shops, dark satanic housing estates and dark satanic police stations——' I broke off, realising that I had never worked out the end of this sentence. I looked at Councillor Duxbury for the feedline but he was away, staring glassily over the Moor.

'—that's different,' I concluded lamely. He did not seem inclined to speak. 'And yet,' I went on, grabbing half-remembered tufts of my Man o' the Dales conversation, 'and yet we've got to remember, this isn't a religion, it's a county. We've, er——'

73

I tailed off again. Councillor Duxbury had the fixed expression that old men have when they are lost in their thoughts, or what they claim are their thoughts, not listening to a word I was saying. A quick gust of wind swept around our ankles. I opened my mouth to speak again, remembering another bit, and then suddenly, without moving, he carved straight into my monologue.

*'Tha's a reet one wi' them calendars, i'n't ta?'*

I blanched, rocked on my heels and nearly fell over the grass edge into the ashpit below. I looked into his face to see if there was any suspicion of a boys-will-be-boys chuckle but he maintained his deadpan look as though he were telling wry jokes at a masonic dinner.

'By, tha's capped me theer, Councillor!' was all I could think of to say.

'Aye, and tha's capped me anall! Ah were reet taken back when Shadrack rang me up on t' telephone. Ah'd ha' thowt a lad like thee would have had more sense.' He spoke easily and not sternly, like a Yorkshire butler filling in plot-lines in a dialect comedy. I fancied that he was peering with keen suspicion at the parcel of calendars, and wondered if it were true that there were wise old men and he was one of them. I didn't know what to make of it. Even if he knew I worked for him, I was surprised that he could distinguish me from Stamp and Arthur. I had a reckless impulse to tell him that I *was* Arthur and that he was getting the two of us mixed up.

I said nothing.

'So tha's going to London, is ta?' he said with mild interest, as though the subject of the calendars had been settled entirely to his satisfaction.

Hopefully, I said: 'Aye, ah'm just about thraiped wi' Stradhoughton.' I remembered too late that 'thraiped' was a word Arthur and I had made up.

'How does ta mean?'

'It's neither muckling nor mickling,' I said, using another invented phrase in my complete panic.

'Aye.' The old man poked the ground with his stick, and said again, 'Aye.' I had no indication what he was thinking

74

about at all. I tried hard to keep talking, but I could not think of a single word of any description.

'Well tha's gotten me in a very difficult position,' he said weightily, at last.

'How does ta mean, Councillor?'

He studied me keenly, and I realised for the first time, with a sinking heart, that he was not as daft as he looked.

'Is ta taking a rise out o' me, young man?'

I felt myself flushing, and found my whole personality shifting into the familiar position of sheepishness and guilt. 'No, of course not.'

'Well just talk as thi mother and father brought thee up to talk then. Ah've had no education, ah had to educate myself, but that's no reason for thee to copy t' way *I* talk.' He spoke sharply but kindly, in a voice of authority with some kind of infinite wisdom behind it, and at that moment I felt genuinely ashamed.

'Now sither. We'll noan go ower t' ins and outs of it, tha's been ower all that down at t' office. But young Shadrack theer thinks ah ought to have a word wi' thi' father about thee. What does ta say to that?'

'I don't know,' I muttered, hanging my head. I wondered how I could ask him, without actually begging for mercy, not to talk to the old man.

'Well don't look as if tha's lost a bob and fun sixpence! Tha's not deead yet!'

I looked up at him and gave him a thin, grateful smile.

'Straighten thi back up! That's better. Now sither. Ah don't know what ah'sll do. Ah'sll have to think about what's best. But sither——' He gripped my arm. I did not feel embarrassed; I was able, even, to look steadily into his eyes. 'Sither. Tha'rt a young man. Tha' got a long way to go. But tha can't do it by thisen. Now think on.'

He released my arm, leaving me feeling that he had said something sage and shrewd, although I was unable to fathom quite what he was getting at. He was stuffing his handkerchief into his overcoat pocket, preparing to go. I did not want him to go. I did not feel afraid. I felt a kind of tentative serenity and I

wanted him to go on with his old man's advice, telling me the
things I should do.

'My grandma's poorly,' I said suddenly, without even knowing that I was talking. But he did not seem to hear.

'Ah'm glad to have had t' chance o' talking to thee,' he said.
He turned and began to make his way gingerly down the
gentlest slope of the ashpit, feeling the way with his shiny
stick. Half-way down he turned back awkwardly. 'Think on,'
he said.

I looked down after him, only just beginning to realise that
for the first time I wanted to tell somebody about it, and that I
could very probably have explained it all to him. I had to
resist an impulse to call back after him.

I stood there until he was safely on the grass perimeter
surrounding the stretch of cinders. I had a feeling, one that I
wanted to keep. It was a feeling of peace and melancholy. I
was not at all afraid. I walked happily along the rough stone
path through the allotments to the quiet moorland beyond,
and even while I was burying the calendars the feeling was
still with me.


SEVEN


The Witch was already fishing in her handbag for an orange,
but I was in a rare mood of optimism, as though I were starting a new life or something. We were on top of the No. 17 bus,
bound for the Coporation Cemetery. I was humming quietly,
and fingering two or three of Stamp's passion pills in my
pocket. The Witch was fuming to herself over the approaches
that had been made to her by various men in raincoats while
she waited for me in St Botolph's Passage. Luckily for me the
experience had put her out of mood for window-shopping.

Half-way to the cemetery, she was still going on about it.
'There *are* some nasty people about.'

'Mm,' I said. 'Have a passion pill.' I held two of the little black beads out in the palm of my hand. 'Energy tablets, they are,' I added hastily, realising what I had just said. 'We always call them passion pills. They're supposed to give you energy.'

The Witch was digging her thumbnail viciously into the peel of her orange. The bus was passing a row of advertising hoardings.

'Look, there y'are,' I cried excitedly, clutching her sleeve and jabbing at the window. '*Too* late. It was an advert for them. P.P., they're called. That's why they're nicknamed passion pills. You're supposed to take two.'

The Witch, stuffing bits of orange into her mouth, gave me her pitying look. 'What *is* the boy talking about?' she said.

I put on the frank and open grin and held out the two black pills. 'Very nice with fruit!' I said in the persuasive voice.

The Witch made some heavy weather over a sigh. 'Better humour the boy,' she said with an attempt at mock-resignation. She took the two pills in her mouth and knocked them back with a slice of orange. 'Satisfied?'

I sat back contentedly and lit a cigarette.

'Fifth today.'

'Last one,' the Witch cautioned.

Life seemed temporarily good. We got off the bus at the cemetery gates and walked up the broad red-gravel avenue between the white gravestones. Sometimes, in expansive moments such as this, I could understand what the Witch found so fascinating about this place. In fact it sometimes fascinated *me*. It was open, tidy and secure, like the campus in an American college musical. After the black, streaky tombs of St Botolph's churchyard there was something pleasantly normal about the symmetrical rows of neat headstones and the tidy oblongs of clean pebbles. All the people here seemed to have died a modern, healthy sort of death.

We strolled on to the grass verge between the graves, making our way to the public shelter outside the red brick chapel at the end of the long drive. The Witch, completely in her element, darted busily from one grave to another, admiring the angels and the September flowers, and crying 'Oh, look, pet, isn't it *sweet!*' whenever she found a stone crib.

From time to time she would stoop reverently over a head-stone and read out one of the verses chipped in gold, square lettering.

> *With you dearest Mother and darling dad,*
> *Happy were the years we had,*
> *And it is comfort in our pain*
> *You are now together again*

I listened to all this benevolently. So far as I was concerned, this was the scene when you see a close-up of a clock and the minute hand moves round a quarter of an hour to show the passage of time. Remembering the fiasco earlier in the day, I decided to give her a good twenty-five minutes this time, and she had quoted enough verses to fill an anthology before we reached the deserted shelter by the mock-Norman door of the burial chapel.

I got her snuggling up to me in the dark corner where we had carved our initials; that was the first step.

'Happy?'

'Mmmmm.'

I kissed her. She responded drowsily.

'Barbara? Tell me, how do you feel?'

'Contented,' she said, squeezing up to me kittenishly.

'You don't feel—you know, restless?'

'No.'

I sat there stroking her sleeve, trying to get some action out of her. I put my mouth close to hers again, but she was messing about making little kissing noises with her lips, and it was impossible to get at her for any length of time.

'Would you like another energy tablet?'

'No thank you, pet. They seem to make me sleepy.'

I grabbed hold of her arms roughly and urgently. She sat up, recognising the signs.

'Barbara,' I said in the pleading voice. 'Barbara!'

'Don't be angry again, pet,' she pleaded, clutching her handbag full of oranges in alarm.

'I'm not angry, just sad. Barbara—you know you're making me ill, don't you?'

'Poor Billy! Why am I making you ill?'

'Dalling! Have you ever heard of repressions? The nervous reactions that affect men who aren't, well——' the only ending I could think of for the sentence was a phrase of Stamp's, 'Getting it regular.' I let the thing peter out.

'I know what you mean, pet,' the Witch said, gently but desperately, as though she were soothing a dangerous lunatic. 'But we must be patient. We must. We'd only regret it.' But I was already regretting it. I found myself, quite suddenly, not caring a damn one way or the other, only wondering what I was doing here in a cemetery with a stone woman, anyway.

I muttered 'Forget it' and leaned back in the hard wooden shelter with my eyes closed, calculating how soon I could get away. I had been meaning to scheme out some way of keeping the Witch out of the Roxy tonight, out of the way of Rita, and I decided that it was high time I got to work on it. A tentative plot began to form in my mind; arranging to meet the Witch outside the Odeon, not turning up, and then explaining the whole unfortunate misunderstanding when she came to tea tomorrow. A warning bell sounded in my brain on the idea of the Witch coming to tea. *See Witch re Captain.* The words I had scribbled down hours before suddenly flashed like a neon sign in my head. I sat up again, sharply.

'Dalling!'

'Mmmm?' She was almost asleep.

'Dalling, are you still coming to tea tomorrow?'

The Witch sat up herself and shot me a keen glance, daring me to wriggle out of it.

'Of course. That's why I was hoping you would have got my engagement ring back.'

'Good.'

I swallowed. I had rehearsed this once, but that was days ago. I tried to visualise the stage instructions, looking studiously down at the stone-flagged floor and tracing one of the cracks with my foot.

'There's something I want to tell you,' I said in the low voice.

The Witch said nothing but, employing her main defence mechanism, stiffened.

'You know what you were saying about loving me even if I were a criminal?'

'Well?' in her icy voice. We had had a fairly tortured evening once when the Witch had cornered me into admitting that I would love her in every conceivable circumstance—age, infirmity, unfaithfulness (the idea of her being unfaithful had rather charmed me) and criminal record being taken into account. I had had no option but to fire the same litany back at her, and had got so far as to make her agree that even if I shot her father and mother she would still, she thought, love me.

'I wonder if you'll still love me when you've heard what I've got to say,' I said.

The Witch was rapidly withdrawing into a cocoon of formality.

'You see—well, you know that I've got a fairly vivid imagination, don't you?'

'Well you have to have, if you're going to be a scriptwriter, don't you?' she said smugly. There were occasions when I would have willingly shot *her*, never mind her relations.

'Well *being* a script-writer,' I continued ponderously, 'I'm perhaps a bit inclined to let my imagination run away with me. As you know.'

The Witch said nothing, but she was beginning to breathe heavily through her nostrils.

'You see, if—if we're going to have our life together, and the cottage, and little Billy and little Barbara and the wishing-well and all that, there's some things we've got to get cleared up.' I nearly added 'and implemented'.

'What things?'

According to my stage instructions I was to give her a frank, honest glance. I was unable to do it, and decided to rely on a frank, honest profile.

'Some of the things I'm afraid I've been telling you.'

The Witch said, in her direct, devastating way: 'Do you mean you've been telling *lies*?'

'Well not lies exactly, but I suppose I've been—well, exaggerating some things. Being a script writer...' Another idea crossed my mind, that of slapping the Witch across the mouth and striding out of the cemetery, never to meet her again. I put it away. 'Well, for instance, there's that business about my father. Him being a sea captain.'

In a weak moment, or rather in a panoramic series of weak moments, I had told the Witch that during the war the old man had been the captain of a destroyer. He had been partly responsible for sinking the *Graf Spee* before being captured —one of the first men to be captured by U-boats, as a matter of fact—and had spent three years in a prisoner-of-war camp. He had been wounded in the leg, which still gave him some trouble.

'You mean he wasn't a sea captain, I suppose?' said the Witch, and I was surprised that *she* didn't seem surprised.

'He wasn't even in the navy,' I said.

'And what about him being a prisoner-of-war? Don't say *that* was all lies.'

'Yes.'

The Witch turned away with a quick movement of the head, bringing tears to her eyes without difficulty. I suspected that she had perfected the whole action in front of a mirror. Its point was to make it quite evident that she was turning away and not just looking away. Reaching out for the most banal remark I could find, I said:

'Are you cross?'

There was a practised silence. The Witch gave it thirty seconds and then said:

'No, I'm not cross. Just disap*poi*nted, that's all. It sounds as though you were *ashamed* of your father.'

I sat bold upright and steamed the heat into my voice. 'I'm *not* ashamed, I'm not, I'm not!'

'Otherwise why say he was a sea captain—? What was he?'

I had to stop myself from saying 'A conscientious objector' and starting the whole thing over again. I said: 'He wasn't anything. He wasn't fit. He has trouble with his knee.'

'The knee he's supposed to have been shot in, I suppose.'

'Yes,' and I was now talking belligerently. 'Another thing, we haven't got a budgie.'

I had told her that we kept a yellow budgerigar called Roger. I had regularly given her communiqués about its antics and there had been a highlight when Roger had flown out of his cage and nearly been caught by Sarah, the tabby.

'Or a cat,' I said.

The Witch was shuffling her handbag about and buttoning her coat to give the impression that she was about to leave.

'How many other lies have you been telling me?'

'My sister.' The Witch had roughly the same story about my imaginary sister as I had given to Arthur's mother.

'Don't tell me you haven't got a *sister*.'

'I did have, but she's dead.' This time it was out before I could prevent it. I ran rapidly over this new turn, and within seconds I had established death from tuberculosis, and a quiet funeral. 'If you still want to come tomorow, they never talk about her,' I said.

'I'm not sure I *shall* be coming, now,' said the Witch. She shuddered elaborately. 'I've always hated—lying.'

A happy thought struck me. In my pocket I still had the miniature silver cross that had spilled out of her handbag in St Botolph's churchyard—the one she was supposed to have given back to her cousin Alec.

'Have you?' I said. I decided against producing the thing triumphantly and waving it under her nose, for the moment at least. I went into the hard voice and said: 'Look, Barbara, we all have our faults. I have mine. You have yours.'

'I don't tell *lies*,' said the Witch.

'Don't you?'

'No!'

'What about that cross or whatever it was that you were supposed to have given back to your cousin?'

'Well, I *did* give it back,' said the Witch. I was satisfied to see the same smooth expression on her face that I wore so regularly myself.

'Did you?' I said cryptically. She looked down at her hand-bag and back at me.

'I told you I'd given it back and I *gave* it back.'

'All right.' I stood up as though washing my hands of the whole business. From the hard voice into the matter-of-fact voice. 'Look. I've got to go into town now. You probably won't believe anything I say after this, but I may as well tell you that I've been offered a job in London. It depends on your attitude whether I take it or not.'

The Witch got to her feet, contriving a dazed expression. I felt like gripping her by the lapels of her coat and saying coarsely: 'Look, chum, I do all these tricks myself. I *know* them. Pack it in.'

'I shall never know whether you're telling the truth after this,' she said. She walked with me down the gravel drive towards the cemetery gates, almost falling over her own feet in her attempts to look straight in front of her.

As we were passing the last grave I said in the bitter voice: 'Well I know what *my* epitaph will be.'

She did not reply at first, so I let her wait for it. At length she said: 'What?' reluctantly.

' "Here lies Billy Fisher," ' I said.

I put just the right amount of ruefulness in my voice, and it took effect. She caught my hand impulsively and said: 'Don't be cross with yourself.'

At the cemetery gates she stopped and held my hands at arm's length, as though for inspection. 'Billy?'

'Yes, dalling?'

'Promise me something?'

'That I'll never lie to you again?' She nodded. 'I'll never lie to you again,' I said.

Holding hands, we walked out of the cemetery. The first person I saw, coming towards us and too near for me to do anything about it, was Arthur's mother, carrying a bunch of pansies.

Out of the side of my mouth I said rapidly: 'Do as I say, explain later!' As Arther's mother came alongside us, I smiled broadly.

'Hullo, Mrs Crabtree. I don't think you've met my sister. Sheila, this is Mrs Crabtree.'

83

Arthur's mother looked at me as though I had hit her. It suddenly struck me that I had made the wrong decision. She said indignantly:

'I'm afraid you've picked the wrong person to play your tricks with *this* time. I happen to know Barbara very well.'

The Witch, for public consumption only, gave me her tolerant, more-in-sorrow look.

'I think it's his queer sense of humour,' she said.

'Got to catch a tram,' I gabbled. 'Bus.' A No. 17 was pulling slowly away from the bus stop. I jumped on and galloped up the stairs, getting the Ambrosian repeater gun into position.

### EIGHT

'What, is *this* for me as well?' asked Rita incredulously.

I nodded, my mouth so full of egg sandwich that my eyes were watering. 'Been robbing a bank,' I chuntered, spluttering food. It was already five o'clock, and the first time I had eaten since breakfast.

'Cugh! Got owt else you don't want?' She was genuinely delighted, more pleased, in fact, than she had been over the engagement ring. She put the silver cross round her neck, fumbling under the metallic blonde hair to fasten the slender chain.

'Joan of Arc,' said Arthur.

'Oo, it's woke up again!' She bared her teeth at him, registering exaggerated scorn. Afraid that she had perhaps been sounding too grateful and had made a fool of herself, she said dubiously, peering down at the cross: 'Aren't you supposed to go to church or summat when you wear one of these?'

Arthur said: 'Yes, you've got to take a vow of chastity.'

'Get back in the knifebox, bighead!' Rita picked up my empty plate, a move I recognised as an obscure gesture of affection. 'You can bring me a fur coat tomorrer,' she said genially. She went back to the counter, leaving us sitting at the rockety table in the corner of the Kit-Kat by the huge, throbbing refrigerator.

'The sexfulness is terrific,' Arthur said, watching her go.

I was back in the buoyant, almost hysterical mood.

'Lo, she is the handmaiden of my desires!' I said, raising a solemn right hand. Arthur took the cue to go into the Bible routine.

'And a voice spake,' he said in a loud, quavering voice. 'And the voice said Lo, who was that lady I saw ye with last cockcrow?'

'And Moses girded up his loins and said Verily, that was no lady, that was my spouse,' I responded.

'Yea, and it was so.'

'Yea, even unto the fifth and sixth generations.'

We finished our coffee and got up, guffawing and blowing kisses at Rita. 'Don't do owt I wouldn't do!' she called, in an unusual mood herself.

We left the glass doors wide open, the doughnut-eaters yelling 'Door!' after us, and walked out into Moorgate and across the road towards Town Arcade.

I had got over the feeling of guilt at meeting Arthur so soon after the hideous contretemps with his mother. I had been thinking of telling him about it, in one form or another, but now I was glad that I hadn't.

We walked into Town Arcade shouting: 'Paymer! Paymer! War declared! Paymer!' and our voices echoed under the arched glass roof. The women shoppers, shuffling miserably after each other with their string bags and their packets of cream biscuits, stared at us. 'Paymer, lady?' I called, flourishing an imaginary *Echo*. To my own surprise, I found that I was still carrying under my arm the gramophone record I had taken out of the house hours ago.

'Let's go take the mickey out of Maurie,' I said.

Maurie was the owner of the X-L Disc Bar at the top of the Arcade, a slight, dapper little man who looked like an Armenian. He was interested in youth work and all the rest of

85

it, and was always going on about showing tolerance and treating everybody as adults. When we had nothing to do we would go in and bully him. 'Hey, Maurie, this record's got all grooves in it.'

'Wonder if we'll get any buckshee records out of him?' said Arthur. We opened the door with our feet and almost fell into the shop.

On Saturday afternoons the X-L Disc Bar was crowded with girls in gipsy ear-rings and youths in drainpipe trousers. They were the same people that we saw in the Roxy every week, but we never saw them anywhere else in Stradhoughton. They seemed to be transported invisibly from one place to another. They made me feel curiously old-fashioned in my stained raincoat and my crumpled suit, and I put on the intellectual act, sloping one shoulder down and trying to look as though the record under my arm was a copy of *Under Milk Wood*. One of the Kit-Kat crowd, doing a sort of skaters' waltz round the shop, called 'Rag-bones!' but nobody else took any notice.

The Disc Bar would not have made a good subject for Man o' the Dales' Yorkshire Sketchbook. It had been a quite passably modern record shop when Maurie first opened it, but under his policy of live and let live it had been quickly reduced to a glass shambles. The cone-shaped ashtray stands, their bright yellow smudged with black, were already tilted, broken and abandoned. The showcases, which were supposed to hang in mid-air on steel wires, sagged and lurched so dangerously that they had to be propped up on old packing cases. One of them was broken, a great jagged crack going along one corner. There were scuff marks all along the orange walls.

The girls in their tartan trousers swarmed around the record booths, leaving the doors swinging open untidily, so that half a dozen melodies—the pop songs, the trumpet specialities and the jazzed-up hymns—met and collided somewhere in the middle of the shop. A boy of about sixteen in a leather lumber jacket was leaning against the counter, juggling with a plastic record sleeve. Little Maurie, in his red braces, was trying to make himself heard. 'Would you mind? I know it's a great temptation, but would you mind?'

Arthur pirouetted across the shop like a dancer, using the peculiar gliding steps that seemed to be more or less obligatory in this centre. He found a cluster of friends from the band that played at the Roxy, and was immediately swallowed up with them in the corner. I stood by myself, hesitating. The odd thing was that he seemed to know everybody and I didn't. In the No. 1 thinking it was sometimes the other way round.

I heard a familiar, grating voice behind me and looked round. It was Stamp, holding up an L.P. and shouting: 'Hey, Maurie, is this a record?'—a joke, if you could call it a joke, that he had used a hundred times before. Stamp was never out of the Disc Bar. Little Maurie was the leader of the youth club whose illiterate posters Stamp was always designing. 'Hey, Maurie! Maurie! Is this a record?' I cuffed his arm so that he almost dropped the L.P. 'No, slipped disc,' I said.

'Oh, they've let *you* out, have they?' jeered Stamp, his eyes narrowing maliciously.

'Yes, they wanted to make room for you,' I said. I was glad to have met even Stamp. I turned away, looking around the shop to see if there was anybody else I knew.

'I say!' Stamp called me back.

'I wouldn't come in on Monday if I were you,' he said.

'I wouldn't come in on *Tuesday* if I were you. Why not?'

He was grinning in the malevolent way he had when he had got hold of a piece of rich bad news. 'I've just been back to the office to get some stuff,' he said. 'Shadrack's adding up your postage book.'

'After you with Shadrack,' I said. I suddenly felt ill. In the light voice: 'Did he say anything?'

'What?'

'Did he *say* anything, dozey! About the stinking postage book?'

'No, he was just muttering to himself. He had all the money and all the stamps out, though. He was adding it all up. How much have you knocked off?'

'Haven't knocked anything off.' Some of Stamp's friends

were hovering round, staring at me. 'Only the book's not up to date, that's all,' I said.

'Borstal here we come,' said Stamp. He turned back to his friends, tittering. Over his shoulder, he said casually: 'Your mate's upstairs.'

I knew at once, with a quick vibration running through me, whom he was talking about, exactly as I had known when he mentioned her this morning. I glanced involuntarily up the stairs where the classical department was, all thought of Shadrack going out of my head before it had time even to take root. One of Stamp's friends, a dopey-looking youth in an Italian striped suit, said: *'Git in there, Charlie!'* I walked slowly up the stairs, the noise fading into a cacophonous backwash. Things I had forgotten came back and I was already steeped in the familiar atmosphere, the sense of freshness, relief, absurd comfort, anticipation, and the hint of some elusive scent that I knew for a fact did not exist. I was already telling her, 'I could remember how you *smelled*, even!' The last thing I heard was Stamp shouting, away in the distance, down in the shop, 'Hey, Maurie, this record's got a hole in it!'

The classical department, usually deserted on a Saturday afternoon, had an almost public library air about it. It was thickly carpeted, with a single glass counter and a row of grey record booths. The rest of it was empty and light and spacious, and quiet. Liz was standing behind the counter, handing a record album to a middle-aged man in a black overcoat. She was talking to him in her comfortable, plummy voice. I knew that she had seen me out of the corner of her eye, and was putting the moment off, the same as I was.

I was trying on expressions, as though I carried a mirror about with me and was pulling faces in it. I tried to look stunned, because after all there was the material for it, and I tried to assemble some kind of definite emotion that I wasn't putting on or concocting out of the ingredients of the atmosphere she carried around with her. I found that what I had was a sensation of singing.

The man picked up the record album and went into one of the record booths, closing the door behind him.

I walked slowly forward to the counter.

'Hullo, Liz.'

'Hullo, Billy.'

I spoke in what I hoped was the low, husky voice, indicating the end of a long journey or something, but she spoke frankly and happily, as though she were delighted to see me and had no reason to hide what she felt.

We grinned at each other, full of relief, like people who have found each other again in a crowd. She was still wearing the same old things, the green suède jacket and the crumpled black skirt. But the crisp white blouse went well with her round, shiny face, the mousy hair and the eyes that laughed aloud.

'It's been a long time,' I said, knowing it was a cliché, in fact selecting it *as* a cliché, but trying to put some meaning into what I was saying.

She shook her head from side to side, happily, considering the point.

'Oh—a month. Five weeks.'

'I ought to say it seemed like years.'

She grinned again. Liz was the only girl I had ever met who knew *how* to grin, or anything about it. 'Isn't this *grand*?' she said.

'I could even remember how you smelled,' I said.

She gave me a mock bow. 'Thank you, kind sir, she said.'

'When did you get back?'

'Yesterday.'

'Thank you very much for ringing me up and telling me.'

She wrinkled her nose, not in the same way as the Witch but in a friendly, candid way. Liz never gave excuses.

'I would have seen you tonight, anyway,' she said. 'Are you going to the Roxy?'

Who isn't? I thought. I started rapidly disposing of personnel. The Witch, for one, would quite obviously be going into a nunnery or somewhere after this afternoon's business. Rita, if I stood her up, would not dream of paying her own way into the Roxy. I did not care, anyway, knowing that I could tell Liz all about it if I wanted to.

'Yes,' I said. 'But I wish you'd rung me up.'

'I hadn't time.' She grinned broadly again, telling me not to believe her and not to worry because it didn't matter, and it didn't. 'Ask me what I'm doing *here.*'

'What are you doing here?'

'Helping Maurie out for the day.' No time to ring me up, but time to help Maurie out. It still didn't matter. The only thing that crossed my mind was the vague question of how Liz knew Maurie. She seemed to know everybody. It was part of the enigma, one of the things about her that I could never get into the test-tube and examine.

'Well what have you been *do*ing all these weeks?' she said, bubbling over with it all. 'How's the script-writing? How are the songs? How's Arthur?' She was the only girl I knew who cared, or who could talk about things as though they really mattered. We began chattering, eagerly interrupting, laughing, grinning at each other as though we knew the whole joke about the world and understood it. We talked until the man in the record booth, whom we had both forgotten, emerged with the record album and paid for it and went away. It was nearly closing time.

'Ask me where I've been all these weeks,' said Liz.

'No,' I said steadily, not laughing this time. It was the one standing challenge between us and I had always told myself that I would never ask. I did not know any longer whether I was afraid to, or whether it was out of some kind of respect for her, or whether it was just an obsession like growing my thumb nail until it was a quarter of an inch long.

'But you might have sent me a postcard,' I said.

'Postcards next time. If there is a next time,' she added softly.

I went downstairs again, waving to her. The crowd had thinned out, leaving a litter of discarded records and cigarette packets on the floor and on the glass showcases. Arthur had gone, and so had his friends from the band. Most of Stamp's crowd had gone too, but Stamp was still there, sniggering with Maurie at the counter.

The old gramophone record still under my arm, I remembered what I had come into the Disc Bar for in the first place. I was loth to approach Maurie without Arthur to back me up, but I decided to do so for Stamp's benefit.

'Hey, Maurie!' I said. 'Can I have the money back on this record?'

He glared at me, a sour look that was unusual for him, and snapped: 'Why?'

'It only *plays* one tune.'

Maurie rang open his cash register. 'Yes, I've been *watch*ing you,' he said venomously. 'I've been *hear*ing about you.' Stamp was leaning on the counter, trying to look as though he didn't know what was going on. 'You're another of these who come in here, thinking you own the shop. Well *I* don't know where you get your money from.'

Maurie always dribbled when he spoke. He sucked in vigorously with his upper lip, retrieving the thin spittle that had been trickling down his chin.

'Well we're having a big clear-out. From now on it's a shop, not a market-place. Take the money and clear out.'

He flung some coins on the scratched glass counter. I had to scrabble at them to pick them up. Stamp was finding it difficult not to break out sniggering again.

'And don't come back again!' said Maurie.

But I was whistling as I walked out of the shop, and I whistled all the way down the Arcade.


NINE


I did nothing but walk around town for an hour and a half, watching Saturday evening begin to happen and the slow queues forming outside the Odeon and the Gaumont. The people walked about as though they were really going some-where. I stood for a quarter of an hour at the time, watching them get off the buses and disperse themselves about the streets. I was amazed and intrigued that they should all be content to be nobody but themselves.

When it was half-past seven I got on a bus myself, on my way to the New House, the pub where I did my club turn. As a rule I could not face this experience without a stiff shot of No. 1 thinking, seeing myself returning to Stradhoughton as the world-famous comedian, doing charity concerts and never losing the common touch. But tonight I did not think about it at all. When Liz was in Stradhoughton I could transport myself from hour to hour like a levitationist, so that all events between one meeting and another were things that happened to other people and not to me.

It was only when I got off the bus at Clogiron Lane and the New House was in sight that I began to unload the ballast and I was left, as usual, with nothing but a kind of desperate inertia.

The New House was an enormous drinking barracks that had been built to serve Cherry Row and the streets around it. The New House was not its proper title. According to the floodlit inn-sign stuck on a post in the middle of the empty car park, the pub was called the Who'd A Thought It. There had been a lot of droll speculation in Man o' the Dales' column about how this name had come about, but whatever the legend was it had fallen completely flat in Clogiron Lane. Nobody ever called the pub anything but the New House.

There was a windy, rubber-tiled hallway where the children squatted, eating potato crisps and waiting for their mothers. Two frosted-glass doors, embossed with the brewery trademark, led off it, one into the public bar and one into the saloon. It was necessary to take one route or the other to get into the concert-room; the only other alternative was to approach the concert-room direct through its own entrance and run the gauntlet of fat women, sitting in rows with their legs apart, shrieking with laughter and gulping down gin and orange. Either that or climb in through the lavatory window.

I decided on the public bar route. I smoothed my hair back, straightened my tie, and went in. I preferred the public bar, anyway. The men who sat here were refugees from the warm terrace-end pubs that had been pulled down; they sat around drinking mild and calling to each other across the room as though nothing had changed. 'Have you got them theer, Charlie?'—'Aye, they're up in our garridge.'—'I'll come down for 'em tomorrow morning.' They seemed to have secrets between them, and they reunited into a world of their own wherever they went. The few items in the New House that gave it anything like the feel of a pub—the dartboard, the cribbage markers, the scratched blind-box and the pokerwork sign that said IYBMADIBYO, if you buy me a drink I'll buy you one—were all part of the same portable world, as if they had been wheeled here in prams in the flight from the old things.

Through the smoke, a voice croaked jubilantly: 'Here he is—*the boy*!' and I realised at once that I had made another mistake. From this point I had to walk through a barricade of Formica-topped tables where all these men sat clacking dominoes and making their observations. I waved my hand flaccidly at one or two of the people I recognised. A man called Freddy Platt, who never did anything else but sit around drinking beer all day, started up.

'Nah lad, Billy! Where's thi dog?' The others laughed, and he looked around eagerly for someone to egg him on. 'He's forgotten t' dog ageean! Ask him what he's done wi' t' dog, Sam!'

'Where's thi dog, Billy?'

Once, in some kind of effort to prise myself into this community of theirs, where they were always selling each other things and sharing the same interests, I had asked Freddy Platt if he wanted to take a dog off my hands. For about five minutes it had worked like an open sesame, with everybody in the bar shouting about dogs, and me in the middle of it, but when they found out the truth I had to pretend it was a joke.

'Nay, it's in t' dogs' home!' I called back in the hearty voice. They laughed indulgently.

Freddy Platt winked elaborately at his mates. 'When's ta bahn off to London, Billy?' he called. He started nudging the man next to him and urging: 'Go on, Sam, ask him when he's off to London.'

They were always bringing that one up, too. I had told them months ago, prematurely as it turned out, that I had a job in London waiting for me. I had been gratified, and then alarmed, at the way the story had spread through the pub, like a dangerous fire. They were still at it with the embers.

'When's ta bahn off to London, Billy?'

'I'll be going, don't you worry!' They laughed again, shaking their heads. 'He's a case, i'n't he?' said Freddy Platt. 'He is. He's a case.' I gave them the deprecating smile, cornered again into the position of village idiot or licensed clown or whatever it was they imagined me to be. Freddy shouted across the room: 'Has ta fetched that stuff down, Walter?' and they were back with their repertoire of secrets.

I walked through into the concert-room, a hideous cork-floored drill hall with buff walls and fancy strip-lighting fitments that looked like rejects from a luxury liner. The concert was already warming up, with the Clavioline thumping away and an Irish labourer, grasping the microphone as though it were a pint pot, singing, *'Blais this house nya Lard we pray.'* Johnny the waiter moved round the room with his tin tray held high above his head, and the fat women sat at the bow-legged tables eating packets of nuts and knocking back the shorts. Their husbands stood at the long bar at the end of the room, where you didn't have to watch the concert if you didn't want to.

The long bar was where the members of the Ancient Order of Stags or whatever it was gathered on Saturday nights, waiting for their lodge meeting to begin upstairs. They were there now, all lean-faced men calling each other brother, for ever shaking hands and digging in their pockets for penny fines. In their own way they were as bad as Freddy Platt and *his* crowd and I gave them the same limp wave and looked away.

There was a patter of applause for the Irish singer, and Johnny the waiter cried: 'Can I 'ave your orders please before the next *turn*!' He started hustling round the room with his tray under his arm and a fistful of silver. Behind me a ponderous voice said: 'Now then, young man!'

I turned round to see another group of Stags padding in from the saloon bar, all holding pints of beer. In the middle of them was Councillor Duxbury, wearing the chain of past grand warden or something. He did not often come to this lodge, and when he did I managed as a rule to avoid him. I was not sure what my status with him was after our encounter on Stradhoughton Moor; I played for safety with a non-committal smile.

One of the men he was with said with heavy jocularity: 'Well, is the worthy brother bahn to give us a turn toneet?'

Councillor Duxbury gave me a solemn wink and said: 'Nay, he is but an untutored apprentice, brother deacon.'

Brother deacon winked too. Practically every man in the pub made a practice of winking before he opened his mouth. 'And what about thee, brother warden? Art thou tutored?'

'Aye, it's not me that wants tutoring.' Councillor Duxbury was looking at me pointedly, and I knew that I was supposed to get some kind of hidden message out of what he was saying. I was wondering already what I had found so understanding about him on Stradhoughton Moor. Then it occurred to me that he had probably heard about Shadrack's audit of the postage book since then.

'Tha'rt initiated, then?' said brother deacon, staggering on with the joke. 'Give t' password.'

'At my initiation I was taught to be cautious. I will letter or half it wi' thee, which you please,' recited Councillor Duxbury.

The Stags spent half their time fooling about in this way, and some of them I knew had long ago stopped speaking in any other manner. Councillor Duxbury and brother deacon were settling down for a long, pedantic cross-talk; but before they had the chance to go rumbling through their passwords, the third man in the group spoke huffily: 'The lodge is not yet tiled, brothers!'

Through the crackling microphone, Johnny the waiter announced: 'Quiet, please! *Can* I 'ave a bit of quiet? And now, two very clever young men who've come all the way over from Dewsbury to entertain us tonight, Bob and *Har*ry! Quiet now, please!' The two young men with fresh, eager-to-please faces bounded on to the low platform and started miming facetiously to a record of 'Baby it's cold outside'. They were making an elaborate strong-man-and-coy-girl act of it, fluttering with the eyelids and slapping each other, and I found it embarrassing to look at them.

'Well we'll go up and get t' lodge tiled, then, if tha'rt so particular,' said Councillor Duxbury.

'Shall we tak' t' untutored apprentice up wi' us?' said brother deacon, clawing at me playfully. 'Come on, lad, ther'll be someone tha knows up theer.'

'The craft will keep its omnipotent eye on t' untutored apprentice,' said Councillor Duxbury.

They were all winking at each other like maniacs, and shoving each other's elbows. Filled with an accumulation of nausea I muttered: 'Excuse me,' and sidled out of their way. I meant to take refuge in the saloon bar but, hardly knowing what I was doing, I found myself slipping through the first door I could find, and I was back in the public bar. The old voice cried: 'Here he is again—*the boy*!' I stopped, feeling trapped in the haze of faces. I looked wildly around the bar, searching for a beer barrel or something that I could focus my eyes on without any harm coming from it. I saw an old man like a tramp, hobbling about the room trying to sell an armful of comic papers. I gazed at him steadily as though trying to place his blank face.

Out of one of the close, anonymous groups I heard the honking voice of Freddy Platt: 'Ther's thi paper here, Billy! Give 'im t' paper, Sam!'

'*Billy's Weekly Liar!*' roared somebody else. 'Go on, Sam, give 'im it!'

'He doesn't want it—he's t' editor!'

We had been through this one before, many a time. *Billy's Weekly Liar* was the comic paper that was peddled about the pub on Saturday nights, along with the *War Cry* and the *Empire News*. They would buy one copy between four of them and sit around pointing at the jokes with their stubby fingers. When they saw me coming they would bring out their own old joke.

'*Billy's Weekly Liar*! Here y'are, Billy!' Somebody was trying to shove the paper into my hand.

'Billy Liar!' laughed Freddy Platt. He was shouting at the top of his voice to compete with the noise from the concert-room next door; the miming act was climbing up to a screaming, oscillating crescendo, and it needed nothing but a couple of policemen running about blowing whistles to complete the sudden, hysterical chaos. 'Billy Liar! We'll call 'im that, eh? We'll call 'im that, Sam! Billy Liar. By! Where's thi dog, Billy?'

He did not get any response from me. I could not even see him. I stared sightlessly around the public bar, darting from one object to another without recognising anything. 'He's a case!' shouted Freddy Platt. 'He is, he makes me laugh! By!'

I felt someone prodding me from behind. I staggered a little under the impetus and wondered whether there would be any future in letting myself go on falling until I was flat on my face on the floor and they would have to carry me out into the cool, quiet air. It was Johnny the waiter with his tray loaded with empty glasses and bottle tops. 'You're on next, Billy boy.' Without caring much what I was doing I stumbled back into the concert-room. 'Billy Liar and his talking dog!' shouted Freddy Platt. I whipped round angrily, and saw that the whole lot of them had got up and were following me into the concert-room. I shambled across the cork floor through the troops of women, buckling at the knees in case I should retrieve the idea of dropping in a dead faint.

'All right, now the best of order now! If you please! Next on the bill to entertain us tonight we 'ave a young man who needs no introduction from me. Quiet, please, for our very own Billee *Fish*ah! Break it up small, you lads!'

I climbed up on the platform, with the Clavioline running meaninglessly through the first few bars of '1 want to be happy.' I looked out across the concert-room at all the people, trying to remember the first line of my act but knowing perfectly well that whatever it was, it was nothing to do with them, and whatever they were, it was nothing to do with me.

97

Some of the women at the round, rocking tables stared at me like cows waiting to be milked, but most of them took no notice at all. Freddy Platt and his friends stood at the end of the room by the public bar door, in a swaying, solid group, still swopping their secrets. I was surprised and depressed to see that Bob and Harry, the two young men involved in the miming act, had sat down with a crowd old enough to be their fathers; they were smoking the same Woodbines and drinking the same mild beer. All the people in the concert-room sat so comfortably, as though they had reached a reasonable agreement with life and death, as though they knew all about it, all that there was to know about it.

I put on my funny face and started on the club turn, wishing that I could whistle 'In a Monastery Garden' through my teeth instead, and please everybody.

'*Ah'm coortin'.*'

A few titters from some of the more impressionable women but, on the whole, dead silence.

'*Ah am. Ah'm coortin'.*'

I jerked my head round with the well-staged, well-practised pop-eyed, indignant look, as though expecting scorn or laughter or disbelief or some reaction of some kind or another from the audience.

'*It's a Wakefield lass.*'

I saw the same people, the women, Freddy Platt and Co., and the few customers at the long bar. Most of the Stags had gone upstairs, knocking three times on the door to get themselves let into the lodge; but there was one man standing by himself at the bar counter, dragging on a cigarette and holding his beer as though it had dealt him an injury. I caught his eye and fear, real fear and not a substitute, clutched me. I forgot the act and bent down urgently to where Johnny the waiter was ladling out gin and pep at the table nearest the platform.

'Johnny! Johnny! *What the bloody hell is our old man doing here?*'

Johnny looked up, surprised. 'He's joining t' Stags, it's initiation night,' he whispered. 'Get on wi' t' turn!'

I muttered, 'Jesus Christ Almighty' and straightened up and faced the microphone, feeling as though somebody had just kicked me in the stomach. I had never seen the old man in a pub before, and had come to depend upon him never using the New House. He was looking at me sardonically; so, if it came to that, was the rest of the audience by now. Some of the women were getting restless. I gave the old man a stiff, formal bow and he turned away with a gesture of contempt and embarrassment. Freddy Platt shouted: 'When's ta bringing t' dog on, Billy?' I ran quickly through my lines. Ah'm coortin.' It's a Wakefield lass.

'She does, she comes from Wakefield. She's a nice lass, only she's got one big fault. She stutters.'

There was some untidy sniggering from various parts of the concert-room. In so far as the act would come to life at all, it was beginning to warm up.

'She does, she stutters.'

I gave them the pop-eyed look again, avoiding the old man's eye. I had just blasted him with the Ambrosian repeater gun; so far as I was concerned he was no longer there.

'But she's a very warm-hearted lass, very warm-hearted. She'll do owt for you. And she likes a cuddle. Oh, yes, she likes a cuddle. Only she stutters.

'We were sitting in t' parlour one night, y'know, just t' two of us, and she were sitting there, and I were sitting here, and she looked at me, she looked at me and she says, would you like a nice cuh cuh cuh cuh cuh cuh cuh cuh——'

The sniggering was well set in by now. The fattest woman of all screamed aloud and the others laughed, this time at her. Freddy Platt was making some kind of noise of his own at the back of the room.

'Would you like a cuh cuh cuh cuh cuh cuh——'

I suddenly realised, with the old sinking feeling, what the low thudding noise I had been hearing for the last minute was. Councillor Duxbury had descended the stairs from the lodge and was clomping deliberately across the concert-room floor towards the gents, the seal of past grand warden swinging round his neck like a prize medal on an old shire horse.

He passed within a yard of the old man, but they did not speak to each other.

'*Would you like a cuh cuh cuh cuh cup of tea?*'

The women shrieked. 'T' record's stuck!' shouted Freddy Platt. I saw Councillor Duxbury off to the door of the lavatory.

'*Then she gets all coy and says yes, ah knows thee, ah bet you thought I were going to ask you if you wanted a cuh cuh cuh cuh cuh cup of cocoa!*'

I got to the end of the stuttering joke, whatever it was. Councillor Duxbury emerged from the gents, buttoning his flies. He walked slowly over to the old man and stood indecisively at the side of him, as though he had forgotten what it was all about.

'*But o' course, ah'm a poor man. Ah can't support her. Ah can't support her. Ah only had one clog on me foot when ah came to Stradhoughton. Only one clog on me foot. But very soon ah were riding about in taxis.*'

The two of them, the old man and Councillor Duxbury, stood talking for a moment. The old man glanced in my direction once, but not malevolently. He finished his beer and the two of them set off towards the stairs, the old man hanging back to keep pace with Duxbury. I had no idea why he should be joining the Stags, but it was obvious that as one Stag to another Councillor Duxbury would tell him all that there was to be told about me.

'*Ah had to take a taxi because ah only had one clog.*'

I was back with the fat women and Freddy Platt and his crowd. I brought out the jokes as I remembered them, trying to bring the act to a finish. Some of the women screeched from time to time, but nobody really cared whether I was on or off the platform. They were beginning to turn round to each other and whisper and light cigarettes, and to pour out beer and hold it studiously to the light, as though I wasn't there at all.

'*Any road*, this *feller stuttered as well. So he goes up to this bookie and y'know, it were t' right busy time, just before t' last race, and he says, ah've backed ah've backed ah've backed ah've backed ah've backed ah've backed——*'

'Ah've backed a loser!' shouted Freddy Platt.

'*Ah've backed ah've backed ah've backed ah've backed. So t'*
*bookie says, gerron wi' it, ah've not got all day*——'

('Neither 'ave we!')

'*So he says ah've backed ah've backed ah've backed ah've*
*backed. So t' bookie says, come on, nark it*——'

'*Nark* it?' exploded Freddy Platt triumphantly. '*Nark* it?
That's not Yorkshire!'

'*So he says nark it*——'

'That's not Yorkshire! That's London talk! He thinks he's
in London!'

'*So he says*——'

Freddy Platt's mate, giving an excruciating imitation of a
cockney, went: 'Eeyah! Ply the gyme, myte! Caw bloimey!'

The whole thing was getting out of hand. The concert-room
was buzzing with talk and laughter, as though they had all
just come out of a meeting. They were beginning to nudge
each other, nodding in my direction and laughing to themselves. Johnny the waiter was making winding motions with
his hand, telling me to get off the platform.

I called back in the bluff, appeasing voice: 'It's all right,
ah'm just practising for when ah get to London! Any road, let
me finish t' story! *So this bookie says give ower, 'ere's five*
*quid, you can tell me what you've backed after t' race. So t'*
*bloke—this feller—says nay, ah've backed ah've backed ah've*
*backed*——'

There was a gale of laughter, the kind of laugh you get for
sheer audacity. Freddy Platt and his friends were beginning to
chant: 'Ah've backed ah've backed ah've backed.' Chairs were
scraping and people were knocking glasses over and rooting in
their handbags. Other people, total strangers, started chanting: 'Ah've backed ah've backed ah've backed.' There was a
mood of pandemonium. I was expecting them any minute to
start flicking pellets at each other.

'*Ah've backed my lorry through thy window*,' I finished,
almost in a whisper. I jumped down from the platform, spray-
ing the lot of them with the Ambrosian repeater gun. There
was a trickle of applause from about four people, but most of

them did not even realise I had finished. The pianist did not bother to give me a few bars on the Clavioline, whether of 'I want to be happy' or any other tune. Staggering across the room I tried to remember how many times I had done this club turn in the past; knowing that each occasion would, in retrospect, become a rich, separate source of acute embarrassment. Some of the women looked at me with a kind of compassionate detachment as I passed. They had stared at me in this way before but I had never realised that it was because they knew things I didn't know, because they were involved in basic matters that I had never even heard about.

I made for the nearest door I could see. 'By! *Tha* dropped a clanger there, Billy!' said Freddy Platt. ' "Nark it?" Tha didn't learn *that* in Yorkshire! Tha what? By!'

I raised my fist in what he was to imagine was a playful gesture. Up on the platform Johnny the waiter, trying to mend the broken illusions and turn the place back into a concert-room, announced that somebody or other would sing a laughing song. A middle-aged, cocky-looking man in a cloth cap, a seasoned club turn with a full diary of engagements, took the microphone. He began singing in a broad, confident voice.

> *Now I think that life is merry,*
> *I think that life is fun,*
> *A short life and a happy one*
> *Is my rule number one,*
> *I laugh when it is raining,*
> *I laugh when it is fine,*
> *You may think I am foolish,*
> *But laughter is my line,*
> *Oh, ha ha ha ha ha ha,*
> *Ha ha ha ha hee,*
> *Ha ,ha ha ha ha ha,*
> *Ho ho ho ho hee.'*

'When's ta bahn off to London, Billy?' cried Freddy Platt. Some of the women nearest to him turned round and went 'Sssh!' They were all watching the singer, their potato crisps untouched. The place was already transformed.

'Billy Liar and his talking dog, the well-known double act!'
'Sssh!'

> '*Ha ha ha ha ha ha,*
> *Ho ho ho ho hee,*
> *Oh, ha ha ha ha ha ha,*
> *Ha ha ha ha hee.*'

I blundered out of the pub and into the car park. I did not stop running until I was clear of Clogiron Lane.

TEN

The Roxy was the last splash of light before Stradhoughton petered out and the moors took over. It was supposed to be a suburban amenity or something; at any rate its red, humming neon sign spluttered out the words 'Come Dancing' six nights a week, and all the grown-up daughters of the cold new houses round about converged on it in their satin frocks, carrying their dance shoes in paper bags advertising pork pies. Youths who had come from all over Stradhoughton for the catch sat around on the low brick banisters by the entrance, combing their hair and jeering at each other.

I approached the place warily, along the shadows, in case Rita was among the girls who promenaded up and down the cracked concrete forecourt, waiting for their escorts to come and pay for them in. I was still full of the evening's fiasco, with selected incidents from it swimming in and out of my head like shoals of bright fish, but as I stepped into the pool of light outside the Roxy I felt an overwhelming relief that another experience was finished with and not still to come. A girl I had once known was waiting by the entrance; I said, 'Hiya, Mavis!' boldly as I passed. I had once written her a poem comparing her bosom with twin melons, and it was always fairly embarrassing to meet her nowadays. But it was something fresh to think about anyway. She said, 'Lo, Billy,' and I walked almost cheerfully up to the paybox.

Inside the Roxy it was hot and bright and, as Stamp had once put it, smelling like a ladies' bog. The foyer, separated from the dance floor by a certain amount of cream fretwork and a lot of big plants, was crowded with the same kind of youths I had seen in the X-L Disc Bar earlier; they were all pulling at their tight clean collars and working their heads round like tortoises. Their girl friends queued for the lavatory, and emerged with their zip-boots and their headscarves discarded, each one making a sort of furtive entry like a butterfly that has turned into a caterpillar. I surveyed this scene with the usual distaste, hunching my shoulders and adopting the attitude of the visiting poet; I was not inclined at this moment towards the bit of No. 1 thinking, fairly standard in this quarter, where I took the floor to a cha-cha with one of the professional exhibition dancers who looked so much like wardresses. I could not see Liz anywhere. I wandered through the fretwork Moorish archway on to the fringe of the dance floor.

The floor was already crowded, with the revolving ball of mirrors overhead catching a hideous violet spotlight and dancing the colours over the pimpled face of, to name the first person I saw, Stamp. He was doing a smirking foxtrot with some girl in a tight, red wool dress; when he turned her in my direction for a piece of cross-stepping that nearly had the pair of them flat on their backs, I saw that his partner was Rita. From her slightly dazed expression, open-mouthed and cloudy-eyed—a kind of facial rigor mortis that touched her whenever she got inside a dance hall—I guessed that Rita had been here about half an hour. I was a little pained that she had not bothered to wait outside for me—she was, after all, still my fiancée, or thought she was—but I was glad to see that Stamp was taking care of her. He looked a little drunk; but that was his problem and not mine. They glided past without seeing me.

At the bandstand Arthur's friends, the Rockets, blew their muted instruments behind little plywood pulpits, the drummer brushing away and grinning round at everybody as though he knew them. Arthur himself, wearing a blue American-cut suit, was swaying about in front of the stick-shaped microphone, waiting to sing. He looked like Danny Kaye or somebody doing a relaxed season at the Palladium, and I could not help admiring his poise and the professional way he stood there doing nothing. I was glad that he had not seen my performance at the New House. I caught his eye and waved to him, a half-wave arrested before it began. Arthur gave me the same mock bow that, in his situation, I had given to the old man; but he did it with a casual dash that made it part of the act.

The people on the dance floor hung around holding hands limply as one tune finished and the Rockets started on the next. Arthur, splaying his hands out, began to sing. *Yooo're my—ev'rthing, ev'ry li'l thing I know-oo.*' He always affected an American accent when he sang. I disliked it, but I had to admit it was good. Then swaying couples brushed past me and, as Stamp and Rita came round for the second time, I began to pick my way upstairs to the balcony.

Liz was sitting by herself at one of the wickerwork tables, gazing down over the dance floor with her chin resting on her plump arms, and smiling happily to herself. I sat down without saying anything to her. She reached out her hand across the table and I took it.

'Late,' said Liz reprovingly as the song finished.

'Yes,' I said. 'I've had an exciting day.'

'I bet you have. Where've you been?'

'Oh, here and there——'

'—up and down,' said Liz, joining in the chant.

'—round and about.' This was a common exchange between us. We used it most when I brushed, without actually asking, on the subject of where Liz kept disappearing to for weeks at a time. I took her hand again. She was still wearing her old black skirt, but with a fresh white blouse. Her green suède jacket hung on the back of the basket chair. I was happy to be with her; it was like being in a refuge, her beaming, comfortable presence protecting me from the others.

'Tell me some plans,' said Liz luxuriously.

'What plans?'

'Any plans. *Your* plans. You *always* have plans. What are you going to do next?'

'I'm thinking of going to London,' I said.

'Only thinking?'

'Well, *going*. Soon, anyway.'

'When's soon?' Liz and I could talk like this for hours, batting the same moonbeams backwards and forwards across the table, enjoying ourselves enormously.

'Well, *soon*.'

'That sounds remote. Why not now?'

'Difficult,' I said.

'No, it's easy. You just get on a train and four hours later, there you are in London.'

'Easy for you,' I said. 'You've had the practice. Liz——?' We were both leaning over the balcony, our hands dovetailed together. On the packed dance floor, near the bandstand, there was a small arena of space where Stamp and Rita, gyrating dangerously, were working out a dance of their own invention. They were both looking down at the floor to see what their feet were doing.

'Yes?' said Liz.

'Stamp calls you Woodbine Lizzie,' I said.

'You should hear what I call Stamp,' said Liz.

I scanned the dance floor idly, and then sat up with a jolt. I had once read about Shepheard's Hotel in Cairo that if you sat there long enough everyone you knew would pass your table. The Roxy was this sort of establishment too and why someone didn't blow *that* up I could never understand, because the next person I picked out, bouncing along the pine-sprung floor with fresh chalk on his uppers was Shadrack himself, doing the quickstep as it might be performed by a kangaroo. The girl he was with, just to complete the wild pattern of coincidence, was Mavis, the one with the twin-melon bosom I had spoken to outside the Roxy. They were no doubt talking about me. Stamp and Rita were still milling around near the bandstand, and I suddenly knew for certain that somewhere on the premises the Witch, too, was waiting, breathing through her nose and swinging her skirt and looking in general as though she had come to dance the Gay Gordons over a couple of swords.

'Let's go for a walk,' I said.

'Soon,' said Liz, mocking me.

Downstairs the drums rolled and Arthur came to the microphone, lifting his hands to quell the faint suggestion of applause. He put his face close to the mike and, in his half-American accent, began the smooth talk that went down so well.

*'Lazengenelmen, are we all happy? Thank you, madam. Next week at the Roxy we have another all-pop night, feat'ring the Rockets, that golden songstress Jeannie Lewis— Jeannie Lewis, I'm not saying she's fat but she's the only girl I know who when she has a chest complaint, she gets her treatment wholesale—and by popular request, yours truly.* Success! *Lazengenelmen, when I came to Stradhoughton I only had one clog. Now I ride around in taxis. I have to take a taxi, I've only got one clog.'*

There were waves of relaxed laughter for Arthur, a cabaret sort of atmosphere that suited him perfectly. Jeannie Lewis, the singer, was sitting on a cane chair by the band, heaving her sequined bosom. Arthur waited for silence, clicking his fingers and smiling confidently.

*'And now a special treat for us all. I want to continue the dance with a little number which I wrote in conjunction with my very good friend Billy Fisher. Where are you, Billy?'* The spotlight played hopefully about the floor, while the Rockets' drummer made a facetious clacking on the kettle-drum.

'That's *you*!' said Liz excitedly.

'I'm all right,' I muttered, hiding my face.

*'Well I know he's out there somewhere,'* said Arthur. *'Maybe he's celebrating the big news, because I know you'll all be glad to know that Billy has just landed himself a big job in London, writing scripts for that verywellknown comedian Danny Boon! I'm sure we wish him all the best in the world.'*

'You stupid *cow*!' I hissed. There was a bit of desultory applause, and one or two of the people on the balcony who knew me slightly looked at me curiously. In spite of it all, I tried to look reasonably famous.

'*Now on with the dance with the little number by Billy Fisher and yours truly—"Can't get along without you"!*' He said it in the coy way that television disc jockeys have, putting the eye on a random girl when he pronounced this soft word 'you.'

'I wish he'd stop calling himself yours truly,' I said through my teeth.

'Shush,' said Liz. 'I want to hear your song.'

The band struck up far too slowly for the number and Arthur, the wry creases in his forehead, began to sing.

> *'Soon you will be saying good-bye,*
> *Just let me mention that I*
> *Can't get along without you.*
> *You seem to have changed with the moon,*
> *Now my heart beats out of tune,*
> *Can't get along without you.'*

I squinted craftily at Liz, hoping she would think the song was dedicated to her. Then I looked down over the balcony at the people dancing below. Nobody seemed to be taking much notice of the song, and in fact Arthur's American accent had become so pronounced that it was difficult to understand what he was singing about. Shadrack and the girl Mavis had vanished, and so had Rita. Stamp was loitering on the brass-rimmed edge of the dance floor, obviously trying to find some way of sabotaging the number. I thought Arthur was doing that effectively himself.

> *'I want to discover*
> *If I'm to blame,*
> *Because as a lover*
> *You're not the same so tell me why.'*

'He's singing it all wrong,' I muttered, getting up. 'Anyway, I suppose I'd better go and congratulate him.' Liz wrinkled her nose at me, and I ran self-consciously down the stairs, keeping my eyes peeled for people who might want to see me.

> *Please tell me why we must part,*
> *Darling it's breaking my heart,*
> *Can't get along without you.'*

I reached the bandstand as Arthur, his arms outstretched, touched the last note. The Rockets went straight into 'American Patrol' and he jumped down, flexing his shoulders and waving to his friends.

'And then I wrote——' I began, striking a dramatic pose for the beginning of our song-writer routine.

'Ah yes, and do you remember the little tune that went something like this,' said Arthur, clutching his heart with one hand and cupping the other to his ear.

'*You made me love you, I didn't want to do it, I didn't want to do it,*' I sang dutifully in the cracked phonograph voice.

'To think I wrote that song on the back of a menu in a fish restaurant——'

'——and today that menu is worth hundreds of pounds.'

'Yes, the price of fish rose steeply between the two wars,' said Arthur, finishing the routine. But it was not the usual thing between me and him; this time he was talking loudly, addressing an audience, the admiring girls who stood around the band giggling and doing little solo jigs.

'And then I wrote——' he said, looking round. I drew him on one side.

'Bloody good, man,' I said. 'How did you manage to persuade them to let you sing it?'

'In your honour,' said Arthur, and now that we had dropped the routine I thought that he was talking in a curiously formal sort of voice.

'Bloody good. Wish you hadn't announced that bit about Danny Boon, though.'

'Why not. It's all fixed up, isn't it?' For the first time, I noticed the slight glint of malice in his eye and the corner of his lower lip twitching.

'Yes, course it is. Only I just didn't want anyone to know just yet, that's all. We ought to get that song recorded and send it up to a publisher.'

'We're going to do it,' said Arthur, meaning him and the Rockets, and also meaning without any help from me.

'Only one thing,' I said in the light voice. 'You want to sing it with a bit less of an American accent.'

Arthur turned to me full-face, and I got the whole effect of the studied, indifferent approach.

'I'll sing it with a *Yorkshire* accent if you like.'

I flared up. 'I don't want you to sing it with *any* flaming accent. Just sing it as it's flaming well written, that's all.'

'Listen, boy, if I sang that song the way you wrote it it'd clear the bleeding hall. You've still got a lot to learn, cocker.'

'Oh, for Christ's sake——'

Arthur nodded his chin. 'Yes, I can see them taking *you* down a peg or two when you get to London. *If* you get to London, I should say. Anyway, don't tell *me* how to sing, matey. Anyone'd think you were going to work for bleeding Glenn Miller.'

'Oh, it's like that, is it?' I said.

'Yes, it's like that. And another thing. I don't know what bloody lies you've been telling my mother about the Witch being this bloody sister of yours, but she's been doing her nut all afternoon. So bloody lay off, for Christ sake.'

He strode back to the bandstand, grabbing the microphone and switching on the American voice. '*And now folks*, by request—*the Hokey-Cokey!*' I turned away, miserable and depressed.

I had almost reached the stairs to the balcony when I saw Stamp leering over the banisters, beckoning his grimy fingers at me. I swung back abruptly and made for the cafeteria under the balcony, at the side of the dance floor. I meant to lose myself for a few minutes among the squealing girls scoffing cream buns and spilling lemonade down their dresses. I hurried through the rows of enamelled tables towards the dark corner by the band's changing-room, and it was only when I was in the middle of it that I realised what kind of bear-pit I had walked into down here. Immediately in front of me stood the Witch in a revolting green blouse and tartan skirt. She was confronting Rita, and Rita's vivid red dress seemed to have been designed especially to set off the miniature silver cross on its silver chain round her neck, and the engagement ring that she brandished on her finger.

'That's *my* cross,' I heard the Witch say in her loud, clear voice.

My heart, familiar with its duty on occasions such as this, did a full cartwheel. I dodged behind a sort of Corinthian column that was holding the balcony up, but too late to avoid the cold eye of the Witch.

'Talk of the devil,' she said coolly.

Rita turned round. 'Oo, look what's jumped out of the corned beef,' she said in her grating voice. She looked flushed and bewildered.

I said faintly: 'What's this—a deputation?' I skimmed through my mind, more or less in despair, to see if I could find a piece of skilful double-talk, aimed at their different intellectual levels, that would succeed in fooling them both. I opened my mouth to speak but I felt the yawn welling up in my throat and I finished up standing there with my mouth open, gaping at them. 'What's up with him, is he catching flies or summat?' said Rita. It was obviously too late for the academic niceties, anyway.

'May I ask why you gave my cross to this—girl?' asked the Witch without any preamble.

My first thought was: 'May I ask why you said you'd given it back to your cousin?' But I still hankered after the subtle approach. 'Yes, it *is* very similar, isn't it?' I said.

'It's my cross. It's got the tooth-mark on it where you bit it that day when you made that ridiculous scene.'

'Do you mean that day at Ilkley, which I am sure Rita is anxious to hear about?' I said, with the intention of embarrassing her.

'It's my cross,' said the Witch.

'No it isn't,' I said. 'You gave yours back to your cousin. I

**III**

just happen to have one similar. If you want to know, your cousin got it from me in the first place.'

'Oh. So you make a *prac*tice of giving these things away, do you?'

'No, I don't make a *prac*tice of it. I just happened to have half a dozen of them to spare. They're what Unitarians wear when they're dead,' I said. It was only a matter of time before the Witch realised who was wearing her engagement ring, and I was beginning to gabble a bit.

'And another thing,' the Witch said. 'Which one of us is supposed to be coming to tea at your house tomorrow?'

'Well neither of you, I'm afraid,' I said, giving them each the frank smile. 'We did hope to have a sort of family party— there were a lot of people coming, including yourselves—only the old man's been called away to Harrogate and he won't be back until Monday.'

'I suppose he's gone to a naval reunion,' said the Witch with her heavy sarcasm. She turned to Rita. 'You know his father's supposed to be a retired sea captain, don't you?'

'Thought he was supposed to be a cobbler or summat,' said Rita.

They started chewing the fat about what the old man did for a living. The Witch, in her bottle-green blouse, stood there looking like the cub-mistress Stamp claimed to have ravished on passion pills. A happy thought struck me, the first happy thought of the evening. I felt in my pocket for the little black beads that were still spilled there. I scooped up a handful, about a dozen or fourteen of them. On the table nearest to us, next to the Witch's handbag and the pile of blood oranges that she had got in as a treat for herself, there was a cup of black coffee, untouched. I moved my hand behind me and, as the two of them got on to the subject of the imaginary budgerigar, I unloaded the fistful of passion pills into the Witch's coffee.

'And now, if it's not too much to ask,' said the Witch, 'perhaps you'll tell us which one of us you invited to the Roxy tonight.'

'Oh, my God,' I said. 'Why don't you ask Rita why she's

112

wearing your engagement ring?' I strode rapidly away, leaving them both open-mouthed as though being filmed at the end of a comedy sequence. I charged through the cafeteria to the foot of the balcony stairs. Stamp, still clinging hold of the banisters, clawed at me as I passed. He was definitely drunk.

'Go to hell, Stamp,' I said curtly.

'*You've* had it,' he said thickly, grabbing my sleeve. '*You've* had it.'

'Keep you mucky hands to yourself.'

'You've *had* it,' drooled Stamp. 'Just been talking to Shad- rack. You've *had* it, Fisher.'

I pulled his hand angrily off my sleeve. 'Well you get your hands off my cowing, mucking, stinking *sleeve*!'

'You've had it,' he mumbled, sinking down on the stairs. I ran up two at a time and found Liz still sitting contentedly, looking over the balcony.

'Sorry I was so long. Let's go for a walk.'

She looked up and smiled. 'You're looking het up.'

'I'm feeling het up,' I said. I edged over to where she was sitting to check that she could not have seen what had been going on. 'I've just had an almighty barney with Arthur about the song. He finished up threatening to sing it with a York-shire accent.'

'Well, he could do worse,' said Liz judiciously.

I sat down, breathing deeply, glad of any opportunity for a bit of normal conversation. The band was playing a soft waltz and there was something soothing about the bobbing heads below us.

'Don't say you're another of these Yorkshire fanatics,' I said.

'No. But there's lots of nice things in Yorkshire. Nice people. To name only one,' she said, squeezing my hand.

'Which is why you keep leaving it, I suppose?'

'Could be.'

To break the silence I said: 'I was talking to that bloke who does the Man o' the Dales' column in the *Echo* the other day——'

'Who? Do you mean John Hardcastle?' Liz broke in. 'I *know* him.' She knew everybody.

113

'That's him,' I said with the sinking feeling. 'At least, I *think* it was him. *One* of the blokes on the *Echo*, anyway. We were going over all this satanic mills lark that he's always doing, and *I* said, Dark Satanic mills I can put up with, they're part of the picture. But when it comes to dark satanic power stations, dark satanic housing estates and dark satanic dance halls——'

'That's good. You ought to use that.'

'So *he* said, That's the trouble with you youngsters, you want——'

'Youngsters? *He's* got a nerve! He's not much older than you are! Are you sure it was John Hardcastle?'

'Oh, for God's sake,' I said desperately. 'A big chap with a moustache—is that him?'

'That's right,' said Liz calmly. 'He's sitting over there.' She nodded casually to a young man with a crowd of people three or four tables away, handlebar moustache and all. Why wasn't Man o' the Dales an old man? And why the handlebar moustache? He looked up, saw Liz and waved. I sat back, exhausted. By now I would not have been surprised to see Councillor Duxbury himself, dancing the Boston Two-Step down below and change out of fourpence.

'Let's go for a walk,' I said weakly.

'Don't you want to have a chat with John?'

Over the tannoy, breaking into the music, a crackling voice announced: *'Mist' William Fisher. Mist' William Fisher. Wanted on the telephone. Mist' William Fisher. Than' you.'*

'Mr William Fisher, wanted on the telephone,' said Liz.

My palms gritty with sweat, I gripped the balcony rail and peered into the bright depths of the dance floor. As in some maniac kaleidoscope I could see Arthur, looking belligerent, about to sing; the Witch striding purposefully out of the cafeteria with her handbag swinging on her shoulder; Rita, standing around looking dazed; to the left, Stamp, standing at the bottom of the staircase, and Shadrack brushing past him. I saw them, or thought I saw them, all in the same shrieking moment, and looking up, there was the youthful Man o' the Dales, glaring with what looked like suspicion at our table. I had a sudden histrionic urge to stand up on my chair and shout: 'Ladies and gentlemen, here are my fountain pen and my suède shoes. Crucify me the modern way!'

'*Mist*' William Fisher, *wanted on the telephone.*'

'Let's go for a walk,' I said. I felt a hand on the back of my chair. I looked up, and I was not surprised to see Shadrack bending over us, flashing his yellow teeth and breathing his bad breath.

'*Could* I have a word with you, Fisher?'

I stood up, feeling punchdrunk. 'Next for shaving,' I said hysterically.

Shadrack turned solicitously to Liz. 'You *will* excuse us for a moment?' She smiled at him. He took me over to the top of the stairs, holding my arm in an alarmingly friendly way.

'Look, this is neither the time *nor* the place, of *course*,' he began confidentially. 'But I just thought I'd better have a word with you about our conversation this afternoon.'

'Oh, yes?' I said, swallowing.

'Yes. The fact is, under the circ'stances we think it prob'ly a good idea if you didn't come in on Monday after all. Prob'ly if you didn't come in until we sent for you. I just thought I'd let you know.'

'Oh. Does that mean——?'

'No, I'm vair much afraid it doesn't mean you've finished with us. Not by a long chalk. I'm afraid you've still got a lot of explaining to do, Fisher.'

'Oh?' I seemed to be beginning every sentence with 'Oh.'

'Yes, I'm afraid it's come to light that you've been carrying on in an alarming fashion for a vair lengthy period of time. An al*arm*ing fashion. To say the least of it. Anyway, the upshot is, we want you to regard yourself as being temp'rarily suspended until we can get it all cleared up.'

He released my arm.

'As I say, this is neither the time nor the place, we realise that. I don't want to stop you enjoying yourself tonight, far from it. But you've got a lot of vair serious explaining to do, sooner or later.'

'"Have a good holiday, Jenkins, I've got some bad news for you when you get back,"' I muttered.

'Wha'? What's that?'

'It was a cartoon,' I said unhappily. 'In the paper.'

'Yes, I'm vair much afraid you think too *much* about cartoons,' said Shadrack. He gave me a strange look and went off down the stairs. I watched the tail of his hacking jacket flapping after him, and murmured *'Bastard'* under my breath.

*'Mist' William Fisher, wanted on the telephone.'*

I beckoned to Liz, and followed Shadrack at a respectful distance down the stairs.


ELEVEN


It was quiet outside the Roxy. The evening was warm, but on the crisp side. The sodium lamps were beginning to flicker on and off dismally. The old gaffers who manned the Alderman Burrows memorial bench at the abandoned tram terminus were beginning to crane themselves stiffly to their feet and adjust their mufflers. The last children had left the piles of builders' sand that marked every exit from Stradhoughton, warning of new territorial ambitions in the way of brittle new roads across the moors.

I stood at the entrance to the Roxy, looking at the showcases full of cracked, shiny photographs and the glue-streaked placards advertising the Autumn Leaf Ball. There was one showcase devoted to the Miss Stradhoughton contest and Rita, with her cardboard crown and her satin sash, smiled toothily down at me. On the broad brick steps, the commissionaire in his threadbare uniform, dry-cleaned to a thin blue and tied with an army webbing belt dyed navy, eyed passing youths with his fixed, policeman's stare. Two of them, shiny-haired and wearing dazzle ties, strolled self-consciously up towards the paybox. I recognised them as friends of Stamp from the crowd he had been with at the X-L Disc Bar that afternoon.

The commissionaire moved forward. 'Not tonight, my friends,' he said, putting his arm out. 'Not after last week.'

'Why, what's up?' said one of the youths.

'Never mind what's up, or what's down. You don't come in, that's Mr Bottomley's strict orders.'

'After you with Mr Bottomley,' said the other youth.

'We're not coming in, we just want to get a mate out.' said the first one.

'You're getting nobody out,' said the commissionaire. The two youths retired into the shadows.

I looked up the blue-carpeted foyer at the cluster of girls gossiping outside the Ladies, and saw them part to let Liz through. Some of them stared after her. I noticed, not for the first time, how scruffy she was in her old suède jacket and her dusty black skirt, and it occurred to me that I had rarely, if ever, seen her wearing anything else. She came and went in her green suède coat as though it were a uniform or something, and even when I pictured her at the celebration parade after the November riots in Ambrosia, she was still wearing it.

She came and stood beside me, by the showcases.

'Miss Stradhoughton,' she said mechanically.

'They gave the title to the wrong girl,' I said with a clumsy attempt at gallantry.

We strolled away from the Roxy and the block of tobacconists' shops, chemists and hairdressers that was built in with it, and over the waste ground to the New Road. We walked up New Road past the Houghtondale Arms, the bus sheds and the crematorium and then, where the dump of cracked drainpipes and the crusty little hills of tar marked the last gasp of housing development, we turned into the unadopted road that led down into Foley Bottoms.

At some point during the evening, probably in the flight from the pub concert-room, I had started walking like a man with flat feet, and I was trying hard to stop it. 'Do you find life complicated?' I said as we walked along. I was long past caring one way or the other about anything very much, and what I said was the first thing that came into my head.

'Hmm-hmm,' said Liz happily.

I said: 'I wish it was something you could tear up and start again. Life, I mean. You know, like starting a new page in an exercise book.'

'Well, it's been done,' said Liz. 'Turning over a new leaf.'

'I turn over a new leaf every day,' I said. 'But the blots show through.' I was rather pleased with this.

We came to the end of the unadopted road and crossed over the broken-down chestnut fencing and the backwash of old bricks and bottles that was the entrance to Foley Bottoms.

'Why are you walking like that?' said Liz.

'Like what?'

'Sort of leaning forwards as though you were on roller skates.'

About half a dozen selected falsehoods skimmed through my mind, ranging from bad shoes to middle ear disease. 'I'm pretending I've got flat feet,' I said at length.

'Fathead.'

Stradhoughton clung tenaciously on to the woods for the first few yards: old prams, cement bags flapping, an electricity sub-station, the trees dying on their feet. But wading through the soggy cardboard boxes and the rust-rimmed bicycle wheels we came to the woods with the acorns falling and the ferns waist-high and green about us.

'I turn over a new leaf every day,' I said. 'But the blots show through the page.'

'Well,' said Liz. 'Perhaps a new leaf isn't good enough. Perhaps you need to turn over a new volume.'

She was even better than I was at carrying metaphor to inscrutable lengths. I thought of pursuing the theme a little further, and was weaving a pleasant fancy about trying not only a new volume but a new library, when Liz started on the problem afresh with an entirely new set of illustrations.

'You know, my lad, the trouble with you is that you're—what's the word—introspective? You're like a child at the edge

118

of a paddling pool. You want very much to go in, but you think so much about whether the water's cold, and whether you'll drown, and what your mother will say if you get your feet wet——'

I hesitated to go with her into the paddling pool zone, which seemed to me to be fraught with peril, but there was nothing for it but to interrupt her.

'All I'm doing is wondering whether to dive or swim,' I said obscurely.

'Perhaps you need a coach,' said Liz, giving me the sly glance. It was perfectly apparent where this one was leading to, and I decided to leave her floundering in her own paddling pool for the time being. We picked our way over the low blackberry branches in silence.

I searched around in my mind for some fresh nonsense to keep us pleasantly occupied. I felt a quick gust of warmth for Liz for her readiness to go so far with me along the well-trodden paths of fantasy. I decided to try her on the London theme.

'Do you know why I'm so fascinated by London?' I said.

'No, Mr Bones, why are you so fascinated by London?' She was not consciously imitating Arthur.

'A man can lose himself in London,' I said. 'London is a big place. It has big streets and big people——' I tailed off, because she would not be drawn, and in any case I had forgotten the end of the sentence. Liz stopped abruptly, and I turned back to face her, expecting the sudden, rash embrace that was a feature of her impetuous temperament.

But she folded her arms and looked at me with her inscrutable, chubby smile that only faintly looked as though, like the Witch before her, she had practised it in a mirror.

'Billy?'

'Uh-huh?'

'Tell me something?'

I said in the soft voice: 'Of course.'

'Do you really know Man o' the Dales?'

In the hard, defiant voice: 'Course I do.'

'Really and truly?'

'Well, know him, it depends what you mean by *know* him. I've *met* him——'

'Count five and tell the truth,' said Liz. It was an old recipe of hers, and one that I always found distasteful. I said in the high-pitched voice, putting an elaborate hand to my heart, 'I cannot tell a lie, I've never met the man.' The phrase, 'I've never met the man' was just not suited to the range of voice I had chosen, and the whole thing sounded forced and ridiculous.

Liz grinned composedly. 'You *are* a fool.'

I wiped the whole matter out with the repeater gun levelled at Man o' the Dales, and we walked on. 'Perhaps I need to turn over a new paddling pool,' I said.

'Write that down,' said Liz, just as Arthur would have said.

Foley Bottoms was largely a botanic clump of nothing, but just before you started getting out of the woods again and on your way to the Strad Lee housing estate—a hideous zoo of orange brick which it would have done Man o' the Dales a power of good to walk through, cobblestones, handlebar moustache and all—there was a knoll or hill of what I always thought of as picnic grass, a kind of lush, tropical green velvet that looked as though you could buy it by the yard in Marks and Spencers. It was a regular custom for me to stop here with whoever it was, Liz, Rita or the Witch; thereafter the custom would vary according to the personality involved. With Rita, it was the film finale clinch prior to sinking down on the grass; with the Witch, a moment of studied casualness in which we both sat down apparently independently, about a yard from one another. I wondered how the Witch was getting on with her cupful of passion pills. In the case of Liz, part of the regular custom was to hold each other at arm's length, scrutinising faces and then, as at a given signal, sit down.

'Who d'you love?' said Liz.

'Thee, lass,' I said, finding refuge in the Duxbury dialect.

'Yes, it sounds like it, doesn't it?'

'Ah do, lass.'

'Say it properly, then.'

'I do, Liz, I do,' I  said soberly, and wondering if I meant it.

I knelt down on the grass and reached my arm up to her. Liz remained standing.

'What about Barbara?'

So rarely did I think about the Witch under her given name that I had to think for a minute who Barbara was when she was at home.

'Well what about her?'

'Well *what* about her?' said Liz. I began pulling at her hands, trying to decide whether to pass the ball back again with another 'Well what about her?' Finally I said: 'All over.'

'You've said *that* before.'

'I know. This time the goose is cooked.' I did not explain whose goose I had in mind. I tightened my grip on her hands and pulled her down, so successfully that she fell on top of me. This should have been the signal for the beginning of some rural by-play but in fact the weight of her knocked me sprawling and by the time I had recovered she was sitting beside me, lighting a cigarette—a delaying trick as annoying in its way as the Witch's oranges.

'I want to marry you, you know, Billy,' Liz said, holding her cigarette to a blade of grass.

I said: 'I know, Liz, I know. We will, one day.'

'Not one day. Now.'

The idea of actually getting married now was so incomprehensible to me that I thought it was part of some new ritual, and I played along with it.

'Tonight?'

'Next week will do. Before you go to London. Or when you get there. Whichever you prefer.'

I began plucking at the glass buttons of her blouse, imagining the court scene where my mother, weeping, opposed my application to marry. The unfastening of Liz's blouse had become a more or less routine affair and it was done in a detached way, rather as if I were helping her off with her coat.

'I think I get engaged a bit too often,' I said.

'I don't want to get engaged. I want to get married.'

'Is that why you keep sloping off every few weeks, because you want to get married?'

'I want to get married,' said Liz stubbornly.

'All right,' I said. 'All right.'

By now I had begun to grow fairly absent-minded in my responses, for it had suddenly struck me that there was somebody in the bushes, listening to us. There was no wind, but every so often one of the rhododendrons behind us would rustle and there would be a crackling of twigs. I looked up sharply, but there was nothing to see.

'How do you mean, all right?' said Liz. 'I've just pro*posed* to you, and you say all right. Aren't you supposed to say this is so sudden, or yes, or something?'

I was groping for some obscure phrase that would comfort her and at the same time leave me uncommitted. I distinctly saw something moving in the bushes behind us. The notion that the Witch had followed us here and was taking everything down in her faultless Gregg shorthand possessed me with an unpleasant vividness.

'If I'm going to dive in,' I said, 'I think it might as well be at the deep end.'

Even if the Witch had got down this remark satisfactorily, there was little that she could make of it in a breach of promise trial. *'Now Mr Fisher, according to these notes you said that if you were going to dive in, it might as well be at the deep end. Now what did you mean by that?'* I got Liz's blouse out of her skirt and began stroking her, like a cat.

Liz screwed her eyes up tightly in the way she did when she was going to say something she thought brazen. Without seeing, she stubbed her cigarette out on the grass.

'You know what you wanted me to do that night on Stradhoughton Moor, and I said another night?'

I remembered very well the cold night on Stradhoughton Moor, in the old folks' shelter, the night before Liz had last disappeared. On that night I had actually proposed, a pretend proposal that we had used for kindling, toasting our hands on it until the early hours when, stiff with cold, we wandered home quietly, the future spent like fireworks.

'I remember,' I said. My heart had begun to beat swiftly. Stamp's phrase, 'Are you getting it regular?' sprang irreverently back into my head. The bushes stirred again, and this time I thought that it might be Stamp himself with his German camera, fitted with infra-red. Either him or the Witch with a portable tape recorder, one or the other.

'Well,' said Liz. 'It's another night tonight, isn't it?'

I kissed her eyes meditatively. So far our relations had been on a thus-far-and-no-further basis, frustrating to both of us but of such a well-established pattern that it came as a slow shock to suggest that the barriers now be taken down.

'Are you sure?' I said, clearing my throat. She nodded, her face full of meaning. Out in the rhododendron bushes the Witch put on another spool. A new notion, that Shadrack was crouching there with a warrant for my arrest, seized me for a moment, then I put it aside to deal with current problems.

'Er—what do you think we ought to do about, you know, babies?'

'Have them,' said Liz luxuriously. 'Lots and lots of them.'

'No, I mean tonight. I mean, I haven't got—you know.'

'It's all right,' said Liz. I peered unhappily out into the bushes. The Witch turned up her volume control, Stamp changed his film and Shadrack crouched forward in the dusk, licking his lips. Liz nestled plumply up to me and bit my ear. We held each other helplessly, doing nothing, the passion seeping away at a dangerous rate.

Liz said: 'Billy?'

'Uh-huh?'

'Ask you something?'

'Uh-huh.'

She screwed up her eyes again and said: 'Do you know what virgo intacta means?'

'Yes.'

'Well. I'm not.'

I sat there quietly, listening. Something had gone wrong with the Witch's tape recorder. Stamp and Shadrack, fiddling with the batteries were adjusting it for her. 'No,' I said finally. 'I somehow didn't think you were.'

'Want me to tell you about it?'

'No.'

I began to fondle her breast, spanning it in my hand and pressing gently with each finger in turn, compulsively. Liz began to breathe heavily and to tremble out of all proportion to the ardour I thought I was drumming up. 'Tell me about it,' I said.

'No, not now.'

'Tell me about it.'

Liz sat up, almost impatiently, pulling her suède coat around her. She stared out into the darkness. Then she began to trace little circles in the grass with her fingers.

'You think that's why I'm always going away, don't you?' she said.

I shrugged, saying and thinking nothing.

'Ask me where I've been for the past five weeks.'

'Does the geographical location make any difference?' I said with simulated bitterness, hoping to keep it all on this same sparring level.

'No, I don't suppose it does,' said Liz. I reached out and touched her breast under her coat, but it was cold and lifeless. She began to speak in a rhythmical, reasoning sort of prose, as though she had rehearsed all the words before she met me.

'Every so often I just want to go away. It's not you, Billy, I want to be here with you. It's the town. It's the people we know. I don't like knowing everybody, or becoming a part of things—do you see what I mean?'

We had been over this before, but from a different route. It had never led so beautifully into the point of contact between us. I began to feel excited, as though on the verge of a discovery.

'What I'd like is to be invisible,' said Liz. 'You know, to do everything without people knowing, and not having to worry about them, not having to ex*plain* all the time. That's why I so enjoyed that night on Stradhoughton Moor. We were both invisible. We——'

'Liz,' I said urgently. 'Liz, listen, listen.' I took her hands, trembling almost, and began to speak rapidly, leaving staccato, deliberate pauses between my words.

'Liz, do you know what I do? When I want to feel invisible?' I had no experience of wanting to feel invisible, but the text was perfect. I was doctoring my words as I went along, quickly and carefully. 'I've never told anybody. I have a sort of—well, it's an imaginary country, where I go. It has its own people——'

'Do you do that? I *knew* you would,' cried Liz triumphantly. 'I knew you would. Why are we so alike, Billy? I can read your thoughts. A town like Stradhoughton, only somewhere over by the sea, and we used to spend the whole day on the beach. That's what I used to think about.'

I was full of excitement, frustrated, painful excitement at not being able to tell her properly, yet at the same time knowing she would understand it, knowing that she would *know*. I wanted to drag her into my mind and let her loose in it, free to pick and choose.

I began counting to myself to slow myself down, and said, only half-feverishly:

'This is more than a town, it's a whole country. I'm supposed to be the Prime Minister. You're supposed to be the Foreign Secretary or something——'

'Yes sir,' said Liz with grave, mock obedience.

'I think about it for hours. Sometimes I think, if we were married, and living somewhere in that house in the country, we could just sit and imagine ourselves there——'

'By a log fire,' said Liz softly. 'And the fir trees all around, and no other house for miles.'

I looked at her squarely. She was as excited as I was in her own settled way. I was tossing a coin in my head, teetering on a decision. Heads I tell her, tails I don't. Heads I tell her this last thing.

'I want a room, in the house, with a green baize door,' I began calmly. 'It will be a big room, and when we pass into it, through the door, that's it, that's Ambrosia. No one else would be allowed in. No one else will have keys. They won't know where the room is. Only we will know. We'll make models of the principal cities, you know, out of cardboard, and we could use toy soldiers, painted, for the people. We could draw maps. It would be a place to go on a rainy afternoon. We could go there. No one would find us. I thought we would have a big sloping shelf running all the way down one wall, you know, like a big desk. And we'd have a lot of blank paper on it and design our own newspapers. We could even make uniforms, if we wanted to. It would be our country.' I stopped, suddenly aware of the cold and the black, peeling branches round about us and the ticking quiet of it all. I had talked myself right through the moment of contact. Liz, her old self, was grinning, pleased with life, seeing it all as our old fantasy, a kind of mental romp in the long grass. 'And let's have a model train, that the kids won't be allowed to use,' she said. 'And a big trench in the garden.'

I sank back, spreadeagling my hands in the grass to rid them of the webbed sensation that was coming back into them like a nervous tic.

'Liz,' I said, all the thoughts exhausted in me. 'Will you marry me?'

She leaned over me and whispered: 'Tomorrow,' in a throaty way. I pulled her down with a feeling of peace and misery, running my hands heavily down her back. She began to kiss me, not knowing that my eyes were open and staring. Her body was warm under the suède jacket and I found some kind of comfort, losing myself, not allowing anything into my head, but sinking into a kind of numb passion. Soon the whole incident had passed into history, to be exhumed and dissected soon, but not now. I felt the black dusty skirt give way as she fumbled at the zipper. I brushed my fingers against the smooth surface of her stomach, feeling her contract gingerly under the touch of them. She rolled over on to her back and I fell on top of her, grateful and easy in my mind, lost in her soft ways.

In the moment of satisfaction I said: 'There's somebody watching us.' From the bushes there was the sharp crack of breaking twigs and a resounding: 'Tskkkkkkkkkkk!'

I called: 'Whoever's out there is going to get their bastard teeth knocked down their throat in a minute!'

I scrambled to my feet, gathering my clothes about me like an Arab. Three youths leaped up from behind the bushes and began to run out of the woods, shouting directions at each other. Two of them were the youths who had been turned away from the Roxy, while I waited for Liz; the third was Stamp. I raced after them almost as far as the road. Stamp, stumbling drunkenly through the ferns, called in a falsetto voice: 'Oh, darling——,' repeating some words I happened to have used a few minutes earlier. I let them go. As if it were far away, I heard Stamp call: 'Can I draw your maps for you, to play with?'

I walked back to the green grass, tucking my shirt into my trousers. Liz was sitting up and combing her hair. 'We should've stayed on the dance floor and let everybody have a look,' she said carelessly.

The idea, fanciful to her, made me go hot all over. Then I shivered. 'Let's go,' I said.

We began to walk back towards the Roxy. 'I'll wrap his cowing posters round his neck, next time I see him,' I said. But the idea of ever seeing Stamp again, or indeed anybody, filled me with horror.

## TWELVE

There was no sense in going back into the Roxy, and so I waited outside while Liz went in to fetch her handbag. It was getting late now, anyway. The commissionaire had changed into civilian clothes and was taking in the sandwich-boards and propping them against the wall inside the foyer. I could hear the Rockets playing tinnily inside, underlined by a steady thump-thump like a ship's engine. After the music there was some announcement over the tannoy which I could not hear. Mist' William Fisher, wanted on the telephone, no doubt; I wondered who had been ringing up for me at the Roxy and why. An inch of white ash fell from my cigarette. I began to walk up and down the parade of shops that lined the Roxy, staring at the gaunt, old-fashioned heads in the window of Molly, hair-stylist, and at the forlorn-looking estate agent's with its little cards buckling in their grained wooden slots. None of the shops looked as though anything had ever happened in them.

I had an instinct that I sometimes used, looking into the future and deciding whether an event would take place or not. I tried to project myself forward, to see whether Liz would come out again. I could not form any definite picture of her coming out and smiling at me, and I concluded that on the whole she would not. I decided to give her five more minutes, counting them off in sixties and folding a finger back for every minute gone. At the third finger I lost count over a commotion behind me. I turned round to see Stamp and his two idiot friends, reeling back from the Houghtondale Arms. Stamp was even drunker than he had been before, and was shouting at the top of his voice: *'To the woods! No, no, not the woods, anything but the woods!'* I stepped back into the estate agent's doorway. The commissionaire had gone round the back of the building with a coke shovel in his hand, and the Roxy was unguarded. They dodged in, giggling and shoving each other. 'Where's yer pass-outs, you two?' yelled Stamp. 'Hey, mister, they're getting in for nix!'

I was dog-tired and feeling gritty round the eyes, and hungry. I walked up to the entrance of the Roxy and looked down the length of the foyer, but I could not see Liz. She was probably already whooping it up with Man o' the Dales inside. At the door of the Ladies, Stamp was talking beerily to Rita, lending her a penny or something. I was hungry and cold and tired.

I walked away, dipping into my mind for a morsel of No. 1 thinking to get me home. Ambrosia was closed for the night, or seemed to be. I came up as chairman of the Stradhoughton Labour Party, in fact M.P. for the division, the youngest member in the House, writing letters to Councillor Duxbury. *Dear Councillor Duxbury, As you know, the proposal to nationalise the undertaking business is already in the committee stage. You are well versed not only in this particular field but in public life also, and before concluding this piece of legislation we would greatly appreciate your comments. (You may remember me as a clerk in your employ, many years ago now ...)*

At the corner of Clogiron Lane was a fish shop, a small area of brightness among the discreet drawn blinds and the concrete lamps. I stepped almost automatically over the hollowed step into this tiled, light womb of warmth, and joined the small queue among the Tizer bottles, the stacked sheets of clean newspaper and the advertisements for cinemas and jumble sales. I leaned in gratitude on the salty marble counter and savoured the high aroma of steam and vinegar and buxom sweat. Written in whitewash on the burnished battery of mirrors above the frying-range was the sign: 'Under completely new management.' The usual fat women were serving in their chip-stained white aprons, but the man at the range, tall and dour like all fish shop proprietors, was a new one. He turned half-round to the trough of batter by his side, and I recognised him instantly as the leading man in an old No. 2 daymare which even now I revived from time to time. Long ago, in a different neighbourhood, I had caused some consternation up and down the street by telling everybody that the man who ran the fish shop had hanged himself. This was undoubtedly the same man. He recognised me too, and gave me one of the keen, contemplative looks that were so much a feature of Stradhoughton life. I had a quick fancy that all my enemies had secretly taken office around Clogiron Lane and were hustling into position, preparing for the coup. I bought my bag of chips and walked out of the shop.

*Dear Mr Shadrack, As you know, the nationalisation of the undertaking business is imminent, and we are very keen to get someone knowledgeable in charge of casket production. I well remember as an 'old boy' of Shadrack and Duxbury's (I was the wretch who forgot to post the calendars!!!) being shown some drawings of a fibreglass casket which you thought could be produced very cheaply ...*

The chips lasted me all the way home to Hillcrest. I threw the greasy bag into our own privet hedge, wiped my hands and lit a cigarette before going indoors. I felt a lot better.

The old man was in the lounge, straddling the fawn tiled fireplace, the back of his balding head glimmering faintly through what little of the mirror you could see behind its crust of frosted bambis. His certificate of membership from the Ancient Order of Stags, thick with Gothic writing and seals and all the rest of it, was propped up on the mantelpiece. I was surprised to see the old man still up. He stood with his waistcoat open and eyed me as I went into the room.

I said: 'Did you want some chips bringing in?'

The old man said: 'I'm surprised t' bloody chip shop's still open, this time o' night.' He nodded towards the cuckoo clock, swinging its lead weights against the sad wallpaper. He turned to chuck his cigarette end in the fire and said, tossing the remark casually across to me: 'They're down at t' Infirmary.

'Who is?'

'Your mother and your grandma, who the bloody hell do you think? Your grandma's been taken badly again. We've been trying to get word to you for t' last hour. Where've you been?'

I felt a twinge of alarm at the idea of Gran being carted off to the Infirmary. Normally, after one of her fits, she would sit ticking broodily in a chair until she was more or less normal again. If the fit recurred, it was supposed to be serious or something. I was glad that they had got her out of the house.

I said, harshening my voice to make it acceptable: 'Why, what's up with her?'

'What's up wi' *you*, that's what I want to know,' the old man snarled, beginning to boil up into his slow rage. 'I thought you were off to t' bloody dance hall when you'd been to t' pub. Why don't you go where you say you're going, we've been ringing up half the bloody night.'

'I had a pass-out——' I began.

'Pass-out, you'll do more than pass out if you don't bloody frame! You'd better ring up for a taxi, your mother wants to see you down at t' Infirmary.'

'Why, what's up wi' me grandma?' I said.

'What's allus up wi' your grandma, what do you think? Get ringing up t' taxi!'

Reluctantly, I went into the hall and rang up New Line Taxis. The old man was shouting: 'And bloody come home on a night in future, not at this bloody time!' but there was something oddly restrained and preoccupied about his abuse. I felt that he had something more to say. I put down the telephone and started to walk up the stairs. That was the trigger for it. With a bound of fury the old man reached the hall door.

'*You don't go up there!*'

'Why, I'm just waiting for t' taxi.'

'I said you don't go up there!'

I leaned against the wall, trying to look resigned and reasonable. 'Well ah've got to have a wash, haven't I?'

'You can go mucky. You don't go up*stairs*. We've had enough of you up there, with your bloody hiding and meddling and I don't know what else.'

'What, I don't know what you're talking about,' I said, screwing my face up to look puzzled.

'You know bloody well what I'm talking about.' And then, sharply: 'What have you done with that letter of your mother's?'

I stood, cold, on the stairs.

'Do you hear me? I'm talking to you!'

'What letter?' I said.

'What, what, what,' the old man mimicked, his face cracking into an ugly sneer. 'Don't keep saying bloody what! You know bloody well what letter! That what she gave you to post to t' Housewives' Choice.'

I leaned back again, my face in a mask of panic, reviewing breakneck all the things they must know if they had found out about my mother's letter.

'I've *told* her once, I posted it,' I said.

'You posted bloody nowt! You've had it in that box! It was given to you to post, you bloody, idle little bastard!'

A small wave of relief touched me, at the hope that the old man would put it all down to nothing more than idleness, I said, with desperate nonchalance: 'I *did* post it. That was just the rough copy.'

'What yer talking about, rough copy? It's your mother's letter. How *could* you have posted it?'

I came down one stair to meet him, trying to talk in the patient, explanatory voice. 'Look. The letter my mother wrote was full of mis*takes*, that's all. I just thought it would have a better chance if I wrote it out *again*, properly, that's all.'

'Well who told you to write it out again? And who told you to open it? You keep your thieving hands off other people's things! And where did you get all them bloody calendars from, anall?'

'What calendars?' It was a purely automatic reflex, like kicking up the knee against a hammer. I was trapped without time to think or to stall or to rig the facts.

The old man took a deep breath and started fingering the shredding, concave belt around his trousers. 'By bloody hell, I'll give you bloody what if you don't stop saying what, what, my lad! You know bloody well what! Don't think I've not been talking to Councillor Duxbury, cos I have! I've heard it all. You make me a bloody laughing-stock, you can't keep your hands off owt. And where's that monkey-wrench out of my garage? I suppose you know nowt about *that*?'

'No, course I don't. What do *I* want with a monkey-wrench?'

'What do you want wi' two hundred bloody calendars? And what have you been doing wi' their bloody nameplates anall? You're not right in the bloody head!'

I had no refuge except in rage. '*I'm* not right, *I'm* not right,' I shouted, coming down the stairs at him. '*I* didn't want to work for Shadrack and flaming Duxbury's. You put me there, now you can answer for it!'

'Don't bloody shout at me, you gormless young get! Or I'll knock your bloody eyes out.'

'God give me strength,' I murmured, closing my eyes at the threat.

'God give you strength, he wants to give you some bloody sense! You're like a bloody Mary Ann!' He was slowing down, like a spent volcano. I sat down on the stairs with my head in my hands, trying to look defeated and hoping he would go away. He turned, muttering to himself. 'Well I hope yer mother gets more sense out o' you. And don't go chelping back at her like you chelp at me, else you'll know about it.' He stood at the hall door, fingering the lock, experimenting with the turning mechanism, and trying hard to effect the transition from shouting into normal speech, I tried to help him.

'Well I *told* you I didn't want to work for Shadrack's when I first started, didn't I?'

'You didn't want to work for nobody, if you ask me owt,' the old man said. 'You thought you'd live on me, didn't you?'

'No, I didn't. I could have kept myself.'

'How?'

'Writing scripts,' I said thickly.

'Writing bloody scripts, you want to get a day's work done, never mind writing scripts. Who do you think's going to run *this* bloody business when *I'm* gone?' He jerked his thumb in the direction of the garage outside, and it was so exactly like the trouble at t' mill routine that Arthur and I had between us that the response flicked immediately into my mind: *'But father, we all have our lives to lead, you yours and I mine!'*

Aloud, I said: 'You said you didn't *want* me in the business.'

'Only because you were so bloody idle! *Some* bastard's got to carry on wi' it. Who's going to keep your mother?'

*Father, the men! They're coming up the drive!*

'Why, you're not retiring, are you?' I said with a forced jocularity. The old man turned away in disgust and walked into the lounge. I sat where I was for a minute or so, and then I started to go upstairs. 'And keep out of your grandma's bedroom!' he called venomously.

I tiptoed into my room and went straight over to the Guilt Chest, already convinced that the whole thing had been a gigantic hoax. But the chest had definitely been moved; it was lying slantwise across the linoleum, only half-under the bed, and the stamp edging was gone. It was almost a relief to know at last for certain that they had been into it. I knelt down and

pulled the Guilt Chest clear of the bed and lifted the tinny lid.
The calendars were still stacked in their heavy piles, though
they had been disturbed. The Housewives' Choice letter had
gone. I felt under a pile of calendars for the stack of invoices
the old man had once given me to post. They were still there. I
grabbed them first, the calendars toppling over into the chest,
and stuffed them into my inside pocket. Liz's postcards were
still there, and so was the copy of Ritzy Stories. The letters
from the Witch had been interfered with. I ran rapidly
through their contents and turned the repeater gun on the
Witch and her silly, daft prose.

I sat on the bed, making a weak effort to translate the scene
with the old man into No. 1 thinking, with my No. 1 father
ushering me into the library for the manly talk. I tried again
to project myself into the future. I could see myself, quite
plainly see myself, sitting on the train, knocking on a peeling
door in Earl's Court, sitting in Danny Boon's office, eating
beans on toast in the A.B.C. I took out my wallet and counted
the notes again, eight pounds ten now, and seventeen shillings
in silver.

I dug out the letter from Danny Boon again and smoothed
it out and read it. *'Several of the boys do work for me, you
might be interested in this.' I* jumped to my feet and grabbed
the old suitcase from under the chest of drawers, throwing out
the store of blankets and Polythene-wrapped cardigans my
mother kept in it. Pulling open drawers, I began to assemble
shirts and handkerchiefs and socks together. I took down my
best suit and folded it in two, still on its hanger, inside the
suitcase. Then I looked in the Guilt Chest, reckoning that
there must be about a hundred and seventy calendars left. I
got a great heap of calendars and put them, in three rows, in
the suitcase. Then I began packing in earnest, putting a
calendar in between each shirt and placing the calendars like
lining all the way round the case. The lid would not close. I
took out two shirts and one calendar. I tore the calendar out of
its envelope and propped it up on the bedroom mantelpiece
behind the Coronation tin. I pushed the envelope behind the
sheet of newspaper in the fireplace, and got the case shut by

pressing on it. There was a rubble of old letters and torn pieces of envelope left in the Guilt Chest. I put Liz's postcards and the letters from the Witch in my raincoat pocket, and left the rest.

I was humming as I went into the bathroom to fetch my toothbrush.

The old man shouted up the stairs: 'Do you hear? T' taxi's come!'

I shouted: 'All right! Just coming,' and put out the light.

## THIRTEEN

The old man did not see the suitcase, and so there was no trouble in getting out of the house. The taxi driver was one we knew slightly, a man who sometimes came round to Hillcrest to help on jobs. I leaned back against the spent and slithery leather-work, pretending he was a stranger. I clicked without real interest into the piece of No. 1 thinking I always reserved for taxis; my chauffeur-driven Bentley running through the home counties and stopping at the prosperous, half-timbered pub. 'Have you eaten, Benson? Better put the car round the back and join me, hadn't you?'

'What's up, then?' said the real taxi-driver as we turned into Clogiron Lane. 'Is somebody poorly?'

'Yer, me grandma,' I said. 'She's had one o' them turns again.'

'Well, you can expect it, can't yer? She's not getting any younger.'

'No.'

'She's a grand old lass, though, i'n't she?'

'Yer.'

Stradhoughton Infirmary was a white Portland stone building, rusting round the window-sills and mottled with the bleaching it had had from the so-called brackish air. In the light of the concrete lamps it looked even more like a mad-house than ever. We pulled up outside the scratched swing doors and I told the taxi to wait. I took the suitcase in with me. I was met by the dead smell of lavender polish; it was like breathing through a furry yellow duster. The portraits of aldermen and benefactors looked down over the deserted central hall. I went through the white door into the casualty department.

It was busy in its late-night, sleep-walking way. On the high-backed benches a knot of women were joined in a litany of bad doctors, inadequate pensions and leaky houses. They whiled away the time indignantly while their husbands had emergency operations or their children suffered. They were the same women, or seemed to be the same women, I had seen earlier in the New House, the ones who knew about life and death and all the rest of it. I no longer envied them. A man with his arm in a sling sat alone and perplexed, wondering why he had come. He was the one I warmed to. Over by the ambulance bay the porters looked as though they did not care about anything, sitting in their little glass office smoking Woodbines crooked in the hollow of their hands. They distended their necks and frowned and altered their mouths into an oblong shape to expel the smoke. A young char in spectacles swilled at the parquet floor. Nurses in white and purple held huddled conferences that were not to do with the dying. The women talked: 'He put me on port wine.'

I found my mother sitting alone in the corridor on a padded bench that had been ripped and sawed at with a knife until the grey stuffing spilled out like brains. I put down the suitcase and went over and stood in front of her. She looked up.

'We looked all over,' she said weakly, and cleared her throat.

'Where's me grandma?'

She nodded towards the flapping doors where the corridor came to an end. 'They've got that black doctor to her. She can't talk. We're just waiting.' She spoke hoarsely, in a resigned way, yet at the same time excitedly. These were the headlines. I knew, for I had seen her lips moving, that she was already rehearsing the text of this eventful day, plucking at the details of it like pomegranate seeds and stringing them together in a long rosary that would be fingered on and off long after anyone had ceased to care. 'We've been trying to get you since half-past nine,' she said. 'I wanted you to come down with me.'

'I know, my dad was saying,' I said, trying to sound like his son. 'He says she's badly this time.'

My mother sucked in her cheeks and moistened her tongue ready for the first run of her long narrative.

'She was all right again at four o'clock, just after you went out,' she began. 'She had a cup of tea at half-past, when we had ours, but she wouldn't have any brown bread. Then she had a sleep. And she was all right at *nine* o'clock, when your father got back from the pub, because she woke up and asked him if he were putting t' television on. Then we were all just sitting watching television——' (later she would add the name of the programme and of the singer and possibly of the song) —'when she just slumped forward in her chair. We thought she were having a fit, but no, she just gave a little jerk with her head, uh, like that there'—she imitated the jerk, and searched with her magpie memory to see if there was some pin she had left unaccounted for in the first five minutes of my grandmother's dying. 'Then she started to slaver. She were just like a baby. It was pitiful, pitiful. Just like a baby, slavering and gasping for breath.

'Anyway, your father said, if it isn't a fit, we'd better ring for Dr *Mor*gan. So we waited five more minutes and she was still slavering, she wet four handkerchiefs through, them big handkerchiefs of your dad's, so I said you'd better ring up and get t' doctor.'

The account droned on until we had covered every paving-stone on the way to the Infirmary. I was not listening but I knew all that she was saying; I responded, Mm, Mm, Mm, at every pause. I did not want the details of it, not every detail, and I began concentrating on objects in the corridor and thinking the wall, the wall, the ceiling, the ceiling, so that the things my mother was saying could ricochet off them and lose what force they had.

'The last thing she said before they got her on t' stretcher was Where's my Jack. I had to think who she was talking about, then I remembered she must have meant your grandad. Only she always used to call him John. She *never* called him Jack, never. Then she said, *I love you, Jack*'—my mother had difficulty in pronouncing this word love. I had never heard her say it before, and it sounded strange on her lips. I tried to imagine it on the lips of the yellow woman on the other side of the swing doors, but it was impossible. I—love—you. My mother said it as though the word had just been invented, like Terylene.

'Oh, before that she said, What are you thinking about. I think she must ha' been talking to your grandad.' My mother stopped and took a long breath, the breath coming out in a staircase of sighing. 'But you had to listen close to, to hear what she was saying. She could hardly speak, and by the time we got here she couldn't speak at all. She was just slavering.'

She seemed to have finished. I had been trying on various expressions and by now I was searching feverishly for one that really belonged to me. I found it difficult to feel anything beyond indignation that my grandmother should be seen off with this gossiping commentary. Even as my mother was speaking, the phrases with which Arthur and I dissected the conversations around us kept slotting into my head like price tabs ringing up on a cash register. 'Never use a preposition to end a sentence with.' 'I must ask you to not split infinitives.' I felt disgust at myself but when I shopped around for some deeper emotion, there was none. I had a nervous urge to laugh, and I found myself concentrating entirely on keeping my face adult and sad.

My mother said: 'They're a long time.' I had no idea how long she had been here, in spite of the time-table she had given me. She stirred on the creaking couch and seemed to shake herself free of her drama. She turned to me, seeing me probably for the first time as her son and not only as a listener.

'Well, you've got yourself into a fine mess, lad, haven't you?' she said.

I got up and stretched, elaborately, turning away from her.

'So it would seem.'

'I'm only thankful *she* knows nowt about it,' my mother said. She was silent for a minute or so. It seemed to me that she did not want to discuss the subject but was pushing herself into it.

'Why didn't you post that letter of mine?'

'I *did* post it. I was telling me dad. I just wrote it out again, that's all.' I had been working on the story since leaving the old man and got it into convincible shape, but I was tired and it no longer seemed to matter.

'What did you want to write it out again for?'

'There were some mistakes in it. I just thought it would stand a better chance if it was better written, that's all.' I was beginning to feel annoyed with her for picking at trivialities at a time like this.

'Yes, well we can't all be Shakespeares, can we,' she said, in a way that was supposed to shame me. She glanced down the corridor at my suitcase against the wall. She showed no surprise, and I knew that she must have noticed it already and decided to say nothing.

'And what have you been saying to Arthur's mother about having a sister?' she said in sharper tones.

'Why, it was only a joke,' I said, not even bothering to try and sound convincing. I did not know how she knew about Arthur's mother, and I did not care.

'A joke, it *sounds* like a joke. And I thought you told me she'd broken her leg?'

'I didn't know you *knew* Arthur's mother,' I said.

'Yes, you don't know who I know and who I don't know, do you? If you want to know, she rang me up. And what did you do with that cardigan she gave you?'

I remembered this. Arthur's mother had once given me a red cardigan for my imaginary sister. I had carted it around town all day and then left it on a bus.

'Gave it to Barbara, thought I told you about it,' I said.

'You tell me nothing. You didn't tell me about giving her cheek outside t' cemetery this afternoon, did you? When you were *with* Barbara. Anyway, she's coming round tomorrow, when Barbara comes for her tea. So you've got a new cardigan to find.'

I decided to speak. She had seen the suitcase, so she knew, but I decided to tell her.

'I won't be here tomorrow,' I said.

My mother sat bold upright and pursed her lips, pulling in any expression she might have had on her face. She could not disguise a look of restrained shock, as though I had suddenly struck her and she was trying not to show it.

'I'd have gone already if it hadn't been for me grandma,' I said, as gently as I could.

She looked at me, a long, sorrowing look. 'If you're in trouble, Billy, it's not something you can leave behind you, you know,' she said in a shaky voice. 'You put it in your suitcase and take it with you.'

My mother was so little given to this kind of imagery that I wondered if she had got rush reports on the calendars in my suitcase.

'Well I'm still going,' I said doggedly. 'I told you I'm going and I'm going.'

The swing doors opened softly. A nurse came padding along the corridor, walking like an actress. She stopped by my mother and said: 'Mrs Fisher?' in the tones of somebody trying to wake somebody else up from sleep. '*Would* you come this way?' Infected by the mood of feigned solicitude, I stood up as my mother, the light of fear in her eyes, rose and walked slowly with the nurse through the swing doors. I sat down, suddenly tense and frightened. I said to myself, clenching my fists, Don't let's have any scenes, don't let's have any scenes, don't let's have any scenes. I wondered rapidly whether to go now, but I knew I would not. I began pawing the floor with embarrassment. I picked up an old newspaper that had been shoved down the back of the bench, and began to read aimlessly. '*Three passengers on a Belfast plane recently were Mr GOOSE, Mr GANDER and the Rev Mr GOSLING. They did not know each other.*' Beneath this news item was a cartoon, of a little boy saying: 'Can I see this gab that daddy says you have the gift of, Mrs Jones?' I chucked the paper down and began walking from one side of the corridor to the other, heel to toe as though measuring out a cricket pitch. Don't let's have any *scenes*.

It was only a few minutes before my mother came back, holding her handbag between her hands, her face marked with grief and dignity as she imagined it to be. She was helped as far as the doors by a grave-faced doctor, and it looked to me like some corny act on television. I could not help these thoughts. I prayed: please, God, let me *feel* something. Let me feel something, only don't let's have any scenes.

'Your grandma died at fourteen minutes past twelve,' my mother said, as though making a formal announcement. I wanted to say: 'I'm sorry' or something, but anything I said would have sounded ridiculous. 'I shall have to sit down,' my mother said. I sat by her, legs apart, head bowed, staring down at my feet and counting the stains on my suède shoes. I examined what I was feeling and it was nothing, nothing.

My mother was already in the luxury of reminiscing. 'She would have wanted it this way,' she said, a platitude so inept that I could only marvel at the clichés that she used like crutches to take her limping from one crisis to another. And at the same time I was relieved to hear her talk like this; I thought, They're as bad as I am, they don't feel it, they only say it. But I did not believe what I was telling myself.

'Do you want to go in and see her?' my mother said. I mumbled 'No,' mingling shock and shame.

She sighed, drawing on her gloves. 'Well, we'll have to carry on as best we can,' she said. She stared at the wall, moving her lips again. 'Her last words were just Jack, Jack, what are you thinking about.'

And she died with a slavered smile and not a genuine thought from anybody. No one had been capable of a genuine thought. All those women, who were supposed to know it all, all about life and death, they didn't know any more than I did.

'Can we get a cup of tea, I've had nothing to eat since half-past four,' my mother said.

'Yer, there's a canteen out in the waiting-room,' I mumbled.

I hovered about, pretending to help her up, and we walked down the corridor.

'We shall have to ring up Mr Shadrack,' my mother said. I had been fearing this, ever since I had heard that Gran was ill, and often in the past I had worked out how to get out of it if they ever wanted a Shadrack and Duxbury funeral for her.

'You don't want to get them, you want to get the Co-op,' I said.

My mother, speaking as though she was ashamed, said: 'Why, do they pay a divi?' and it was as though her voice was being pulled back on a lead, like a dog.

I said: 'No, but they're better than blinking Shadrack and Duxbury's.'

We were back in the hall of the casualty department. The canteen was still open. I went over to the steamy aluminium-ridged counter with the pale milky rings on it, and ordered sloppy tea in a thick mug marked SGI, Stradhoughton General Infirmary. I took the cup over to my mother and then went back and fetched my suitcase. I stood it almost in front of her and sat down. All the women had gone. There was only an old tramp in a dirty raincoat, his foot bandaged, sitting like a lost man in the corner.

My mother put her cup on the floor, shaking her head. 'I can't drink it.' She twisted her wedding ring.

'What train are you supposed to be catching?' she said.

'I don't know, when there is one.' And then, in the gentle voice: 'I've *got* to go tonight, because I want to see Danny Boon on Monday morning.'

My mother opened her handbag. 'Well you haven't got any money, have you?'

I said, flushing for the first time: 'I've got a few pounds. I've been saving up.' I was beginning to get embarrassed. I wanted to be away and finished with it all. I said: 'You'd better be getting back. I've got a taxi waiting for you outside.'

'I've got some papers to sign first,' my mother said. She stared down at the cup of tea on the floor. 'We don't say much,' she said—a straight lie, for a start—'but we need you at home, lad.'

The sudden editorial 'we' made me feel uncomfortable. 'Well, I'll be coming home,' I said. With a rush of generosity I added: 'I'll just get fixed up with Danny Boon and then I'll come home next week-end.'

She shook her head slightly from side to side, saying nothing.

'Well I'll *have* to go, because I don't know what time the train is,' I said. 'T' taxi's just outside, when you're ready.' I shuffled about in front of her, trying to say some words that I had practised for this moment, but I could not say them. I walked away slowly, trying to look as though I were reluctant to go. By the time I reached the white door I was already thinking of Gran as an article in the *Reader's Digest*. '*Ma Boothroyd said what she thought. Everyone feared her blunt tongue. Came the day when Ma Boothroyd had to go to hospital...*' Twenty-three, twenty-four, twenty-five. The Lord is my shepherd, I shall not want, he maketh me to lie down in green pastures.

I did not have the courage to turn round and look at my mother, but I knew that her face would be flawed and crumpled like an old balloon, and that for the first time she would be looking as though these things had really happened.

## FOURTEEN

The strange, poppy-like flowers seen nowhere else in the world were in full bloom in Ambrosia, or what was left of it. We had won the elections, and I was pressing forward with my visionary plan to build an entire city over the dunes on a gigantic wooden platform. The reactionary Dr Grover had got a commission set up to investigate me, but I knew for a fact that he had been bribed to put forward a rival plan for another city to the west, over the marshes. In the inner layers of No. 1 thinking, Grover got his way and the houses began to sink, seventy-

one dead and fourteen unaccounted for. 'We will rebuild,' I
announced in the *Ambrosia Poppy*. 'We will build on the
dunes.' Now I was home on a visit to my parents, my full-dress
uniform unbuttoned at the throat. The telephone rang, and I
spoke rapidly in Ambrosian to one of my lieutenants. '*Monay.
D'cra d'njin, intomr nay nay Grover. D'cra Grover, n'jnin
repost. Finis.*' My mother was impressed, but no, she was not
impressed. How could she be, that one? I tried to fit in my
No. 1 mother, but she was a piece from another jigsaw. I
began to slide off into some hate thinking about my real
mother and her clichés and her knitting, about my dead
grandmother snickering 'Good night' at the television set
and the old man, stolid and daft, pulling his faces and
banging nails all over the garage. '*Dad, I shall want the van.
Don't ask questions. There may be people here. You don't
know where I've gone or when I'm coming back. O.K.?*' I was
sick and tired of it all, of it all.

I walked with my suitcase, following the pitch-pocked
channels in the road where the tramlines had been. I was
beginning to feel like a man made entirely of sawdust. I tried
to get back to Ambrosia but none of it would click and I had
nothing but hate for anybody. I fired off the repeater gun at all
the people who knew my secrets, but none of the secrets really
mattered, they were like dead wounds with the bandages falling off. I started to get clear, frightening thoughts. Nine
pounds. Less the fare, call it seven. Seven pounds. If I can get a
room for two pounds ten a week, that's two weeks and a quid a
week for food. I can always get a job of some kind, maybe
washing-up. I began to imagine myself in the tradition of
American writers, driving lorries, sweeping up, South American revolution, soda jerk, newspaper boy. Then the No. 1
thinking switched off, this time at the mains. I knew that it
would probably be a job as a clerk, in an office, but by myself,
by myself. No Stamps, no Shadracks. I could be an eccentric.
The surly one, the man with the past.

Saturday night was over and done with. Along Infirmary
Street a low wind caught and held a sheet of brown paper and
wrapped it round a lamp-post. I could hear cars whining up

Houghtondale Hill two miles away. One or two rashly-hired taxis, piled high with people splitting the fare, ran past me on their way to the Strad Lee housing estate, and I caught the idiot murmur of their radios instructing the drivers as they passed. The late bus went by, looking as though it was the last bus that would ever run again anywhere, its occupants reading the *Empire News* under the blue glare. A dog padded across the road. A man stamped home in his raincoat and I knew that he was counting the lamp-posts to get there quicker. The pavement was dry and hollow, here and there etched with the trickle of long-stale urine. The streets were cold and the girls on the posters were grinning in their sleep.

I walked like a ghost down Moorgate, the suitcase making red ridges on my hand and turning into loot at every sight of a policeman. I turned into Bull Ring, dodging the slow-moving road-sweeper vans emerging like snails from the cleansing department and leaving their trickling smear along the gutters. I walked across Bull Ring into New Station.

The station was ablaze with cold, white light. The booking hall was deserted except for a fleet of electric trollies piled high with newspaper parcels. The last Harrogate diesel was just pulling sleekly away from platform two.

The enquiry office was closed. I walked up to the roller indicator where the trains were listed: 1.05 Wakefield, Doncaster; 1.35 Leeds (City), Derby, Kettering, London (St Pancras); 1.50 Selby, Market Weighton, Bridlington, Filey, Scarborough. There were no other trains to London that night. All the windows but one at the ticket office were boarded up. I waited under A-G until a tired man in his shirt-sleeves appeared, and I bought a single second-class to St Pancras. It cost thirty-five shillings. I looked up at the big station clock. It was ten minutes to one.

Below the ticket office was the buffet and main waiting-room. The buffet end was closed, its counter still lined with thick cups and the floor littered with crusts of bread, but there were about a dozen people still in the waiting-room, most of them asleep with their feet up on the scratched tubular chairs or their heads down on the rockety tables, among the flattened straws and empty lemon-squash cartons. I went in and stood by the door, under one of the large, empty-looking pictures of fields and hills that lined the walls. A few people were awake: half a dozen soldiers, all in civvies, going home on leave, three old prostitutes, a man in a large black coat. I was sleepy, recognising everything about five seconds after it happened. I did not see Rita, or Stamp, until I had settled down on my suitcase and was lighting a cigarette.

They did not see me either. Stamp, savouring the dregs of his dull, drunken evening, was leaning against one of the gilded pillars that separated the waiting-room from the buffet, sweating and muttering to himself. Rita was pulling in-effectually at his arm, like a tired wife trying to get her husband out of the pub. '*Come* on, they're all *looking* at you,' I heard her say impatiently. She stood indecisively and then let go of his arm and said, obviously not for the first time: 'Oh, well I'm going, you can look after yourself.' Stamp, lost in the biley swamps of his own suffering, gripped the pillar for support and comfort, retched, swallowed and then, in his thin and watery way, was sick all over the floor. Rita tutted and phewed and looked rapidly from side to side to find sympathy for her own predicament. She walked a few steps away and turned her back, standing with a formal casualness, pretending not to be anything to do with Stamp. A few of the sleeping people stirred. One of them half-awoke.

'Christ sake, shift outside if you wanna spew!'

Some of those who were already awake began tittering. One of the soldiers imitated a man in the toils of sickness. '*Wyyach!*' Stamp, clawing at the air, reeling and watery-eyed, caught some kind of hazy glimpse of me sitting in the corner, watching him. The image passed straight though into his sub-conscious and he peered at me without recognition, fixing his eyes on me only as an object while he strained and sweated and gasped for air.

The man in the big black coat, red-faced and beery in his own right, was enjoying it all. For the benefit of the soldiers he called: 'Get that man in the guard-house! C.O.'s prade, morrow morning. Hat off, left right left right left right

HALT!' One or two of the soldiers grinned weakly; the one sitting next to me muttered: 'He wants to get back in the blasted army if he's so blasted keen.'

Stamp, mopping grimily at his damp forehead, staggered to the wall and sat down on the floor under a picture of Lake Windermere, head down like a sleeping Mexican. Rita walked over and began plucking at him again, pleading: '*Come* on, then. You shouldn't drink and then you wouldn't *be* like this.'

In the middle of the room, the tableau changed. The three old prostitutes were haggling with a half-drunk, fair-haired lad who had just come in. 'Well do you want *her*, then? You should have said. *She* doesn't care, one way or t' other.' They were all about fifty years old, and they did not look like prostitutes, more like housewives who baked loaves. They talked like mothers anxious to please their grown-up sons with a good tea. 'Well get a taxi and take her home then. She'll take fifteen shillings, she doesn't care, she doesn't want to skin you.'

The soldiers next to me were muttering. '*He* must be hard up for it, they look like three old grandmothers.'

'Three old grandmothers, bet they'll be getting their pensions in the morning!'

'Ha! Be funny if one of 'em pegged out on the job. Three dirty old grandmothers.'

It was wit to the taste of Stamp, but Stamp saw nothing of what was going on around him. He had got up and was leaning over his pillar again, slavering into the thin green mess which he had padded about the floor with his sick-speckled shoes.

'*Wyyach!*' went one of the soldiers.

'That time me and Jacko got them German drinks. *Wyyach!*'

I got up and walked to the other side of the waiting-room, skirting round Stamp in a broad arc. As soon as Rita saw me I regretted that I had moved.

'Look what's crawled out of the cheese!' she said, neither raising nor lowering her voice. She was wearing a blue swagger coat over her tight red dress. The silver cross was no longer round her neck.

'I should think some people ought to crawl back *into* the cheese,' I said, nodding towards Stamp.

'Oo, where's yer rubber halo?' jeered Rita. We looked at each other, or at least I looked at her. Rita had a habit of looking at nothing, her eyes glazing over with a sort of gormless preoccupation.

'What happened to the Witch?' I said.

She screwed her face up into an ugly scowl. *Who?*'

'Barbara. Her you were talking to in the Roxy.'

'Don't know, don't care,' said Rita.

'Did she say anything?'

'Ask no questions and you'll get no lies told,' she said in the same level voice.

'I bet she got that cross out of you,' I said recklessly. 'Hope you didn't give her the ring back, did you?'

Rita's voice suddenly took on the same pitch and colour as the voices of the three old prostitutes still haggling away in the middle of the room:

'You what? Do you think I'm daft, or what? It might be her cross, but you gave that ring to *me!*'

I looked around, but nobody was listening.

'I know, only it's a bit of a mix-up,' I said. 'You see, I thought Barbara had broke the engagement off——'

'Yer, well you've another think coming if you think I'm as daft as she is! You gave that ring to *me,* in front of a witness.'

'How do you mean, what's witnesses got to do with it?'

Rita stared at me, thin-lipped like all the people I had known that day. She made as if to speak twice and then, spitting the words out with such force that her head shook, she said in the lowest range of her coarse voice:

'You're just *rot*ten, aren't you?'

I looked wildly across the room to my suitcase, and from my suitcase to the door, planning the shortest route out into the booking hall.

'Y'are! You're rotten! All through! I've met some people in my time but of all the lying, scheming—— Anyway, you gave that ring to *me!*'

I said quietly and urgently: 'Look, nobody's asking for the ring. You can have it——'

'Don't talk to me, you rotten get!' Rita's voice was rising with each word, and even the prostitutes were beginning to stare. 'Get back to '*er*! You rotten get! You rotten, lying get! Gar, you think you're summat, don't you? But you're nowt! You miserable, lying, rotten, stinking get!'

White-faced, I turned my back on her and walked quickly towards my suitcase, skidding and almost losing my balance where Stamp had been sick on the floor. 'You think you're it but you're spit!' shouted Rita. One of the soldiers caught my eye and jerked his head up, raising his eyes and going: 'Cuh!' I grabbed my suitcase blindly and made for the door. Two railway policemen walked into the waiting-room, looking ponderously about them, and Rita shut up. One of them walked over to where Stamp was leaning helplessly against the pillar and began talking to him in a low, dangerous voice.

The man in the black coat called: 'Two men, buckets, mops. Floor cleaned. Port to me when you've finished. Double!' I slid out of the waiting-room and stood irresolutely in the booking hall, still shaken.

It was just on one o'clock. I stood contemplating the gigantic advertisement for Ovaltine that filled one whole end of the booking hall. Running my eyes down the wall, I began to count the loaded parcel trolleys that stood around the station. I got up to nineteen, and then the waiting-room door opened again and one of the policemen came out, helping Stamp towards the lavatory. Stamp saw me with his boiled, steaming eyes and muttered through the spit on his face: 'Know somethn bou' you, Fisher. *I* saw you. Wai' Monday, you jus' wai'.' The policeman led him off, as he muttered again: 'Wai' Monday.'

I had lost my place among the parcel trolleys. I began counting the tiles on the dirty, unwashed floor of the station. I counted them in a line, screwing up my eyes, and numbering each tile only with great difficulty after I had passed twenty. Raising my head slightly I saw a pair of heels by the one window of the ticket office that was still open. I opened my eyes again and looked, and there was no mistaking the casual black skirt, the green suède jacket and the unkempt hair. Liz was just turning away from the ticket office as I picked up my case and began to stumble towards her, walking drunkenly in the manner of Stamp being led off to the lavatory.

She saw me just as she was turning off to make for the platform where the Doncaster train was waiting. I waved, and she came towards me. I flapped my hand again, airily.

'Goin' London,' I mumbled, grabbing her arm and lurching about in front of her. 'You goin' London? I'm goin' London. Go' catch a train. Goin' London.'

'So you keep saying,' said Liz, beaming comfortably.

'You come London, me. Goin' London. Pla'form three, S' Pancra', ge's all London.'

'Where did you get it?' said Liz, still beaming as though she relished the whole thing.

'Where ge' wha'?'

'The booze. Or did you find some little dive to go to after you so mysteriously disappeared?'

'Go' go London,' I said. 'Carn stay Stradanan. Go' go London.'

The station announcer, as inarticulate as myself, crackled out some message about the Doncaster train. Liz looked up at the station clock.

'Well *I'm* not going to London. I've got to go to Doncaster——'

I took hold of her arm again, wagging my head heavily.

'No, you come London. Need you London. Ge' nother ticket, come London.'

Liz gave me one of her long looks, and slowly took hold of me, inspecting me at arm's length.

'Drop it,' she said, stern behind the smile.

I said in my normal voice: 'Drop what?'

'That's better. You may be a brilliant scriptwriter, Billy, but you're a rotten actor.'

I put on an elaborate mock-sheepish act, standing on one foot, pulling out a grin and spreading my arms about.

'*All* right,' said Liz. 'Now where did you get to tonight?'

'Where did *I* get to? Where did *you* get to?'

Lovingly, in detail, we reconstructed the half hour I had waited outside the Roxy, charting and justifying our movements, forgiving and understanding, and everything so simple. Liz had been having a long talk with the Witch, whom she had discovered weeping and slobbering and sick on the floor of the Ladies. Everything that could be told had been told.

'Are you really going to London, or just pretending?' said Liz.

I took the ticket out of my pocket and showed it to her.

She looked at me steadily and there was love in her dark eyes, the first time I had seen it, a liquid, far-reaching thing, too deep to touch.

'I'm not coming, you know, Billy.'

'Please.'

She shook her head. 'I won't live with you, Billy.'

'Come anyway,' I said. 'Live next door. Blimey, you've been everywhere else, you might as well come and live in——' I broke off as a suspicion crossed my mind. 'Why are you going to Doncaster?'

She grinned again, in the frank manner that gave nothing away.

'Oh, just—Doncaster,' she said, shrugging amiably.

I said bluffly, in the man of the world voice: 'Well whatever you want in Doncaster, they've got it in London. Yes? Yes?'

She was shaking her head, smiling.

'One condition,' she said.

I closed my eyes tightly and smote my forehead, teetering on the brink of a decision. All the details of it were there, in a compact parcel of No. 1 thinking, from the register office ceremony to the Chelsea attic. All it needed was the decision.

'And *I* wouldn't want the communal ring,' said Liz. But *I* did not answer, and she knew that there was no answer.

A porter was rattling the gate at the entrance to the Doncaster platform. Liz picked up her bag, a small, well-worn grip. She regarded me steadily for a few seconds and, standing a foot in front of me, blew me a kiss.

'Postcards?' she said, whispering it.

'Postcards,' I said.

I struck the farewell attitude, legs apart, arms akimbo, the sad figure fading into silhouette as the train steams away. But she did not look back. The porter banged the gate shut and I saw Liz clamber into the last carriage after two soldiers. I watched the train disappear. I knew that she would already be in bright conversation, grinning engagingly at some item of army news.

It was twelve minutes past one. I picked up my suitcase and walked back towards the waiting-room. Rita, the three old prostitutes and most of the others had gone, and there was sawdust on the floor where Stamp had been. Two soldiers slept on, their feet extended across a couple of chairs apiece. The man in the black coat was still there, but dozing.

I stood by the wall and, raising one leg, balanced the suitcase on my knee. I took out the top layer of calendars and began rooting about among the shirts and socks for more. I stacked the calendars on the tubular table beside me until I had got them all out. Then I closed the suitcase and pushed it under the table. I scooped the calendars up into two heavy parcels, one under each arm, and barged the door open with my back. I looked up and down the booking hall but there was nobody watching. There was a deep wire litter bin, labelled 'Keep Your Borough Clean.' I bent over and tipped the calendars into it. The basket toppled slightly. I gathered up some newspapers from a nearby seat and stuffed them in on top of the calendars.

I turned to go and then, struck by a second thought, I felt in my pocket for the wad of invoices that I should have posted for the old man. I dropped those in the basket too. I found the letters from the Witch, and ripped them in pieces, scattering the bits in the litter bin and on the floor around it. I began going methodically through my pockets, discarding practically everything: the fragment of script for Danny Boon, the letter I had started to write to him, a couple of Stamp's passion pills, a cigarette packet. When I had finished I had nothing left but the note from Danny Boon, Liz's postcards, and my railway ticket. I walked back into the waiting-room and got my suitcase. It needed fourteen minutes before the London train was due to go.

Ambrosia came softly into my head, the beginning of it all, with the march-past and the one-armed soldiers and the flags. I muttered to myself, almost aloud: 'Seventy-eight ninety-six, a hundred and four, the Lord is my Shepherd, I shall not want, he maketh me to lie down in green pastures, he leadeth me beside the still waters.' The No. 1 thinking fused into a panic-panorama with the No. 2 daymares and the quick sharp shafts of ordinary, level thought. I imagined myself as a modern clergyman, pipe-smoking, twinkling, arranging a contemporary funeral with Shadrack; but nasally he was saying, 'It's vair vair unsatisfactory, vair unsa'sfactory.' I could not summon up my No. 1 mother, only the real one, with her pressed, depressed mouth and her petty frown. Seven pounds, seven pounds ten actually, get a room for thirty bob a week, call it three weeks, three quid left, half a crown a day, egg and chips one and threepence, cup of tea threepence, bus fares a tanner. He restoreth my soul, he leadeth me in the paths of righteousness for his name's sake. I saw Liz in the Chelsea attic, and Rita whoring it in the streets outside, and the Witch as the reactionary Dr Grover's mistress. I tried hard to shut it down and find myself, myself, but not knowing what to do for characteristics. Yea, though I walk through the valley of the shadow of death, I will fear no evil.

The station announcer began to list the stations to London. Leeds (City), Derby, Kettering, London (St Pancras). Change at Leeds for Bradford, Ilkley, Bolton Abbey. The man in the big black coat, chastened now, began to arrange his things. I got up and began to walk hurriedly up and down the waiting-room; I had the sensation of a water-tap running in my stomach. I picked up my suitcase and put it down twice. I took out the ticket and looked at it, vaguely noting the price and the details. I could not think, except in confused snatches. I began to count ten; at the end of the count I would oblige myself to answer one way or the other. One. Two. Three. Four. The train now leaving platform three is the one thirty-five for London, calling at. Five. Six. Seven. There was no need to count to the end. I picked up the suitcase, feeling deflated and defeated. I walked out of the waiting-room and across the booking hall to the ticket barrier on platform three, hoping that I would make a quick decision but knowing that there was no question of it. The man in the black coat and three or four soldiers walked through, showing their tickets.

The ticket collector looked at me.

'You gettin' on this train?' I shook my head, taking a step forward at the same time.

I did not wait for the train to leave. I transferred the suitcase to my left hand and walked out of the station. In Bull Ring I stopped and lit a cigarette and buttoned up my coat. The suitcase felt absurdly light. I began to breathe great gusts of air, but there was little air to breathe.

I walked across Bull Ring and up Moorgate. Suddenly I began to feel excited and buoyant, and I was almost running by the time I reached Town Square. I began to whistle 'March of the Movies' and to march in step with it. There was nobody about. When I came to the War Memorial I transferred my suitcase to my right hand and at the correct moment I saluted with the left—up, two, three, down, two, three, head erect, shoulders back. I brought the whistling to a huffing crescendo and wheeled smartly into Infirmary Street. I dropped into a normal step, and then I began the slow walk home.

# The Loneliness of
# The Long-distance Runner

## ONE

As soon as I got to Borstal they made me a long-distance cross-country runner. I suppose they thought I was just the build for it because I was long and skinny for my age (and still am) and in any case I didn't mind it much, to tell you the truth, because running had always been made much of in our family, especially running away from the police. I've always been a good runner, quick and with a big stride as well, the only trouble being that no matter how fast I run, and I did a very fair lick even though I do say so myself, it didn't stop me getting caught by the cops after that bakery job.

You might think it a bit rare, having long-distance cross-country runners in Borstal, thinking that the first thing a long-distance cross-country runner would do when they set him loose at them fields and woods would be to run as far away from the place as he could get on a bellyful of Borstal slum-gullion—but you're wrong, and I'll tell you why. The first thing is that them bastards over us aren't as daft as they most of the time look, and for another thing I'm not so daft as I would look if I tried to make a break for it on my long-distance running, because to abscond and then get caught is nothing but a mug's game, and I'm not falling for it. Cunning is what counts in this life, and even that you've got to use in the slyest way you can; I'm telling you straight: they're cunning, and I'm cunning. If only 'them' and 'us' had the same ideas we'd get on like a house on fire, but they don't see eye to eye with us and we don't see eye to eye with them, so that's how it stands and how it will always stand. The one fact is that all of us are cunning, and because of this there's no love lost between us. So the thing is that they know I won't try to get away from them: they sit there like spiders in that crumbly manor house, perched like jumped-up jackdaws on the roof, watching out over the drives and fields like German generals from the tops of tanks. And even when I jog-trot on behind a wood and they can't see me anymore they know my sweeping-brush head will bob along that hedge-top in an hour's time and that I'll report to the bloke on the gate. Because when on a raw and frosty morning I get up at five o'clock and stand shivering my belly off on the stone floor and all the rest still have another hour to snooze before the bells go, I slink down-stairs through all the corridors to the big outside door with a permit running-card in my fist, I feel like the first and last man on the world, both at once, if you can believe what I'm trying to say. I feel like the first man because I've hardly got a stitch on and am sent against the frozen fields in a shimmy and shorts—even the first poor bastard dropped on to the earth in midwinter knew how to make a suit of leaves, or how to skin a pterodactyl for a topcoat. But there I am, frozen stiff, with nothing to get me warm except a couple of hours' long-distance running before breakfast, not even a slice of bread-and-sheepdip. They're training me up fine for the big sports day when all the pig-faced snotty-nosed dukes and ladies—who can't add two and two together and would mess them-selves like loonies if they didn't have slavies to beck-and-call—come and make speeches to us about sports being just the thing to get us leading an honest life and keep our itching finger-ends off them shop locks and safe handles and hairgrips to open gas meters. They give us a bit of blue ribbon and a cup for a prize after we've shagged ourselves out running or jumping, like race horses, only we don't get so well looked-after as race horses, that's the only thing.

So there I am, standing in the doorway in shimmy and shorts, not even a dry crust in my guts, looking out at frosty flowers on the ground. I suppose you think this is enough to make me cry? Not likely. Just because I feel like the first bloke in the world wouldn't make me bawl. It makes me feel fifty times better than when I'm cooped up in that dormitory with three hundred others. No, it's sometimes when I stand there feeling like the *last* man in the world that I don't feel so good. I feel like the last man in the world because I think that all those three hundred sleepers behind me are dead. They sleep so well I think that every scruffy head's kicked the bucket in the night and I'm the only one left, and when I look out into the bushes and frozen ponds I have the feeling that it's going to get colder and colder until everything I can see, meaning my red arms as well, is going to be covered with a thousand miles of ice, all the earth, right up to the sky and over every bit of land and sea. So I try to kick this feeling out and act like I'm the first man on earth. And that makes me feel good, so as soon as I'm steamed up enough to get this feeling in me, I take a flying leap out of the doorway, and off I trot.

I'm in Essex. It's supposed to be a good Borstal, at least that's what the governor said to me when I got here from Nottingham. 'We want to trust you while you are in this establishment,' he said, smoothing out his newspaper with lily-white workless hands, while I read the big words upside down: *Daily Telegraph*. 'If you play ball with us, we'll play ball with you.' (Honest to God, you'd have thought it was going to be one long tennis match.) 'We want hard honest work and we want good athletics,' he said as well. 'And if you give us both these things you can be sure we'll do right by you and send you back into the world an honest man.' Well, I could have died laughing, especially when straight after this I hear the barking sergeant-major's voice calling me and two others to attention and marching us off like we was Grenadier Guards. And when the governor kept saying how 'we' wanted you to do this, and 'we' wanted you to do that, I kept looking round for the other blokes, wondering how many of them there was. Of course, I knew there were thousands of them, but as far as I knew only one was in the room. And there *are* thousands of them, all over the poxeaten country, in shops, offices, railway stations, cars, houses, pubs—In-law blokes like you and them, all on the watch for Out-law blokes like me and us—and waiting to 'phone for the coppers as soon as we make a false move. And it'll always be there, I'll tell you that now, because I haven't finished making all my false moves yet, and I dare say I won't until I kick the bucket. If the In-laws are hoping to stop me making false moves they're wasting their time. They might as well stand me up against a wall and let fly with a dozen rifles. That's the only way they'll stop me, and a few million others. Because I've been doing a lot of thinking since coming here. They can spy on us all day to see if we're pulling our puddings and if we're working good or doing our 'athletics' but they can't make an X-ray of our guts to find out what we're telling ourselves. I've been asking myself all sorts of questions, and thinking about my life up to now. And I like doing all this. It's a treat. It passes the time away and don't make Borstal seem half so bad as the boys in our street used to say it was. And this long-distance running lark is the best of all, because it makes me think so good that I learn things even better than when I'm on my bed at night. And apart from that, what with thinking so much while I'm running I'm getting to be one of the best runners in the Borstal. I can go five miles round better than anybody else I know.

So as soon as I tell myself I'm the first man ever to be dropped into the world, and as soon as I take that first flying leap out into the frosty grass of an early morning when even birds haven't the heart to whistle, I get to thinking, and that's what I like. I go my rounds in a dream, turning at lane or footpath corners without knowing I'm turning, leaping brooks without knowing they're there, and shouting good morning to the early cow-milker without seeing him. It's a treat, being a long-distance runner, out in the world by yourself with not a soul to make you bad-tempered or tell you what to do or that there's a shop to break and enter a bit back from the next street. Sometimes I think that I've never been so free as during that couple of hours when I'm trotting up the path out of the gates and turning by that bare-faced, big-bellied oak tree at the lane end. Everything's dead, but good, because it's dead before coming alive, not dead after being alive. That's how I look at it. Mind you, I often feel frozen stiff at first. I can't feel my hands or feet or flesh at all, like I'm a ghost who wouldn't know the earth was under him if he didn't see it now and again through the mist. But even though some people would call his frost-pain suffering if they wrote about it to their mams in a letter, I don't, because I know that in half an hour I'm going to be warm, that by the time I get to the main road and am turning on to the wheatfield footpath by the bus stop I'm going to feel as hot as a potbellied stove and as happy as a dog with a tin tail.

It's a good life, I'm saying to myself, if you don't give in to coppers and Borstal-bosses and the rest of them bastard-faced In-laws. Trot-trot-trot. Puff-puff-puff. Slap-slap-slap go my feet on the hard soil. Swish-swish-swish as my arms and side catch the bare branches of a bush. For I'm seventeen now, and when they let me out of this—if I don't make a break and see that things turn out otherwise—they'll try to get me in the army, and what's the difference between the army and this place I'm in now? They can't kid me, the bastards. I've seen the barracks near where I live, and if there weren't swaddies on guard outside with rifles you wouldn't know the difference between their high walls and the place I'm in now. Even though the swaddies come out at odd times a week for a pint of ale, so what? Don't I come out three mornings a week on my long-distance running, which is fifty times better than boozing. When they first said that I was to do my long-distance running without a guard pedalling beside me on a bike I couldn't believe it; but they called it a progressive and modern place, though they can't kid me because I know it's just like any other Borstal, going by the stories I've heard, except that they let me trot about like this. Borstal's Borstal no matter what they do; but anyway I moaned about it being a bit thick sending me out so early to run five miles on an empty stomach, until they talked me round to thinking it wasn't so bad—which I knew all the time—until they called me a good sport and patted me on the back when I said I'd do it and that I'd try to win them the Borstal Blue Ribbon Prize Cup For Long Distance Cross Country Running (All England). And now the governor talks to me when he comes on his rounds, almost as he'd talk to his prize race horse, if he had one.

'All right, Smith?' he asks.

'Yes, sir,' I answer.

He flicks his grey moustache: 'How's the running coming along?'

'I've set myself to trot round the grounds after dinner just to keep my hand in, sir,' I tell him.

The pot-bellied pop-eyed bastard gets pleased at this: 'Good show. I know you'll get us that cup,' he says.

And I swear under my breath: 'Like boggery, I will.' No, I won't get them that cup, even though the stupid tash-twitching bastard has all his hopes in me. Because what does his barmy hope mean? I ask myself. Trot-trot-trot, slap-slap-slap, over the stream and into the wood where it's almost dark and frosty-dew twigs sting my legs. It don't mean a bloody thing to me, only to him, and it means as much to him as it would mean to me if I picked up the racing paper and put my bet on a hoss I didn't know, had never seen, and didn't care a sod if I ever did see. That's what it means to him. And I'll lose that race, because I'm not a race horse at all, and I'll let him know it when I'm about to get out—if I don't sling my hook even before the race. By Christ I will. I'm a human being and I've got thoughts and secrets and bloody life inside me that he doesn't know is there, and he'll never know what's there because he's stupid. I suppose you'll laugh at this, me saying the governor's a stupid bastard when I know hardly how to write and he can read and write and add-up like a professor. But what I say is true right enough. He's stupid, and I'm not, because I can see further into the likes of him than he can see into the likes of me. Admitted, we're both cunning, but I'm more cunning and I'll win in the end even if I die in gaol at eighty-two, because I'll have more fun and fire out of my life than he'll ever get out of his. He's read a thousand books I suppose, and for all I know he might even have written a few, but I know for a dead cert, as sure as I'm sitting here, that what I'm scribbling down is worth a million to what he could ever scribble down. I don't care what anybody says, but that's the truth and can't be denied. I know when he talks to me and I look into his army mug that I'm alive and he's dead. He's as dead as a doornail. If he ran ten yards he'd drop dead. If he got ten yards into what goes on in my guts he'd drop dead as well—with surprise. At the moment it's dead blokes like him as have the whip-hand over blokes like me, and I'm almost dead sure it'll always be like that, but even so, by Christ, I'd rather be like I am—always on the run and breaking into shops for a packet of fags and a jar of jam—than have the whip-hand over somebody else and be dead from the toe nails up. Maybe as soon as you get the whip-hand over somebody you do go dead. By God, to say that last sentence has needed a few hundred miles of long-distance running. I could no more have said that at first than I could have took a million-pound note from my back pocket. But it's true, you know, now I think of it again, and has always been true, and always will be true, and I'm surer of it every time I see the governor open that door and say Good morning lads.

As I run and see my smoky breath going out into the air as if I had ten cigars stuck in different parts of my body I think more on the little speech the governor made when I first came. Honesty. Be honest. I laughed so much one morning I went ten minutes down in my timing because I had to stop and get rid of the stitch in my side. The governor was so worried when I got back late that he sent me to the doctor's for an X-ray and heart check. Be honest, It's like saying: Be dead, like me, and then you'll have no more pain of leaving your nice slummy house for Borstal or prison. Be honest and settle down in a cosy six pounds a week job. Well, even with all this long-distance running I haven't yet been able to decide what he means by this, although I'm just about beginning to—and I don't like what it means. Because after all my thinking I found that it adds up to something that can't be true about me, being born and brought up as I was. Because another thing people like the governor will never understand is that I *am* honest, that I've never been anything else but honest, and that I'll always be honest. Sounds funny. But it's true because I know what honest means according to me and he only knows what it means according to him. I think my honesty is the only sort in the world, and he thinks his is the only sort in the world as well. That's why this dirty great walled-up and fenced-up manor house in the middle of nowhere has been used to

163 F*

coop-up blokes like me. And if I had the whip-hand I wouldn't even bother to build a place like this to put all the cops, governors, posh whores, penpushers, army officers, Members of Parliament in; no, I'd stick them up against a wall and let them have it, like they'd have done with blokes like us years ago, that is, if they'd ever known what it means to be honest, which they don't and never will so help me God Almighty.

I was nearly eighteen months in Borstal before I thought about getting out. I can't tell you much about what it was like there because I haven't got the hang of describing buildings or saying how many crumby chairs and slatted windows make a room. Neither can I do much complaining, because to tell you the truth I didn't suffer in Borstal at all. I gave the same answer a pal of mine gave when someone asked him how much he hated it in the army. 'I didn't hate it,' he said. 'They fed me, gave me a suit, and pocket-money, which was a bloody sight more than I ever got before, unless I worked myself to death for it, and most of the time they wouldn't let me work but sent me to the dole office twice a week.' Well, that's more or less what I say. Borstal didn't hurt me in that respect, so since I've got no complaints I don't have to describe what they gave us to eat, what the dorms were like, or how they treated us. But in another way Borstal does something to me. No, it doesn't get my back up, because it's always been up, right from when I was born. What it does do is show me what they've been trying to frighten me with. They've got other things as well, like prison and, in the end, the rope. It's like me rushing up to thump a man and snatch the coat off his back when, suddenly, I pull up because he whips out a knife and lifts it to stick me like a pig if I come too close. That knife is Borstal, clink, the rope. But once you've seen the knife you learn a bit of unarmed combat. You have to, because you'll never get that sort of knife in your own hands, and this un-armed combat doesn't amount to much. Still, there it is, and you keep on rushing up to this man, knife or not, hoping to get one of your hands on his wrist and the other on his elbow both at the same time, and press back until he drops the knife.

You see, by sending me to Borstal they've shown me the knife, and from now on I know something I didn't know before: that it's war between me and them. I always knew this, naturally, because I was in Remand Homes as well and the boys there told me a lot about their brothers in Borstal, but it was only touch and go then, like kittens, like boxing-gloves, like dobbie. But now that they've shown me the knife, whether I ever pinch another thing in my life again or not, I know who my enemies are and what war is. They can drop all the atom bombs they like for all I care: I'll never call it war and wear a soldier's uniform, because I'm in a different sort of war, that they think is child's play. The war they think is war is suicide, and those that go and get killed in war should be put in clink for attempted suicide because that's the feeling in blokes' minds when they rush to join up or let themselves be called up. I know, because I've thought how good it would be sometimes to do myself in and the easiest way to do it, it occurred to me, was to hope for a big war so's I could join up and get killed. But I got past that when I knew I already was in a war of my own, that I was born into one, that I grew up hearing the sound of 'old soldiers' who'd been over the top at Dartmoor, half-killed at Lincoln, trapped in no-man's land at Borstal, that sounded louder than any Jerry bombs. Government wars aren't my wars; they've got nowt to do with me, because my own war's all that I'll ever be bothered about. I remember when I was fourteen and I went out into the country with three of my cousins, all about the same age, who later went to different Borstals, and then to different regiments, from which they soon deserted, and then to different gaols where they still are as far as I know. But anyway, we were all kids then, and wanted to go out to the woods for a change, to get away from the roads of stinking hot tar one summer. We climbed over fences and went through fields, scrumping a few sour apples on our way, until we saw the wood about a mile off. Up Colliers' Pad we heard another lot of kids talking in high-school voices behind a hedge. We crept up on them and peeped through the brambles, and saw they were eating a picnic, a real posh spread out of baskets and flasks and towels. There must have been about seven of them, lads and girls sent out by their mams and dads for the afternoon. So we went on our bellies through the hedge like crocodiles and surrounded them, and then dashed into the middle, scattering the fire and batting their tabs and snatching up all there was to eat, then running off over Cherry Orchard fields into the wood, with a man chasing us who'd come up while we were ransacking their picnic. We got away all right, and had a good feed into the bargain, because we'd been clambed to death and couldn't wait long enough to get our chops ripping into them thin lettuce and ham sandwiches and creamy cakes.

Well, I'll always feel during every bit of my life like those daft kids should have felt before we broke them up. But they never dreamed that what happened was going to happen, just like the governor of this Borstal who spouts to us about honesty and all that wappy stuff don't know a bloody thing, while I know every minute of my life that a big boot is always likely to smash any nice picnic I might be barmy and dishonest enough to make for myself. I admit that there've been times when I've thought of telling the governor all this so as to put him on his guard, but when I've got as close as seeing him I've changed my mind, thinking to let him either find out for himself or go through the same mill as I've gone through. I'm not hard-hearted (in fact I've helped a few blokes in my time with the odd quid, lie, fag, or shelter from the rain when they've been on the run) but I'm boggered if I'm going to risk being put in the cells just for trying to give the governor a bit of advice he don't deserve. If my heart's soft I know the sort of people I'm going to save it for. And any advice I'd give the governor wouldn't do him the least bit of good; it'd only trip him up sooner than if he wasn't told at all, which I suppose is what I want to happen. But for the time being I'll let things go on as they are, which is something else I've learned in the last year or two. (It's a good job I can only think of these things as fast as I can write with this stub of pencil that's clutched in my paw, otherwise I'd have dropped the whole thing weeks ago.)

By the time I'm half-way through my morning course, when after a frost-bitten dawn I can see a phlegmy bit of sunlight hanging from the bare twigs of beech and sycamore, and when I've measured my half-way mark by the short-cut scrimmage down the steep bush-covered bank and into the sunken lane, when still there's not a soul in sight and not a sound except the neighing of a piebald foal in a cottage stable that I can't see, I get to thinking the deepest and daftest of all. The governor would have a fit if he could see me sliding down the bank because I could break my neck or ankle, but I can't not do it because it's the only risk I take and the only excitement I ever get, flying flat-out like one of them pterodactyls from the 'Lost World' I once heard on the wireless, crazy like a cut-balled cockerel, scratching myself to bits and almost letting myself go but not quite. It's the most wonderful minute because there's not one thought or word or picture of anything in my head while I'm going down. I'm empty, as empty as I was before I was born, and I don't let myself go, I suppose, because whatever it is that's farthest down inside me don't want me to die or hurt myself bad. And it's daft to think deep you know, because it gets you nowhere, though deep is what I am when I've passed this half-way mark because the long-distance run of an early morning makes me think that every run like this is a life—a little life, I know—but a life as full of misery and happiness and things happening as you can ever get really around yourself—and I remember that after a lot of these runs I thought that it didn't need much know-how to tell how a life was going to end once it had got well started. But as usual I was wrong, caught first by the cops and then by my own bad brain, I could never trust myself to fly scot-free over these traps, was always tripped up sooner or later no matter how many I got over to the good without even knowing it. Looking back I suppose them big trees put their branches to their snouts and gave each other the wink, and there I was whizzing down the bank and not seeing a bloody thing.

167

I don't say to myself: 'You shouldn't have done the job and then you'd have stayed away from Borstal'; no, what I ram into my runner-brain is that my luck had no right to scram just when I was on my way to making the coppers think I hadn't done the job after all. The time was autumn and the night foggy enough to set me and my mate Mike roaming the streets when we should have been rooted in front of the telly or stuck into a plush seat at the pictures, but I was restless after six weeks away from any sort of work, and well you might ask me why I'd been bone-idle for so long because normally I sweated my thin guts out on a milling-machine with the rest of them, but you see, my dad died from cancer of the throat, and mam collected a cool five hundred in insurance and benefits from the factory where he'd worked, 'for your bereavement,' they said, or words like that.

Now I believe, and my mam must have thought the same, that a wad of crisp blue-back fivers ain't a sight of good to a living soul unless they're flying out of your hand into some shopkeeper's till, and the shopkeeper is passing you tip-top things in exchange over the counter, so as soon as she got the money, mam took me and my five brothers and sisters out to town and got us dolled-up in new clothes. Then she ordered a twenty-one-inch telly, a new carpet because the old one was covered with blood from dad's dying and wouldn't wash out, and took a taxi home with bags of grub and a new fur coat. And do you know—you wain't believe me when I tell you—she'd still near three hundred left in her bulging handbag the next day, so how could any of us go to work after that? Poor old dad, he didn't get a look in, and he was the one who'd done the suffering and dying for such a lot of lolly.

Night after night we sat in front of the telly with a ham sandwich in one hand, a bar of chocolate in the other, and a bottle of lemonade between our boots, while mam was with some fancy-man upstairs on the new bed she'd ordered, and I'd never known a family as happy as ours was in that couple of months when we'd got all the money we needed. And when the dough ran out I didn't think about anything much, but just roamed the streets—looking for another job, I told mam—hoping I suppose to get my hands on another five hundred nicker so's the nice life we'd got used to could go on and on for ever. Because it's surprising how quick you can get used to a different life. To begin with, the adverts on the telly had shown us how much more there was in the world to buy than we'd ever dreamed of when we'd looked into shop windows but hadn't seen all there was to see because we didn't have the money to buy it anyway. And the telly made all these things seem twenty times better than we'd ever thought they were. Even adverts at the cinema were cool and tame, because now we were seeing them in private at home. We used to cock our noses up at things in shops that didn't move, but suddenly we saw their real value because they jumped and glittered around the screen and had some pasty-faced tart going head over heels to get her nail-polished grabbers on to them or her lip-stick lips over them, not like the crumby adverts you saw on posters or in newspapers as dead as doornails; these were flickering around loose, half-open packets and tins, making you think that all you had to do was finish opening them before they were yours, like seeing an unlocked safe through a shop window with the man gone away for a cup of tea without thinking to guard his lolly. The films they showed were good as well, in that way, because we couldn't get our eyes unglued from the cops chasing the robbers who had satchel-bags crammed with cash and looked like getting away to spend it—until the last moment. I always hoped they would end up free to blow the lot, and could never stop wanting to put my hand out, smash into the screen (it only looked a bit of rag-screen like at the pictures) and get the copper in a half-nelson so's he'd stop following the bloke with the money-bags. Even when he'd knocked off a couple of bank clerks I hoped he wouldn't get nabbed. In fact then I wished more than ever he wouldn't because it meant the hot-chair if he did, and I wouldn't wish that on anybody no matter what they'd done, because I'd read in a book where the hot-chair worn't a quick death at all, but that you just sat there scorching to death until you were dead. And it was when these cops were chasing the crooks that we played some good tricks with the telly, because when one of them opened his big gob to spout about getting their man I'd turn the sound down and see his mouth move like a goldfish or mackerel or a minnow mimicking what they were supposed to be acting—it was so funny the whole family nearly went into fits on the brand-new carpet that hadn't yet found its way to the bedroom. It was the best of all though when we did it to some Tory telling us about how good his government was going to be if we kept on voting for them— their slack chops rolling, opening and bumbling, hands lifting to twitch moustaches and touching their buttonholes to make sure the flower hadn't wilted, so that you could see they didn't mean a word they said, especially with not a murmur coming out because we'd cut off the sound. When the governor of the Borstal first talked to me I was reminded of those times so much that I nearly killed myself trying not to laugh. Yes, we played so many good stunts on the box of tricks that mam used to call us the Telly Boys, we got so clever at it.

My pal Mike got let off with probation because it was his first job—anyway the first they ever knew about—and because they said he would never have done it if it hadn't been for me talking him into it. They said I was a menace to honest lads like Mike—hands in his pockets so that they looked stone-empty, head bent forward as if looking for half-crowns to fill 'em with, a ripped jersey on and his hair falling into his eyes so that he could go up to women and ask them for a shilling because he was hungry—and that I was the brains behind the job, the guiding light when it came to making up anybody's mind, but I swear to God I worn't owt like that because really I ain't got no more brains than a gnat after hiding the money in the place I did. And I—being cranky like I am—got sent to Borstal because to tell you the honest truth I'd been to Remand Homes before—though that's another story and I suppose if ever I tell it it'll be just as boring as this one is. I was glad though that Mike got away with it, and I only hope he always will, not like silly bastard me.

So on this foggy night we tore ourselves away from the telly and slammed the front door behind us, setting off up our wide street like slow tugs on a river that'd broken their hooters, for we didn't know where the housefronts began what with the perishing cold mist all around. I was snatched to death without an overcoat: mam had forgotten to buy me one in the scrummage of shopping, and by the time I thought to remind her of it the dough was all gone. So we whistled 'The Teddy Boys Picnic' to keep us warm, and I told myself that I'd get a coat soon if it was the last thing I did. Mike said he thought the same about himself, adding that he'd also get some brand-new glasses with gold rims, to wear instead of the wire frames they'd given him at the school clinic years ago. He didn't twig it was foggy at first and cleaned his glasses every time I pulled him back from a lamp-post or car, but when he saw the lights on Alfreton Road looking like octopus eyes he put them in his pocket and didn't wear them again until we did the job. We hadn't got two ha-pennies between us, and though we weren't hungry we wished we'd got a bob or two when we passed the fish and chip shops because the delicious sniffs of salt and vinegar and frying fat made our mouths water. I don't mind telling you we walked the town from one end to the other and if our eyes worn't glued to the ground looking for lost wallets and watches they was swivelling around house windows and shop doors in case we saw something easy and worth nipping into.

Neither of us said as much as this to each other, but I know for a fact that that was what we was thinking. What I don't know—and as sure as I sit here I know I'll never know—is which of us was the first bastard to latch his peepers on to that baker's backyard. Oh, yes, it's all right me telling myself it was me, but the truth is that I've never known whether it was Mike or not, because I do know that I didn't see the open window until he stabbed me in the ribs and pointed it out. 'See it?' he said.

'Yes,' I told him, 'so let's get cracking.

'But what about the wall though?' he whispered, looking a bit closer.

'On your shoulders,' I chipped in.

His eyes were already up there: 'Will you be able to reach?' It was the only time he ever showed any life.

'Leave it to me,' I said, ever-ready. 'I can reach anywhere from your ham-hock shoulders.'

Mike was a nipper compared to me, but underneath the scruffy draught-board jersey he wore were muscles as hard as iron, and you wouldn't think to see him walking down the street with glasses on and hands in pockets that he'd harm a fly, but I never liked to get on the wrong side of him in a fight because he's the sort that don't say a word for weeks on end—sits plugged in front of the telly, or reads a cowboy book, or just sleeps—when suddenly BIFF—half kills somebody for almost nothing at all, such as beating him in a race for the last *Football Post* on a Saturday night, pushing in before him at a bus stop, or bumping into him when he was day-dreaming about Dolly-on-the-Tub next door. I saw him set on a bloke once for no more than fixing him in a funny way with his eyes, and it turned out that the bloke was cock-eyed but nobody knew it because he'd just that day come to live in our street. At other times none of these things would matter a bit, and I suppose the only reason why I was pals with him was because I didn't say much from one month's end to another either.

He puts his hands up in the air like he was being covered with a Gatling-Gun, and moved to the wall like he was going to be mowed down, and I climbed up him like he was a stile or step-ladder, and there he stood, the palms of his upshot maulers flat and turned out so's I could step on 'em like they was the adjustable jack-spanner under a car, not a sound of a breath nor the shiver of a flinch coming from him. I lost no time in any case, took my coat from between my teeth, chucked it up to the glass-topped wall (where the glass worn't too sharp because the jags had been worn down by years of accidental stones) and was sitting astraddle before I knew where I was. Then down the other side, with my legs rammed up into my throat when I hit the ground, the crack coming about as hard as when you fall after a high parachute drop, that one of my mates told me was like jumping off a twelve-foot wall, which this must have been. Then I picked up my bits and pieces and opened the gate for Mike, who was still grinning and full of life because the hardest part of the job was already done. 'I came, I broke, I entered,' like that clever-dick Borstal song.

I didn't think about anything at all, as usual, because I never do when I'm busy, when I'm draining pipes, looting sacks, yaling locks, lifting latches, forcing my bony hands and lanky legs into making something move, hardly feeling my lungs going in-whiff and out-whaff, not realising whether my mouth is clamped tight or gaping, whether I'm hungry, itching from scabies, or whether my flies are open and flashing dirty words like muck and spit into the late-night final fog. And when I don't know anything about all this then how can I honest-to-God say I think of anything at such times? When I'm wondering what's the best way to get a window open or how to force a door, how can I be thinking or have anything on my mind? That's what the four-eyed white-smocked bloke with the note-book couldn't understand when he asked me questions for days and days after I got to Borstal; and I couldn't explain it to him then like I'm writing it down now; and even if I'd been able to maybe he still wouldn't have caught on because I don't know whether I can understand it myself even at this moment, though I'm doing my best you can bet.

So before I knew where I was I was inside the baker's office watching Mike picking up that cash box after he'd struck a match to see where it was, wearing a tailor-made fifty-shilling grin on his square crew-cut nut as his paws closed over the box like he'd squash it to nothing. 'Out,' he suddenly said, shaking it so's it rattled. 'Let's scram.'

'Maybe there's some more,' I said, pulling half a dozen drawers out of a rollertop desk.

'No,' he said, like he'd already been twenty years in the game, 'this is the lot,' patting his tin box, 'this is it.'

I pulled out another few drawers, full of bills, books and letters. 'How do you know, you loony sod?'

He barged past me like a bull at a gate. 'Because I do.'

Right or wrong, we'd both got to stick together and do the same thing. I looked at an ever-loving babe of a brand-new typewriter, but knew it was too traceable, so blew it a kiss, and went out after him. 'Hang on,' I said, pulling the door to, 'we're in no hurry.'

'Not much we aren't,' he says over his shoulder.

'We've got months to splash the lolly,' I whispered as we crossed the yard, 'only don't let that gate creak too much or you'll have the narks tuning-in.'

'You think I'm barmy?' he said, creaking the gate so that the whole street heard.

I don't know about Mike, but now I started to think, of how we'd get back safe through the streets with that money-box up my jumper. Because he'd clapped it into my hand as soon as we'd got to the main road, which might have meant that he'd started thinking as well, which only goes to show how you don't know what's in anybody else's mind unless you think about things yourself. But as far as my thinking went at that moment it wasn't up to much, only a bit of fright that wouldn't budge not even with a hot blow-lamp, about what we'd say if a copper asked us where we were off to with that hump in my guts.

'What is it?' he'd ask, and I'd say: 'A growth.' 'What do you mean, a growth, my lad?' he'd say back, narky like. I'd cough and clutch myself like I was in the most tripe-twisting pain in the world, and screw my eyes up like I was on my way to the hospital, and Mike would take my arm like he was the best pal I'd got. 'Cancer,' I'd manage to say to Narker, which would make his slow punch-drunk brain suspect a thing or two. 'A lad of your age?' So I'd groan again, and hope to make him feel a real bully of a bastard, which would be impossible, but anyway: 'It's in the family. Dad died of it last month, and I'll die of it next month by the feel of it.' 'What, did he have it in the guts?' 'No, in the throat. But it's got me in the stomach.' Groan and cough. 'Well, you shouldn't be out like this if you've got cancer, you should be in the hospital.' I'd get ratty now: 'That's where I'm trying to go if only you'd let me and stop asking so many questions. Aren't I, Mike?' Grunt from Mike as he unslung his cosh. Then just in time the copper would tell us to get on our way, kind and considerate all of a sudden, saying that the outpatient department of the hospital closes at twelve, so hadn't he better call us a taxi? He would if we liked, he says, and he'd pay for it as well. But we tell him not to bother, that he's a good bloke even if he is a copper, that we know a short cut anyway. Then just as we're turning a corner he gets it into his big batchy head that we're going the opposite way to the hospital, and calls us back. So we'd start to run ... if you can call all that thinking.

Up in my room Mike rips open that money-box with a hammer and chisel, and before we know where we are we've got seventy-eight pounds fifteen and fourpence ha'penny *each* lying all over my bed like tea spread out on Christmas Day: cake and trifle, salad and sandwiches, jam tarts and bars of chocolate: all shared and shared alike between Mike and me because we believed in equal work and equal pay, just like the comrades my dad was in until he couldn't do a stroke anymore and had no breath left to argue with. I thought how good it was that blokes like that poor baker didn't stash all his cash in one of the big marble-fronted banks that take up every corner of the town, how lucky for us that he didn't trust them no matter how many millions of tons of concrete or how many iron bars and boxes they were made of, or how many coppers kept their blue pop-eyed peepers glued on to them, how smashing it was that he believed in money-boxes when so many shopkeepers thought it old-fashioned and tried to be modern by using a bank, which wouldn't give a couple of sincere, honest, hardworking, conscientious blokes like Mike and me a chance.

Now you'd think, and I'd think, and anybody with a bit of imagination would think, that we'd done as clean a job as could ever be done, that, with the baker's shop being at least a mile from where we lived, and with not a soul having seen us, and what with the fog and the fact that we weren't more than five minutes in the place, that the coppers should never have been able to trace us. But then, you'd be wrong, I'd be wrong, and everybody else would be wrong, no matter how much imagination was diced out between us.

Even so, Mike and I didn't splash the money about, because that would have made people think straightaway that we'd latched on to something that didn't belong to us. Which wouldn't do at all, because even in a street like ours there are people who love to do a good turn for the coppers, though I never know why they do. Some people are so mean-gutted that even if they've only got tuppence more than you and they think you're the sort that would take it if you have half the chance, they'd get you put inside if they saw you ripping lead out of a lavatory, even if it weren't their lavatory—just to keep their tuppence out of your reach. And so we didn't do anything to let on about how rich we were, nothing like going down town and coming back dressed in brand-new Teddy boy suits and carrying a set of skiffle-drums like another pal of ours who'd done a factory office about six months before. No, we took the odd bobs and pennies out and folded the notes into bundles and stuffed them up the drainpipe outside the door in the backyard. 'Nobody'll ever think of looking for it there,' I said to Mike. 'We'll keep it doggo for a week or two, then take a few quid a week out till it's all gone. We might be thieving bastards, but we're not green.'

Some days later a plain-clothes dick knocked at the door. And asked for me. I was still in bed, at eleven o'clock, and had to unroll myself from the comfortable black sheets when I heard mam calling me. 'A man to see you,' she said. 'Hurry up, or he'll be gone.'

I could hear her keeping him at the back door, nattering about how fine it had been but how it looked like rain since early this morning—and he didn't answer her except to snap out a snotty yes or no. I scrambled into my trousers and wondered why he'd come—knowing it was a copper because 'a man to see you' always meant just that in our house—and if I'd had any idea that one had gone to Mike's house as well at the same time I'd have twigged it to be because of that hundred and fifty quid's worth of paper stuffed up the drainpipe outside the back door about ten inches away from that plain-clothed copper's boot, where mam still talked to him thinking she was doing me a favour, and I wishing to God she'd ask him in, though on second thoughts realising that that would seem more suspicious than keeping him outside, because they know we hate their guts and smell a rat if they think we're trying to be nice to them. Mam wasn't born yesterday, I thought, thumping my way down the creaking stairs.

I'd seen him before: Borstal Bernard in nicky-hat, Remand Home Ronald in rowing-boat boots, Probation Pete in a pit-prop mackintosh, three-months clink in collar and tie (all this out of a Borstal skiffle-ballad that my new mate made up, and I'd tell you it in full but it doesn't belong in this story), a 'tec who'd never had as much in his pockets as that drainpipe had up its jackses. He was like Hitler in the face, right down to the paint-brush tash, except that being six-foot tall made him seem worse. But I straightened my shoulders to look into his illiterate blue eyes—like I always do with any copper.

Then he started asking me questions, and my mother from behind said: 'He's never left that television set for the last three months, so you've got nowt on him, mate. You might as well look for somebody else, because you're wasting the rates you get out of my rent and the income-tax that comes out of my pay-packet standing there like that'—which was a laugh because she'd never paid either to my knowledge, and never would, I hoped.

'Well, you know where Papplewick Street is, don't you?' the copper asked me, taking no notice of mam.

'Ain't it off Alfreton Road?' I asked him back, helpful and bright.

'You know there's a baker's half-way down on the left-hand side, don't you?'

'Ain't it next door to a pub, then?' I wanted to know.

He answered me sharp: 'No, it bloody well ain't.' Coppers always lose their tempers as quick as this, and more often than not they gain nothing by it. 'Then I don't know it,' I told him, saved by the bell.

He slid his big boot round and round on the doorstep. 'Where were you last Friday night?' Back in the ring, but this was worse than a boxing match.

I didn't like him trying to accuse me of something he wasn't sure I'd done. 'Was I at that baker's you mentioned? Or in the pub next door?'

'You'll get five years in Borstal if you don't give me a straight answer,' he said, unbuttoning his mac even though it was cold where he was standing.

'I was glued to the telly, like mam says,' I swore blind. But he went on and on with his looney questions: 'Have you got a television?'

The things he asked wouldn't have taken in a kid of two, and what else could I say to the last one except: 'Has the aerial fell down? Or would you like to come in and see it?'

He was liking me even less for saying that. 'We know you weren't listening to the television set last Friday, and so do you, don't you?'

'P'raps not, but I was *looking* at it, because sometimes we turn the sound down for a bit of fun.' I could hear mam laughing from the kitchen, and I hoped Mike's mam was doing the same if the cops had gone to him as well.

'We know you weren't in the house,' he said, starting up again, cranking himself with the handle. They always say 'We' 'We', never 'I' 'I'—as if they feel braver and righter knowing there's a lot of them against only one.

'I've got witnesses,' I said to him. 'Mam for one. Her fancy-man, for two. Ain't that enough? I can get you a dozen, more, or thirteen altogether, if it was a baker's that got robbed.'

'I don't want no lies,' he said, not catching on about the baker's dozen. Where do they scrape cops from anyway? 'All I want is to get from you where you put that money.'

Don't get mad, I kept saying to myself, don't get mad—hearing mam setting out cups and saucers and putting the pan on the stove for bacon. I stood back and waved him inside like I was a butler. 'Come and search the house. If you've got a warrant.'

'Listen, my lad,' he said, like the dirty bullying jumped-up bastard he was, 'I don't want too much of your lip, because if we get you down to the Guildhall you'll get a few bruises and black-eyes for your trouble.' And I knew he wasn't kidding either, because I'd heard about all them sort of tricks. I hoped one day though that him and all his pals would be the ones to get the black-eyes and kicks; you never knew. It might come sooner than anybody thinks, like in Hungary. 'Tell me where the money is, and I'll get you off with probation.'

'What money?' I asked him, because I'd heard that one before as well.

'You know what money.'

'Do I look as though I'd know owt about money?' I said, pushing my fist through a hole in my shirt.

'The money that was pinched, that you know all about,' he said. 'You can't trick me, so it's no use trying.'

'Was it three-and-eightpence ha'penny?' I asked.

'You thieving young bastard. We'll teach you to steal money that doesn't belong to you.'

I turned my head around: 'Mam,' I called out, 'get my lawyer on the blower, will you?'

'Clever, aren't you?' he said in a very unfriendly way, 'but we won't rest until we clear all this up.'

'Look,' I pleaded, as if about to sob my socks off because he'd got me wrong, 'it's all very well us talking like this, it's like a game almost, but I wish you'd tell me what it's all about, because honest-to-God I've just got out of bed and here you are at the door talking about me having pinched a lot of money, money that I don't know anything about.'

He swung around now as if he'd trapped me, though I couldn't see why he might think so. 'Who said anything about money? I didn't. What made you bring money into this little talk we're having?'

'It's you,' I answered, thinking he was going barmy, and about to start foaming at the chops, 'you've got money on the brain, like all policemen. Baker's shops as well.'

He screwed his face up. 'I want an answer from you: where's that money?'

But I was getting fed-up with all this. 'I'll do a deal.'

Judging by his flash-bulb face he thought he was suddenly on to a good thing. 'What sort of a deal?'

So I told him: 'I'll give you all the money I've got, one and fourpence ha'penny, if you stop this third-degree and let me go in and get my breakfast. Honest, I'm clambed to death. I ain't had a bite since yesterday. Can't you hear my guts rollin'?'

His jaw dropped, but on he went, pumping me for another half hour. A routine check-up, as they say on the pictures. But I knew I was winning on points.

Then he left, but came back in the afternoon to search the house. He didn't find a thing, not a French farthing. He asked me questions again and I didn't tell him anything except lies, lies, lies, because I can go on doing that forever without batting an eyelid. He'd got nothing on me and we both of us knew it, otherwise I'd have been down at the Guildhall in no time, but he kept on keeping on because I'd been in a Remand Home for a high-wall job before; and Mike was put through the same mill because all the local cops knew he was my best pal.

When it got dark me and Mike were in our parlour with a low light on and the telly off, Mike taking it easy in the rocking chair and me slouched out on the settee, both of us puffing a packet of Woods. With the door bolted and curtains drawn we talked about the dough we'd crammed up the drainpipe. Mike thought we should take it out and both of us do a bunk to Skegness or Cleethorpes for a good time in the arcades, living like lords in a boarding house near the pier, then at least we'd both have had a big beano before getting sent down.

'Listen, you daft bleeder,' I said, 'we aren't going to get caught at all, *and* we'll have a good time, later.' We were so clever we didn't even go out to the pictures, though we wanted to.

In the morning old Hitler-face questioned me again, with one of his pals this time, and the next day they came, trying as hard as they could to get something out of me, but I didn't budge an inch. I know I'm showing off when I say this, but in me he'd met his match, and I'd never give in to questions no matter how long it was kept up. They searched the house a couple of times as well, which made me think they thought they really had something to go by, but I know now that they hadn't, and that it was all buckshee speculation. They turned the house upside down and inside out like an old sock, went from top to bottom and front to back but naturally didn't find a thing. The copper even poked his face up the front-room chimney (that hadn't been used or swept for years) and came down looking like Al Jolson so that he had to swill himself clean at the scullery sink. They kept tapping and pottering around the big aspidistra plant that grandma had left to mam, lifting it up from the table to look under the cloth, putting it aside so's they could move the table and get at the boards under the rug—but the big headed stupid ignorant bastards never once thought of emptying the soil out of the plant pot, where they'd have found the crumpled-up money-box that we'd buried the night we did the job. I suppose it's still there, now I think about it, and I suppose mam wonders now and again why the plant don't prosper like it used to—as if it could with a fistful of thick black tin lapped around its guts.

The last time he knocked at our door was one wet morning at five minutes to nine and I was sleep-logged in my crumby bed as usual. Mam had gone to work that day so I shouted for him to hold on a bit, and then went down to see who it was. There he stood, six-feet tall and sopping wet, and for the first time in my life I did a spiteful thing I'll never forgive myself for: I didn't ask him to come in out of the rain, because I wanted him to get double pneumonia and die. I suppose he could have pushed by me and come in if he'd wanted, but maybe he'd got used to asking questions on the doorstep and didn't want to be put off by changing his ground even though it was raining. Not that I don't like being spiteful because of any barmy principle I've got, but this bit of spite, as it turned out, did me no good at all. I should have treated him as a brother I hadn't seen for twenty years and dragged him in for a cup of tea and a fag, told him about the picture I hadn't seen the night before, asked him how his wife was after her operation and whether they'd shaved her moustache off to make it, and then sent him happy and satisfied out by the front door. But no, I thought, let's see what he's got to say for himself now.

He stood a little to the side of the door, either because it was less wet there, or because he wanted to see me from a different angle, perhaps having found it monotonous to watch a bloke's face always telling lies from the same side. 'You've been identified,' he said, twitching raindrops from his tash. 'A woman saw you and your mate yesterday and she swears blind you are the same chaps she saw going into that bakery.'

I was dead sure he was still bluffing, because Mike and I hadn't even seen each other the day before, but I looked worried. 'She's a menace then to innocent people, whoever she is, because the only bakery I've been in lately is the one up our street to get some cut-bread on tick for mam.'

He didn't bite on this. 'So now I want to know where the money is'—as if I hadn't answered him at all.

'I think mam took it to work this morning to get herself some tea in the canteen.' Rain was splashing down so hard I thought he'd get washed away if he didn't come inside. But I wasn't much bothered, and went on: 'I remember I put it in the telly-vase last night—it was my only one-and-three and I was saving it for a packet of tips this morning—and I nearly had a jibbering black fit just now when I saw it had gone. I was reckoning on it for getting me through today because I don't think life's worth living without a fag, do you?'

I was getting into my stride and began to feel good, twigging that this would be my last pack of lies, and that if I kept it up for long enough this time I'd have the bastards beat: Mike and me would be off to the coast in a few weeks time having the fun of our lives, playing at penny football and latching on to a couple of tarts that would give us all they were good for. 'And this weather's no good for picking-up fag-ends in the street,' I said, 'because they'd be sopping wet. Course, I know you could dry 'em out near the fire, but it don't taste the same you know, all said and done. Rainwater does summat to 'em that don't bear thinkin' about: it turns 'em back into hoss-tods without the taste though.'

I began to wonder, at the back of my brainless eyes, why old copper-lugs didn't pull me up sharp and say he hadn't got time to listen to all this, but he wasn't looking at me anymore, and all my thoughts about Skegness went bursting to smithereens in my sludgy loaf. I could have dropped into the earth when I saw what he'd fixed his eyes on.

He was looking at *it*, an ever-loving fiver, and I could only jabber: 'The one thing is to have some real fags because new hoss-tods is always better than stuff that's been rained on and dried, and I know how you feel about not being able to find money because one-and-three's one-and-three in anybody's pocket, and naturally if I see it knocking around I'll get you on the blower tomorrow straightaway and tell you where you can find it.'

I thought I'd go down in a fit: three green-backs as well had been washed down by the water, and more were following, lying flat at first after their fall, then getting tilted at the corners by wind and rainspots as if they were alive and wanted to get back into the dry snug drainpipe out of the terrible weather, and you can't imagine how I wished they'd be able to. Old Hitler-face didn't know what to make of it but just kept staring down and down, and I thought I'd better keep on talking, though I knew it wasn't much good now.

'It's a fact, I know, that money's hard to come by and half-crowns don't get found on bus seats or in dustbins, and I didn't see any in bed last night because I'd 'ave known about it, wouldn't I? You can't sleep with things like that in the bed because they're too hard, and anyway at first they're....' It took Hitler-boy a long time to catch on; they were beginning to spread over the yard a bit, reinforced by the third colour of a ten-bob note, before his hand clamped itself on to my shoulder.

## THREE

The pop-eyed potbellied governor said to a pop-eyed pot-bellied Member of Parliament who sat next to his pop-eyed potbellied whore of a wife that I was his only hope for getting the Borstal Blue Ribbon Prize Cup For Long Distance Cross Country Running (All England), which I was, and it set me laughing to myself inside, and I didn't say a word to any potbellied pop-eyed bastard that might give them real hope, though I knew the governor anyway took my quietness to mean he'd got that cup already stuck on the bookshelf in his office among the few other mildewed trophies.

'He might take up running in a sort of professional way when he gets out,' and it wasn't until he'd said this and I'd heard it with my own flap-tabs that I realised it might be possible to do such a thing, run for money, trot for wages on piece work at a bob a puff rising bit by bit to a guinea a gasp and retiring through old age at thirty-two because of lace-curtain lungs, a football heart, and legs like varicose bean-stalks. But I'd have a wife and car and get my grinning long-distance clock in the papers and have a smashing secretary to answer piles of letters sent by tarts who'd mob me when they saw who I was as I pushed my way into Woolworth's for a packet of razor blades and a cup of tea. It was something to think about all right, and sure enough the governor knew he'd got me when he said, turning to me as if I would at any rate have to be consulted about it all: 'How does this matter strike you, then, Smith, my lad?'

A line of potbellied pop-eyes gleamed at me and a row of goldfish mouths opened and wiggled gold teeth at me, so I gave them the answer they wanted because I'd hold my trump card until later. 'It'd suit me fine, sir,' I said.

'Good lad. Good show. Right spirit. Splendid.'

'Well,' the governor said, 'get that cup for us today and I'll do all I can for you. I'll get you trained so that you whack every man in the Free World.' And I had a picture in my brain of me running and beating everybody in the world, leaving them all behind until only I was trot-trotting across a big wide moor alone, doing a marvellous speed as I ripped between boulders and reed-clumps, when suddenly: CRACK! CRACK!—bullets that can go faster than any man running, coming from a copper's rifle planted in a tree, winged me and split my gizzard in spite of my perfect running, and down I fell.

The potbellies expected me to say something else. 'Thank you, sir,' I said.

Told to go, I trotted down the pavilion steps, out on to the field because the big cross-country was about to begin and the two entries from Gunthorpe had fixed themselves early at the starting line and were ready to move off like white kangaroos. The sports ground looked a treat: with big tea-tents all round and flags flying and seats for families—empty because no mam or dad had known what opening day meant—and boys still running heats for the hundred yards, and lords and ladies walking from stall to stall, and the Borstal Boys Brass Band in blue uniforms; and up on the stands the brown jackets of Hucknall as well as our own grey blazers, and then the Gunthorpe lot with shirt sleeves rolled. The blue sky was full of sunshine and it couldn't have been a better day, and all of the big show was like something out of Ivanhoe that we'd seen on the pictures a few days before.

'Come on, Smith,' Roach the sports master called to me, 'we don't want you to be late for the big race, eh? Although I dare say you'd catch them up if you were.' The others catcalled and grunted at this, but I took no notice and placed myself between Gunthorpe and one of the Aylesham trusties, dropped on my knees and plucked a few grass blades to suck on the way round. So the big race it was, for them, watching from the grandstand under a fluttering Union Jack, a race for the governor, that he had been waiting for, and I hoped he and all the rest of his pop-eyed gang were busy placing big bets on me, hundred to one to win, all the money they had in their pockets, all the wages they were going to get for the next five years, and the more they placed the happier I'd be. Because here was a dead cert going to die on the big name they'd built for him, going to go down dying with laughter whether it choked him or not. My knees felt the cool soil pressing into them, and out of my eye's corner I saw Roach lift his hand. The Gunthorpe boy twitched before the signal was given; somebody cheered too soon; Medway bent forward; then the gun went, and I was away.

We went once around the field and then along a half-mile drive of elms, being cheered all the way, and I seemed to feel I was in the lead as we went out by the gate and into the lane, though I wasn't interested enough to find out. The five-mile course was marked by splashes of whitewash gleaming on gateposts and trunks and stiles and stones, and a boy with a waterbottle and bandage-box stood every half-mile waiting for those that dropped out or fainted. Over the first stile, without trying, I was still nearly in the lead but one; and if any of you want tips about running, never be in a hurrry, and never let any of the other runners know you are in a hurry even if you are. You can always overtake on long-distance running without letting the others smell the hurry in you; and when you've used your craft like this to reach the two or three up front then you can do a big dash later that puts everybody else's hurry in the shade because you've not had to make haste up till then. I ran to a steady jog-trot rhythm, and soon it was so smooth that I forgot I was running, and I was hardly able to know that my legs were lifting and falling and my arms going in and out, and my lungs didn't seem to be working at all, and my heart stopped that wicked thumping I always get at the beginning of a run. Because you see I never race at all; I just run, and somehow I know that if I forget I'm racing and only jog-trot along until I don't know I'm running I always win the race. For when my eyes recognise that I'm getting near the end of the course—by seeing a stile or cottage corner—I put on a spurt, and such a fast big spurt it is because I feel that up till then I haven't been running and that I've used up no energy at all. And I've been able to do this because I've been thinking; and I wonder if I'm the only one in the running business with this system of forgetting that I'm running because I'm too busy thinking; and I wonder if any of the other lads are on to the same lark, though I know for a fact that they aren't. Off like the wind along the cobbled footpath and rutted lane, smoother than the flat grass track on the field and better for thinking because it's not too smooth, and I was in my element that afternoon knowing that nobody could beat me at running but intending to beat myself before the day was over. For when the governor talked to me of being honest when I first came in he didn't know what the word meant or he wouldn't have had me here in this race, trotting along in shimmy and shorts and sunshine. He'd have had me where I'd have had him if I'd been in his place: in a quarry breaking rocks until he broke his back. At least old Hitler-face the plain-clothes dick was honester than the governor, because he at any rate had had it in for me and I for him, and when my case was coming up in court a copper knocked at our front door at four o'clock in the morning and got my mother out of bed when she was paralytic tired, reminding her she had to be in court at dead on half past nine. It was the finest bit of spite I've ever heard of, but I would call it honest, the same as my mam's words were honest when she really told that copper what she thought of him and called him all the dirty names she'd ever heard of, which took her half an hour and woke the terrace up.

I trotted on along the edge of a field bordered by the sunken lane, smelling green grass and honeysuckle, and I felt as though I came from a long line of whippets trained to run on two legs, only I couldn't see a toy rabbit in front and there wasn't a collier's cosh behind to make me keep up the pace. I passed the Gunthorpe runner whose shimmy was already black with sweat and I could just see the corner of the fenced-up copse in front where the only man I had to pass to win the race was going all out to gain the half-way mark. Then he turned into a tongue of trees and bushes where I couldn't see him anymore, and I couldn't see anybody, and I knew what the loneliness of the long-distance runner running across country felt like, realising that as far as I was concerned this feeling was the only honesty and realness there was in the world and I knowing it would be no different ever, no matter what I felt at odd times, and no matter what anybody else tried to tell me. The runner behind me must have been a long way off because it was so quiet, and there was even less noise and movement than there had been at five o'clock of a frosty winter morning. It was hard to understand, and all I knew was that you had to run, run, run, without knowing why you were running, but on you went through fields you didn't understand and into woods that made you afraid, over hills without knowing you'd been up and down, and shooting across streams that would have cut the heart out of you had you fallen into them. And the winning post was no end to it, even though crowds might be cheering you in, because on you had to go before you got your breath back, and the only time you stopped really was when you tripped over a tree trunk and broke your neck or fell into a disused well and stayed dead in the darkness forever. So I thought: they aren't going to get me on this racing lark, this running and trying to win, this jog-trotting for a bit of blue ribbon, because it's not the way to go on at all, though they swear blind that it is. You should think about nobody and go your own way, not on a course marked out for you by people holding mugs of water and bottles of iodine in case you fall and cut yourself so that they can pick you up—even if you want to stay where you are—and get you moving again.

On I went, out of the wood, passing the man leading without knowing I was going to do so. Flip-flap, flip-flap, jog-trot, jog-trot, crunchslap-crunchslap, across the middle of a broad field again, rhythmically running in my greyhound effortless fashion, knowing I had won the race though it wasn't half over, won it if I wanted it, could go on for ten or fifteen or twenty miles if I had to and drop dead at the finish of it, which would be the same, in the end, as living an honest life like the governor wanted me to. It amounted to: win the race and be honest, and on trot-trotting I went, having the time of my life, loving my progress because it did me good and set me thinking which by now I liked to do, but not caring at all when I remembered that I had to win this race as well as run it. One of the two, I had to win the race or run it, and I knew I could do both because my legs had carried me well in front—now coming to the short cut down the bramble bank and over the sunken road—and would carry me further because they seemed made of electric cable and easily alive to keep on slapping at those ruts and roots, but I'm not going to win because the only way I'd see I came in first would be if winning meant that I was going to escape the coppers after doing the biggest bank job of my life, but winning means the exact opposite, no matter how they try to kill or kid me, means running right into their white-gloved wall-barred hands and grinning mugs and staying there for the rest of my natural long life of stone-breaking anyway, but stone-breaking in the way I want to do it and not in the way they tell me.

Another honest thought that comes is that I could swing left at the next hedge of the field, and under its cover beat my slow retreat away from the sports ground winning post. I could do three or six or a dozen miles across the turf like this and cut a few main roads behind me so's they'd never know which one I'd taken; and maybe on the last one when it got dark I could thumb a lorry-lift and get a free ride north with somebody who might not give me away. But no, I said I wasn't daft didn't I? I won't pull out with only six months left, and besides there's nothing I want to dodge and run away from; I only want a bit of my own back on the In-laws and Potbellies by letting them sit up there on their big posh seats and watch me lose this race, though as sure as God made me I know that when I do lose I'll get the dirtiest crap and kitchen jobs in the months to go before my time is up. I won't be worth a threpp'ny-bit to anybody here, which will be all the thanks I get for being honest in the only way I know. For when the governor told me to be honest it was meant to be in his way not mine, and if I kept on being honest in the way he wanted and won my race for him he'd see I got the cushiest six months still left to run; but in my own way, well, it's not allowed, and if I find a way of doing it such as I've got now then I'll get what-for in every mean trick he can set his mind to. And if you look at it in my way, who can blame them? For this is war—and ain't I said so?—and when I hit him in the only place he knows he'll be sure to get his own back on me for not collaring that cup when his heart's been set for ages on seeing himself standing up at the end of the afternoon to clap me on the back as I take the cup from Lord Earwig or some such chinless wonder with a name like that. And so I'll hit him where it hurts a lot, and he'll do all he can to get his own back, tit for tat, though I'll enjoy it most because I'm hitting first, and because I planned it longer. I don't know why I think these thoughts are better than any I've ever had, but I do, and I don't care why. I suppose it took me a long time to get going on all this because I've had no time and peace in all my bandit life, and now my thoughts are coming pat and the only trouble is I often can't stop, even when my brain feels as if it's got cramp, frostbite and creeping paralysis all rolled into one and I have to give it a rest by slap-dashing down through the brambles of the sunken lane. And all this is another uppercut I'm getting in first at people like the governor, to show how—if I can—his races are never won even though some bloke always comes unknowingly in first, how in the end the governor is going to be doomed while blokes like me will take the pickings of his roasted bones and dance like maniacs around his Borstal's ruins. And so this story's like the race and once again I won't bring off a winner to suit the governor; no, I'm being honest like he told me to, without him knowing what he means, though I don't suppose he'll ever come in with a story of his own, even if he reads this one of mine and knows who I'm talking about.

I've just come up out of the sunken lane, kneed and elbowed, thumped and bramble-scratched, and the race is two-thirds over, and a voice is going like a wireless in my mind saying that when you've had enough of feeling good like the first man on earth of a frosty morning, and you've known how it is to be taken bad like the last man on earth on a summer's afternoon, then you get at last to being like the only man on earth and don't give a bogger about either good or bad, but just trot on with your slippers slapping the good dry soil that at least would never do you a bad turn. Now the words are like coming from a crystal-set that's broken down, and something's happening inside the shell-case of my guts that bothers me and I don't know why or what to blame it on, a grinding near my ticker as though a bag of rusty screws is loose inside me and I shake them up every time I trot forward. Now and again I break my rhythm to feel my left shoulder-blade by swinging a right hand across my chest as if to rub the knife away that has somehow got stuck there. But I know it's nothing to bother about, that more likely it's caused by too much thinking that now and again I take for worry. For sometimes I'm the greatest worrier in the world I think (as you twigged I'll bet from me having got this story out) which is funny anyway because my mam don't know the meaning of the word so I don't take after her; though dad had a hard time of worry all his life up to when he filled his bedroom with hot blood and kicked the bucket that morning when nobody was in the house. I'll never forget it, straight I won't, because I was the one that found him and I often wished I hadn't. Back from a session on the fruit-machines at the fish-and-chip shop, jingling my three-lemon loot to a nail-dead house, as soon as I got in I knew something was wrong, stood leaning my head against the cold mirror above the mantelpiece trying not to open my eyes and see my stone-cold clock—because I knew I'd gone as white as a piece of chalk since coming in as if I'd been got at by a Dracula-vampire and even my penny-pocket winnings kept quiet on purpose.

Gunthorpe nearly caught me up. Birds were singing from the briar hedge, and a couple of thrushes flew like lightning into some thorny bushes. Corn had grown high in the next field and would be cut down soon with scythes and mowers; but I never wanted to notice much while running in case it put me off my stroke, so by the haystack I decided to leave it all behind and put on such a spurt, in spite of nails in my guts, that before long I'd left both Gunthorpe and the birds a good way off; I wasn't far now from going into that last mile and a half like a knife through magarine, but the quietness I suddenly trotted into between two pickets was like opening my eyes underwater and looking at the pebbles on a stream bottom, reminding me again of going back that morning to the house in which my old man had croaked, which is funny because I hadn't thought about it at all since it happened and even then I didn't brood much on it. I wonder why? I suppose that since I started to think on these long-distance runs I'm liable to have anything crop up and pester at my tripes and innards, and now that I see my bloody dad behind each grass-blade in my barmy runner-brain I'm not so sure I like to think and that it's such a good thing after all. I choke my phlegm and keep on running anyway and curse the Borstal-builders and their athletics—flappity-flap, slop-slop, crunchslap-crunch-slap-crunchslap—who've maybe got their own back on me from the bright beginning by sliding magic-lantern slides into my head that never stood a chance before. Only if I take whatever comes like this in my runner's stride can I keep on keeping on like my old self and beat them back; and now I've thought on this far I know I'll win, in the crunchslap end. So anyway after a bit I went upstairs one step at a time not thinking anything about how I should find dad and what I'd do when I did. But now I'm making up for it by going over the rotten life mam led him ever since I can remember, knocking-on with different men even when he was alive and fit and she not caring whether he knew it or not, and most of the time he wasn't so blind as she thought and cursed and roared and threatened to punch her tab, and I had to stand up to stop him even though I knew she deserved it. What a life for all of us. Well, I'm not grumbling, because if I did I might just as well win this bleeding race, which I'm not going to do, though if I don't lose speed I'll win it before I know where I am, and then where would I be?

Now I can hear the sportsground noise and music as I head back for the flags and the lead-in drive, the fresh new feel of underfoot gravel going against the iron muscles of my legs. I'm nowhere near puffed despite that bag of nails that rattles as much as ever, and I can still give a big last leap like gale-force wind if I want to, but everything is under control and I know now that there ain't another long-distance cross-country running runner in England to touch my speed and style. Our doddering bastard of a governor, our half-dead gangrened gaffer is hollow like an empty petrol drum, and he wants me and my running life to give him glory, to put in him blood and thobbing veins he never had, wants his potbellied pals to be his witnesses as I gasp and stagger up to his winning post so's he can say: 'My Borstal gets that cup, you see. I win my bet, because it pays to be honest and try to gain the prizes I offer to my lads, and they know it, have known it all along. They'll always be honest now, because I made them so.' And his pals will think: 'He trains his lads to live right, after all; he deserves a medal but we'll get him made a Sir'—and at this very moment as the birds come back to whistling I can tell myself I'll never care a sod what any of the chinless spineless In-laws think or say. They've seen me and they're cheering now and loudspeakers set around the field like elephant's ears are spreading out the big news that I'm well in the lead, and can't do anything else but stay there. But I'm still thinking of the Out-law death my dad died, telling the doctors to scat from the house when they wanted him to finish up in hospital (like a bleeding guinea-pig, he raved at them). He got up in bed to throw them out and even followed them down the stairs in his shirt though he was no more than skin and stick. They tried to tell him he'd want some drugs but he didn't fall for it, and only took the pain-killer that mam and I got from a herb-seller in the next street. It's not till now that I know what guts he had, and when I went into the room that morning he was lying on his stomach with the clothes thrown back, looking like a skinned rabbit, his grey head resting just on the edge of the bed, and on the floor must have been all the blood he'd had in his body, right from his toe-nails up, for nearly all of the lino and carpet was covered in it, thin and pink.

And down the drive I went, carrying a heart blocked up like Boulder Dam across my arteries, the nail-bag clamped down tighter and tighter as though in a woodwork vice, yet with my feet like birdwings and arms like talons ready to fly across the field except that I didn't want to give anybody that much of a show, or win the race by accident. I smell the hot dry day now as I run towards the end, passing a mountain-heap of grass emptied from cans hooked on to the fronts of lawnmowers pushed by my pals; I rip a piece of tree-bark with my fingers and stuff it in my mouth, chewing wood and dust and maybe maggots as I run until I'm nearly sick, yet swallowing what I can of it just the same because a little birdie whistled to me that I've got to go on living for at least a bloody sight longer yet but that for six months I'm not going to smell that grass or taste that dusty bark or trot this lovely path. I hate to have to say this but something bloody-well made me cry, and crying is a thing I haven't bloody-well done since I was a kid of two or three. Because I'm slowing down now for Gunthorpe to catch me up, and I'm doing it in a place just where the drive turns in to the sportsfield—where they can see what I'm doing, especially the governor and his gang from the grandstand, and I'm going so slow I'm almost marking time. Those on the nearest seats haven't caught on yet to what's happening and are still cheering like mad ready for when I make that mark, and I keep on wondering when the bleeding hell Gunthorpe behind me is going to nip by on the field because I can't hold this up all day, and I think Oh Christ it's just my rotten luck that Gunthorpe's dropped out and that I'll be here for half an hour before the next bloke comes up, but even so, I say, I won't budge, I won't go for that last hundred yards if I have to sit down cross-legged on the grass and have the governor and his chinless wonders pick me up and carry me there, which is against their rules so you can bet they'd never do it because they're not clever enough to break the rules—like I would be in their place—even though they are their own. No, I'll show him what honesty means if it's the last thing I do, though I'm sure he'll never understand because if he and all them like him did it'd mean they'd be on my side which is impossible. By God I'll stick this out like my dad stuck out his pain and kicked them doctors down the stairs: if he had guts for that then I've got guts for this and here I stay waiting for Gunthorpe or Aylesham to bash that turf and go right slap-up against that bit of clothes-line stretched across the winning post. As for me, the only time I'll hit that clothes-line will be when I'm dead and a comfortable coffin's been got ready on the other side. Until then I'm a long-distance runner, crossing country all on my own no matter how bad it feels.

The Essex boys were shouting themselves blue in the face telling me to get a move on, waving their arms, standing up and making as if to run at that rope themselves because they were only a few yards to the side of it. You cranky lot, I thought, stuck at that winning post, and yet I knew they didn't mean what they were shouting, were really on my side and always would be, not able to keep their maulers to themselves, in and out of cop-shops and clink. And there they were now having the time of their lives letting themselves go in cheering me which made the governor think they were heart and soul on his side when he wouldn't have thought any such thing if he'd had a grain of sense. And I could hear the lords and ladies now from the grandstand, and could see them standing up to wave me in: 'Run!' they were shouting in their posh voices. 'Run!' But I was deaf, daft and blind, and stood where I was, still tasting the bark in my mouth and still blubbing like a baby, blubbing now out of gladness that I'd got them beat at last.

Because I heard a roar and saw the Gunthorpe gang throwing their coats up in the air and I felt the pat-pat of feet on the drive behind me getting closer and closer and suddenly a smell of sweat and a pair of lungs on their last gasp passed me by and went swinging on towards that rope, all shagged out and rocking from side to side, grunting like a Zulu that didn't know any better, like the ghost of me at ninety when I'm heading for that fat upholstered coffin. I could have cheered him myself: 'Go on, go on, get cracking. Knot yourself up on that piece of tape.' But he was already there, and so I went on, trot-trotting after him until I got to the rope, and collapsed, with a murderous sounding roar going up through my ears while I was still on the wrong side of it.

It's about time to stop; though don't think I'm not still running, because I am, one way or another. The governor at Borstal proved me right; he didn't respect my honesty at all; not that I expected him to, or tried to explain it to him, but if he's supposed to be educated then he should have more or less twigged it. He got his own back right enough, or thought he did, because he had me carting dustbins about every morning from the big full-working kitchen to the garden-bottoms where I had to empty them; and in the afternoon I spread out slops over spuds and carrots growing in the allotments. In the evenings I scrubbed floors, miles and miles of them. But it wasn't a bad life for six months, which was another thing he could never understand and would have made it grimmer if he could, and it was worth it when I look back on it, considering all the thinking I did, and the fact that the boys caught on to me losing the race on purpose and never had enough good words to say about me, or curses to throw out (to themselves) at the governor.

The work didn't break me; if anything it made me stronger in many ways, and the governor knew, when I left, that his spite had got him nowhere. For since leaving Borstal they tried to get me in the army, but I didn't pass the medical and I'll tell you why. No sooner was I out, after that final run and six-months hard, that I went down with pleurisy, which means as far as I'm concerned that I lost the governor's race all right, and won my own twice over, because I know for certain that if I hadn't raced my race I wouldn't have got this pleurisy, which keeps me out of khaki but doesn't stop me doing the sort of work my itchy fingers want to do.

I'm out now and the heat's switched on again, but the rats haven't got me for the last big thing I pulled. I counted six hundred and twenty-eight pounds and I am still living off it because I did the job all on my own, and after it I had the peace to write all this, and it'll be money enough to keep me going until I finish my plans for doing an even bigger snatch, something up my sleeve I wouldn't tell to a living soul. I worked out my systems and hiding-places while pushing scrubbing-brushes around them Borstal floors, planned my outward life of innocence and honest work, yet at the same time grew perfect in the razor-edges of my craft for what I knew I had to do once free; and what I'll do again if netted by the poaching coppers.

In the meantime (as they say in one or two books I've read since, useless though because all of them ended on a winning post and didn't teach me a thing) I'm going to give this story to a pal of mine and tell him that if I do get captured again by the coppers he can try and get it put into a book or something, because I'd like to see the governor's face when he reads it, if he does, which I don't suppose he will; even if he did read it though I don't think he'd know what it was all about. And if I don't get caught the bloke I give this story to will never give me away; he's lived in our terrace for as long as I can remember, and he's my pal. That I do know.

# INTRODUCTION
## by
DAVID ELLOWAY

# INTRODUCTION

Both *Billy Liar* and *The Loneliness of the Long-distance Runner* were published in 1959, the latter being the longest of a collection of short stories to which it gave its name. Previously, in 1957, Waterhouse had published *There is a Happy Land*, a sensitive study of childhood in a northern industrial town, and *Jubb* followed in 1963. Sillitoe's first novel, *Saturday Night and Sunday Morning*, caused a considerable stir when it appeared in 1958 because of its grimly realistic portrayal of one side of working-class life, and he has subsequently published *Key to the Door*, *The General*, and a volume of poetry, *The Rats and Other Poems*.

Both writers have an intimate knowledge of the working- or lower-middle-class provincial life that they describe. Waterhouse was born in Leeds, the son of a greengrocer. He left school at the age of fifteen and, like Billy Fisher, was for a time clerk in an undertaker's office—one of various jobs he tried before becoming a journalist. Sillitoe was the son of a labourer in a Nottingham bicycle factory and after leaving school at fourteen he too worked in a bicycle factory, as do Arthur Seaton and his father in *Saturday Night and Sunday Morning*. He was called up in the R.A.F. and while on service in Malaya contracted tuberculosis. He began to write during the year he spent in hospital and has since made writing his career.

Sillitoe and Waterhouse are only two of a group of authors concerned with working-class life whose first books appeared at about this time. Stan Barstow, the son of a Yorkshire coalminer, published *A Kind of Loving* in 1960, and John Braine, the son of a sewage works inspector and also a Yorkshireman, published his first novel, *Room at the Top*, in 1957. They all achieved a wide popularity; both the last two novels mentioned, as well as *Saturday Night and Sunday Morning* and the two stories in this volume, have been turned into sucessful films. Even more striking was the impact of working-class writers on the theatre, often with the support of the Royal Court Theatre or Joan Littlewood's East End Theatre Workshop. It seemed sometimes as if nearly all the more exciting new plays were being written by such authors as Harold Pinter, who came from the East End Jewish community and began to write for the theatre in 1957; Arnold Wesker, a former plumber's mate and kitchen porter, or Shelagh Delaney, 'failed 11-plus' and employee in an engineering works, both of whom had their first plays produced in 1958.

A decade before—in 1945—the first really effective Labour Government had been elected and had set out to destroy the remaining class barriers. The social changes since the war provide the background for many of these books and plays, but—surprisingly perhaps—are often regarded with little enthusiasm. These writers are concerned less with social reform than with people, and with the effect on them of the changes that had already taken place. Wesker's theme is the undermining of pre-war socialist idealism by post-war prosperity, Sillitoe's heroes defiantly refuse to accept the new opportunities that are offered them, while Braine shows the effect on the character of a working-class man when he ruthlessly adopts the competitive attitudes of middle-class society in order to rise in the world. Such works are inevitably concerned with the contrast in outlook between the older generation, who lived through the years of industrial depression before the war, and their children, born into an era of moderate affluence. They deal with one aspect of that more general and classless antagonism between youth and age which is the theme of *Billy Liar*.

This, too, is a topic of special significance in post-war Britain. Of course, no older generation has ever known 'what youth is coming to', but the normal healthy rebellion of the young against the ways of their fathers has been unusually violent in recent years.

The two stories in this volume present the two extremes of

youthful rebellion: the cheerful—and even attractive—irresponsibility of the frustrated teenager and the determined malevolence of the hardened criminal. Billy Fisher may have stolen a few pounds from the postage account but he still remains within society and one feels that society will probably 'deal with' him without resort to the police court. Sillitoe's hero, however, was born to delinquency. We know nothing of how his family has been reduced to such uncompromising hostility to society, but we are left with the impression that he had no alternative but to become one of the 'Out-law blokes like me and us,' inevitably opposed to the 'In-law blokes like you and them'. He presents in an extreme form that opposition between 'them' and 'us' that Professor Hoggart sees as a major factor in the ordinary person's attitude to society. The world of 'them' is the largely impersonal world of the 'Authorities' and the 'Bosses', in sharp contrast to the intimate and human world of one's own family and neighbourhood:

> 'They' are 'the people at the top', 'the higher-ups', the people who give you your dole, call you up, tell you to go to war, fine you, made you split the family in the thirties to avoid a reduction in the Means Test allowance, 'get yer in the end', 'aren't really to be trusted', 'talk posh', 'are all twisters really' ...[1]

Since the larger world of government and administration is little understood it is generally mistrusted and its interference in the private individual's affairs resented. The 'authorities' tend to increase this distrust by hiding defensively behind official forms and procedures; in *The Loneliness of the Long-distance Runner* they speak impersonally in the plural: 'they always say "We" "We", never "I" "I"—as if they feel braver and righter knowing there's a lot of them against only one.' Even Shadrack adopts the same formula, or an even more impersonal one:

> 'It's been noticed that you were half an hour late again this morning.' He always said 'It's been noticed'.

[1] R. Hoggart, *The Uses of Literacy*. Penguin Books, 1958, pp. 72-3.

We all find it difficult to feel the same responsibility to something as impersonal as an 'organisation' or a 'community' as we do to individual acquaintances we meet in the pub or gossip with in the shop on the corner. The company director who would not think of cheating the business rival he plays golf with may still be prepared to fiddle his income tax, just as the housewife who would tell the local greengrocer if he had given her too much change might well feel satisfied to have got away without paying her fare on the Corporation Bus Service—' "They" won't miss it'. But this attitude is likely to be strongest among those who have least experience of the larger community, and therefore among the younger generation whose experience of social relationships has been largely confined to the family and to personal friends. To no small extent it is the blind antagonism of 'us' to 'them' that lies behind those waves of youthful irresponsibility that have become identified in popular thought first with the Teddy Boys and later with their successors, the Mods and Rockers.

The disturbing feature of much of this behaviour was its pointless violence. Teenage self-assertion—expressed more innocently in flamboyant dress and hair styles, or an enthusiasm for the aggressive rhythms of beat music—was always liable to flare out in truculent behaviour and brutality for its own sake. Stabbing, the beating up of one individual by a gang, the wrecking of cafés and youth clubs, seemed to have become a fashion. The gang-fights on Margate and Brighton beaches, the earlier riots in cinemas showing rock-'n-roll films, the hysterical behaviour of teenage girls about the current pop idol, suggested that even entertainment was acceptable only when it was accompanied by similar violence.

What was especially puzzling was that all this was taking place in a 'Welfare State'. There was much greater social security than existed in the days of inadequate doles and national assistance before the war; some form of secondary education was provided for every child; there was virtually no unemployment, and in spite of inflation the real value of wages had risen considerably, especially for the teenage employee. Theft and violence are understandable in times of genuine poverty and violent social injustice, but now it was the beneficiaries of the new society who were rebelling against it.

There were many reasons for this. The first Teddy boys had spent the most important years of their childhood during the war, with fathers away in the Forces and mothers often out on war work. This weakening of family ties was continued to some extent by the rapid increase in the number of divorces and by the growing practice for women to continue to go out to work after marriage. The disruption of the family is by far the commonest cause of delinquent behaviour—the conflict in the Long-distance Runner's family emerges as one cause of his aggressive attitude. Another reason, and one resulting directly from improved economic conditions and health services, was the earlier maturing of adolescent boys and girls. They were becoming physically adult several years before society was prepared to consider them as other than children. But probably the most important cause was the new social security itself. Before the war the uncertainty of finding a job when one left school and the struggle to make ends meet on inadequate wages were disciplines enough. Now, however, the virtual certainty of finding adequately paid employment gives the teenager a degree of independence from the time he leaves school. His energies are no longer consumed in making a living and supplementing the family income. The apparently pointless self-assertion of the adolescent is a luxury that can be enjoyed only in a comparatively affluent society. Billy Fisher's family, trained in habits of frugality and caution by years of pre-war depression, cannot begin to understand the dreams of freedom that their son indulges in—they respond automatically with 'shouts of "What about your job at Shadrack and Duxbury's" and "Who do you think's going to keep you?"'

But if post-war prosperity has loosened the bonds that tied the teenager to his local community, it has often left him with the sense of belonging to no community at all. Although he enjoys economic security he lacks the security of feeling himself a part of an organised society, and it is those who feel insecure and insignificant who find it necessary to compensate for this by aggressive self-assertion. The conditions of our commercialised society make it increasingly difficult for the individual to feel that he has a significant part to play in it. He will probably have a dull, routine job on an assembly line, in an office or behind a shop counter. His contribution will be a meaningless fragment in the vast system of modern industry and commerce. Boredom is probably as important as insecurity in causing delinquency. Together they breed that barren cynicism that finds expression in pointless rebellion.

Meanwhile the most insistent voices of this society unite to encourage these superficial and irresponsible attitudes. The more popular press reduces the important issues that will determine the course of our lives to tabloid fragments, rarely paying much attention to them unless they can be given a sensational or 'human' twist. Mass entertainment provides a continuous stream of background noise—enabling Billy Fisher to tell the time in the morning—and is turning us into a nation of passive spectators. The advertisers cajole us to provide a market for the increasing flow of goods that will have become obsolescent in a few years' time, and if we do not happen to need their products they are adept at inventing that need for us. The basic impulses in human nature—love, ambition, the desire for security—are sentimentalised and debased into slick selling slogans. Social success is to be achieved by buying the right deodorant, athletic success by using the right hair cream, success in love by smoking the right cigarettes. We live in an age of substitutes, in which goods are sold by their packaging, by TV. jingles or by free gifts of plastic roses, and the life the commercial world offers us is a form of 'substitute life'. Teenagers are an obvious target for the advertisers—their incomes have increased more than those of any other section of the population and as they have few family responsibilities they can spend a much higher proportion of their earnings on themselves. Even their self-assertion is commercialised: they must demonstrate their individuality by wearing the same style of clothes as every other self-assertive teenager, by having their hair cut in the same way as the latest pop idol, by buying records that have reached the top ten because every other teenager is buying them, and by drinking instant coffee from a plastic cup at a chromium topped bar in one of thousands of similar cafés. Life is becoming as mass-produced and tasteless as a broiler fowl: it is the life of Stradhoughton.

* * * * *

We all know Stradhoughton: its main street is

exactly like any other High Street in Great Britain. Woolworth's looked like Woolworth's, the Odeon looked like the Odeon, and the *Stradhoughton Echo's* own office ... looked like a public lavatory in honest native white tile,

and this is

the usual Saturday morning down in town, the fat women rolling along on their bad feet like toy clowns in pudding basins, the grey-faced men reviewing the sporting pinks.

Waterhouse portrays the sordid reality of an industrial town:

the bookies' shops, the stinking urinal, the sly chemist's with red rubber gloves and big sex books in the window, and the obscure one-man businesses mooning behind the dark doorways.

Its character is caught in the evocative detail—the cards buckling in the estate agent's window, the Tizer bottles and 'high aroma of steam and vinegar' in the fish and chip shop, the flattened straws in the station waiting room. The debris of civilisation pollutes the surrounding countryside, spreading from the building sites around Foley Bottoms and over the 'pastoral slum' of Stradhoughton Moor; and the urban filth is most bleakly exposed in the pallor of the night, when you can hear the 'idiot murmur' of the taxi radios and see the pavements 'etched with the trickle of long-stale urine'.

This is the very raw material of life that its inhabitants try to conceal with an even shoddier chromium-plate sophistication. Stradhoughton is 'with it': it has an 'Arcade', an 'X-L Disc Bar' and the Roxy. Behind the 'glassy, glacial doors' of the Kit-Kat café the throbbing urns of an older way of life have been replaced by a 'cackling' espresso machine. But the thinness of this glossy veneer is exposed by the people who live within it. The Roxy and the X-L Disc Bar are the natural haunts of the coarsely animal Stamp, whose mind moves habitually amongst 'mucky books' and 'getting it regular'. His colleagues flaunt their drainpipe trousers and Italian striped suits, but have reduced the Disc Bar to a glass shambles. The buxom Rita is equally destructive of the sophistication of the Kit-Kat:

> With her shiny white overall, her mottled blonde hair, and her thick red lips, she could have transmogrified the Great Northern Hotel itself into a steamy milkbar with one wipe of her tea-cloth.

Her natural habitat is a transport café in the Huddersfield Road; but at least she brings an earthy reality to the flashy pretence of the Kit-Kat. She, too, is Miss Stradhoughton, smiling toothily in a cardboard crown from the cracked, shiny photographs outside the Roxy, where the girls undermine their cosmetic glamour by 'carrying their dance shoes in paper bags advertising pork pies'.

As an alternative to this escape into a tinny modernity there is the attempt by Man o' the Dales and his readers to live in the past, to romanticise the lost 'regional' character of Strad-houghton. The very name

> conjures up sturdy buildings of honest native stone, gleam-ing cobbled streets, and that brackish air which gives this corner of Yorkshire its own especially *piquancy*.

The self-conscious italic print of *'piquancy'*—like the very name 'Man o' the Dales'—has the same sentimental whimsy that one finds in imitation Tudor 'Olde Worlde Tea Shoppes'. It is only an attempt to dress Stradhoughton up in period fancy-dress, and this sturdy old Dalesman himself turns out to be an urban young man with a handle-bar moustache.

Together, Shadrack and Duxbury sum up these two attempts to conceal the depressing reality of Stradhoughton. Shadrack tries to jazz up the undertaking business by fitting useless radios in his funeral cars and designing a streamlined fibre-glass coffin, while Duxbury—one of Man o' the Dales' regular contributors—lapses into senility with his unintelligible but carefully preserved Yorkshire accent and his probably imaginary recollections of the past. Shadrack has replaced Duxbury's fake 'Dickensian windows, bottle-glass and all' with 'modern-plate glass and a shop sign of raised stainless steel lettering', and the incongruous mixture of this with Duxbury's antiquated window dressing makes their establishment an epitome of the muddle of bogus cultures that jostle in the town. Everything is commercialised and degraded. Shadrack can even commercialise death, applying to it the methods of the car-salesman. He has joined every religious denomination in the town and visits St Botolph's church to pick up custom—religion is merely a means of 'getting round old ladies'. Throughout the book the notorious calendars are a reminder of this combination of the commercial and the sentimental: their simpering picture and mottoes are intended for distribution to useful business contacts and likely customers—doctors, clergymen, mother superiors and old peoples' homes.

Stradhoughton is a quagmire of mass-produced sentimentality, of crinoline ladies and frosted Bambis that clutter up the mirror in Hillcrest. It infects both the old and the new: the Witch can find her beloved little angels and 'sloppy verse' in the tidy oblongs of the Corporation Cemetery as well as in St Botolph's churchyard—near the urinal. Everyone seems occupied in escaping into sentimental fantasies. The thought of marriage sparks off in Rita's mind an advertiser's vision of a 'dream house'—with seagrass stools, and novel horseshoe companion-set—while the Witch dreams of 'a thatched cottage in the middle of some unspecified field in Devon ... the Windsor chairs, the kettle singing on the hob, the bloody cat', *and* a wishing well. The commercial world has stamped its trivial monotony on these dreams. They are to be found illustrated on the pages of any woman's magazine, which is doubtless where they originated. The characters are perpetually converting their real lives into conventional and meaningless routines. Instead of falling in love they go through the motions that films and novelettes have taught them to regard as evidence of a 'grand passion'. They destroy any genuine intimacy or individuality in the relationship by transforming it into a stereotyped and unfelt pattern. So Billy Fisher obliges the Witch with an absurd pretence of exaggerated jealousy and acts out a pseudo-passionate scene of confession in the Corporation Cemetery as if he were on the stage, while the Witch indulges in 'practised silences' and brings tears automatically to her eyes by turning away with a quick movement of the head. The 'elaborate shudder' with which she announces her hatred of lying is as bogus as the ineffectual aphrodisiac tablets with which Billy—however improperly—tries to inject some sort of reality into their relationship. The prospect of death prompts a similarly artificial response. The fact of Gran's death sinks in a morass of conventional platitudes—'She would have wanted it that way', 'Well we'll have to carry on as best we can'—until Billy can only marvel at the clichés that his mother uses, 'like crutches to take her limping from one crisis to another'.

Waterhouse catches the quality of Stradhoughton life most unerringly in the way the characters speak—in the cliché, the stock phrase that springs to mind merely because it has been used so many times before, not because it is appropriate or genuinely meant. Man o' the Dales's 'blunt Yorkshire individuals' have become 'interchangeable like spare wheels on a mass-produced car'. Instead of being live persons, responding to the particular circumstances of each new situation, they have become automatons; every situation produces an automatic response. 'Everyone in Stradhoughton spoke in clichés': the Fisher family monotonously trot out their limited repertoire of phrases like No. 14 trams; Stamp's corny jokes rattle out 'with the mindlessness of a Pavlov dog'; Councillor Duxbury clicks into his reminiscences 'as though he were himself an old gramophone that has just been kicked back into action'; and Rita indulges in 'mechanical badinage' in the Kit-Kat with 'standard, ready-to-use repartee'. The cliché is the verbal equivalent of the mass-produced civilisation in which they live: 'Rita spoke as though she got her words out of a slot machine, whole sentences ready-packed in a disposable tinfoil wrapper.' Her bosom is 'itself a cliché, like a plastic relief given away by the women's magazines'.

Billy Fisher sees the whole of Stradhoughton life as a series of music-hall acts, the sort of cross-talk scenes in which he and Arthur burlesque their fellows. One can only sympathise with the guerilla warfare of mockery that he wages against humbug. He ought not to have stolen the postage money, but this seems a venial sin compared with the hypocrisy of Shadrack, and of the calendars on which it should have been spent. His indiscriminate use of the communal engagement ring is no more dishonest than the fake courtship scenes in which it figures. He may be 'a pathological bloody liar', but the world he lives in is one big lie, and at least his lies are entertaining, both in themselves and in their disastrous consequences. And one sympathises the more because he is as much a prey to Stradhoughton as the people he despises. He also flies from reality into one impossible dream after another. On the first page we are plunged directly into the fantasy world of Ambrosia into which he escapes from the triviality of his own life, and his Ambrosian repeater gun is always at the ready to be turned on unpleasant facts and to annihilate them in his thoughts. The novel opens and closes with the 'March of the Movies', the national anthem of this musical comedy world. His dreams of success are no more realistic. The glossy No. 1 father and mother—sophisticated and understanding substitutes for his own parents—would be thoroughly at home with Rita's seagrass stools to go with their 'rubber-plants on the low-slung shelves', and the vision of an apple-cheeked Grandma and Councillor Duxbury living in a thatched cottage is as sentimental as the Witch's marriage dreams. Even when he exposes the romantic fantasies about Yorkshire tradition he assumes the character of one of Man o' the Dales's own bluff Yorkshiremen, with pipe and tobacco pouch.

The difference, of course, is that Billy is well aware of the absurdity of it all. When the Witch contrives a dazed expression he feels like saying, 'Look, chum, I do all these tricks myself. I *know* them. Pack it in.' He is Stradhoughton made conscious of itself: his life is a deliberate burlesque of its fantasies, stock responses and clichés. But although he recognises this he cannot stop it. He can distinguish his deliberate No. 1 thinking from his involuntary No. 2 thinking, but even that distinction has become mechanical. He can face unpleasant situations only by preparing appropriate poses, which collapse when put to the test. He cannot rid himself of absurd obsessions about 'Fisher's Yawn', ingrowing hair on the chin or the overpowering feeling that his fingers are webbed. Stock phrases slot into his head 'like price tabs ringing up on a cash register'. Even his deliberate burlesques of Yorkshire sentimentality are automatically 'triggered off' by such objects as Josiah Olroyd's memorial vase. Worse still, they become mixed up with his real life. He is an awful example of the old nursery adage, 'if you go on pulling faces like that you will grow to look like them'. Just as he deliberately acts his prepared scene with the Witch in the Corporation Cemetery, so in his interview with Shadrack he sounds unintentionally 'like something out of amateur dramatics'. His gift for imitating other people is itself an obsession. He slips into Shadrack's pronunciation when he is talking to him, he falls 'chameleon like' into Rita's accent in the Kit-Kat, and on the Moor he not only imitates Councillor Duxbury's dialect, 'half-mockingly, half-compulsively', but finds himself involuntarily using the mock-dialect of his and Arthur's Duxbury dialogues. He becomes a victim of his own burlesque of others.

Thus the novel acquires its complex comic tone. Simultaneously one is laughing both at Billy and with him at the people he burlesques, and yet, at the same time sympathising with the predicaments in which he is entangled by his forlorn attempts to escape from his environment. As these entanglements are drawn into a tight knot at the comic climaxes on Stradhoughton Moor, in the Roxy and at Foley Bottoms, pathos and humour mingle and heighten each other with increasing poignancy.

It is on the Moor that his vulnerability is first decisively exposed. Councillor Duxbury's *'Tha's a reet one wi' them calendars, i'n't ta?'* slices through the fragments of cynical poses that Billy tries desperately to assemble. Beneath them is only the awkward and embarrassed adolescent, while the world he mocks suddenly acquires an unexpected solidity. The question 'Is ta taking a rise out o' me, young man?' shows Duxbury to be well able to meet such youthful impertinence with calm, and even amused, assurance. The advice he gives Billy—

Tha's got a long way to go. But tha can't do it by thisen. Now think on—

would once have seemed merely raw material for another 'Duxbury dialogue', but now it sounds 'sage and shrewd'. When put to the test this antiquated dialect is found to be capable of saying something worth saying. Councillor Duxbury remains an absurd figure, but at this point one senses a genuine kindness and a genuine wisdom. Billy Fisher is forced to look at reality—to realise that Duxbury recognised his imitations and knew all about the calendars. He begins to realise for the first time that he wants to tell him about them.

There is a sudden sense of release: 'I had a feeling, one that I wanted to keep. It was a feeling of peace and melancholy.'

The value of Duxbury's advice is confirmed by the increasing evidence of Billy's separation from his fellows. He 'had no friends, only allies'; his relations with Arthur are only on the level of Music Hall cross-talk—'Even our ordinary conversations were like the soft-shoe shuffle routine with which we enlivened the ordinary day.' In the X-L Disc Bar his isolation, in his stained raincoat and crumpled suit, is painfully apparent. Arthur, on the other hand, 'seemed to know everyone'. He is thoroughly at home in Stradhoughton's 'sophisticated' society: in the Roxy 'his poise and the professional way he stood there doing nothing' contrasts vividly with the fiasco of Billy's own performance in the New House and with his acute embarrassment when Arthur has at last persuaded 'his friends, the Rockets' to play one of their songs. Billy's basic insecurity, his inability to feel a part of this dance-hall society even when he has achieved this moderate success, makes him curl up in himself with shame. He must assert his superiority over

Arthur to cover his embarrassment, so provoking the breach between them. The very poses he adopts in order to face these alien groups—as a visiting poet in the Roxy and as a world-famous comedian in the New House—ironically accentuate his isolation from them, just as his attempt to prise himself into the society of the New House with his lie about having a dog to sell leads only to fresh embarrassment and a fresh sense of his isolation. Increasingly one sees his cynical self-assertion as a defence mechanism to cover his sense of social isolation.

The New House has all the tinny vulgarity of Strad-houghton, the shoddy glitter of formica tables and strip light-ing mixed up with a few out-of-place relics of 'warm terrace-end pubs'. Its occupants spend all their time in apparently meaningless winking and unintelligible questions and answers, yet it seems that this expresses a secret communal life that may also be a relic of the older pubs and retains something of their social warmth:

> They seemed to have secrets between them, and they re-united into a world of their own wherever they went.... All the people in the concert-room sat so comfortably, as though they had reached a reasonable agreement with life and death, as though they knew all about it, all that there was to know about it.

The grotesque women stare at him with a kind of compassion-ate detachment

> because they knew things I didn't know, because they were involved in basic matters that I had never even heard about.

One begins to suspect that all the absurd ritual of the Ancient Order of Stags also expresses the genuine sense of community to be found in the working man's club, which has survived even in the tawdry and impersonal surroundings of the New House.

How far this is true is left uncertain. Waterhouse shows us Stradhoughton entirely through Billy's eyes. When, in the Infirmary waiting room, he flinches away from the reality of Gran's death, he reassures himself with the thought that 'All those women, who were supposed to know it all, all about life and death, they didn't know any more than I did.... They're as bad as I am, they don't feel it, they only say it.' 'But,' he adds, 'I didn't believe what I was telling myself.' His mother's stock expressions seem at least a clumsy attempt to express, as well as to escape from, genuine emotion. Perhaps, it is implied, we are all a muddle of genuine feeling and cliché, and it is better to accept the cliché for the sake of what is genuine. Human beings cannot be so simply classified as 'sincere' and 'insincere'—that is only one more of Billy's fantasies. The chapter ends with Mrs Fisher's face

> flawed and crumpled like an old balloon ... for the first time ... looking as though these things had really happened.

And it is Billy who does not have the courage to turn round and who proceeds to transform Gran into a stock obituary.

The mother at least faced an emotional situation, even if it made her look 'like some corny act on television'; the son flies from it with all the adolescent's dread of expressing emotion in public. He escapes into cynicism or tries to drive it out of his mind by the more primitive method of meaningless chanting. He repeatedly protests that he is feeling nothing, and this is true because the feeling is overwhelmed in a flood of embarrassment:

> I sat down, suddenly tense and frightened. I said to myself, clenching my fists, Don't let's have any scenes, don't let's have any scenes, don't let's have any scenes.

The same dread of 'scenes' is evident when Gran has a fit. He deliberately avoids being involved in it, he even hopes that she will die so that there will be no more 'scenes'. Any approach to reality embarrasses him: even the way in which he tells his family of the letter from Danny Boon has an unnatural stridency and he confesses to his embarrassment when he tells Arthur about it.

It is only with Liz that Billy is able to escape from his isolation and from the embarrassment and consequent rebellious self-assertion that it produces. The depth of their relationship is felt in the unobtrusive way in which she is introduced, by the casual references to her, the enigmatic cards, her name cut in the desk—even Rita's moments of tenderness are significantly associated with Woodbine smoke. The thought of her continually emerges from the deeper levels of his nature through the deliberate masquerade that makes up most of his conscious life. A fascination gathers like an aroma round her Woodbines and her green suède jacket—'an elusive scent that I knew for a fact did not exist'. The emotion associated with her is the more genuine and the more sensitively defined for not being made definite:

> I had no real feeling about her, but there was always some kind of pain when she went away.

By 'real feeling' Billy means the sort of 'definite emotion' that he tries to 'assemble' in the X-L Disc Bar, but he can get no further than 'a sensation of singing'. In their relationship nothing needs to be defined. Instead of talking in external cliché formulas they have an intuitive understanding: Billy is content not to ask where she has been, although he does not know why he is content, and when Liz gave an obviously untrue excuse for not phoning him

> She grinned broadly again, telling me not to believe her and not to worry because it didn't matter, and it didn't.

In contrast to the mechanical responses that make up the Witch, her personality has a subtle organic unity that defies analysis:

> It was part of the enigma, one of the things about her that I could never get into the test tube and examine.

Instead of the self-conscious poses adopted by all the other characters she has a realistic impulsiveness—'bubbling over with it all':

> She was the only girl I knew who cared, or who could talk about things as though they really mattered. We began chattering, eagerly interrupting, laughing, grinning at each

other as though we knew the whole joke about the world and understood it.

With her he feels that real relation to the world that he attributes, rightly or wrongly, to the women in the New House:

Sometimes I could think about Liz, think properly on the ordinary plane, for a full minute, before we were both whisked off into Ambrosia.

Liz frequently figures in the unreality of Ambrosia—as 'a kind of white-faced Eva Peron' or with a pony tail in his Chelsea flat—but these are glossy perversions of the warm humanity of Liz herself. Her cheerful openness is caught in the frankness of her grin—'Liz was the only girl I had ever met who knew *how* to grin'. She is quietly and cheerfully self-contained and poised. She, too, knows everyone, she is as much at home in the Roxy as Stamp or Arthur, 'with her chin resting on her plump arms, and smiling happily to herself'—she even knows Man o' the Dales. She is at ease with all those things that send Billy into blind exasperation or embarrassment, but apparently uncontaminated by them: that their lovemaking in the wood has been spied on merely amuses her. She is able to accept this artificial and vulgar society and yet preserve her own integrity. That is why Billy feels that she protects him from other people.

Billy's relations with her are a continual struggle between his wish to be honest with himself and his self-conscious tendency to degrade everything into cheap fiction. He is still 'trying on expressions' with her in the X-L Disc Bar and even his awareness of that 'elusive scent' is turned into a stock formula—'I could remember how you *smelled*, even!' He tries the Man o' the Dales pose on her, and it is sympathetically punctured; he takes refuge in the Duxbury dialect from a serious confession of love, and when forced to 'say it properly' wonders if he meant it. He confuses her genuine proposal with his own pretend proposal and 'plays along with it', hoping 'to keep it all on the same sparring level'. In the end he cannot bring himself to take the decision of marrying her, but there is a genuine intimacy when Liz's confession that she, too, wants to be 'invisible' persuades him to admit her into his most personal fantasy world—which she can indulge in as 'a kind of mental romp in the long grass', not as a form of compulsive escape. Billy is left with that same 'feeling of peace and misery' that he had previously experienced when Councillor Duxbury forced him to face reality on Stradhoughton Moor.

Liz is not only able to accept Stradhoughton, she is also able to accept Billy Fisher, his fantasies and his absurdity. She can tell him 'You *are* a fool' and grin composedly as she says it. That is what Billy has to learn from her. She recognises his trouble when she tells him he is introspective. His life is a series of self-conscious postures, periodically shattered by panic emotion which he refuses to recognise as his own and thrusts away from him. He analyses his own character as he analyses the behaviour of other people until there is hardly one natural feeling left. There is his No. 1 thinking, his No. 2 thinking, his hate thinking—even his conscience is separated from the rest of his character and locked away in the 'Guilt Chest'. There seems to be no personality, only a collection of routines, rituals, obsessions, catch-phrases, exasperations and embarrassments, loosely tied together by this self-consciousness. He tries to assert himself, but there is no 'self' to assert: so, on the station, caught in a 'panic-panorama' of No. 1 thinking and No. 2 daymares, he confesses, 'I tried hard to shut it down and find myself, myself, but not knowing what to do for characteristics.' He has to learn to accept himself, and that means accepting the society that has made him what he is.

It is obvious for most of the story that Billy will not escape to London; he is himself too much a part of Stradhoughton. His very prospect of escape is only another Stradhoughton fantasy; the letter from Danny Boon is much too vague to give him any real hope of establishing himself as a script writer, as his No. 2 thinking frequently tells him. But he is also perhaps a part of Stradhoughton in a more significant sense. As his disastrous day mounts to its hilarious but almost tragic climax there are increasing hints that real people and a real society might be found there, and that he cannot separate himself from them either by cynicism or by physical flight. Councillor Duxbury's 'tha can't do it by thisen' is supported by his mother's unexpected insight:

'If you're in trouble, Billy, it's not something you can leave behind you, you know,' she said in a shaky voice. 'You put it in your suitcase and take it with you.'

In her final words—'but we need you at home lad'—the 'we' is not the generalised, impersonal 'we' that Shadrack uses: Billy describes it as 'editorial' but it makes him feel uncomfortable. This may be only another platitude, but it seems to be used to express a human relationship.

\* \* \* \* \*

Billy Fisher is no long-distance runner. The most he can manage is a short sprint to the station, encumbered as he is by the load of calendars from his Guilt Chest and all the other dead lumber of society that he drags around with him. Sillitoe's hero has no Guilt Chest and no connection with society except mutual hostility. He is the free, untrammelled runner, and throughout the story we share his loneliness, feeling 'like the first and last man on the world, both at once'.

The story is told entirely from his point of view and in his language. The vocabulary is crude and blunted, as if it had actually been written with a stub of pencil clutched in his paw. The narrative gives the impression of being the disordered thoughts of an uneducated mind, although in fact these thoughts are assembled skilfully to give a picture of his past and present life and are gathered together into a unified climax. They are given direction by the running. They plod on to the accompaniment of the 'trot-trot-trot, slap-slap-slap, over the stream and into the wood', through to the 'crunchslap end'. The style is as hard, spare and wiry as the runner's muscles and as uncompromisingly blunt as the 'scruffy head' of the Borstal boy. It has the continuous monotony of a long-distance run. Facts and ideas emerge as they spring to mind when one is occupied in steady physical activity. Certain ideas recur and become especially persistent as one jogs on, especially those ideas that one has tried not to think about but which are now released by the hypnotic effect of the running. They become fixed in the otherwise fluctuating train of thought and acquire new significance and power. Thus the death of the Runner's father is referred to casually to explain why they had to buy a new carpet, but returns at the climax of the story and forces its way more and more insistently into his consciousness—'which is funny', he comments,

> because I hadn't thought about it at all since it happened and even then I didn't brood much on it.

The narrative is inseparable from the running because running has enabled him to think. It makes him 'think so good': 'I get to thinking, and that's what I like.' For him running *is* thinking:

> I feel that up till then I haven't been running and that I've used up no energy at all. And I've been able to do this because I've been thinking; and I wonder if I'm the only one in the running business with this system of forgetting that I'm running because I'm too busy thinking.

Previously he had had no opportunity to think:

> I've had no time and peace in all my bandit life, and now my thoughts are coming pat and the only trouble is I often can't stop, even when my brain feels as if it's got cramp, frostbite and creeping paralysis all rolled into one and I have to give it a rest by slapdashing down through the brambles of the sunken lane—

the equivalent for him of Billy Fisher's 'counting and quoting method' to banish unwelcome thoughts. Thus running has made him aware of himself in a new way. Previously he had asserted himself negatively against society by breaking its laws and annoying policemen; now he has found his individuality in his running, he knows himself as a human being 'and I've got thoughts and secrets and bloody life inside me'. He experiences his isolation from society positively now, as the 'loneliness' of the long-distance runner. We learn incidentally that his name is Smith, but only the Governor calls him that: he is simply the 'Long-distance Runner', for it is in his running that he has found his identity. His mind is his 'barmy runner-brain'. For him running is life.

This is subtly supported by the feeling of freedom and life in the description of the running. Nothing is idealised, everything is described in simple, primitive terms: the 'phlegmy bit of sunlight hanging from the bare twigs of beech and sycamore', the smoky breath 'going out into the air as if I had ten cigars stuck in different parts of my body', the piece of treebark that he stuffs into his mouth,

> chewing wood and dust and maybe maggots as I run until I'm nearly sick, yet swallowing what I can of it just the same because ... for six months I'm not going to smell that grass or taste that dusty bark or trot this lovely path.

At first 'everything's dead, but good, because it's dead before coming alive, not dead after being alive'. In contrast, the Governor lives in the dead, impersonal world of 'them', dead because it is a world of empty conventions and slick platitudes about 'playing ball with us and we'll play ball with you' that make no human contact with the living world of the Long-distance Runner. He hopes to exploit the vitality of this world for himself, to have put in him 'blood and throbbing veins he never had'. He regards the Runner as he would a race-horse. For him running is merely a means of winning races.

Thus the Long-distance Runner had either 'to win the race or run it'; he could not do both. 'Running' is asserting his independence; 'racing'—running to win—would be sacrificing that independence to conform with the wishes of the Governor and his 'dead' society. It is identified with the principles of competition and success that control the Governor's middle-class world: if he wins the Governor's pals will be impressed and 'get him made a Sir', while it could lead the Long-distance

Runner himself to respectability and fame—to a wife, a car and his face in the papers. The race-track becomes a symbol of this organised bourgeois life:

> a course marked out for you by people holding mugs of water and bottles of iodine in case you fall and cut yourself so that they can pick you up—even if you want to stay where you are—and get you moving again

—a welfare state designed to keep you in training for the rat-race. Thus winning the race would mean 'running right into their white-gloved wall-barred hands,' not only because it would please the Governor but also because it would be an acceptance of these middle-class values as the Runner's own. To use his running in order to win would be to desecrate the only thing in which he has found real value:

> I knew what the loneliness of the long-distance runner running across country felt like, realising that as far as I was concerned this feeling was the only honesty and realness there was in the world.

With twisted integrity he sacrifices the prospect of comfort and success for a principle. He is honest, as he continually asserts: honest to the personal identity he has discovered in his running.

This honesty is not merely self-assertion, the 'honest' expression of his spite against the Governor. The climax of the story makes this clear. The physical experience of the running becomes more intense—'slippers slapping the good dry soil', 'the fresh new feel of underfoot gravel'—and more intimately involved with the thoughts that come with mechanical persistence, 'like a wireless in my mind'. But the physical rhythm is disturbed, and with it the easy flow of the thoughts:

> Now the words are like coming from a crystal-set that's broken down, and something's happening inside the shell-case of my guts that bothers me and I don't know why or what to blame it on.... But I know it's nothing to bother

about, that more likely it's caused by too much thinking that now and again I take for worry.

'Worry' recalls his father, 'who had a hard time of worry all his life up to when he filled his bedroom with hot blood'. Images of his father become more and more insistent: 'I see my bloody dad behind each grass-blade in my barmy runner-brain.' He is made to re-live all the details of the death, when he found his father

> looking like a skinned rabbit, his grey head resting just on the edge of the bed, and on the floor must have been all the blood he'd had in his body.

Earlier he had declared, 'It's daft to think deep, you know, because it gets you nowhere', but his running forces him to think deeper and deeper, and to acknowledge the horror he had felt at an event which earlier in the story had merely been a means of providing him and his family with 'such a lot of lolly'. The thoughts that had been repressed throughout his 'bandit life' and that could not be fathomed by the Borstal psychiatrist are now being brought into his conscious mind by this uniquely athletic form of depth analysis. He is being taught things about himself that he does not want to know: his weakness when—like Billy Fisher when Gran has a fit—he was afraid to go into his father's bedroom; the pity he felt for his father because of his mother's behaviour; and the conflict within him when he had to stop his father punching her even though he knew she deserved it. He begins to understand the nature of his own defiance of society and recognises this last act of defiance as a repetition of the 'Out-law death' his father died, refusing to go to hospital. It is only his father's example that gives him the resolution to continue to defy the Governor:

> By God I'll stick this out like my dad stuck out his pain and kicked them doctors down the stairs.

The final run becomes his life in miniature, as it might be recalled on the psychiatrist's couch:

a little life ... but a life as full of misery and happiness and things happening as you can ever get really around yourself.

Like Billy Fisher the Long-distance Runner discovers that he cannot run away from his own past—that 'you put it in your suitcase and take it with you'. His running is no longer merely an assertion of his independence, it has become a means of revealing his own nature to himself. In consequence he is no longer sure that he likes to think; once he had despised the Borstal authorities for giving him this opportunity to be independent and to hit back at them, but now he suspects that they have

> maybe got their own back on me from the bright beginning by sliding magic-lantern slides into my head that never stood a chance before.

The brash self-sufficiency of the 'bright-beginning' has been humanised until at the end he is 'blubbing like a baby'. But the emotion is still held firmly in the defiant rhythm of his running:

> Only if I take whatever comes like this in my runner's stride can I keep on like myself and beat them back.

He accepts the burden of his past, which all this 'thinking' has disclosed to him, with a genuinely tragic strength:

> What a life for all of us. Well, I'm not grumbling, because if I did I might just as well win this bleeding race—

to grumble would be disloyal to his out-law caste, it would be equivalent to appealing for the sympathy of all the 'In-laws' clustered round the winning-post. Being a long-distance runner is no longer 'a treat ... out in the world by yourself with not a soul to make you bad tempered'; now it symbolises the stark desolation of his own life—and perhaps of all human life if we could see behind the superficial appearances:

> all I knew was that you had to run, run, run, without knowing why you were running, but on you went through fields

you didn't understand and into woods that made you afraid, over hills without knowing you'd been up and down, and shooting across streams that would have cut the heart out of you had you fallen into them. And the winning post was no end to it, even though crowds might be cheering you in, because on you had to go before you got your breath back, and the only time you stopped really was when you tripped over a tree trunk and broke your neck or fell into a disused well and stayed dead in the darkness forever.

So, with this clear insight into the tragedy of such loneliness, he still resolves to be a long-distance runner, 'crossing country all on my own no matter how bad it feels'.

*　*　*　*　*

Neither of these stories ends 'on a winning post'—as did those books which Sillitoe's hero had read and which consequently taught him nothing. They are both 'open-ended', they start in the middle of things and, to an external observer, they end with things much the same as when they began. A Saturday has slipped by; a race has been lost. But both writers have used these opportunities to reveal human values in situations that seem particularly devoid of them. Things are not just the same. Billy Fisher returns home still whistling the Ambrosian national anthem, but his suitcase feels absurdly light now that he has disposed of its guilty load of calendars, just as his spirit was momentarily lightened by the knowledge that Councillor Duxbury knew all about them. His secrets no longer matter: 'they were like dead wounds with the bandages falling off'. His proposed job with Danny Boon was an illusory 'winning post', such as the Long-distance Runner knows from the start that he must reject, and Billy also rejects it decisively when he turns away from the London train. Several times in the course of the day he has been forced to recognise the possibility of there being real ties between himself and Strad-houghton, although he consciously resists the thought, and his final decision, taken beneath an indecisive welter of No. 1 and No. 2 thinking, suggests a tacit admission of them. The Long-distance Runner continues to cross country all on his own, but he now understands what this involves. He understands, too, the real nature of the 'honesty' that he has discovered in running. It is not merely an honest expression of his own feelings, but an honest recognition of the real nature of those feelings, which he has concealed from himself, as well as from the 'In-laws', by means of a protective mask of cynicism. He now knows that it is not only cunning 'what counts in this life'.

Both stories start with blind self-assertion, but end with at least a degree of self-knowledge. Their humanity is equally evident in their humour. This springs less from a deliberate attempt to be amusing than from their authors' acute awareness of human psychology—as when Billy Fisher recognises Rita's removal of his empty plate as 'an obscure gesture of affection' or Waterhouse deftly traces the movement of Billy's thoughts, first in self-conscious confession—

> I was now talking belligerently, 'Another thing, we haven't got a budgie.'
> I had told her that we kept a yellow budgerigar called Roger. I had regularly given her communiqués about its antics and there had been a highlight when Roger had flown out of his cage and nearly been caught by Sarah, the tabby.
> 'Or a cat,' I said.

—and then in compulsive lying—

> 'Don't tell me you haven't got a sister.'
> 'I did have, but she's dead.' This time it was out before I could prevent it. I ran rapidly over this new turn, and within seconds I had established death from tuberculosis, and a quiet funeral.

Sillitoe's humour is less full-blooded but is equally important in humanising his bleak story. It ranges from the coldly unfunny comedy of the happiness of the family after the father's death to the incidental absurdity of Mike's preoccupation with his glasses. The doggedly realistic exchanges with the detective, the bullying and cheap cunning on the one side and the truculent impertinence on the other, are permeated with an equally realistic humour until the episode dissolves into almost farcical comedy as the notes are washed out of the drainpipe and spread with damning particularity over the yard —the detective stares in blank incomprehension and the culprit can only continue to jabber irrelevantly, like Billy Fisher patching together his poses before Councillor Duxbury on the Moor.

The amused detachment of such humour gives to both stories a sense of proportion. The reader is reminded of the limitations of the Long-distance Runner's point of view by the wry irony that plays over his less egotistical moments—his fellow-feeling for the policeman's 'honest' spite in waking his mother up at 4 a.m., or his disgust with his own shortsighted spite in keeping the detective out in the rain where he could see the banknotes. It dissolves away any trace of sentimentality in *Billy Liar*. There is tragedy in the disruption of Billy's brief idyll in Foley Bottoms, but he himself transforms the intrusion of Stamp into absurd comedy as his fantasies get to work on the rustling in the bushes, the Witch puts another spool on her tape recorder and Stamp and Shadrack fiddle with the batteries and adjust it for her. The mixture of tragedy and comedy is sometimes grotesque—when Billy, seeing a hostile face behind every Corinthian column in the Roxy, has a histrionic impulse to stand on his chair and shout 'Ladies and gentlemen, here are my fountain pen and my suède shoes. Crucify me the modern way'—and sometimes tender—in the endearing absurdity of Billy's final meeting with Liz amongst the cardboard models and toy soldiers of Ambrosia. Both stories demand a sensitive complexity of response from the reader.

Their humour is one aspect of their 'honesty'. They are honest, as the Long-distance Runner would say, in accepting what they find and seeking to understand it. They show the emergence of rebellion from a sense of isolation and insecurity and the adoption of a cynical pose as a defence against this insecurity—a pose that only increases the isolation of their heroes. They challenge our more comfortable assumptions, especially the belief that, like the Governor, we know what the winning post is, that our principles are self-evidently the correct ones. Having no winning posts themselves they raise questions rather than offer solutions, but their sympathetic penetration into two rebellious minds helps to break down the barriers of complacency and cynicism that are the chief obstacles to the reconciliation of the rebel and society.

1966

DAVID ELLOWAY

NOTES

# NOTES

*The notes in this edition are intended
to serve the needs of overseas students
as well as those of English-born users*

## BILLY LIAR

*Dialect:* overseas readers may find difficulty with the passages in
Yorkshire dialect. Some individual idioms are annotated as they
appear in the text, but the most frequently recurring variations
from Standard English are listed below. The right-hand columns
give the normal spelling, when this has been changed to indicate
dialect pronunciation, and the approximate meaning of the idioms.

| | | | |
|---|---|---|---|
| *afore* | before | *ha'* | have |
| *ageean* | again | *i'n't* | isn't |
| *Ah* | I | *ivvery* | every |
| *Ah'd* | I'd | *lass* | girl |
| *Ah'm* | I'm | *mah* | my |
| *Ah'sll* | I shall | *mun* | must |
| *Ah've* | I've | *nah* | now |
| *allus* | always | *nay* | no |
| *an'* | and | *neether* | neither |
| *anall* | and all (as well) | *noan* | not |
| *any road* | anyway | *nobbut* | nothing but |
| *'appen* | happen (perhaps; | *nowt* | nothing |
| | I suppose) | *ower* | over |
| *aye* | yes | *owt* | anything |
| *bahn* | bound (going) | *sither* | see thee here |
| *coortin'* | courting | | (pay attention) |
| *cos* | because | *summat* | something |
| *eether* | either | *t'* | the |
| *fair* | really | *ta* or *tha* | thou (you) |
| *fun* | found | *tha'd* | thou'd (you would) |
| *gerron* | get on | *th'art* | thou'rt (you are) |
| *gi'* | give | *theer* or *ther'* | there |
| *gormless* | senseless | *thi* | thy |

231

| | | | |
|---|---|---|---|
| *think on* | go on thinking about that | *wun't* | wouldn't |
| *thisen* | thyself (yourself) | *yer* | your *or* yes |
| *toneet* | tonight | *yon* | that |
| *wanna* | want to | | |
| *wi'* | with | | |

*Page*

3 *Ambrosia:* the fanciful country that Billy Fisher has invented so that he can escape into it from the reality of his own insignificance in Stradhoughton and imagine himself to be a hero. Its name is appropriate for an imaginary ideal, for in Greek mythology ambrosia was the food of the gods.

*Town Square:* in Stradhoughton. The imaginary march-past began in Ambrosia, but he transfers it to his own town so that he can imagine his friends watching his triumphant return.

*The Lord . . . to lie down:* the opening of the 23rd Psalm.

4 *passe-partout:* a form of black, sticky tape used as an inexpensive means of framing pictures.

5 *'Calendars . . . Captain':* the meaning of these notes becomes clear later in the novel. *S* is Shadrack; *re* (from the Latin *res*) is a commercial and legal abbreviation for 'about'. See *Witch re Captain* is explained on p. 81.

*pitch-painted:* creosoted.

*white-haired boy:* outstanding pupil, favoured by the art teacher.

*Technical:* Technical School.

6 *'Yesterday in Parliament':* the report on the previous day's proceedings in Parliament broadcast by the B.B.C. before the 9 a.m. news.

*the old man:* familiar slang for 'my father'.

*When Did You Last See Your Father?:* the well-known 19th century picture of a Cavalier's son being interrogated by Roundheads who are trying to discover where his father is hidden.

*invoices:* bills.

7 *gallivanting:* roving about idly.

8 *chuntering:* mumbling—generally a mumbled complaining.

9 *benediction:* blessing—spoken by a priest over the congregation at the end of a religious service. Billy implies ironically that his family's conversations resemble a church service in following a set pattern or ritual; he would be assuming the

232

superior position of the priest and having the last word.

9 *rhubarb-rhubarb:* the word traditionally muttered by the chorus in a play to give the impression of a general buzz of conversation in which the individual words are inaudible.

*Stradhoughton Empire:* the local music-hall.

*catchline:* a phrase frequently repeated by a comedian, the mere repetition giving a humorous effect.

10 *back-doubles:* back streets—the routes by which one 'doubles back' to avoid pursuit, as Mrs Fisher escapes from the subject being discussed into irrelevant topics.

*'Ere, rear, rear:* 'Here, here, here'—slurred together by Mr. Fisher's careless pronunciation.

*For crying out loud!:* modern slang equivalent of 'for goodness sake!'

*Woodbine:* a low-priced brand of cigarette.

11 *don't have so much off:* when he has his hair cut—an example of a 'back-double' (see note above).

*machine-turned:* mass-produced on a machine, instead of being carved by a craftsman. Billy no longer expresses his contempt for these cheap commercial products because he has given up the attempt to make his family understand it.

*Player's Weights:* another low-priced brand of cigarette.

*No. 1 thinking and No. 2 thinking:* Billy's No. 1 thinking is his daydreaming—such as that about Ambrosia—which he indulges in deliberately. His No. 2 thinking, he says, is *obsessional.* An obsession is a thought that one cannot control or dismiss from one's mind. Generally it concerns some subject that one fears and so has tried not to think about. One has 'repressed' it, tried to prevent it from entering the conscious mind, but it returns of its own accord and haunts one. Behaviour can also be obsessional, when one feels an uncontrollable impulse to do something that one knows to be absurd. This is also the result of some secret tension or repressed fear inside one. Billy suffers from many of these trivial physical obsessions (see p. 4), of a kind with which we are probably all familiar.

*sarcoma:* tumour.

12 *Bertrand Russell:* the celebrated contemporary English logician and philosopher. At the time this book was written he was especially prominent as an advocate of nuclear disarmament.

*Councillor:* the official title of a member of the Borough Council responsible for the local administration of Stradhoughton.

12 *Marcovitch:* a superior brand of cigarettes.

*solitaire:* a game played with counters on a board by a single player; here it represents the typical amusement of a socially superior woman with little to occupy her time.

*tight:* drunk.

*vacuum annexe to the No. 2 thinking:* the empty state of mind that is attached to his No. 2 thinking—like an annexe to a building—because it is when he is in such a vacant mood that his No. 2 thoughts begin to get a grip on him.

13 *efforts:* productions—used generally in a somewhat derogatory sense.

14 *standing account:* permanent account—they buried so many people from the Old People's Home that instead of charging separately for each funeral they sent the Home a quarterly bill.

*saccharine:* sweetening agent used as a substitute for sugar, here suggesting over-sweet sentiments.

15 *aphrodisiac:* causing sexual excitement.

*Ritzy Stories:* a cheap sexy magazine.

*'Housewives' Choice':* a B.B.C. programme on which records requested by housewives are played.

*Basildon Bond:* a brand of writing paper.

*Just a Song at Twilight:* the first line of *Love's Old Sweet Song*, at one time a very popular sentimental ballad.

*motif:* theme, subject.

*Eva Peron:* wife of the former President Peron of the Argentine. She was a romantic figure in the popular agitation that brought him into power.

17 *semis:* semi-detached villas.

*Man o' the Dales:* the pen-name of the journalist who writes a regular column in the local paper, chiefly on Stradhoughton's history and its 'Yorkshire character'. The 'Dales' are valleys leading up into the Pennine hills.

18 *piquancy:* sharp, stimulating flavour.

*X-L Disc Bar:* a gramophone record shop, in very modern style. 'X-L' is a whimsical form of 'Excel'.

*Woolworth's:* one of the large chain of department stores of that name.

*Odeon:* a cinema.

*Dark satanic mills:* a phrase from William Blake's poem *Jerusalem*. As 'mills' can mean 'factories' (as in 'cloth mills') the poem is often thought to be a comment on the effects of the industrial revolution.

19 *toy clowns in pudding basins:* wooden clowns that wobble along on semi-circular bases.

*sporting pinks:* newspapers devoted to giving news about sport, printed on pink paper.

*half-digested grievances:* half-understood complaints about their rates. Rates are a form of local taxation levied on property.

*Dickensian windows, bottle-glass and all:* windows of the type common in the 18th and early 19th centuries which one meets in the illustrations to Dickens's novels, such as *The Old Curiosity Shop.* They would probably have been bow-windows, with small panes of green glass resembling bottle-ends.

20 *Pavlov dog:* The Russian physiologist, Ivan Pavlov (1849-1936), was the first to study the 'conditioned reflex' by accustoming dogs to hearing a bell when they were to be fed and, later, causing them by involuntary association to salivate when the bell was rung even in the absence of food.

*bog:* lavatory (slang).

*'clurk':* uneducated pronunciation of 'clerk'.

*tart:* girl (slang).

*telly:* television (slang).

21 *'subs':* subscriptions.

*The Two Schools at Gripminster:* evidently a school story of a very conventional type which exploits the glamour attached to the English public school. The schoolboy heroes are crudely idealised, distinguished athletically rather than academically, and talk in an exaggerated form of the slang that is supposed to be widely used in such institutions. The appeal of such stories is similar to that of Billy's Ambrosia: they enable boys who are unable to go to public school—the great majority of their readers—to escape imaginatively into the life of an upper-class boarding school.

*Omnibus:* collected stories.

22 *Mr Bones and Mr Jones:* typical names adopted by two cross-talk comedians.

*rod:* gun (U.S. underworld slang).

*curtains:* the end, the final curtain (U.S. underworld slang).

23 *Odd Man Out Club:* a typical name for a sophisticated London club.

23 *Chelsea:* a district in the West End of London frequented by writers and artists.

*theatre in the round:* an 'advanced' type of theatre in which the audience surrounds the stage or acting-area.

*the Embankment:* tramps and unsuccessful writers are traditionally supposed to sleep wrapped in newspaper on the seats along the Embankment on the north side of the Thames.

*doss down:* sleep in a cheap lodging-house, or 'doss-house' (slang).

*Rowton House:* the best known of the London institutions providing cheap beds for tramps.

*Petticoat Lane:* in the East End of London, famous for its street-market.

24 *Lord Harewood:* Councillor Duxbury probably refers to the present Earl of Harewood's father, who married the Princess Royal, George V's daughter, and died in 1947.

*thraiped:* this word and many of the other 'dialect' words that follow have no meaning, but have been invented merely to sound like Yorkshire dialect.

*took the Michael:* made fun of (slang); commonly phrased as 'took the micky'.

*course:* of course.

*end on it:* end of it.

*I'll use that:* in his music-hall act.

25 *Roxy:* a dance-hall.

*'Woodchopper's Ball':* a popular song, especially associated with Woody Herman.

*bint:* girl (slang).

*'s morning:* this morning.

*randy:* sexually excitable.

*bohemianism:* unconventional behaviour.

26 *tarting:* acting as a prostitute (slang).

*alchemist:* medieval chemist, occupied in trying to transmute base metals into gold.

*soft-shoe shuffle:* a dance often performed by a pair of comedians at the end of their act, in which both have exactly parallel steps which are aptly described by this name.

*Who's Who?:* an annual publication giving personal information about celebrities. The grammatical form of its title is in fact correct.

27 *gingivitis:* disease of the gums.

29 *naff off:* go away (slang).

*gaberdines:* sports trousers of fine worsted cloth.

30 *first account:* first customer—to be buried.

*R.A.F.:* Royal Air Force.

*card-carrying:* holding a membership card—here used metaphorically to mean that Shadrack was an official member.

*Unitarian . . . Low Church:* various religious denominations which would have had churches or chapels in Stradhoughton. The *Unitarians* insist on the unity of God and so deny the divinity of Christ; the *Baptists* practise adult instead of infant baptism; the *Methodists* follow the teaching and church organization developed by John Wesley when he broke with the established Anglican Church (Church of England) in the 18th century. *High* and *Low Church* are two forms of Anglicanism. The Anglican Church developed as a 'middle way' between Roman Catholicism and the more extreme Protestant Churches. High Church beliefs and ritual remain closer to those of the Catholics, while the Low Church is more Protestant.

31 *Able-Peter:* the 'call-sign' Shadrack uses to contact a funeral car by radio. 'Able' and 'Peter' are words adopted by the armed forces to send the letters 'A' and 'P' by radio, since many letters of the alphabet are easily mistaken for each other.

*The Loved One:* a novel by Evelyn Waugh, published in 1948, satirising the extravagant practices of undertakers—or 'morticians'—in the U.S.A.

*Lady Chatterley's Lover:* the novel by D. H. Lawrence, published in 1928 but banned for many years in England because of its frank descriptions of sexual intercourse.

32 *Tommy Atkins:* colloquial name for a soldier.

*Max Miller:* a cockney comedian—the 'cheeky chappie'—who flourished both before and after the last war and was distinguised by his high-speed patter.

*trouble at t' mill routine:* a burlesque of the conventional, melodramatic play concerned with industrial relations.

33 *peg-board notices:* advertisements pegged on to a board in which parallel rows of holes are drilled to receive the pegs.

*schizophrenic:* schizophrenia is a psychological disease in which the personality is split into two or more parts which operate separately from each other—as Billy's attention is divided here between Liz and Rita.

34 *ticking:* so quiet that the ticking of the clocks can be heard.

*pathological:* diseased—compelled to lie by his warped mentality.

*Vim:* a brand of scouring powder.

35 *glacial:* literally, 'made of glass', but also suggesting 'cold and impersonal'—like a glacier.

*slophouse:* either a doss-house (see Note for p. 23) or an eating-house of the lowest type—'slop' is slang both for 'tramp' and for food of very poor quality.

*espresso machine:* a sophisticated machine for making and dispensing coffee.

*transmogrified:* transformed.

*Penguins:* a brand of chocolate biscuit.

36 *go bloody bald:* be furious (slang).

*The liefulness is terrific:* Arthur imitates the way in which the Indian boy, Hurree Jamset Ram Singh, always speaks in the 'Billy Bunter' stories by Frank Richards. These school stories were first published before the 1914-18 war and are still popular to-day. Billy Fisher adopts their style in *The Two Schools at Gripminster.*

*Perspex:* trade name of a transparent plastic material.

*How much . . . I can't?:* What authority have you for saying I can't?

*Jesus wept:* the shortest verse in the Bible (John 11:35), used as an oath.

*badinage:* banter.

*naffing:* a vulgar expletive that has lost its original meaning.

37 *mill-tinged:* with the accent of a worker in a cloth mill.

*loaftins:* tins for baking loaves.

*Gimme . . . pie:* Arthur imitates an American accent. *Gimme:* give me. *cawfees:* coffees. *rye:* rye bread. *blueberry:* the U.S. form of 'bilberry'.

*drugstore:* U.S. snackbar.

*Marlon Brando:* very popular U.S. film star.

*Gerroff yer knees:* get off your knees—Rita implies that Billy is excessively polite.

38 *an 'A' picture:* a film to which children under 16 years are admitted only if they are accompanied by adults.

*clichés:* see Introduction p. 210.

*crackers:* mad—with anger (slang).

*Western Brothers:* two popular radio comedians from before

the last war who adopted an affected public school accent and idiom.

38 *oral footy-footy:* 'footy-footy' is an amorous game that lovers play with their feet, often secretly beneath a table. Rita's spoken expressions of love are no more articulate.

'*Tramp . . . marching*': popular song from the 1914-18 war.

39 *platitudes:* conventional and meaningless remarks.

*free coupon:* an almost valueless addition, like the free coupons given away by manufacturers with their goods to help sales.

*Government surplus:* surplus Government stores sold off cheaply.

*knocked it off:* stole it (slang).

40 *ta:* thank you (slang).

*seagrass:* a type of reed that is used as raffia.

*companion-set:* set of fire-irons.

*satin-brass:* brass polished with a fine wire brush or mop to give it a dull gloss finish.

41 *Jammy:* lucky (slang)—metaphorically, he gets jam on his bread.

*snooping:* spying.

*tutting:* from 'tut-tut', the conventional expression of impatience.

42 *two-timing her:* deceiving her—by having a second girl-friend and so dividing his time between the two of them.

*lych-gate:* roofed gateway to a churchyard.

*Black Death:* the plague that killed over a third of the population of England in 1348-9.

*wayside pulpit:* board displaying texts or moral exhortations.

*saw:* proverbial saying.

44 *sugar-mouse kisses:* kisses resembling sugar mice—a form of confectionery—in being coyly sweet.

*sententiously:* with self-conscious solemnity.

*necking fodder:* food to promote love-making.

45 *claustrophobia:* morbid fear of confined spaces.

46 *Baloo . . . Wolf Cub pack:* Wolf Cubs are the junior branch of the Boy Scouts. The cub-mistress who is second-in-command of a pack is called 'Baloo' after the bear of that name who taught the wolf cubs in Kipling's *The Jungle Book*.

*prototypes:* original versions.

47 *poker-work:* a simple form of decoration consisting of designs, mottoes, etc. burnt on to wood with a hot poker.

47 *Windsor chairs:* upright wooden chairs with straight backs
consisting of vertical wooden rods set in a hooped frame;
associated with cottages, kitchens, etc.

    *tarmacadam:* the ordinary form of road surfacing with tar
and closely packed stone, first used by John Macadam at the
beginning of the nineteenth century.

48 *alfo, fon:* 'also', 'son'—spelt with the archaic long 's' that looks
like an 'f'.

    *College of Commerce:* college of further education where the
Witch would have learnt typing and shorthand after leaving
school.

51 *Pretty:* a sentimentally whimsical addition to 'please', suggesting 'be pretty'.

52 *packets of twenty:* cigarette packets.

    *'Pennies from Heaven':* title-song of a pre-war film starring
Bing Crosby.

    *Morris Thousand:* type of small car.

53 *'Cal. Witch . . . A's ma (sister)':* see Note for p. 5. *Cal:* calendars. *Ldn:* London. *Hswvs:* Housewives. *Namepl:* see pp. 33-4.
*A's ma:* Arthur's mother, see pp. 33-4.

54 *thought-stream monologue:* a monologue that faithfully re-
produces the confused movement of a single person's thoughts
—with all their irrelevant associations and often punning
connections between ideas—before they have been ordered
into articulate speech.

    *Nevah! . . . conflict!:* the beginning of Churchill's tribute to
the Battle of Britain fighter-pilots, concluding '. . . has so
much been owed by so many to so few.' *Nevah* imitates his
pronunciation of 'never'.

    *voiceofemall:* voice of them all—the catch-phrase used by a
music-hall entertainer who imitates the voices of well-known
people.

    *Hay:* affected pronunciation of 'I'.

    *Mickey Mouse:* Walt Disney's most famous cartoon character.

    *Joycean:* in the manner of James Joyce, whose style in *Ulysses*
(1922) and *Finnegans Wake* (1939) is developed from the
'thought-stream' technique.

55 *like a drowning man's life story:* a drowning man is supposed
to re-live his whole life at the moment of death.

    *sanctum:* literally, holy place.

    *executive:* appropriate to the office of a business 'executive'—a term that covers the higher salaried employees and managers in the commercial world.

56 *'Abide With Me':* the hymn by H. F. Lyte (d. 1847); especially appropriate for funerals.

*glass-fibre:* a very strong and rigid plastic material.

*doodling:* sketching idly, in vacant moments.

*siddown:* sit down.

*anarchism:* the political doctrine that rejects all forms of government. Shadrack misuses the word.

*Anachronism:* something inappropriate to the historical period in which it has been placed.

*manilla file:* thin cardboard folder.

*dossier:* set of records concerning one individual.

57 *y're:* you are.

*memo-sheets:* paper on which notes or 'memoranda' are recorded.

*vair:* Shadrack's affected pronunciation of 'very'.

58 *Fact:* In fact; Shadrack clips all his words.

59 *implemented:* put into practice—business jargon, generally used of a decision or plan.

*goodwill:* good relations with their customers.

60 *R.I.P.:* abbreviation of 'Requiescat in Pace' or 'Rest in Peace'. A Methodist might object both to its original Latin form, which associates it with the Roman Catholic Church, and to the fact that it implies a prayer for the dead; such prayers were rejected by most of the reformed—i.e. Protestant—churches.

61 *exhumation order:* official authorization for a corpse to be dug up.

*d'y'think:* do you think.

*penal servitude:* imprisonment with hard labour.

*charge sheet:* record of the crimes with which an accused person is 'charged' in a police court.

*In Memoriam column:* the newspaper column in which relatives and friends of the dead pay tribute to their memories on the anniversary of their deaths.

62 *testing it for strength:* considering how seriously it had been meant.

63 *sink tidy:* small refuse container placed in the sink.

*replete doom:* in fact it was the house that was *replete*—'filled' —with a sense of doom.

63 *sick:* sick of it—had too much of it.

   *grammatical pleasantry:* joke that depends on a point of grammar.

64 *gadding:* wandering about idly.

   *hiding:* beating.

   *learned:* taught—a common error in uneducated speech.

   *melodramatics:* extravagantly dramatic speech and actions.

65 *beautiful Josiah Olroyd lines:* appropriate lines for the 'trouble at t' mill' routine—see Note for p. 32.

   *histrionic:* dramatic. Billy wants his family to be able to understand the dramatic significance of the expression he adopts.

66 *widow's mite:* proverbial for a small contribution—see Mark 12:42.

67 *frame yourself:* hurry—similar in meaning to 'get stuck in'.

   *conning:* examining.

68 *funeral policy:* insurance policy to provide a sum of money to pay for funeral expenses.

   *gags:* jokes.

   *staff job:* regular post as a script-writer.

69 *humping:* carrying clumsily.

70 *pastoral:* rural.

   *slag:* usually the waste material from metal smelting, but here the solid refuse from any furnace or fire; clinker.

   *allotments:* area of ground divided into plots and let out to local residents, generally for the purpose of growing vegetables.

   *Council yearbook:* annual brochure published by the Borough Council to advertise and give information about Stradhoughton.

   *pot-hole:* deep hole worn by natural processes in rock, common in limestone.

   *reactionary:* extreme conservative.

   *Quisling:* treacherous—from the name of the Norwegian Nazi who collaborated with the Germans when they occupied Norway in 1940.

71 *terrace-end:* at the end of a row of terraced houses.

   *Bile Beans:* trade name of a purgative pill.

   *Dr Johnson:* the critic, essayist, poet, novelist and dictionary compiler who dominated English letters for some thirty years before his death in 1784. Councillor Duxbury's 'reputation as a wag in the council chamber' (p. 72) might have led him to dream of matching Johnson's blunt wit and wisdom, much of which was recorded by Boswell in his *Life of Samuel Johnson.*

71 *George Borrow:* author of *Lavengro* (1851), *The Romany Rye* (1857) and other books about gipsy life. His interest in their ancient traditions and way of life probably explains his association with Duxbury.

*Yorkshire relish:* a pungent sauce.

*sunny 'un:* sunny one, i.e. day.

72 *deadpan:* with no sign of irony or humour.

*fot'ty:* forty.

*Messiah:* oratorio by Handel, first performed in 1742. Choral singing is especially popular in northern England, and Duxbury must have heard *Messiah* on many occasions.

*whether or no:* whether I can or not.

73 *council houses:* houses built by the local Council and let at low rents.

*mills:* cloth mills.

*feedline:* line spoken by the subordinate partner in a comic dialogue to introduce the next joke—he 'feeds' it to the main comedian.

74 *Tha's a reet one:* 'You're a right one'—a 'complete idiot': a fairly light-hearted ironic comment implying that the person addressed has distinguished himself by his stupidity.

*i'n't ta?* aren't you?

*masonic dinner:* dinner held by the Freemasons, an organization of professional and business men with branches in most towns.

*capped:* defeated, baffled. Billy uses it to imply that he knows nothing of any calendars, and so Councillor Duxbury has the advantage of him in any conversation about them; Councillor Duxbury uses it to mean that Billy has astounded him by his stupid dishonesty.

*reet taken back:* right taken aback—completely astounded.

*Ah'd ha' thowt:* I should have thought.

*filling in plot lines:* speaking lines whose only purpose is to supply additional information about the plot.

75 *taking a rise out o' me:* making fun of me.

*noan go ower t' ins and outs:* not go over all the details.

*tentative:* uncertain.

77 *made some heavy weather over:* made it a complicated and absorbing business.

77 *campus:* open area in which the college is built; its grounds.

*crib:* cradle carved on a child's tombstone.

78 *mock-Norman:* imitating Norman architecture, with round arch and 'dog-tooth' ornament.

79 *repressions:* impulses that one has resisted and tried to 'repress' or dismiss from one's mind.

80 *litany:* literally, part of a church service, consisting of a sequence of petitions by the priest alternating with formal responses by the congregation—as Billy and the Witch follow a set pattern in their questions and answers.

*and implemented:* see Note for p. 59.

81 *Graf Spee:* German pocket battleship scuttled in 1939 off Buenos Aires after an engagement with British cruisers.

*conscientious objector:* someone who objects on religious or moral grounds to being conscripted into the armed forces.

82 *tabby:* cat with greyish mottled or striped fur.

84 *more-in-sorrow look:* a look suggesting great forbearance—the full expression is 'more in sorrow than in anger'.

*Cugh!:* Coo!—an ejaculation of surprise.

*Joan of Arc:* referring to the cross that Joan was given when she was about to be burnt.

*Get back in the knifebox:* implying that he is too 'sharp', or witty.

*bighead:* swollen headed, conceited.

85 *The sexfulness is terrific:* compare 'The liefulness is terrific' (see p. 36).

*Lo, she is . . . desires:* probably intended as a parody of the Song of Solomon.

*contretemps:* unlucky accident.

*Paymer:* paper—an imitation of the almost unintelligible shout of a news-vendor.

86 *buckshee:* free (slang).

*drainpipe:* narrow, with no turn-ups.

*'Under Milk Wood':* the 'play for voices' written by Dylan Thomas for the B.B.C. and first produced in 1954.

*Rag-bones:* a reminiscence of the cry of the 'Rag and Bones Man' who used to push a cart round the streets buying up old clothes and other derelict articles.

*tartan:* patterns of variously coloured stripes crossing at right-angles, characteristic of Scottish national dress.

*lumber jacket:* leather jacket, originally worn by lumber-jacks.

87 *L.P.:* long-playing record, at 33⅓ r.p.m.

*slipped disc:* displacement of one of the discs of cartilage separating the vertebrae in the spinal column—punning on the use of 'disc' for a gramophone record.

*After you with Shadrack:* a coarse expression of contempt.

*Borstal:* see Note for p. 157.

88 *cacophonous backwash:* receding wave of discordant noise.

*concocting:* making up, by mixing the various ingredients.

89 *personnel:* literally, group of persons engaged in some activity. Billy has to get rid of the other girls he has arranged to meet at the Roxy.

*stood her up:* 'left her standing'—outside the Roxy: failed to meet her and pay for her admission, as he had promised.

90 *enigma:* riddle, mystery.

91 *Gaumont:* another cinema.

92 *club turn:* performance for the working-men's club that arranges a weekly variety show at the New House.

*levitationist:* someone, generally a spiritualist, who purports to be able to rise and float in air.

93 *mild:* mild beer.

*them theer:* them there—a dialect expansion of 'them'.

*garridge:* familiar pronunciation of 'garage'.

*cribbage markers:* pegs for scoring at cribbage, a card game.

*blind-box:* box for donations to assist the blind.

*Formica:* trade name of a hard plastic material.

*open sesame:* the magic formula that opened the treasure cave in the tale of 'Ali Baba and the Forty Thieves'.

94 *a case:* a case for a lunatic asylum.

*deprecating:* mildly protesting.

*drill hall:* literally, the hall used for training and social activities by the part-time Territorial units of the British army—bleak and impersonal.

*Clavioline:* an electronic instrument with a keyboard, like a piano, but also with stops that enable it to reproduce the tones of other instruments.

*'Blais this house, nya Lard we pray':* 'Bless this house, now Lord we pray'—the first line of a very popular religious song, sung here with a mixture of Irish accent and conventionally sentimental emphasis.

*knocking back:* drinking.

*shorts:* short drinks—small measures of spirits.

94 *Ancient Order of Stags:* a working-man's club, resembling a
number that still flourish, chiefly in the industrial towns of
the Midlands and North. This one imitates the middle-class
Freemasons in its organization and complicated rituals of
initiation ceremonies and passwords, and even in having a
special and secret way of shaking hands so that 'brother' members can recognize each other. Each branch is known as a
*lodge* and is run by a *warden*, with several *deacons* subordinate to him. A *grand warden* presides over the central organization.

*penny fines:* for failing to observe some detail in their ritual.

95 *apprentice:* used here as part of the special jargon of the Stags
—someone who has not been initiated or instructed ('tutored')
in the secrets of their order.

*letter or half it wi' thee:* spell out the individual letters or
divide the words into half—so that the full password should
not be heard by anyone who was not initiated and might be
within earshot.

*tiled:* ready for the meeting to begin; completed. Like the
Masons, if less appropriately, the Stags borrow much of their
jargon from the processes of building a house.

96 *'Baby it's cold outside':* a popular song from the post-war film
*Neptune's Daughter*.

*The craft:* the Order of Stags—again like the Masons, the Stags
trace their origin back to the craft guilds into which the
various trades were organized in the Middle Ages, hence their
use of 'apprentice' for someone not yet fully initiated in their
order.

*Billy's Weekly Liar:* a comic periodical that circulates chiefly in
the midlands and north of England.

*peddled:* sold by visiting salesmen—compare 'pedlar'.

*War Cry:* the official periodical of the Salvation Army.

*Empire News:* a Sunday newspaper since amalgamated with
the *Sunday Express*. First editions of Sunday papers are often
sold on Saturday evening.

97 *By!:* meaningless interjection, expressing astonishment.

*'I want to be happy':* popular song from the pre-war musical
comedy *No, No, Nanette* by Vincent Youmans.

98 *'In a Monastery Garden':* very popular light orchestral work
by Albert Ketèlbey.

99 *sardonically:* with scornful irony.

99 *clomping:* walking heavily.

    *gents:* lavatory.

    *shire horse:* largest breed of cart-horse.

100 *flies:* trouser buttons.

    *feller:* fellow.

    *bookie:* bookmaker.

    *t' right busy:* the busiest.

101 *nark it:* stop it, forget about it; Billy Platt is correct in saying that this is not Yorkshire but Cockney slang.

    *Eeyah! Ply the gyme, myte! Caw bloimey!:* 'Here! Play the game, mate! Cor blimey!'—the last phrase is a corruption of 'may God blind me' (Cockney dialect).

    *give ower:* 'give over'—Billy substitutes the Yorkshire equivalent for 'nark it' (see above).

102 *dropped a clanger:* made a mistake (Forces slang).

    *turn:* used here for the performer.

103 *amenity:* something that contributes usefully or pleasantly to society.

    *fiasco:* disaster.

    *Hiya:* hullo—in U.S. style.

104 *cha-cha:* South American dance.

    *rigor mortis:* stiffening of the body after death.

105 *Danny Kaye:* very popular U.S. entertainer and film star.

    *Palladium:* probably the most famous London variety theatre.

    *'Yoo're—my—ev'rthing, ev'ry li'l thing I know-oo':* 'You're my everything, every little thing I know'—first line of a popular song, as crooned in an American accent.

106 *Shepheard's Hotel:* the leading hotel for Europeans in Cairo, before it was blown up in 1952 by rioters protesting against French and British control of the Suez Canal.

107 *Gay Gordons:* Scots dance tune; sword dancing is a Scots custom, the steps being performed over several swords with the blades facing upwards. Billy compares the Witch in her tartan skirt to a Highlander in the kilt.

    *mike:* microphone.

    *Lazengenelmen:* ladies and gentlemen.

    *all-pop:* consisting only of 'pop' music. 'Pop' (short for 'popular') is light music in a jazz or 'beat' style, but is much less demanding than serious jazz, which attracts a smaller and more discriminating audience.

108 *yours truly:* an affected way of referring to oneself, from the

conventional phrase used before signing one's name at the end of a letter.

108 *disc jockeys:* radio personalities who introduce record-request programmes.

109 *American Patrol:* dance tune in march tempo, especially associated with Glenn Miller.

'*You made me love you . . .*': Very popular ragtime song of the time of the 1914-18 war.

*phonograph:* early form of gramophone.

110 *cocker:* often used to address another person in a friendly way, but here implying that he is too 'cocky', or conceited.

*taking you down a peg or two:* reducing your self-esteem.

*Glenn Miller:* one of the most famous U.S. dance band leaders. He directed U.S. forces broadcasting during the war until his death in 1944.

*doing her nut:* 'going off her head'—with anger (slang).

*lay off:* stop it (slang).

*Hokey-Cokey:* light-hearted dance performed communally in a circle.

*scoffing:* eating greedily (slang).

111 *bear-pit:* the arena in which bears were chained to be baited by dogs. Billy is playing the part of the bear.

*Corinthian:* the most ornate style in Greek architecture.

*Talk of the devil:* a proverbial expression—if you talk of the devil he always appears.

*double-talk:* statement that can mean different things to different people.

112 *Unitarians:* see Note for p. 30.

*naval reunion:* meeting of former shipmates.

*chewing the fat:* energetically discussing (slang).

113 *You've had it:* You've been found out (slang).

*het up:* agitated (slang).

*barney:* quarrel (slang).

114 *lark:* literally, frolic; used contemptuously for something intended seriously but which one cannot take seriously (slang).

*handlebar moustache:* Long and curled up at the ends like bicycle handlebars.

*Boston Two-Step:* American ball-room dance from the 19th century.

*change out of fourpence:* recalls Councillor Duxbury's remini-

scences on how much one used to be able to buy for fourpence
(see p. 24).

*tannoy:* trade name of a loudspeaker system.

115 *punchdrunk:* like a boxer stupified by punches.

*Next for shaving:* Billy envisages himself as a barber having
to tolerate a succession of unwelcome customers.

*by a long chalk:* by any means.

116 *hacking jacket:* sports coat with slits extending a few inches
up either side of the back—originally designed for riding,
or 'hacking'.

*sodium lamps:* street lamps giving a yellow light.

*gaffers:* very old men, generally used of countrymen.

117 *Ladies:* cloakroom.

*scruffy:* untidy (slang).

*Houghtondale Arms:* a public house.

118 *Fathead:* humorously affectionate name for someone who is
stupid.

*electricity sub-station:* concrete hut housing a transformer
which reduces the voltage in the grid system to that used by
ordinary consumers.

*introspective:* self-consciously examining his own psychological
condition.

120 *power of:* great deal of.

*Marks and Spencers:* one branch of a large chain-store.

*film finale clinch:* prolonged embrace that concludes a film.

121 *the goose is cooked:* that affair is finished. 'To have your goose
cooked' is to be defeated or exposed, but Billy's application of
this saying is deliberately vague.

*rural by-play:* incidental amorous play. In this context 'rural'
suggests love-making—as in Hamlet's 'country matters'.

*sloping off:* slipping away (slang).

122 *Gregg:* the system of shorthand taught by the Gregg secretarial
schools.

*breach of promise trial:* trial of, generally, a woman's claim for
damages from a man who has broken his promise to marry
her.

*kindling:* wood used for lighting a fire.

123 *infra-red:* invisible rays, below the wave-length of the red end
of the spectrum, enabling pictures to be taken in the dark.

*spool:* of tape.

*virgo intacta:* legal term for 'virginity'.

124 *drumming up:* arousing (slang).

*simulated:* pretended.

*sparring:* make-believe, not serious—as one 'spars' without actually hitting.

125 *doctoring:* attending carefully to; cunningly improving on his ordinary way of speaking.

126 *exhumed:* dug up—in memory.

127 *sandwich-boards:* two boards hinged together at the top, used for displaying advertisements.

128 *pass-outs:* passes enabling them to leave the Roxy and return without being charged a second time.

*nix:* nothing (slang).

*whooping it up:* having a hilarious time (slang).

*beerily:* drunkenly.

*M.P. for the division:* Member of Parliament for the constituency.

*nationalise:* transfer it from private to public ownership.

*in the committee stage:* after a bill has been first introduced in the House of Commons it is passed to a small committee which scrutinises and sometimes amends it in detail.

129 *fish shop:* shop selling fried fish and chips, either to be eaten on the premises or taken away wrapped in newspaper.

*Tizer:* trade name of a brand of soft drink.

*jumble sales:* sales of secondhand and unwanted articles, held to raise funds by organizations such as churches and games clubs.

*daymare:* an adaptation of 'nightmare'.

*coup:* sudden and decisive action.

*casket:* a more elegant term for a coffin.

*old boy:* former member—usually confined to a former pupil of a school.

130 *crust of frosted bambis:* Bambi was the fawn in Walt Disney's film of the same name, his most sentimental cartoon character. These would be plastic reproductions, probably in some bright and glittering material.

*Gothic writing:* imitation medieval script.

*taken badly:* taken ill (dialect).

*ticking:* complaining (slang).

*frame:* see Note for p. 67.

131 *Get ringing up:* start ringing up (slang).

*on a night:* at night (dialect).

132 *stall:* prevaricate, avoid the issue.

    *rig:* distort.

    *monkey-wrench:* large adjustable spanner.

    *get:* a term of indiscriminate abuse (slang).

    *Mary Ann:* effeminate half-wit—the term has been used to refer both to an effeminate actor and to a stand on which dresses are hung.

133 *chelping:* answering impertinently.

134 *Earl's Court:* district in West London.

    *the A.B.C.·* one of a chain of self-service restaurants of that name.

    *Polythene:* soft transparent plastic material.

    *Coronation tin:* a tin produced at the time of the Coronation and probably bearing a portrait of the Queen.

135 *Bentley:* very expensive make of car.

    *half-timbered:* constructed with a visible framework of timber beams, in mock-Tudor style.

    *turns:* attacks of illness.

    *Portland stone:* limestone quarried on Portland Bill in Dorset.

136 *madhouse:* lunatic asylum.

    *aldermen:* co-opted members of a Borough Council, senior to the elected councillors.

    *casualty department:* the department that receives emergency cases.

    *litany:* see Note for p. 80.

    *parquet:* made of small wooden blocks.

137 *pomegranate seeds:* small seeds that need to be picked out with care.

    *rosary:* string of black beads fingered by Roman Catholics as a guide to their daily sequence of prayers.

    *magpie memory:* a reference to the magpie's tendency to carry off and hoard useless objects.

    *some pin:* some trivial detail amongst all the facts that she is laboriously collecting.

138 *Terylene*: trade name of an artificial fabric resembling silk.

139 *convincible:* capable of convincing.

    *cardigan:* knitted woollen jacket.

140 *solicitude:* sympathetic concern.

    *scenes:* used in the special sense of situations in which powerful emotion is expressed.

    *Can I see this gab . . . gift of?:* the point of this characteristic newspaper joke is that 'to have the gift of the gab' is a proverbial expression for being able to talk fluently.

141 *corny:* cheaply conventional (slang).

142 *Co-op:* Co-operative Society—a trading organization founded on socialist principles and supplying a wide range of goods and services from retail branches throughout Great Britain. Most of its regular customers are members of the society and its profits are distributed to them in the form of a dividend on the value of the purchases that each has made.
*divi:* dividend.

143 *editorial 'we':* this impersonal plural form is often adopted in the editorial column of a newspaper as it expresses the policy of the paper, not the opinion of the individual writer.
*Reader's Digest:* a periodical that specializes in printing abridged versions of books and articles that have already been published elsewhere.

144 *Monay. D'cra d'njin . . . :* invented 'Ambrosian' language.
*snickering:* sniggering.
*pitch-pocked:* spotted with patches of tar.
*dead wounds:* healed wounds.
*quid:* pound (slang).
*soda jerk:* assistant in a snack-bar, serving soft drinks (U.S. slang).
*at the mains:* at the main electricity supply, i.e. permanently.

145 *roller-indicator:* train departure indicator, winding up automatically on rollers.
*St Pancras:* London railway station serving the North.
*tubular:* with frames made of metal tubing.

146 *civvies:* civilian clothes.
*biley:* bilious.
*wanna spew:* want to vomit (slang).
*guard-house:* building occupied by the camp guard, where army offenders would be detained.
*C.O.'s p'rade:* Commanding Officer's parade. The rest of the sentence imitates the orders given when a man charged with an offence is marched in.

147 *picture of Lake Windermere:* a British Railways poster advertising trips to the Lake District in N.W. England.
*tableau:* dramatic scene.
*skin you:* take all your money (slang).
*pegged out:* died (slang).

148 *yer rubber halo:* your artificial halo—because Billy has suggested that he is more virtuous than Stamp.

*you've another think coming:* you'll have to change your
thoughts.

149 *Gar:* a snarl.

*you're it:* you're the only person who matters.

*'Port:* report—more imitation of military orders.

*Double:* double march—the military equivalent for 'run'.

*Ovaltine:* trade name of a well-known beverage.

*Know somethn bou' you . . . Wai' Monday, you jus' wai':*
I know something about you. . . . Wait until Monday, you
just wait.

150 *Go' catch:* got to catch—Billy imitates Stamp's drunken speech.

*You come London, me . . . ge's all London:* you come to London with me . . . get us all to London.

*ge' wha'?:* get what?

*booze:* drink (slang).

*dive:* club, in a basement. The word generally suggests something disreputable, or at least unconventional.

*Go' go London . . . Carn stay Stradanan:* got to go to London
. . . can't stay in Stradhoughton.

*Need you London. Ge' nother ticket:* I need you in London.
Get another ticket.

*Drop it:* stop it (slang).

151 *man of the world:* experienced.

*registry-office ceremony:* civil marriage in a registry office, without a religious ceremony.

*communal:* for common use.

*grip:* canvas or leather hold-all.

152 *akimbo:* with hands on hips and elbows turned out.

153 *bob:* shillings (slang).

*tanner:* sixpence (slang).

*He restoreth my soul . . . name's sake:* from the 23rd Psalm.

*shut it down:* stop his No. 1 and No. 2 thinking.

*Yea, though I walk . . . no evil:* from the 23rd Psalm.

*chastened:* sobered.

154 *huffing:* bombastic.

# THE LONELINESS OF THE LONG-DISTANCE RUNNER

*Page*

157 *Borstal:* Borstal institutions were first established under the Prevention of Crime Act of 1908 for young criminals between the ages of 16 and 21, as an alternative to sending them to prison. Discipline is strict but its purpose is to reform rather than to punish. The inmates are encouraged to play a constructive part in society after their release by being given training in various trades, continuing their general education and developing their physical fitness. The period of detention, normally about three years, depends on the rate of progress made by each detainee, and they are progressively allowed more freedom as they show they can be trusted. The name comes from the village of Borstal in Kent, where the first of these institutions was situated.

*did a very fair lick:* ran fast (slang).

*cops:* police—an abbreviation of 'coppers' (slang).

*bakery job:* theft at a bakery; 'job' is used in this sense throughout the story.

*slumgullion:* abusive term for 'stew' (slang).

*daft:* stupid (slang).

*make a break for it:* try to escape.

*mug's game:* situation only a fool would find himself in (slang).

*see eye to eye:* agree.

*there's no love lost:* because there has never been any love between them to be lost.

*manor house:* large country houses that could no longer be maintained by their owners were often used to house Borstals.

*jumped-up:* promoted too quickly (slang).

158 *jogtrot:* trot with an easy 'jogging' stride.

*bloke:* man (slang).

*snooze:* sleep lightly.

*permit running-card:* the card showing he is permitted to train outside the Borstal grounds.

*shimmy:* vest (slang).

*pterodactyl:* prehistoric winged reptile; for the source of the Long-distance Runner's confused knowledge of pterodactyls see p. 167.

*sheep-dip:* dripping, or animal fat which has been used for cooking and left to cool (slang).

158 *loonies:* lunatics (slang).

    *slavies:* servants (slang).

    *to beck-and-call:* ready to be summoned by the slightest gesture.

159 *kicked the bucket:* died (slang).

    *Nottingham:* the Long-distance Runner's home town.

    *Daily Telegraph:* a newspaper whose outlook is generally conservative.

    *play ball:* cooperate, as when both sides observe the rules of a game.

    *poxeaten:* literally, diseased with syphilis—used as a general term of abuse.

160 *lark:* game—used as a term of mild contempt for any activity.

161 *mams:* mothers (dialect).

    *they'll try to get me in the army:* as a conscript; compulsory national service was not finally abolished until 1959.

    *kid:* deceive (slang).

    *swaddies:* soldiers (slang).

    *so what?:* what difference does it make? (slang).

    *boozing:* drinking (slang).

    *a bit thick:* rather unreasonable (slang).

162 *keep my hand in:* keep in practice.

    *'Like boggery, I will':* an expression implying that he has no intention of doing so (slang).

    *tash:* moustache (slang).

    *barmy:* idiotic (slang).

    *hoss:* uneducated pronunciation of 'horse'.

    *didn't care a sod:* didn't care at all (slang).

    *sling my hook:* run away (slang).

    *the likes of him:* the sort of person he is (slang).

    *for a dead cert:* with absolute certainty (slang).

    *mug:* face (slang).

163 *whip-hand:* mastery.

    *fags:* cigarettes (slang).

164 *posh:* smart, socially superior (slang).

    *penpushers:* office workers (slang).

    *got the hang of:* learnt the art of, learnt how to (slang).

    *crumby:* decayed, derelict (slang).

    *pal:* friend (slang).

    *a bloody sight more:* considerably more (slang).

    *dole office:* Employment Exchange; where unemployment relief pay is 'doled out'.

164 *dorms:* dormitories (slang).

*get my back up:* annoy me (slang).

*clink:* prison (slang).

165 *Remand Homes:* where offenders under the age of 17 are detained while they are awaiting trial or, should they be convicted, transfer to an approved school. They may also be used for the punitive detention of first offenders for periods of up to a month.

*it was only touch and go:* the effect was indecisive.

*kittens:* knuckle-dusters (slang).

*dobbie:* an assault with the fists (slang).

*pinch:* steal (slang).

*called up:* conscripted.

*do myself in:* commit suicide (slang).

*been over the top:* attacked over the parapet of a trench—an expression from the 1914-18 war, used figuratively here to mean that they had been in action against the forces of the law.

*Dartmoor, Lincoln:* prisons.

*no-man's-land:* the open area between opposing armies, another term from the 1914-18 war.

*Jerry:* German (slang).

*nowt:* nothing (dialect).

*kids:* children (slang).

*scrumping:* stealing apples.

*high-school:* superior grammar school.

166 *batting:* hitting (slang).

*tabs:* ears (slang).

*clambed:* frozen (dialect).

*chops:* jaws (slang).

*spouts:* talks volubly (slang).

*wappy:* stupidly sentimental (slang).

*the same mill:* the same hard experience.

*quid:* pound (slang).

*on the run:* escaping from prison (slang).

167 *scrimmage:* scramble.

*flat out:* at full speed.

*the 'Lost World':* a wireless adaptation of Conan Doyle's novel *The Lost World*, the setting of which is an isolated plateau in South America where prehistoric animals still survive.

*cut-balled:* castrated (slang).

*Page*
167 *get really around yourself:* make a part of your life.
  *know-how:* experience, practical knowledge.
  *scot-free:* in complete safety; a 'scot' was originally a form of
    tax.
168 *scram:* make off (slang).
  *telly:* television (slang).
  *on a milling-machine:* in a factory.
  *fivers:* £5 notes (slang).
  *ain't a sight of:* isn't very much (slang).
  *dolled-up:* dressed smartly (slang).
  *grub:* food (slang).
  *wain't:* wouldn't (dialect).
  *didn't get a look in:* wasn't considered at all (slang).
  *lolly:* money (slang).
169 *fancy man:* lover (slang).
  *dough:* money (slang).
  *nicker:* pounds (slang).
  *adverts:* advertisements (slang).
  *tart:* girl (slang).
  *grabbers:* fingers (slang).
  *blow:* squander (slang).
  *rag-screen:* screen made of woven fabric.
  *half-nelson:* a hold in wrestling.
  *knocked-off:* killed (slang).
  *nabbed:* captured (slang).
  *hot-chair:* the electric chair used for executions in the U.S.A.
    (slang).
170 *worn't:* wasn't (dialect).
  *gob:* mouth (slang).
  *Tory:* member of the Conservative Party.
  *bumbling:* talking in a ponderously confused manner.
  *stunts:* tricks, jokes.
  *probation:* the probation system was introduced by the Pro-
    bation of Offenders Act of 1904 as a means of dealing with
    first offenders or those convicted of several trivial offences. The
    culprit is placed under the supervision of a probation officer
    to whom he has to report regularly and who watches over his
    conduct and welfare.
  *owt:* anything (dialect).
  *ain't:* haven't.
  *cranky:* stupid.

257

171 *perishing:* freezing—to death (slang).

*snatched:* frozen (dialect).

'*The Teddy Boys Picnic*': an adaptation of the pre-war song, *The Teddy Bears' Picnic*, popularised by Henry Hall. 'Teddy Boy was first used in the early 1950s to refer to youths who adopted an Edwardian style of dress, 'Ted' being an abbreviation for 'Edward'. This fashion was often associated with aggressive and anti-social behaviour.

*twig:* realise, grasp (slang).

*looking like octopus eyes:* looking larger than usual because of the light diffused from them by the fog.

*bob:* shilling (slang).

*nipping into:* entering nimbly and unobtrusively.

*latch:* fasten (slang).

*peepers:* eyes (slang).

*get cracking:* get rapidly to work (slang).

172 *ham-hock*: as thick and solid as a joint of bacon.

*nipper:* small boy (slang).

*scruffy:* worn out and dirty (slang).

*plugged:* stuck (slang).

*Football Post:* newspaper giving the football results.

*Dolly-on-the-Tub:* pregnant woman (slang).

*cock-eyed:* cross-eyed (slang).

*Gatling-Gun:* heavy machine-gun developed in the U.S.A. in the later 19th century.

*upshot*: uplifted.

*maulers:* hands (slang).

*jags:* sharp edges.

173 *I came, I broke, I entered:* an adaptation of Julius Caesar's famous 'veni, vidi, vici'—'I came, I saw, I conquered'. 'Breaking and entering' is a legal term for breaking into a building with the intention of robbing.

*clever-dick:* contemptuous term for something or someone superficially clever.

*draining pipes . . . yaling locks:* climbing drain pipes and picking locks (slang). The second is adapted from 'Yale', the name of a brand of locks.

*scabies:* irritating skin disease.

*flies:* trouser buttons.

*four-eyed, white-smocked bloke:* the Borstal psychiatrist, wearing glasses and a white overall-coat (slang).

173  *caught on:* understood (slang).

*you can bet:* you can be sure (slang).

*tailor-made fifty-shilling grin:* puns on the name of a former tailoring firm, The Fifty Shilling Tailors; 'tailor-made' means 'of high quality'. The expression might imply that Mike was looking as pleased as the advertising models wearing their suits.

*crewcut:* close-cropped hair style.

*nut:* head (slang).

*in the game:* in the practice of thieving (slang).

174  *everloving:* very desirable—it will never let you down (slang).

*Hang on:* wait (slang).

*splash:* squander (slang).

*narks:* police spies (slang).

*tuning in:* listening—as to a wireless set.

*with a hot blowlamp:* as one melts the ice in a frozen pipe.

*growth:* cancer.

*narky:* irritated (slang).

*tripe-twisting pain:* pain that seems to twist one's entrails (slang).

*Narker:* used here as the name for a policeman.

*punchdrunk:* like a boxer stupified by punches.

175  *ratty:* annoyed (slang).

*cosh:* bludgeon.

*outpatient department:* the department that treats patients who are not confined to hospital.

*batchy:* stupid (slang).

*comrades:* gang of thieves.

*a stroke:* a stroke of work (slang).

*stash:* hide (slang).

*pop-eyed:* with protruding eyeballs (slang).

*smashing:* magnificent, extremely fortunate (slang).

*as clean:* as efficient.

176  *diced:* distributed, thrown out—as in dice (slang).

*mean-gutted:* mean spirited (slang).

*put inside:* imprisoned (slang).

*let on about:* disclose (slang).

*skiffle drums:* drums used by skiffle groups—small groups of amateur and unconventional musicians which flourished in the late 1950s. Their instruments usually included drums, guitar and wash-board.

176 *doggo:* secret (slang).

    *green:* inexperienced.

    *dick:* detective (slang).

    *nattering:* chattering (slang).

    *snotty:* irritated (slang).

177 *Borstal Bernard . . . pitprop mackintosh:* impertinent names
    for policemen; *nicky-hat* puns on the word 'nick', meaning
    'prison'; *rowing-boat boots* refers to the proverbial size of a
    policeman's feet; a *pitprop mackintosh* is one as long and
    straight as a pit-prop, military in style.

    *smell a rat:* become suspicious.

    *'tec:* detective (slang).

    *jackses:* spout (slang).

    *paintbrush tash:* neat rectangular moustache. The comparison
    with a paintbrush was probably suggested by the fact that
    Hitler was once a house-painter.

    *rates . . . income tax:* rates (see Note for p. 19) are often
    included in the rent paid for property, and income tax is
    generally deducated from wages before they are paid out.

    *Ain't:* isn't.

    *pub:* public house.

178 *swore blind:* asserted emphatically—from the oath 'may God
    blind me' used to confirm the truth of a statement.

    *P'raps:* perhaps.

    *baker's dozen:* thirteen, instead of the usual twelve.

    *mad:* angry (slang).

179 *lip:* impertinence (slang).

    *Guildhall:* the name often given to the building housing the
    administrative offices of a city. In this case the police station
    is situated in it.

    *kidding:* lying, fooling (slang).

    *like in Hungary:* as the secret police were attacked during the
    rebellion against the Communist government of Hungary in
    1956.

    *blower:* telephone (slang).

    *got me wrong:* misunderstood, misjudged me (slang).

    *fed-up:* exasperated (slang).

    *do a deal:* come to an arrangement, compromise.

180 *flash-bulb face:* his face lit up hopefully.

    *on to a good thing:* following a promising line of inquiry
    (slang).

180 *third-degree:* the most severe form of examination of an accused
person by the police in the U.S.A.

*batting an eyelid:* displaying the least sign of uncertainty
(slang).

*got nothing on me:* had no evidence against me (slang).

*high-wall job:* burglary that involves climbing a high wall, as
did the theft at the bakery.

*Woods:* Woodbine cigarettes.

*do a bunk:* run away (slang).

*Skegness, Cleethorpes:* seaside resorts on the east coast.

*arcades:* amusement arcades.

*beano:* celebration (slang).

181 *buckshee:* free; not restricted by known facts (slang).

*Al Jolson:* U.S. musical comedy entertainer, who usually performed as a negro with a blackened face. His voice was the
first to be heard in a talking film, *The Jazz Singer*, in 1927.

*sleep-logged:* deep in sleep—formed on the analogy of 'water-
logged'.

*hold-on:* wait.

182 *make it:* be able to perform it.

*cut bread:* loaf that is already sliced.

*on tick:* on credit (slang).

*bite:* take the bait, like a fish.

*telly-vase:* vase on the television set.

*tips:* cork-tipped cigarettes.

*jibbering:* inarticulate gabbling.

*Course:* of course.

*summat:* something (dialect).

*don't bear thinkin' about:* too unpleasant to be thought about.

*hoss-tods:* horse droppings (dialect).

183 *copper-lugs:* 'lugs' is a slang expression for 'ears'; 'copper' may
pun on two uses of the word—(a) a metal, (b) slang expression
for policeman.

*smithereens:* small fragments.

*sludgy loaf:* stupid head (slang).

*jabber:* talk rapidly and incoherently.

*greenbacks:* £1 notes, coloured green (slang).

184 *flaptabs:* ears (slang).

*on piece work:* according to the amount of work produced, instead of being paid a fixed wage.

*lace-curtain lungs:* perforated like a lace curtain.

184 *a football heart:* enlarged to the size of a football.

*like varicose beanstalks:* with varicose veins protruding round them like beanstalks growing round a pole.

*clock:* face (slang).

*Woolworth's:* one branch of a large chain store.

*whack:* defeat (slang).

185 *gizzard:* literally, a bird's second stomach for grinding food.

*Gunthorpe:* name invented for another Borstal.

*a treat:* magnificent.

*opening day:* the day when the Borstal is open to visitors.

*Hucknall:* another invented name for a Borstal.

*Ivanhoe:* the film version of Sir Walter Scott's novel. The Long-distance Runner is probably thinking of the tournament in it.

*cat-called:* made derisive comments.

*Aylesham trusties:* 'trusty' is Borstal slang for a boy who can be trusted with special privileges. 'Aylesham' is another fictional Borstal.

186 *dead cert:* absolute certainty to win (slang).

*die on the big name:* fail to live up to the high reputation.

*Medway:* this name for a Borstal was probably suggested by the fact that the village of Borstal is on the river Medway.

187 *on to the same lark:* aware of the advantages of this practice.

*had it in for:* intended to hurt or punish (slang).

*paralytic tired:* so tired that she was almost paralysed (slang).

*dead on:* precisely (slang).

*whippets:* cross between a greyhound and a terrier, trained to race after a dummy rabbit.

*collier's cosh:* coal-miner's bludgeon; whippet racing is especially popular amongst miners.

189 *wall-barred:* refers to the barred windows in the walls of prisons.

*my natural long life of stonebreaking:* stonebreaking is one of the traditional occupations for convicts. The Long-distance Runner sees the whole of his 'outlaw' life as a form of stonebreaking.

*thumb:* give the conventional gesture with the thumb to indicate that one wants a lift.

*crap:* rubbish (slang).

*cushiest:* most comfortable (slang).

*get what-for:* be punished—'for what' he has done (slang).

190 *collaring:* seizing (slang).

*chinless wonder:* term of abuse, suggesting a person who is lacking in character although he has a superficially important position.

190 *tit for tat:* blow for blow.

*pat:* readily, easily.

*uppercut:* blow struck upwards.

*kneed and elbowed:* jostled by the other runners' knees and elbows or by branches in the lane.

191 *crystal-set:* early form of wireless set.

*shell-case:* outer framework.

*ticker:* heart (slang).

*take after:* resemble.

*fruit machines:* automatic gambling machines; pictures of different fruits are whirled round and the gambler wins if a certain combination is showing when the machine stops.

*three-lemon loot:* money won on the winning combination of three lemons in the fruit machine.

*nail-dead:* contraction of the expression 'dead as a door nail'.

*Dracula-vampire:* in Bram Stoker's novel, *Dracula,* Count Dracula is a human vampire who sucks the blood of his victims. The Long-distance Runner would probably have known one of the several horror films that have been made from it.

*penny-pocket winnings:* money won on penny-in-the-slot machines.

*pickets:* boys marking the route.

192 *croaked:* died (slang).

*tripes and innards:* entrails (slang).

*knocking-on with:* knocking about with, associating with (slang).

*lead-in drive:* entrance drive of the Borstal, leading to the winning post.

193 *doddering:* decrepit.

*gaffer:* literally, an old man; used popularly to refer to the senior person in any organization.

*made a Sir:* knighted.

*never care a sod:* won't care at all (slang).

*scat:* clear out (slang).

*guinea-pig:* used for medical experiments.

*guts:* courage (slang).

*Boulder Dam:* the dam across the Colorado River in the U.S.A.

194 *a bloody sight:* much (slang).